# JAMES W HALL

# GONE WILD

**A DELL BOOK**

Published by
Dell Publishing
a division of Bantam Doubleday Dell Publishing Group, Inc.
1540 Broadway
New York, New York 10036

ISBN: 0-440-21781-4

Reprinted by arrangement with Delacorte Press

Printed in the United States of America

Published simultaneously in Canada

February 1996

10  9  8  7  6  5  4  3  2  1

OPM

For Leslie, who is determined to take me to a higher level. Damn her.

And a deep thanks to the many people who helped me research and write this book. For my lovely "sister," Laura Boniske, who got me pointed in the right direction in the first place. Couldn't have done it without her. John Witty, my jungle escort and backstreets culinary buddy. Shirley McGreal, whose passion is fierce and inspiring. For Lennie Jones, the real thing. A man of dignity, purpose and good taste. For Joe Wasilewski, who took me into the heart of the heart of snake country. For Vaughn Morrison, my faithful friend and birder without par. For Patti Ragan, whose love for orangutans gave this book its heart. For Marjorie Doggett and Stella Brewer-Marsden, great hosts in the Far East, wonderful ladies. For Diane Taylor-Snow, the leech specialist and much more. For Birute Galdikas, who hovers like a powerful presence above all this. And for my great friends Les Standiford and Mary Jane Elkins, who patiently read and reread my manuscript.

And as ever, for Evelyn, who is always there, full of wisdom and love, the best friend I could ever wish for.

What would the world be, once bereft
Of wet and wildness? Let them be left,
O let them be left, wildness and wet;
Long live the weeds and wilderness yet.
                    —Gerard Manley Hopkins

# C H A P T E R

## 1

Allison Farleigh felt the dull tingle of a leech on her neck. Her fourth this week. With her right hand she reached back and touched the thing, fixed to her flesh like a damp strand of dough. She couldn't see it, but knew the leech was black with an eerie inner shine like a dark tube of neon.

Probably tumbled out of a casuarina tree, or brushed onto her poncho from a palm frond as she and her daughters passed. Devious bastards, they secreted a blend of anesthetic and meat tenderizer as they anchored their twin mouths. Apparently it had been drinking her blood for several minutes, because Allison could feel the warm numbness beginning to seep down her backbone.

She shut her eyes and dug her thumb under the flattened worm, tried to picture it as nothing but a strip of adhesive, not some living creature fattening itself on her blood. She pinched the leech, took a long breath, set her teeth, and ripped it off.

Eyes watering, she slung the thing onto the soft ground, felt the warm trickle of blood on her neck and the itch of a rising welt. She bent over and watched the creature squirm. Then she squatted, drew out her trail knife, and sliced it in two. Both halves continued to wriggle, then both began to bleed. Allison Farleigh's blood leaked into the earth, that swampy foreign soil, thirteen time zones from Florida, as far from home as it was possible to go.

For if someone were to drill a hole into Allison's backyard in Coral Gables, tunnel straight down, directly through the molten center of the globe, eventually they would pop out in that thicket of banyan and durian, jambu-batu and liana vines. That swampy tropical forest on the exact opposite side of the earth.

The island of Borneo, a few miles north of the equator. For the last week Allison and her two daughters had been tramping through that airless jungle swarming with pythons and mosquitoes, scorpions, tiger ants, and great mobs of hornbills and garish pigeons. Along with twenty other international volunteers, they were working on the annual Borneo orangutan census, helping to calculate how much the population had dwindled in the last year, how much closer those great apes had moved to extinction.

Allison pushed herself back to her feet and rubbed at her neck, then stumbled as a dizzy swirl passed behind her eyes. She felt the dull cramp begin to pulse once again in her stomach. Probably from something she'd eaten, like that fish-head curry ladled out onto banana leaves on a backstreet in Singapore last week, or maybe it was the lingering jet lag, her body still twelve hours out of synch.

She steadied herself against the tree and waited for the swoon to pass, pressing a hand to her sore belly. She listened as Winslow and Sean marched back down the trail, retracing their steps. They'd finally noticed old Mom wasn't with them anymore.

Allison nudged herself away from the tree and took a deep breath.

"I'm back here!" she called out.

A moment or two later Winslow rounded a kink in the trail, her bright, coppery red hair tucked up under a Marlins baseball cap, a couple of wisps of it broken loose, trailing down her neck. She wore baggy khaki pants and pink tennis shoes, a blousy denim shirt that concealed her lanky body, the sleek physique of a distance runner. There was a blue bandanna knotted at Winslow's throat and two Nikons hung around her neck.

Twenty-two, Winslow was the older daughter by one year, inheriting Allison's green Irish eyes, her chalky, un-tannable skin, long limbs, and the same thick blaze of hair. Like Allison, the girl could eat mountains of food and not an extra ounce attached itself to her. She was five-nine, Allison's height, and had chipped-glass cheekbones, oversize eyes, the severe and edgy beauty of the women on the covers of fashion magazines.

Several steps behind Winslow, Sean came tramping down the path. Faded jeans, hiking shoes, a dark green University of Miami long-sleeve jersey. Shorter than Wins-low by several inches, a few pounds heavier. Hair cut short, the way she'd worn it since that morning when she was twelve years old. Snipping her long blond tresses with pinking shears in the bathroom, coming downstairs to model the new look and announce to the shocked break-fast table that she was no longer a girl. And what are you now? Harry asked. I'm a tomboy now, she said.

And a tomboy she remained, with more or less that same Prince Valiant cut, hair the color of late summer wheat. Gray-blue eyes. A spray of freckles across her fore-head. Harry's looks, Allison's spunk.

Always a wisecrack bubbling on her lips. Her eyes flitting from one thing to the next as if she was searching out the target for her next quip. A college athlete, Sean was a specialist in the hundred-meter breaststroke, fourth on the tennis team, point guard in intramural basketball. Sean the irreverent, never seemed to brood or fret. Didn't have the haunted shadows that sometimes darkened Winslow's eyes. Yet, it was Sean who Allison worried more about. Sean who she suspected would take the news harder. The disclosure that Allison had brought them to the other side of the world to make.

"Chalk up another one," Sean said, touching one of the leech halves with the toe of her hiking shoe. "Ms. Allison Farleigh has stretched her leech lead out even fur-ther. It now stands at an insurmountable four leeches, while her daughters, bless their hearts, are not even on the scoreboard yet. So, tell us, Ms. Farleigh, how do you do it? What exactly is your secret for leech enticement?"

"It's my animal magnetism," Allison said. "Has them falling out of the trees."

Sean smiled and kicked the leech off into the underbrush.

"So what do you think, do the Dayak natives eat these things? I mean, they eat everything else in the jungle, right?"

Winslow made a disgusted noise, sat down on a fallen log, and watched her sister.

Sean said, "Yeah, I can see it. Your hardworking Dayak wife is sitting in her hut holding the bag of leeches she's pulled off her kids today, she's paging through her *Joy of Cooking,* Borneo edition. Tired of the same old recipes. Let's see, how about some leech chowder tonight? No, that was last night. Maybe barbecued leech on yellow rice. Then, of course, there's always the old standby, leech français."

Winslow shrugged off her knapsack.

"Here we go again," said Winslow. "Off to the races."

"Romantic Borneo," said Sean, intoning it in the hokey travelogue voice she'd been using all week. "Come with us for a visit to the home of the Ibans and the Dayaks, those romantic headhunters. Experience every colorful lower bowel disease known to modern man. Only seventy-two vaccinations stand between you and alluring, rain-drenched Borneo, vacation capital of the Far East. You can leave your American Express at home, but don't forget your malaria tablets."

Allison smiled as she reached back to rub at the welt on her neck. Above them, from the high branches of a ficus, a gibbon sang out, and in the distance a hornbill seemed to reply, its scream sounding like some child's gruesome tantrum.

Winslow took the waxed paper off her sandwich and began to eat. Sean popped open her Tupperware jug and drank half her iced tea in one long guzzle, then sat down on the log beside Winslow.

"Does this mean we're doing lunch?"

"Well, I am," Winslow said. "I'm starved."

"Lunch it is then."

Through the thick undergrowth twenty yards away, Allison caught a flit of movement. She peered past Winslow at a stand of tree ferns and bamboo, but whatever she'd seen had vanished back into the blur of greenery. Another bird perhaps, or one of the heavy durian fruits falling from a limb. That sharp-spiked gourd weighed three or four pounds, could knock you unconscious if you took a direct hit. Just one more of the jungle's surprises.

They were working a quadrant of the Semonggoh rain forest two hours up the Lupar River by speedboat from Kuching. Every morning for the last week they'd left the Holiday Inn in the dark, and arrived by seven-thirty at the base camp in Serasam. Then each group of volunteers was given a rough map of the area they were responsible for that day and dispatched in different directions for the day's count. Sweeping her binoculars across the treetops, Sean was their spotter, while Winslow handled the photographic work. Bringing up the rear, Allison was the tabulator, carefully filling out the forms. Time, date, place of sighting, size, approximate age, weight, sex. Notable behaviors.

It was Allison's fifth orangutan count, her daughters' first. Once again Dr. Sidra Tindusiri, who headed the Semonggoh orangutan sanctuary, had courted and bribed the necessary Malay officials to secure the permits the volunteers needed to be able to assist in the annual tally. Dr. Tindusiri knew within a few square miles where each of her rehabilitated orangutans was *supposed* to be, but it was the volunteers' job to confirm that each of those apes was still alive. A task it would have taken Sidra months to accomplish with her limited staff.

This year there was a sense of dread among the volunteers, because for the last few months there had been steady reports that a band of poachers had been working this part of the jungle. The bastards used high-powered rifles to blast mother apes out of the trees so they could steal their newborns and sell them as pets or to unscrupulous zoos. As the orangutan population declined, its price soared. Forty thousand dollars a head was this season's rate for wild-born babies. A reward so high, apparently the poachers had grown brazen enough to hunt in even that well-patrolled national preserve.

Poaching orangutans anywhere was bad enough, but hunting down the rehabilitated animals that roamed this preserve was particularly horrific. Years of work went into reestablishing each ape into the wild. Most of the adult apes in this part of the jungle had once been domesticated pets. Abandoned on the streets of Taipei when they'd grown too large and threatening, or voluntarily handed over to the Malaysian government's rehab program, these apes were getting a second chance. But in their years as household pets or as nightclub entertainment, they'd lost their natural fear of humans, and often made easy prey.

One of Allison's goals this year was to take home a stack of photographs of this section of the jungle; the apes at play, at rest, mothers and their babies. She was hoping Winslow's shots would be strong enough to help sell an article to *Nature* or *National Geographic,* a passionate piece that would detail the orangutan's plight, plug Sidra's work and Allison's organization on a huge scale. Get more money flowing in this direction.

While Allison's watchdog league was devoted to shutting down the buying, selling, and smuggling of *all* endangered wildlife, Allison specialized in orangutans. *Pongo pygmaeus.* People of the forest, the orange apes, wild men of Borneo. Their long, reddish hair standing out from their bodies as if it were charged with static electricity. Bulging stomachs and eyes full of melancholy wisdom. They spent their lives in the forest canopy, dangling from limber branches hundreds of feet up, or bending saplings like pole vaulters to reach down for pieces of fruit, jambu-air, longsat, nangka.

Same number of teeth as man; blood pressure, body

temperature the same. Ninety-eight percent of their genetic material identical to humans. And as far as she was concerned, whatever comprised that other two percent was pretty damned wonderful. The orangutans Allison had spent time with were a hell of a lot more intelligent and certainly more trustworthy than most of the humans she'd run into.

Seven years ago it had begun for her. Returning from Harry's consulate job in Brunei, Allison had gone with Harry and her daughters into a back room at customs at the Singapore airport to check on their Labrador before their long flight home. It was a muggy afternoon, everyone cranky.

The Lab was fine, thumping its tail against the wire mesh as they approached. But in a far corner of the room, Allison noticed a stack of cages filled with primates. Chimps, macaques, gibbons, orangutans.

As she veered toward them, gooseflesh broke out on her arms and neck. While she stood before the cages, some of the animals gibbered and peeped, but most were silent, staring at her with the look she came to recognize as forlorn and confused.

At that moment, gazing into their baffled eyes, Allison felt a deep ache growing inside her. Spellbound, she watched as the apes shifted in their cages, as one grabbed the bars and rattled, and from inside another cage a hairy hand reached out through the bars toward her, then suddenly drew back.

"You going to eat, Mother?"

Allison said yes, took off her backpack, found a dry spot at the base of a *neram* tree and sat. She opened her canteen and took a long sip.

"So, Winslow," Sean said. "You read about the palangs yet? The penis ornaments?"

"Penis ornaments?" Winslow eyed her sister suspiciously. "Get out of here, Sean."

"No, it's real, I swear. Isn't it, Mother?"

Allison nodded that it was.

"It's true," Sean said. "They stand in the cold river, get all shriveled and numb, then they drill holes in the tips of their penises. And later when they're healed, they pull out the retainer plug and insert colorful, interesting thingamajigs in the holes. Feathers, small bones, wood carvings. Something pretty. Part decoration, partly to please their women. Like a French tickler or something."

"You read this?"

"Yeah, in one of the books Mother brought. Palangs."

"And their women are supposed to like that? A bone through the penis? Jesus."

Sean took a bite of her sandwich. A slug of iced tea.

"Maybe what it is, it's a trick the Dayak women play on their guys," Winslow said. "They tell them what they want, so the men go off, drill holes in their wieners. Their women are sitting around laughing about it: 'Those idiots, they fell for it again.'"

Allison chuckled.

"What I was thinking," Sean said, "maybe we could open a shop back home. Be the first to introduce palangs to America. A little stall at the mall like the Piercing Pagoda."

Winslow let out a whoop. The two of them matched laughs for a few moments, then Winslow folded up her waxed paper, slipped it back into her pack, the chuckles fading.

"No, no," Winslow said, "it would never fly. American men are too spineless."

"I don't know," Sean said. "You present it the right way, put the proper spin on it. Get some celebrity spokesman, Stallone, Schwarzenegger, one of those guys: 'My woman can't get enough of my new palang. Are you man enough?'"

Winslow chuckled.

"Never work. The only guys who'd do palangs would be ones you wouldn't want to be around anyway. Motorcycle guys, tattoo geeks, like that. The nose ring crowd."

"What do you think, Mother? Is this an idea or

what? Maybe a whole new career path. Forget law school. Open a little kiosk at Dadeland Mall. Drill and Fill. Introduce palangs to Middle America. We wouldn't have to pay the staff. I know a dozen girls who'd do that work for nothing."

Allison felt her smile drifting away.

Sean swung back to Winslow and said, "Okay, here it is. I got it now. So, yeah, maybe some American men don't have the guts for something like this. Then we'd have to offer a whole different product line. Fake palangs."

"Fake palangs?"

"Yeah, yeah, like that arrow-through-the-head thing by that comedian, Steve Martin. You know, a flesh-colored spring that fits around their penis, looks like they drilled a hole, but they didn't really. An optical illusion palang. We could have bones, arrows, maybe some yuppie stuff, miniature golf clubs, little tennis rackets. Customize your own palang. Go home, pull down your shorts, it's 'Honey, look what I did for you.' "

Winslow was laughing now. Sean on a roll.

"I mean, it's all in how we market it. We could provide both services, fake or real. Make it like a test: 'If you really love her, you'll have your penis drilled. But then again, if you're not ready to commit, we've got just the thing for you.' "

"Kurt would never do it."

"Yeah, that's true, not Kurt. But I bet Patrick Sagawan would."

"Knock it off, Sean."

"He could be one of our poster guys. Patrick Bendari Sagawan, the Malaysian hunk, nephew of the richest man in the world. He palanged himself for his sweetheart. Will you?"

All week Sean had been kidding Winslow about Patrick, the sultan's nephew. Seven years ago in Brunei, Winslow had nursed a fierce crush for him. The boy was two years older. Back then, at seventeen, he was already a lady's man with silky, cosmopolitan manners. Allison suspected, but never heard for sure, that Winslow had lost her virginity that year.

When the orangutan count was done, the three of them were planning to spend a few days in Brunei, an hour's plane ride east. Visit old friends. Probably the only reason the girls came along on the trip at all was because of the Brunei part. They had romantic memories of the place, very different memories from Allison's. Harry had told the girls that Patrick was still a bachelor. Winslow had blushed, looking at her lap. Ohmygod, ohmygod, Sean said. Think of it, Winslow. Still mooning for you.

"Kurt would never do it," Winslow said. "He gets a paper cut on his finger, he passes out. My big, brave boy-friend. You'd think a vet would be tougher."

"But Patrick Sagawan would do it," Sean said. "And Thorn would too. Old Nature Boy. Now, there's a guy we can always count on."

"Yeah," Winslow said. "Thorn would do it if we asked him. And I bet if Mother asked Dad, we could sign him up too."

They both looked at Allison with teasing smiles. She moved her eyes to the trees.

"Yeah, how about Dad?" Sean said. "Think he'd be willing? I mean, just as a promotional thing? Harry Farleigh, famous ex-diplomat, had himself fitted for one. How about you?"

Allison brought her eyes back to them. They were both watching her. Sean grinning, Winslow's smile losing a little of its energy as she saw her mother's expression. Allison feeling her own face collapse. Her blood harden-ing.

"What do you think, Mother? Dad go for this?"

"I'm leaving him," Allison said. Lowering her eyes.

Something howled in the trees nearby. Neither of her daughters spoke. By slow degrees Sean's grin sank away.

"I'm leaving Harry." Allison screwed the cap back on her canteen, set it aside. She took a breath, looked at each of them, and said, "I wanted to tell you over here, let you have time to get used to the idea before we get back home. Give us a chance to talk it over."

Sean stood up. She dropped the Tupperware jug of tea.

"You're kidding."

Allison shook her head, watching Sean's eyes darken, her mouth twisting into a bitter grin.

"Jesus Christ! Jesus H. Mother of Christ."

"Sean," Winslow said. "Come on. Cool it."

Sean took a step toward Allison, made fists. Veins rising.

"So that's what this trip was all about? Not counting apes, not shooting photos. You had this on your mind the whole time. That's why you made such a big deal—the Farleigh women get to spend some time together, female bonding. But no. All along it was to spring this bullshit on us."

"I *did* want to spend time with you. I wanted us to be able to confront this, talk it all through."

Sean kicked the Tupperware into the bushes. Turned and stood staring at the lush greenery, her back to Allison.

"Goddamn it," she said, and swung around. "Twenty years, all of a sudden, out of the blue, you dump him. What? Is there somebody else? That's it, isn't it? You're having an affair."

Allison looked into Sean's eyes and slowly told her no, there was nobody else, nobody.

"Come on, Sean," Winslow said. "Back off."

"Hey, she wanted to talk about it. We're talking about it."

"It's been twenty-*three* years," Allison said. "And things haven't been right for a while, not since we came back from Brunei."

Sean's face was red, mouth quivering. Not used to suppressing anything. Eyes growing damp, her mouth moving as if she were chewing a wad of gum.

"Why now?" Winslow said quietly.

"It's time. I've waited too long as it is."

Winslow said, "Have you already told him?"

"No, I wanted to tell you first. I wanted to talk with you."

"It's your life," Winslow said. "You don't need our approval."

"When we get back," Allison said, "I'm moving out. I'm going to live at the Shack."

"The Shack!"

"I'll be fine out there. It's where I want to be."

Still silent, Sean shifted her glare back and forth between Allison and Winslow. Then she shook her head savagely, turned her back on them, and stalked down the trail in the direction they'd come.

"She'll be all right," Winslow said. "You know how she is about Dad."

"I know."

"I'll go get her."

Winslow took her baseball hat off, dropped it with her pack. She looped the Nikons around her neck and headed off down the trail after her sister.

The male orangutan sat in his mother's nest high in an ironwood tree playing with a rambutan that she'd given him earlier in the day. The fruit was rare in this part of the jungle. A delicacy.

The young orangutan was tearing free the meat of the rambutan and pitching the excellent food out of the nest onto the ground a hundred feet below, leaning out from a branch, watching it fall into the bushes near where the three humans sat. The mother did not try to restrain him. She simply let him play.

The male orangutan was four years old. For the next two or three years he would live alongside her every moment of the day just as he had done since birth. His mother would protect him from the dangers of the jungle, but never once would she discipline him.

Orangutans lived solitary lives, mainly because their food sources were spaced too widely for them to live successfully in groups. But living alone was not easy. The loneliness, the quiet. A thousand acres of dense forest were necessary to support just one adult male. Very likely the only contact her son would ever have with other orangutans would be on those rare occasions when he grew lustful and sought out a female.

Because of this, there was no need for the mother orangutan to teach her offspring manners. It was best that he make his own decisions. So, if he found it amusing to throw away such precious food, it was all right. To be able to amuse himself, however he accomplished it, would be crucial to his survival.

# C H A P T E R

## 2

In the clearing beside the Lupar River Allison waited for her daughters to return. Weary, angry at herself. She hadn't intended to blurt it out like that. She'd meant to choose a quieter time, in the room at the hotel, or after dinner. Lay the groundwork, circle around to it, prepare them for the shock. But just the mention of Harry's name had made her heart lurch, loosened the feelings, and it had all erupted.

Now it was done, the words spoken. Sean angry, Winslow shaken. And though Allison had handled it clumsily, she was at least relieved it was done. What she'd debated for so many painful months, the words she'd harbored in the silent hours of the night, were out. Hearing them come from her own lips a few moments ago, Allison was struck by how natural it sounded—leaving her husband of twenty-three years.

Allison watched a harem of proboscis monkeys pass through the trees overhead, the male with his large crooked nose hooting at his women, moving them along. And a flock of noisy hornbills, a single owl, a scattering of parrots, a dozen gibbons.

She propped her back against the smooth bark of a *neram* tree. One of the magnificent *Dipterocarpus oblongifolius* that grew alongside so many Malaysian rivers and sent their great arches of shade over the water. Allison listened to the flitter of insects and cries of birds. Honks and whistles, and a host of frenzied shrieks like dozens of locomotives jamming on their brakes at once. The cicadas and frogs and small sparrows were setting up a pandemonium of clicks and clatters, belches and kronks, as though the jungle were some great rail yard where all the axles and gears and pistons had gone for years without grease.

She inhaled the dense, sulfurous air, filled with a stifling bloom of decay. Above her the branches of the *neram* were cluttered with bright orchids and ferns. She closed her eyes, rested her head against the tree, let her breath ease. Oddly, she found the jungle racket to be soothing.

Her heart was just finding its normal pace again when she heard a loud clattering of brush nearby. She opened her eyes and turned toward the rustle. And there, shoving the thick foliage aside, approaching her with his nimble, bowlegged gait, was a young orangutan, a male of three or four. In his right hand he carried a piece of fruit. Rambutan.

The ape halted a yard in front of her, staring into her eyes. There was a peculiar streak of silver in the hair above his left eye as if someone had dabbed a painted finger against his forehead. It gave the ape a slightly clownish look, one frosted sprig in his otherwise deep red hair.

After another moment, Allison slowly extended her right hand, and the young ape stepped forward, his eyes on hers. Alert, curious, maybe a trace of wariness. When he was only a foot or two away, he looked down at her hand, reached out and put the gooey remains of the rambutan into it. Allison smiled and brought the fruit close to her mouth and made a pleasurable gurgling noise. The orangutan came closer, touched the knee of her jeans, pinched the fabric, rubbed it between thumb and forefinger as if he were judging its value.

Dream-slow, Allison set the rambutan aside and opened her arms. The ape held his ground, showing his teeth, a mischievous grin. He brushed his hand against his hairy thigh as if to wipe the sticky fruit juice away.

Then he made several small peeps like an Easter chick and took a half step toward her, and then another, coming slowly inside her arms. He halted and brought his face close to her hair, lifted a handful from her shoulder and examined it.

Bringing a strand to his mouth, he rubbed it against his lips, and sucked it inside and chewed on it for a moment, then in a flatulent burst he blew the hair out.

The ape stepped to the side and examined Allison's face, then he glanced down and took hold of her left hand, held it in both of his. His grip was sensitive but powerful. And before she knew what he was doing, he had slipped her wedding ring off, her grandmother's four-carat diamond, and popped it into his mouth.

He grinned at her, the glimmer of gold suspended for a moment on his drawn-back lips. Then he stretched out his long, hairy right arm to encircle her shoulders. She yielded for a moment or two, then gingerly Allison drew back from his embrace, raised her right hand, and touched the orangutan's face. She hadn't actually seen him swallow the ring. It was likely he'd merely tucked it into his cheek to examine later.

Very carefully, she slid a finger along his lower lip and into his mouth, the ape beginning to peep rapidly, but not drawing away. With her forefinger she probed his gums, one side then the other, the slobbery cavities of his cheeks. On the right side, she wriggled her hand deeper into the damp hollow until her finger touched something cold and loose in the far back pocket of his jaw.

The orangutan didn't draw away, didn't struggle, seemed to be enjoying this sloppy sport. His eyes on hers. Letting Allison teach him how this game was played.

Allison poked the tip of her finger through the ring, dug it free. Carefully she drew it forward, had it almost to his lips, when the orangutan gave a startled screech, lurched away from her, and rose a foot into the air and hung there.

Squeaking madly, the ape rocked his head back and stared up into the branches of the *neram*. From a thick limb several feet above Allison's head, the ape's mother hung by her feet. Two hundred pounds, many times more powerful than a human that size, the big orangutan bared her teeth and made a sharp guttural noise, a single fierce bark as she ripped her baby from Allison's arms. Then she gave Allison one final, loathsome glare and dragged her wayward son away, up the side of the giant tree.

Allison came to her feet and watched the mother ape haul her young son roughly, one powerful arm slung around her son's waist. Mother and child scooted up the tree until they disappeared into the dense branches forty feet up. Allison stepped back into the center of the clearing for a better view. She watched the branches shift and sway, but the mother orangutan kept herself hidden from view as she climbed.

Allison tore open her knapsack and found her binoculars. For half a minute more she searched the canopy till finally she heard a loud jostling in the trees and shifted her glasses to the right, and found an open corridor in the limbs where a cluster of high branches were rattling and swaying as though a heavy wind were passing through them.

It took her a moment more to spot the dark orange shape of the mother orangutan hoisting herself higher into the limber branches, fluttering the leaves violently as she went, twigs breaking around her, the yawn and shriek of thick wood flexing beneath the great ape's weight as she worked with meticulous speed through the mesh of limbs toward the drab light of an overcast sky.

When the two loud rifle blasts sounded nearby, Allison gasped, jerked the binoculars from her eyes, and stumbled sideways. She caught herself against the *neram* tree, then with jittery hands she pressed the glasses to her eyes again.

She saw the ape hesitate, peer down at the shooter. The orangutan moved her head to one side for a better view, then she glanced upward, selected a route, and began to climb higher into the branches. As she hauled herself upward, her son, hanging around her neck, reached out and nabbed a leaf, stuffed it into his mouth.

A man's shout came from Allison's left, then the sound of several people crashing through the underbrush, their voices low and insistent, the hard breathing of men on the run. Allison lowered her glasses and hurried down the path where Winslow and Sean had disappeared.

A few yards down the path she stopped and stood for a moment, scanning the surrounding jungle. Wax palms and ferns, banyans, tualangs, sagas, creeper vines and broadleaf strangler figs, a thick mass of green. Visibility less than twenty feet in any direction. She hissed out her daughters' names, but there was no reply.

In the time they'd been gone they might have walked out of earshot of the gunfire. And if Winslow had convinced Sean to return, surely they were taking cover, just as Allison should be doing. But she could not. She had to see these men. Intervene if she could. Or at the very least see their faces so she might identify them later.

Taking the most direct route toward the men's voices, Allison moved down a creek bed that angled away from the river path they had been on. Painstakingly she followed the gully toward the noises of the men.

After several yards she stopped and lifted her binoculars again and sighted on the canopy. It took a few moments of scanning right to left and back again, but at last she saw them, mother and son perched together in a crook of one of the hundred-year-old ironwoods that filled this part of the rain forest. Probably the tallest tree for miles around.

The mother ape was staring down through the limbs and leaves and fronds, leaning out from her perch while her child gripped her arm. In her left hand the big orangutan gripped a clump of branches it had ripped free, holding it away from her body as if preparing to bombard her attackers.

Twenty yards below her a flock of hornbills exploded

from the branches, squawking and screaming, and the mother ape recoiled into the deep crotch of the tree.

Allison lowered her glasses and moved on down the creek bed, maneuvering across a slight embankment, then a ten-foot stretch of slippery stones. The gully continued to slope down until Allison's shoulders were below the level of the jungle floor. Her feet slipped and she steadied herself against the muddy walls, and peered into the forest but saw nothing, only the emerald glow of the sunlight filtering through a hundred fine layers of green.

Stretching onto her toes, she craned upward, and there, ten feet off, she glimpsed the coppery red hair, the back of Winslow's head as her daughter aimed her Nikon through the jungle thicket.

Allison whispered her name, and Winslow lowered her camera and turned. When she spotted Allison, she pressed a quick finger to her lips, then reached into her shirt pocket and drew out a roll of film and held it up. By God, she'd got the bastards.

"Where's Sean?"

"She went back to the refuge."

For a moment she held Allison's gaze, giving her a pained smile. As though she'd seen now in the stark and sudden drama playing out before them, the secret, evil heart of all her mother had been fighting against. And though Allison had not known it till that moment, she saw now how much she'd yearned for this. For her daughters to have a glimpse of what drove her, what had inspired her fury and passion these last seven years.

Winslow nodded once, took a long breath, and turned away, stepping back into her blind to aim her Nikon once more.

Allison reached up and touched the slippery walls of the gully. Nothing to hold on to, too high for her to pull herself out. She wanted badly to join her daughter, to stand beside her in this moment. But it looked like she either had to completely retrace her steps or forge ahead another thirty yards to where the ravine sloped back up onto the jungle floor.

She went forward, picking her way across the treacherous rocks, fighting for balance at every step. At the end of the ravine she halted before the embankment and stared up at the slope, which was covered by a tangle of roots and vines. It was a great deal steeper than it had appeared from a distance, almost a vertical climb.

As she hesitated a moment more, searching the walls for a foothold, she noticed, a few feet to her right, a recess hollowed out of the gully wall. It was partially hidden by a mat of overhanging vines. Probably some creature's burrow.

For a moment she had a pang of fear. She wasn't familiar with the nesting habits of wild pigs or sun bears. For all she knew this might be the doorstep of some napping beast.

The jungle floor was now a yard above her head. A simple pull-up away, no different than hauling herself out of the ocean over the gunwale of a sailboat, something she'd done a hundred times. Except here there was nothing to grip but creeper vines, and she knew from past experience that they were not the most securely anchored vegetation.

But what the hell. She blew out a breath, reached out, took hold of one of the large, hairy creepers, and began to hoist herself up the steep embankment. Grunting hard, she dragged her chin to ground level and reached out with her right hand for the base of a small tree, and had to stretch another inch, then another, raking the bark with her fingernails, still a few inches out of range.

She took a deep breath and lunged upward and made a swipe at the sapling, and grabbed hold. Then, as she was dragging herself up and over the edge of the ravine, the sapling broke in half, and Allison lost her balance and slid back down the gully wall, thumping her elbows and knees, bruising her ribs on a protruding root.

Breathing hard, she lay on her back on the muddy floor of the ravine and listened to the men's voices calling out from very close by. She didn't recognize the words at first, thought for a moment the men were speaking Chinese, Malay, some dialect she'd never heard. But it must have been the interference of her own jangling heart, for a second later she heard someone speak in very distinct American English.

"To your right, up there, on that big branch. No, to your right, asshole. Yeah, yeah, there you go."

Then she heard the hard, metallic ratchet of a rifle being cocked, and less than a second later the deafening boom.

From high in the canopy the mother ape bellowed, a soul-shaking noise. Allison saw a hundred birds burst into flight, and lifted her eyes to watch the orangutan pitch forward from its roost, take a final swipe at a limb for balance, but miss it, then tumble forward, her young son gripping her around the neck as the big ape dropped, face forward, flailing its arms like Allison had seen sky divers do, trying to keep their bellies into the wind. The wounded orangutan was still alive, still with enough dim hope for her race to do what she could to shield her son from the crash.

Allison turned her eyes away, but heard the whack and crash of great limbs breaking, and then a long trumpeting scream, the ape's death wail. And a half second later the unbearable concussion. For a few moments the jungle was silent, then came a man's war whoop and other voices cheering and joking as they jogged toward their kill.

# CHAPTER

# 3

Allison had dealt with animals in every ghastly condition imaginable: sickness, deprivation, gross physical abuse. She'd seen the emptiness of their movements after years of gruesome medical experimentation, the lightless eyes, the ghostly gaze of severely tortured creatures. By now she considered herself tough, even a little calloused to the suffering of animals.

But at that moment, as the mother ape and her child crashed to the jungle floor, she could barely breathe, immobilized with sudden grief and disgust. Feeling a murderous rage as well, a great heave of strength swelling in her. She wanted to scream, and felt the first rumbles of it coming up from her bowels, but she set her teeth, and ground her head back against the muddy walls of the ravine and strangled the shriek. Tears blinded her. She wasn't sure how much time passed before she raised her head and sat up.

It was eerily quiet. A single cicada made its electric buzz off to the north, but that was the only sound in the immense silence of the jungle. Then with cold horror, Allison heard one of the motorized gadgets on Winslow's camera engage. An automatic rewind. The loud mechanical whir and clatter lasted nearly half a minute. Afterward the jungle was even quieter than before.

A moment later she heard someone rustling in her

direction. Allison came to her feet. There was a shout, and the sound of men's voices, and the clamor of several people barging through the underbrush. Winslow's outraged wail: "No!"

Allison raced back to the vine-matted wall, jumped up, took hold of a vine, and writhed upward. She reached the brim in seconds, pulled her head over the edge. She held herself there, chin on the ground, feeling the tremors in her muscles, her grip slowly giving way. She took a breath and heaved up an inch or two, brought her breast even with the level of the ground, tried to lever herself onto the jungle floor. Just a few yards in front of her, below the web of fronds and limbs, she saw three sets of shoes and cuffs shuffling side by side. Twenty yards away she could make out her daughter's pink sneakers.

"Leave her alone!" Allison cried out. "Leave her the hell alone! You bastards."

But at that moment her hands failed and Allison skidded back down the embankment to the floor of the ravine, her leg catching on a jutting rock, twisting violently. She felt the fiery jolt in her ankle, then sensation drained from it, numbness from her shin down. She groaned, lay back against the muddy ground. For a moment she heard only the whisper of a feverish breeze through the tatter of fronds and thick underbrush. Then Winslow's scream.

"Mother!" she called. "Moth—"

Two almost simultaneous rifle blasts cut her daughter's shout in half. The explosions echoed through the forest, swept like icy winds down the dark canyons of Allison's heart. She couldn't breathe, was able to summon only a single image out of the fog of her shock. Winslow sprawled on the ground, her last word spoken, her final breath. Jesus, God.

Lying on her side in the mire, Allison heard a man's voice from somewhere nearby. For a moment she didn't register the words he was yelling. But then her body tensed and she felt a clammy hand rise up inside her, grip and twist.

He was calling out a single word, drawing it out, taunting.

"All-iii-son, All-iii-son. Come out, come out, wherever you are. All-iii-son. We know you're there, Allison. Come on, pretty lady. I got something here. A little present for you, Allison. Come to Papa."

She shrank into a corner of the ravine. Pressed her back hard against the side. Above her was the snap of limbs and rustle of their approach. She pulled herself up into the hollowed recess in the wall, dragged her aching leg inside. She rolled deep into the warm darkness of the burrow.

"All-iii-son. Might as well come out. We know it's you, All-iii-son. We know you're here." The singsongy rhythms of a kid's hide-and-seek game.

She heard the slide of steel against steel, then the snap of the cartridge locking into the chamber. She tucked her body deep into the stuffy recess, a fetal curl. Seeing, through the curtain of vines, movement on the gully's ledge.

She faintly recognized the voice, felt sure it was a man she'd encountered through her work. But she couldn't place it. He might be any of a hundred different people. She'd made at least that many enemies in the last seven years, had accumulated dozens of death threats from animal smugglers, corrupt foreign officials, zookeepers, medical researchers. The list was long.

"All-iii-son! Allison Farleigh. We're going to find you." Singing it out, jeering. "We're going to find you, Allison. And when we do, we're going to fuck you uuuu-up."

"Yeah, just like we did your little girl."

"Only much much much much much worse. All-iii-son. Come out, come out, wherever the fuck you are. Allie, Allie, in come free."

Allison closed her eyes, felt a sob growing in her chest like a great hot blister. Felt it swell, strangling her, but she fought it, choked it back, the howl of despair.

She heard them on the ledge above her. A handful of

pebbles and twigs tumbled into the ravine. She pressed backward, moving farther in, her back nudging against something slick and cool. She held still. Didn't breathe. Cold, sleek, with a rubbery strength, shifting behind her, nestling closer, like Harry used to do, spooning her in his sleep. She reached behind her and touched the dry oiliness of scales.

"I don't know," the man said from somewhere very nearby. "Maybe she ran off already. Went to get the authorities. They got 911 in this fucking country?"

"She's still around here. Don't worry. We'll find her."

"Another hour it gets dark, man. I don't want to be out in this fucking place then. No telling what kind of shit drops out of the trees around here at night."

"Come on, you idiot. Let's find her. She's here. I know she is." Then the same voice singing out, "All-iii-son, come out, come out. We got a nice piece of candy for you, Allison."

She felt the creature stir again. Part of it moving, part of it staying still, as though it were snuggling closer to her. Slowly she turned her head to get a look. In the dim light she could make out its brown and gray camouflage markings, but couldn't tell its size. Some of them, she knew, grew to thirty feet, three hundred pounds of coiling sinew. Nonpoisonous. Crushed their prey. Beyond that, she knew nothing about pythons.

The snake's head began to pry between her ankles. Allison jammed them closed, but it was no use. The python was far stronger. It was already beginning a slow spiral up her body.

She heard the men nearby, and through the curtain of vines she glimpsed three pairs of jeans, hiking boots. They were standing on the opposite bank, facing her.

"Yeah, yeah. I see it."

"If I hadn't pointed it out, you wouldn't've."

"Jesus Christ, man. All right, you get three brownie points for spotting the fucking cave. Is that good enough for you? Ten more points, you win a free dishwasher."

"I just want a little credit, is all. You never give me any goddamn credit for anything."

The python was burrowing beneath her waist, starting its third loop around her. Allison the barber pole. The snake was surprisingly gentle, felt like warm water rising around her. For an instant everything became exquisitely vivid. The smell of the damp cave, the velvety embrace of the snake, the rasp of its body against her flesh, her slow breath entering and leaving her body, the screams and songs of birds. Even the men outside, their footsteps, their voices.

The python coiled around her almost tenderly, as if it were half asleep, as if this were love it was making, nurturing her. Bringing Allison slowly and completely into its own world.

She strained against its constrictions, twisted deeper into the cave as if she might be able to beat the snake at its own game, oozing free like a watermelon seed from its slippery grasp. She wriggled headfirst into a blur of cobwebs, the mess sticking to her hair, turning it to cotton candy. But her approach was working, she was keeping her chest above the snake's coiling grasp, staying one curl ahead. Protecting her lungs, her heart. But there wasn't enough room in the cave. Five feet, six at most. Eventually the python would trap her against the far wall, cram her head against the stone, continue its methodical encircling.

While, outside, the men on the opposite bank called out her name, and she heard the metallic clack of a rifle being cocked.

"We see you moving around in there, Allison. We seeeee you."

She stiffened. And the python glided onward, coiling higher, pressing the air from her chest. Splashing bright pink lights against the backs of her eyes. She felt it harden around her like concrete setting up, heard the crackle and tick of her joints and tendons beginning to give way.

In the same instant that she heard the rifle blast, a clod of dirt blew into her face. Abruptly the python halted its caress. Allison managed a shallow breath. Then, faster than it seemed possible, the snake unwrapped itself from her and poured out of the entrance of the cave; thick as her calf, it flowed across her body, a bloody gash in the flesh behind its head. The snake rushed into the fading daylight to confront who or what had attacked it.

"You fucking idiot," one of the men yelled. "Jesus, shit, look what the hell you stirred up now."

"I thought it was her. You did, too, man. You did."

There was another rifle shot. Then she listened to the men hustle away into the dense brush shouting at each other, and in the distance Allison heard them laughing like jackals.

She waited in the cave. After a short while she heard them approaching again, listened to the scrabbling of men through underbrush, their voices. She pressed herself against the contours of the grotto, in the fetid dark. Every nerve awake, hearing each second as it passed, as the men roamed nearby, and then once again moved away.

For over an hour Allison waited. Listening to each sigh and twitch of the jungle, every scrape of twig and scream of bird. The light dimmed, heat slacked off, and the voices gradually moved out of earshot. Still she waited. Waited until the blackness settled, the night noises began, the flutters and clicks and shrieks of the nocturnal animals.

Allison dragged herself out of the cave. She fully expected to meet the python guarding its lair, was prepared to fight it hand to hand, scratch, gouge, whatever it took. But it had disappeared. And she writhed across the ground to the embankment, took hold of one of the vines and pulled herself up.

Bumping her swollen ankle sent white jolts through her, wrenched the breath from her lungs. At each stab she gasped, but kept on with her climb. She wriggled across the crest, and on her hands and knees went scrambling through the dark snarl of limbs and fronds until she found the clearing where Winslow lay.

In the gloomy moonlight she made out the blood covering her daughter's face, pressed a fingertip to the slender puncture driven into the bridge of her daughter's nose. The ground was saturated with gore.

Both of Winslow's cameras had been taken, her film bag too.

In a numb trance, Allison held back the sobs, drew off her poncho, and draped it over Winslow's body. She fanned the flying insects away from the blood. She lay down beside her, brought her mouth close to Winslow's ear, and spoke her name. Then said the words that she had not spoken often enough in life, the words not a single person had uttered to Allison in years. She repeated them, and repeated them again, like a chant in her beautiful daughter's ear.

When finally Allison allowed herself to weep, the tears came from her quietly. And she felt a vast ache in some part of her that no longer existed, a helpless agony like the phantom pain of a severed limb. The flesh gone, torn away, but still tormenting her beyond the limits of endurance.

All night she battled the ants and flies. Threw sticks and pebbles at large rats or possums that wandered close by. And every second of the night Allison prepared herself for the cool muscularity of the python against her back again. She would fend it off this time, kill it if she had to, cut it in half as she had done with the leech.

But the python didn't return. And an hour after first light, as she was fighting to stay awake, she heard a couple of the park rangers yelling for her. Then she heard Sean's voice singing out her name. Singing it out over and over.

Allison had enough strength left to call back just once.

The ape with the silver swatch of hair was stunned but alive. His mother was dead. Falling from such a great height, even the deep bed of ferns she'd landed in was not enough to save her. The son had lost his breath after the fall, but in a moment or two he revived. He stood beside his mother's body and began to pick leaves and bits of broken branches from her fur.

When the men arrived, one of them scooped him up. The young ape was still groggy from his fall and didn't resist. There was blood on his lower lip, and several fingers on his right hand were broken.

The hunter tied up the silver-haired orangutan with ropes around his ankles and wrists, then attached the rope around the ape's ankles to the man's belt. Upside down, the young ape swung back and forth against the man's hip as he walked.

On the other side of the man another orangutan was lashed up the same way. This orangutan was sick, or very sleepy. The newly captured orangutan poked his fingers at the sick one, but the sick one did not poke back. The young male orangutan had never seen another ape besides his mother.

While he swung from the man's belt, he was able to grab for flakes of bark or leaves as they passed through the jungle. Once or twice as he was reaching out the man halted, took a grip on the orangutan's throat, and rapped him hard on the back of the head with his knuckles.

The ape with the silver streak stopped reaching for things. He contented himself with staring down at the man's shoes as they moved along the path, nipping once or twice at the man's shoelaces.

As darkness fell the men came out of the jungle and stood in a clearing beside a river. They talked and drank from their canteens. There were two more orangutans attached to the other man's belt. Those apes were very quiet. The men drank more water, and joked with each other. Then one of them pulled two cameras out of his knapsack and opened the backs, exposing the film. One after the other the man hurled the cameras far out into the river.

Then two of the men got into a motorized canoe with their orangutans. The other man got into a faster boat without any orangutans. They motored away in different directions, the two men went downriver, the other man sped north.

# CHAPTER

# 4

Friday night they were the only customers in the Gunga Din Bar, one of Singapore's oldest drinking establishments. Rayon and Orlon White, plus the bartender, Harvey Trumbo. Orlon had started calling him Sir Harvey, Your Royal Highness. Pronouncing it *hine ass*. Needling the guy for the pure, brainless fun of it.

The Gunga Din Bar had dark mahogany walls, a crimson rug, a tiger's head on one wall, the heads of a gazelle and a rhino on another. Green leather elbow rests on the bar. Like the smoking room of some big-time Ernie Hemingway safari hunter. Tables scattered around, the lights low. Paintings of the jungle and mountains, each painting with its own dim overhead light. But the main attraction of the Gunga Din was the long metal cage mounted above the shelves of liquor bottles. The cage ran the length of the wall, maybe fifty feet.

Inside it a single gibbon roamed from one end to the other and back again. He would stop to swing on his trapeze for a second, then squawk, make a few spooky hoots, and climb up the side of the cage watching the three humans, then start his boring journey again back and forth along the upper wall of the bar. It was a siamang gibbon, with short black fur all over it except for his face, which was hairless and white, little tufts coming off each side of his head like a punk rocker. Cute little guy, strange too. Only a few thousand of them left in the jungle. Which was the reason some people were willing to pay upward of ten thousand dollars for one of them.

Ray had on his new batik shirt, just bought that afternoon at the Galang marketplace. Red and black batwing designs on the shirt, along with long white pants and white loafers. He'd wet-combed his blond hair straight back. Sleek-looking, two days out of the jungle, all primed and ready to find one of those slinky working girls from Bugis Street, take a few rides on the old Malaysian slippery slide.

Sitting next to him, his brother Orlon was a foot shorter at five-two. Thirty-two years old and slick bald. Every morning Orlon completely shaved his body; plucked his eyebrows and lashes for good measure. Worked at it the way some people gnawed their fingernails down to the quick. Straight-razoring himself till his head, face, his whole damn body was as smooth as an ice cube.

Then he'd go over every inch of flesh for another half hour with a pair of tweezers, plucking out anything he might've missed. Next morning Orlon would start the whole damn process over again. Told Ray he got the idea from those Olympic swimmers, shaving themselves so they'd go faster through the water. He heard one of them say how it made his flesh ultrasensitive. So Orlon tried it, and it gave him such a kick he kept on. And now he was addicted, claimed that every tickle of air, every brush of cloth lit him up, gave him a little rush.

Tonight Orlon had on his usual outfit, ratty blue jeans torn at the knees and the butt, no undershorts, letting the world see the crack of his ass. A white T-shirt with a monster truck-pull logo on the front. Dressed like that, short and soft-bellied, completely hairless, nine times out of ten Orlon could still pick up the prettier lady. Damned if Rayon could say why. Maybe it was a smell thing, some kind of sex dust hovering around him. Apparently it rose off Orlon like sand off the Sahara. And strange as it seemed, that left Ray, handsome as a Tom

Selleck movie star, not getting half the action his twin brother did.

Harvey, their bartender, was red-faced and sinewy, an inch under six feet, with a skinny mustache that looked drawn on with an eyeliner pencil. The guy didn't say much, but he looked like the kind who might've served in the French Foreign Legion for a while or the Royal Gurkhas, been up to his elbows in guts and blood more than once and jolly well liked it, and as a matter of fact was considering jumping over the bar and slinging some blood with the White brothers if the conversation kept heading in the direction it was.

"Another thing I hate about the British," Orlon was saying, "they all talk like queers."

"He means homosexuals," Rayon said to Harvey. Then to Orlon, "The word *queer* is offensive to some people."

"Uppity faggots is what I mean," said Orlon. "Damn British talk like they're yawning at you. Like they went to college too long, now everything bores them. Know what I mean, Harv? See what I'm saying? Uppity, like they still run the world."

"Indeed."

Orlon smiled, getting his licks in. Ray took the folded-up gunnysack off his lap and dropped it down by his feet. He had another sip of his Singapore Sling.

Trumbo was leaning against the liquor shelf, arms crossed over his skinny chest. Head tipped back, his sleepy eyes focusing on the tiger's head across the bar. Been standing like that for the last ten minutes, pretending he was only half listening, all the while the gibbon swung from the ceiling of his cage, hooting and yodeling a few feet above Trumbo.

"Your names," the bartender said without looking their way. "Rayon and Orlon." Slowly he twisted his mouth out of shape like he was trying to pick food out from between his teeth.

"Yeah, that's right. He's Orlon, I'm Rayon."

"Those would be synthetic fibers, would they not?"

Harvey kept his eyes on the tiger's head. "Petroleum products, if I'm not mistaken. Like plastic. Cheap, disposable."

"Whatta you doing, Harvey, trying to piss us off? That your objective here?" Without looking away from the bartender, Orlon sipped his Singapore Sling and wiped his mouth with the back of his hand. Then he glanced at Ray, and back at Harvey. "Well, let me tell you, bud, you're going to have to try harder than that. I been insulted by some major-league assholes in my time. I got a very high threshold of provocation."

"Quite."

The gibbon had stopped roaming, and now it was peering through the weave of his cage at Orlon. The two of them making deep eye contact like they were sending wavelength messages.

"So tell me, gentlemen," Harvey said, clearing his throat. "Are these names of yours derived from American TV? Tom and Jerry cartoon characters, perhaps? Something of that nature?"

"Good, good, Harvey. That's better. I'm starting to get a little pissed. Tiny puffs of steam coming out my ears."

"They're nicknames, is all," Ray said, jumping in to cool it off before anybody fired the first shot. After all, they had business to conduct, then women to locate. Ray said, "We made the names up, gave them to ourselves. Like aliases."

"Yeah," Orlon said. "Like it's any of your goddamn business, Harvey, one way or the other."

"My legal name," Ray said, "is Raimondo and his is Orlando. That's what our mother named us originally."

"I see," Trumbo said, bringing his eyes wearily to the brothers, looking at one, then the other, the trace of a smile. "Then that would make you of Hispanic origin." Putting a little prissy spin on *Hispanic*.

Orlon stiffened, but Ray rested a hand on his arm.

"We're Irish, is what we are," Ray said. "Presbyterians."

"Is that a fact?" Harvey said. "Then where did the Latino appellations come from, if I might be so bold?"

" 'If I might be so bold,' " Orlon said, mincing the words. "Would you listen to this guy? 'Appellations.' Is that faggy or what? Am I wrong, Ray? Am I off base here? 'Indeed.' 'Quite.' 'If I might be so bold.' 'Appellations.' Does this guy dress up like the queen mother or what? Walk around in his high heels, playing with his scepter."

Ray pressed his brother's arm down hard against the bar, kept him in place.

"Our mother," Ray said, "she had a crush on Ricky Ricardo. You know, the bobaloo guy, Desi what's his name on TV. She thought the guy was sexy or something, I dunno, so when me and Orlon came along, she picked these names for us. Raimondo and Orlando."

"What're you telling this fucking guy about our mother for?"

"I take it that when you got older," the bartender said, "the names embarrassed you, so you changed them to something else. Something, I must say, equally grating on the ear."

Trumbo picked up a shot glass and began polishing it with a towel. Keeping his eyes on his work.

"Okay, here's how it is, Harvey," Ray said, feeling Orlon starting to boil beside him. "The town we live in, see, Miami, Florida, if you're called Raimondo or Orlando there, what people think is, you're Cuban."

"And we don't like Cubans," Orlon said. "Almost as much as we don't like smart-ass faggot Brits."

Trumbo put the shot glass down behind the bar. Watching them in his peripheral vision, but keeping his eyes hidden. Sneaky bastard. Ray was about to let go of his brother, let him scramble across the bar, rip the guy's hamster dick off.

The gibbon had taken a seat on a piece of driftwood. He was grunting to himself, eyes fixed on Orlon. Probably never seen anybody so hairless before. The gibbon tipped his head to the right and left, still studying Orlon like he was trying to figure out what species he belonged to.

"So." The bartender turned around looked at them full on for a second, resting his hands on his side of the bar, smiling like they were all great pals. "I'm sorry to inform you that it is now one A.M., and the bar is officially closed. You may settle your accounts, gentlemen, then be on your bloody way."

Orlon eased back on his stool. He squinted hard at the bartender, noisily sucked down the last of his drink, and pushed the empty glass forward. He ran his hands across his smooth head, then slid a finger along the ridges where his eyebrows used to be, and said, "So how much you want for that gibbon?"

While he waited for an answer, he reached into the pocket of his blue jeans and came out with a black-handled jackknife. He opened the largest blade and began to trim his nails.

"I beg your pardon?"

"You heard me, Harv. What'll you take for it? The primate."

"It doesn't belong to me. It belongs to the hotel."

"But you're its keeper, aren't you, Harv?"

"I have nothing to do with that animal."

"We'll go four hundred," Orlon said. "Four hundred U.S. dollars. More'n you make in a week, I'd be willing to bet."

Orlon brushed his nail shavings off the bar and settled his eyes on the bartender.

"Four hundred's a solid offer," said Ray. "More than fair."

"Especially since we're going to take the fucking thing anyway," said Orlon.

"You'll have to speak to the management about that, gentlemen."

"Afraid I can't do that, Harv," Orlon said. "I never been real good talking to the management. Not to cops either. You might say I got a subconscious problem with authority."

Orlon pressed the point of his knife into the teak bar and dug it in.

"My little brother," Rayon said, "in case you haven't noticed it yet, Harvey, he was born with a pathological wild streak. Regulations, rules, closing times, shit like that —it's what sets him off." Ray was catching the mood now, a little contact macho coming off Orlon.

"You see what he's doing now, carving up your bar. That's typical of my little brother. He sees something, a brick wall, something standing in his way, a sign says no trespassing, like that, he'll rip that sign down, or smash himself up against those bricks till he's either knocked himself out or broken a hole in the wall. See what I'm telling you? The man's a natural-born rebel. You tell him he can't do something, it's like throwing gasoline on a campfire. That's no way to put it out."

Harvey wasn't moving. He was staring at the damage Orlon was doing to his bar, moving his eyes fast between that and Ray. Getting the picture.

"What he's doing there, Harvey, he's carving his signature. The letter O."

"I'm almost done. Give me a minute more before you look."

"It stands for Big O. You know, like in recognition of Orson Welles, the movie director. Shot some great movies. So Orlon took it as a second nickname for the same reason. 'Cause he's such a great shooter. Only it isn't movies he shoots. See what I'm driving at with you?"

Harvey was beginning to, but he didn't open his mouth.

"Now why don't you try it, Harvey? Call him Big O. Go on, go ahead. See if he isn't nicer to you as a result. Sometimes it works with him."

Orlon smiled at that, but didn't move his eyes, all focused on his work. A nice round O appearing in the beautiful teak bar. About the size a Coke can would leave.

"Now, see, the reason we came in here tonight, Harvey, it wasn't to drink your drinks. It wasn't to fraternize with you. Tell you about our mother, our names, nothing like that.

"It just so happens the last time we were in here, a

few weeks back, we saw that little fellow in the cage there, and we made a mental note of it, and then yesterday when we got back in town, we realized we had an extra space in one of the cargo crates we're shipping home, so Orlon here, he turns to me and he says, hey, remember that prize monkey, that cocktail lounge exhibit, and I say, yeah, yeah. So he says, hey, Ray, let's go pay a call on the Gunga Din Bar. And that's why we're here, Harvey. The complete story."

"That gibbon, gentlemen, is a member of the siamang species. Very rare. Even if it were in my power to sell it to you, you wouldn't be permitted to ship it out of the country. You can't sell it anywhere. It's endangered."

"Endangered, Harvey? *Endangered?* That the word you used?"

"That's right."

"Hey, Harv," Ray said. "We're all of us endangered. Every single one of us. Isn't that right, Orlon?"

Orlon brushed away the wood shavings, folded up his knife, looked up at the bartender.

"Some of us, Harvey, are a lot more endangered than others."

Once Orlon wrestled Harvey to the floor, it was all over. The man knew how to fight standing up, a stiff-backed play-by-the-rules boxer, got in a couple of right jabs to Orlon's right cheek and mouth, but Orlon bulled in underneath his fists, butted him in the sternum, and once Harvey was flat on his back, Orlon straddling his chest, holding a blade against the man's Adam's apple, the power went right out of his muscles.

"I believe our buddy Harvey needs a drink. His royal hine ass looks a little frayed around the edges."

Ray just stood there.

"Get me a bottle, would you please."

Ray went over to the shelves and took down a quart of Jim Beam and brought it back, handed it to his brother. Orlon tipped it over the bartender's mouth, let some trickle out. Harvey sputtered, spit it out, then tried to twist free, but Orlon gripped him hard with his legs and pressed the naked blade against Harvey's throat. Drew a thin line of blood.

"What's wrong? You not a drinker, Harvey? You a twelve stepper or something? Got yourself one of them higher powers? I heard about guys like you."

He poured more of the bourbon into the bartender's mouth, but again the man spit it out.

"Hey, now, I'd say that's an insult, wouldn't you, Ray? A direct affront to the great state of Kentucky. This man is being thoroughly disrespectful to our land of origin."

"Yes, I believe he is. I believe he's showing a very definite anti-American sentiment."

"Can't have that," Orlon said. "Not and hold our heads up."

Orlon raised the bottle above his head, held it there for a second to let Harvey get a good look at what was about to happen, then he brought it down, smacked it across the side of Harvey's skull just hard enough to put him under.

"Hey, Harvey," Orlon said. " 'I don't like your face. Never have. You got shifty eyes and a weak chin.' " He looked over at his brother. "Know where that's from?"

"No," Ray said. "I don't."

"Edward G. Robinson said it to Byron Foulger in *I Am the Law* just before he threw him out of his office."

"Fascinating."

"Shifty eyes and a weak chin. I like that."

Orlon smiled and got off the man's chest and rolled him over, and Ray tied the bartender's wrists with the braided nylon rope they'd used on the orangutans. Then Ray climbed up on the teak counter behind the bar, kicked a few liquor bottles out of the way to get a better footing. He reached up and pried opened the cage door and waited till Orlon hoisted Harvey up to him. Ray cradled the man in his arms for a second, then hefted him up and rolled the skinny guy into the cage.

In a frenzy, the siamang gibbon chirped as it raced

from one end of the cage to the other. Each time he passed Harvey he touched a finger to the bartender's face. Eyes, mouth, nose.

It took almost twenty minutes before the gibbon quieted enough that they could snag the little bastard. Rayon got him in a headlock, dragged him out of the cage, and held on while Orlon twisted the ape's arms behind his back and secured him with the Velcro handcuffs he'd bought in an adult entertainment complex back in Miami. Red satin with big squares of black Velcro. The gibbon fought and twisted, but the cuffs held.

When they had his ankles done, too, they dropped the siamang into the gunnysack and Ray carried it out to the lobby, right out through the front door of the hotel. No one seemed to notice. Or if they did, they didn't say anything.

Allison was lying in a hospital bed in Singapore, the room dimly lit, hushed bells and voices echoing in the hallways. Heart stopped, blood hardened, breath empty. Hearing the voices, hearing the quiet business of healing going on around her. Hearing Harry's voice, Sean's. Words coming from the thick, dark vacuum. Dead, but hearing the distant sound of Harry describing his meeting with the Malaysian authorities.

"Little bastard sat there not even taking notes. Chief of major crimes division. I told him everything you told me, Allison. Every detail. He didn't even suggest flying over to Singapore to interview you himself. Just sat there listening to what I told him. Three men hunting orangutans, the whole scene, and this self-important little man, smoking cigarettes the whole time, dingy office, he had his eyes closed, he might've been asleep for all I know. When I was finished, he took a minute more, then he opened his eyes, looked out his window, and all he said was, 'We will do our utmost.'

"Our utmost! Can you believe that! We will do our utmost. My daughter dead, my wife in the hospital, and this little man is lighting another cigarette, eyes closing again. He's doing his goddamn utmost just to stay awake."

Sean telling her father to calm down. It's okay. Just relax, okay?

Floating in the exhausted half-light of the room, with the aroma of dying flowers, of aftershave, the discreet vanilla scent of the sheets, the hollow ache of death filling her joints, the bruised, breathless drag of air into her body, mindless respiration, her body's pointless act of self-perpetuation.

Allison spoke the man's name, which had been hovering like a poisonous fume in her head since that afternoon in the jungle.

"What'd she say?"

"Something Bond," said Sean. "James Bond?"

Allison willed herself to pronounce his name again, vile in her mouth.

"Oh," Sean said. "*Joshua* Bond."

"Jesus Christ," said Harry. "It never stops with her. She's practically in a coma and it's still 'Joshua Bond, Joshua Bond, Joshua Bond.' Alpha and omega of everything abominable. Al Capone of animal dealers."

Allison was a shell of flesh, her will departed, mind blank, body rotting with self-hatred. Endless hours stretching in all directions, an eternity of vanilla and flowers and bells chiming in the distance. Caught in the undertow of her loss. Harry speaking, Harry nudging her numb flesh. Sean's voice. But Allison was lifeless. A frail husk, even when she rose from this bed, walked out the door, sat in the plane, strapped herself in, put food in her mouth, drank water, mechanically took what was offered, she was still inert. Allison, embalmed by grief.

# CHAPTER

# 5

When Ray White woke on Monday, last day of October, their final morning in Singapore, he found himself tangled in the mosquito netting. The white gauzy stuff was wrapped from his toes to his waist.

He and Orlon had been sharing a two-room suite in Raffles Hotel, best in Singapore. Old colonial decor, built when Harvey Trumbo's predecessors ruled the world. Lily ponds filled with giant goldfish, cast-iron fountains, Persian rugs, stained glass. A few hundred potted palms in the lobby, ceiling fans as big as DC-3 propellers, Roman columns everywhere. The kind of place where tigers used to wander in from the jungle, prowl the billiard room, guys playing pool had to stop and shoot them.

Orlon kept saying it felt like they were walking around in a Bogart movie. All the time going, "Where's Sydney Greenstreet? I know he's around here somewhere. Where's Peter Lorre, Mary Astor?"

Their plush bedroom had two giant four-poster beds with the mosquito netting rigged up under the canopy on each one so that you could pull a rip cord by your head and the thing would whoosh down around you like a heavy fog. Just don't get twisted up in it.

"King Tut," Orlon said. Standing in the doorway to the bathroom, his tweezers in his right hand, a hand mirror in the other. "That's who you look like wrapped up like that. King Tut."

Ray rolled to his right, but that only tightened the netting around his hips.

"Jesus, I don't know why I associate with you, Rayon. You're such a mongoloid."

Ray lay there for a minute, staring over at his brother.

"You associate with me because if you didn't, you'd be in Raiford serving a dozen life terms. I'm the smart brother, you're the dumb, violent one. Don't get us confused."

Ray rolled to his left, came just to the edge of the bed, and had to stop. The gauze had loosened.

He watched Orlon pluck an eyelash, then open his tweezers over the rug and shake it loose. Ray hated seeing him do that to himself. Every day the same thing. Some screwed up self-mutilation fetish. Though whenever Ray started in on it, suggesting Orlon might want to make an appointment with a qualified health professional about his problem with body hair, Orlon would just stare at him until the words withered up and died in the air. These days Ray had stopped mentioning it altogether. Though he *had* asked his brother to at least refrain from plucking himself in public.

Ray kicked off the last of the mosquito netting and stood up.

"Man, you look just like Boris Karloff in *The Mummy*. Like you're just waking up after three thousand years in your tomb, peeling off your bandages. Karloff's greatest role."

Ray stood there a minute, waiting to see if Orlon was going to go on, educate him further about Hollywood. Man, almost every night back in Miami the guy rented three, four movies, mainly old crime films, the noirs, and he watched them one after the next. Knew all the actors' names, the directors. Always watched the credits roll at the end, wouldn't get up and switch it off like any normal person, had to sit there and study all that shit. Best boy, grips, catering company. Committing it all to memory.

But no, this morning Orlon wasn't handing out any more Hollywood facts. He turned his back toward the mirrored medicine chest, twisted around so he could see himself, then held the hand mirror off to one side and closed the tip of his tweezers around a hair that must've been growing from his shoulders.

Ray groaned, went over to the minibar and got a Perrier, then drank it down in one continuous swallow, keeping his back to his brother. Three weeks in the Far East, and Ray still hadn't had diarrhea once. Which he attributed mainly to good drinking habits. Bottled water and Singapore Slings.

"You finished in there?"

Orlon was bent over the sink, slapping his face with alcohol. He raised up, jerked a towel off the rack and patted himself down with it, then came over to the door.

"What's your hurry, man? You can't wait to get on that plane, strap yourself in for thirty hours?"

"Sooner we're back in Miami, the better. I'm homesick to see a full-figured woman."

"You mean a woman with tits," Orlon said.

"I'm not that uncouth."

"*Tits,*" Orlon said. "A perfectly acceptable word."

"It's demeaning to women, that kind of language."

"Well, personally, I've come to appreciate these Orientals," Orlon said. "What I particularly like is how slick their bodies are. You notice that? Almost hairless. Genetically depilated."

Orlon stood naked in the doorway, no pubic hair, no leg hair, no armpit or nose hair. The guy glistened. His skin was as sleek as the goddamn day he was born.

"Where's Rawi today?" Ray asked the little Malaysian customs guy in his short-sleeved white shirt and black trousers, and some kind of admiral's hat.

"Rawi no here."

"We can see that," said Orlon.

"He coming in later on or what?" Ray asked.

The customs guy looked the White brothers over.

Piss-stained eyes, a sour twist in his mouth. Gold braids on his shirt, epaulets. The squirt thought he was General Pershing, Commander in Chief of the Changi International Airport.

A gang of tourists was gathering behind the White brothers, talking loud; Germans, it sounded like. One of the men peeked over Orlon's shoulder, trying to see what the holdup was.

Ray said, "I mean, usually we deal with Rawi. We do a lot of business here. He's like our personal friend."

"He no come in today," the customs guy said. "No come in tomorrow, or no more. He fire."

"Rawi! Shit. What happened?"

"He taking bribe. Chief fire him. Now let's see papers."

Ray glanced at his brother. The Germans grumbling.

Orlon said, "You want to try back later? Make a few calls first?"

Ray shook his head. "Let's risk it. I'm ready to be home."

Ray took out the documents from the Lampung Zoo and Nature Preserve and slid them across to the customs guy. The address for the Lampung Zoo was Beri Rambai Avenue, in Manila. Nice official seal, a professional-looking logo that showed a gorilla touching one fist to its chest, the other hand reaching up, holding on to a vine. Even had a slogan underneath the zoo's name. Ray'd thought it up. "Life on the Wild Side." A street address, a phone number, all the other hundred and one numbers and signatures required for international transportation of wildlife. All of which were totally phony. No such zoo, no such address. Just the telephone number was real.

Back in Manila, someone was sitting there waiting to answer, say "Lampung Zoo and Nature Preserve," a person who cost the White brothers five hundred a month, but who knew all the export rigamarole inside out: the weird, complicated etiquette, the names of every single relevant Filipino official, the entire chain of command from the president on down; knew all the shipping standards and regulations. Even knew the rules of the CITES charter, the international agreement about which animals were protected, which weren't; which could or couldn't be shipped where. Five hundred a month was a bargain for all that. A smart lady. So valuable to them that neither of the White brothers had hit on her, though she was something of a fox. Of the Asian persuasion.

The brothers stood there waiting while the customs guy had a long look at all the paperwork. Their carry-on bags sat at their feet. Ray, with his hair shampooed and tousled dry, his Beach Boy look. In another batik shirt, loose elastic-waist warm-up pants, black with a white stripe. Going to stay comfortable for the long flight. Orlon in tennis shorts, sandals, a black T-shirt with an ad for a Holly camshaft.

Orlon watched the customs agent as the little guy read over the permits, then picked up their passports and studied them.

"Birds?" the man said.

"That's right," Ray said. "Parrots, songbirds, cockatoos."

He set aside the passports and stared down at the shipping manifest. Stepping out from behind his podium, he went over to the luggage cart where the wooden crate was sitting. Five-by-five box, little breathing holes, but you couldn't see anything through them 'cause Ray had thumbtacked some cheesecloth inside. The box weighed almost four hundred pounds. They'd had to hire a flatbed truck to get them from the bird shop to the airport. Storing the orangs in some back cages at the Jurong bird shop, fifty bucks a day storage fee. A rip-off, but what could you do? One of the problems with smuggling animals, you had to deal with so many criminals.

"We are quite late. We will miss our plane," the German said over Ray's shoulder. "Maybe you might act polite and let us go first before you?"

"Bite my Jockey shorts," Orlon said.

The German stared down at Orlon for a few seconds,

then turned back to his group and consulted with them, working on the translation together.

The customs guy tapped on the crate with his knuckles, bent over and tried peering through a breathing hole. There was a small crowbar sticking out of his back pocket.

"You take to America as excess luggage," the man said. He tapped one of the crates. "Why you not ship birds normal way? Pay cargo rate. Much more cheap."

He stood up, looked at Ray.

"Word is *cheaper*," Ray said, trying to be helpful. The Indonesian guy in his white rooster suit with gold braids eyed Ray for a few seconds. The man was way too eager, paying too much fucking attention. Ray was beginning to perspire.

A big guy behind them made some remark in ugly German and herded his platoon away to another line.

"What you're trying to say is, it's less expensive to send the birds cargo rate. But see, we already know that. And this is how we want them to go anyway. We always do it this way."

The customs man studied Ray some more, his chin jutting out an extra inch. Then he extracted his pint-size crowbar and gave the crate a good whack. Brought his ear close to the wood. There was a faint noise inside it. A warble, a high moan. Christ, that was all they needed, the damn apes starting to act up right there. Throw another whining, peeping fit.

The man straightened up and squinted at Ray.

"You got problem with my English? You not understand me? I go get my boss, he better English."

"What my brother is trying to articulate to you." There was acid rising in Orlon's voice. "We don't care about the expense. This is the way we like to ship our birds. As extra baggage."

"All go in the same place inside airplane," the man said. "Cargo hold. Same place. Either way you ship, box sit in same place." Again he rapped the crate with his knuckles. "Not make sense pay extra for same place in airplane. 'Less maybe you try play game. Want keep from shipping inspection, think we not do as good job, something like that."

The brothers looked at each other. Orlon rolled his eyes, ready to pinch this guy's breathing tubes closed. Ray reached back for his wallet. Took it out, fiddled in there, and withdrew a hundred bucks American. He palmed the bill, then reached out like he was going to take his passport back, and he let the hundred stay there on the guy's podium.

The guy edged back to the desk and peered down at the bill. Then he looked Ray up and down, did the same to Orlon.

"You give me this?"

"Give you what?" Rayon said. "I didn't give you anything."

The man touched the bill with a finger like it was alive, looked over his shoulder briefly, and the bill disappeared.

"Birds?" the customs guy asked.

"That's right, birds. Tweet, tweet. Like that."

"Yeah, birds. Shit on your head, like that," Orlon said.

"I know English," the man said. He picked up his rubber stamper and gave the passports each a whack. "More you think."

As they were passing into the waiting area, Orlon cuffed Ray on the shoulder and smiled.

"Tweet, tweet?"

"Yeah," Ray said. "Tweet, tweet."

"Man, you were pissed, weren't you? You never get pissed."

"Guy irritated me. Officious little prick."

"Tweet, tweet," his brother said. "Tweet, tweet, tweet."

"Oh, here we go. I'm gonna be hearing this for the next twenty-something hours."

\* \* \*

Ray stuffed the *Time* magazine back in the flap on the bulkhead. Christ, he'd already finished two magazines, and they hadn't even reached altitude yet. Gonna be a long damn day, long night too. Long tomorrow.

The White brothers always timed their flights so they made it back to Miami International in the midnight-to-two A.M. time frame. The Fish and Wildlife inspection office was closed then, and a lot of times you could breeze right through, bring in live snow leopards as far as anyone cared. Hell, Ray believed that that was how the entire world should work. Close down all the law enforcement facilities between midnight and dawn, let the lawless element have a few hours of the day to transact their business. Less mess for everybody.

In the seat beside him, Orlon was sulking. Lately the White boys had gotten used to riding first class, but tonight first class on the Singapore to Los Angeles leg was completely booked, and they were bumped back to business.

"It's some rock band up there," Ray said.

"Which rock band?"

"I think it's the moonwalk guy. Or the one with the puffy lips, the skinny blond wife. Mick the dick."

"So which is it?"

"How should I know?" Ray said. "I just heard somebody say something, one of the flight attendants."

"The moonwalk guy, the Stones, shit, they have their own goddamn planes. They're not going to fly with the rabble."

"Maybe their plane is in for repairs."

"I don't like it. I don't like sitting back here with the goddamn subordinate classes."

"Business class is fine," said Ray. "These are leather seats. They're wide. What's the big deal? Only difference is you get caviar up there. We get the liver pâté and cashews. Hell, a year ago this time we couldn't afford to ride in the cargo hold. What's your problem, man?"

"It's the principle of the thing."

"Oh, yeah. I forgot for a minute what a principled guy I'm traveling with."

"What's that mean?"

"You know what it means. I'm referring to your propensity for violence."

"Me? Violent?" Orlon was quiet for a second, then said, "Yeah, and who was it shot that girl in the jungle?"

Ray leaned out in the aisle, looked behind them to see if anybody'd heard. Just an old couple, eyes closed, both of them hooked up to headsets, giving little synchronized jukes to the music. Cute. Dancing together side by side. And across the aisle nobody riding beside them tonight either.

Orlon leaned close and whispered, "I know I didn't shoot her. 'Cause I didn't have a gun. You fucking confiscated it from me. Remember?"

"I didn't shoot the girl," Ray said.

"Bullshit."

"Our esteemed business partner shot her."

"You both aimed," Orlon said. "I saw you."

"But I missed. I saw where my shot went. It hit a tree."

"How do you know it wasn't his shot hit the tree?"

Ray took another look around to see if anybody was eavesdropping. Then he turned back around, looked Orlon dead in the eye.

" 'Cause I aimed at the tree, that's how I know."

"You aimed at the tree? Why the hell'd you do that?"

The flight attendant went by with a bottle of champagne. She opened the curtain to first class and Ray leaned out, but he couldn't see much before she snapped it closed. One black guy in leather pants, tall, skinny, standing in the aisle talking to someone. Could have been the moonwalker himself, or a stagehand from Jagger's band. Could have been anybody.

"I aimed at the tree 'cause—hell, I don't know why. I didn't feel like killing anybody that particular day. I was taking a day off, okay?"

"She was a pretty girl," Orlon said. "Maybe that was it. You saw her, got a good look, pretty red hair, and you couldn't bring yourself to squeeze one off at her."

"Maybe. Maybe that's it. She *was* a pretty woman."

"Jesus, you're getting soft, Ray. You're starting to flab up on me. I think maybe what we're going to have to do, we're going to take you in to the liposuction doctor, have him suck all the softness out of you."

"I'm not going soft."

"Yeah, so why'd you shoot a tree?"

"I had my reasons."

"Liposuction," Orlon said. "It's your only hope."

The stewardess came through the curtain, smiling, carrying two empty champagne bottles. Ray put his arm out across the aisle, blocking her way. Her smile disappeared. She was still showing her teeth, lips still in the right position for a smile, but it wasn't genuine anymore. Unfortunately, Rayon and Orlon had that effect on a lot of women.

"That the moonwalk guy up there?"

"The moonwalk guy?" the stewardess said. An older woman, chubby face, gray in her hair, probably edging up on fifty. Man, what was happening to the airlines? Deregulation, was that it? Ray could remember when all the stewardesses were Playboy bunnies.

"The moonwalk guy, you know. The one with the glove, grabs his crotch and holds on, that guy."

"No," she said. "It's Fresh Meat."

Orlon asked her to repeat the name, and she did.

"Never heard of 'em," Orlon said. "What kind of music, opera?"

"Rap," she said, nudging Ray's arm aside and moving on down the aisle.

"Rap," said Ray.

"Should've known," Orlon said. "First class. Rap stars."

Orlon was squinting at one of his knuckles. Probably spotted a bristle.

Ray shook his head, staring at the closed curtain.

Orlon said, "Christ almighty. What's the class system coming to? I mean, the world's in total turmoil. Those guys make more money faking like they're gangsters than we get for being the real thing."

He smiled at his brother. Then he put his knuckle in his mouth, started chewing off that hair.

"Man, I told you not to do that in public. It's revolting. Upsets my digestive tract."

Orlon lowered his hand.

"Tweet, tweet," he said. "Tweet, tweet."

"Oh, great. Here we go."

"You were saying why you didn't shoot the girl."

"Maybe I didn't shoot her," Ray said quietly, "because I wanted our business partner to do it."

"Why's that?"

Ray looked around again. Nobody paying any attention.

" 'Cause now we got something on him."

"Got what? So he shot somebody. What're we gonna do, testify against him? Guys like us putting our word up against a guy like him?"

Ray reached down and pulled out his carry-on bag. He unzipped one of the compartments, reached in and came out with a little plastic container. He rattled it in Orlon's face.

"What if . . ." said Ray. "What if the dead girl, just before she died, happened to capture a bad deed on extrafine Kodak film? Got a photo of a man shooting a rare animal out of a tree. Would that interest anyone?"

Orlon reached out and took the film container.

"Where the hell did this come from, man?"

"That first little while when you guys ran off looking for Allison," he said. "I took a second and frisked the dead girl. Found this little thing in her breast pocket."

Orlon peeled open the lid, looked inside. He capped it, handed it back.

"Shit, for all we know it could be snapshots of mosques or some other tourist bullshit."

"I don't think so," said Ray. "This girl's out there in

the jungle with her two cameras around her neck, plus she's Allison's daughter. So I don't think she's there to take tourist pictures."

"All right. So, tell me, Ray. Why the hell would we want to get anything on that guy? He's our business partner. We reap major financial benefits from knowing him. Goose that's laying our golden eggs."

"You're asking me why we'd want to get anything on him?"

"Yeah. Why?"

"Think about it, Orlon. I want you to spend the next twenty-two hours—Singapore to L.A., L.A. to Miami with a change in Dallas-Ft. Worth—thinking about it."

The orangutan with the silver streak was in the dark cargo hold. It was cold and noisy. The crate he was in had been partitioned off into six compartments, like a liquor box only larger. His cubicle was just big enough to wedge his shoulders into crosswise. For the most part he had to stand up, but with some effort he could dip his knees slightly and lower himself into a half squat.

Across from him there was one small hole in the wood. Out of it he could see things. Not much, but a few things. Dark shapes out in the cargo hold.

The plywood dividers came up only to his neck, so he could peek into the adjacent compartments and see his traveling companions. The orangutan on his right was smaller, while the one on his left was larger than he was. Both apes were fit into their compartments upside down, their arms pinned to their sides.

They'd each vomited several times, and now both of them were very still. The orangutan twisted his head back and forth, trying to see out the hole in the wood crate. There were things out there, but it was hard to see them clearly. Boxes, other crates, luggage that shifted and creaked. The plane was only half full tonight, the cargo hold even less than that.

He had been offered food back in the bird store, but because he was still young, he was used to eating only things his mother provided, so even though he was very hungry, he didn't eat.

He peeped a few times. Small sounds.

He continued to peer out the hole. It was almost the only thing he could do to entertain himself. When he grew tired of that, he looked down at the upside-down apes' faces, first one, then the other. They appeared to be asleep.

Sometime later, he found he could lean his head to the right and could bring his nose close to the feet of the ape next to him. He could smell the ape's toes. They still smelled like the jungle, trees and leaves. Smelled like the young ape's mother.

He brought his head back, and squinted out the hole in the crate some more. He was hungry. He was thirsty too. The plane was very bumpy, very very cold.

The vomit at the bottom of the crate was starting to smell good. But there was no way he could get to it. He wrestled against the tight fit, but he couldn't loosen himself.

So he looked out the hole some more. There might be food out there somewhere. Maybe there was water too. It sounded like it was raining. Sounded like a storm going on all around him. If he saw food outside the hole, maybe he would be able to get out there and eat it.

Beside him one of the other apes groaned loudly. Then there was a slurping noise. The ape with the silver streak bent his head to the side to see. The upside-down ape next to him was licking up its vomit. Licking it very slowly till it was gone.

# CHAPTER

# 6

November the fourth, Friday, nine days after Winslow was murdered, the funeral service was held at the Plymouth Congregational Church, a one-hundred-year-old coral building on Main Highway in Coconut Grove. One of Harry's partners was a deacon there, which made it as close as the Farleighs came to having a church affiliation.

Sean sat on one side of Allison, Harry on the other, neither of them touching her. Sean was weeping quietly, Harry sniffling from time to time. But Allison was quiet. She'd already done her mourning. She'd wept until she was empty, then wept more. Stayed in her darkened bedroom for the week since returning from the Far East. Couldn't eat, couldn't lift her body from the bed. Only that morning, for the first time in days, she'd pulled herself together, gotten showered and dressed. Shuffled on her sprained ankle out into the sun.

Allison took a long breath, inhaled the halo of expensive cologne that was wafting from the other side of the aisle, where Harry's colleagues sat, a half dozen lawyers from Barker, Hoff, Taylor, and Stern.

Harry had joined the firm a couple of years before, after retiring as assistant undersecretary of state for Asian affairs. Fourth man down from the secretary, rubbing shoulders with senators, even receiving an occasional phone call from the president. They had a condo in

Georgetown that Allison tried to make into a home for a year or two. But it hadn't worked. The dreary dust of bureaucracy settled into her pores, Washington's chalky air suffocating her. She moved back to the Gables house, and Harry commuted back to Miami for long weekends now and then. Less and less as time went on.

Now he was a registered lobbyist, paying calls on his old friends in government, working deals. Barker, Hoff, Taylor, and Stern's main client, possibly their only client, was Rantel Industries, an international construction company based in Miami. High-rise office buildings, glitzy malls, sports arenas, domed stadiums, colossal hotel complexes. At Rantel the investors drove stretch limos to the job sites, wore gold-plated hard hats.

Harry refused to discuss his work, but Allison assumed he was doing what other career diplomats did, trading on a lifetime of quid pro quos. Using his knowledge of the Far East to broaden the financial horizons of Barker, Hoff, Taylor, and Stern.

The rest of the funeral party was made up of a few of Sean's college friends, some members of Allison's Wildlife Protection League, a couple of young women from the photography studio where Winslow had worked since graduation. An aspiring photographer, for the last year and a half Winslow had been developing other people's snapshots, going out to endless weddings and anniversary parties.

Dr. Kurt Franklin sat in the front row along with Thorn and a couple of people Allison didn't know. Kurt was Winslow's fiancé. He was a vet at Metro Zoo, two years older than Winslow. He'd met her months ago at a Wildlife Protection League barbecue Allison had sponsored. He and Winslow hit it off, talked the evening away. A narrow-faced young man, extravagantly polite.

The minister began by admitting that he'd never actually met Winslow, but he had been told by all that she was a truly wonderful soul. He urged the mourners to console themselves by recalling the young woman at her happiest moments, and by praying to God to help them

grow through their hour of grief. For surely Winslow
Farleigh played some important role in God's plan. It had
to be so, even though it was beyond our ability to understand. By helping each other to accept God's mysteries,
surely we would reach our own wisdom and grace.

When Reverend Ruark finished reading the twenty-
third psalm, he closed his Bible and took a seat off to one
side of the altar. In the front row Kurt Franklin cleared
his throat and pushed himself to his feet. He trudged
across the stone floor and climbed the steps to the pulpit.
Earlier this week Kurt had asked the Farleighs if he could
give the eulogy for Winslow, and Harry said yes, yes, of
course.

Allison watched as Kurt steadied himself, a thin hand
on each side of the pulpit. He drew in a couple of labored
breaths, then took some papers from his pocket, unfolded
them, flattened them out before him. He stared down at
them for a moment, then refolded them carefully. He
cleared his throat, looked down at Sean, then Allison,
then Harry. Back at Sean. Tears shone on his cheeks.

"I can't do this," he said. He swallowed deeply,
looked down at the first row. "Thorn? Would you?"

Kurt came out from behind the pulpit and held out
his speech. Hesitantly Thorn stood up, let out a sigh, then
crossed the stone floor and took the pages. Kurt went
back to his seat, slumped over and put his face in his
hands.

Thorn climbed the steps, went behind the pulpit, and
spread the pages out before him and looked them over.
He was an inch on the other side of six feet, medium
build, long arms, scruffy hair that was tortured by the sun
to a bright blond. His skin was coppery, eyes somewhere
between blue and turquoise. He walked in a loose-gaited
way, almost a saunter, though there was nothing insolent
about him. He was in his early forties, roughly Allison's
age.

She'd known Thorn for thirty years. Allison's father
used to take Allison fishing with Thorn's adoptive mother,
Captain Kate Truman, young Thorn acting as first mate.

And twenty years later when Sean and Winslow were ten and eleven, Allison hired Thorn to take the girls out a few times, teach them about the water, fishing, boats. The girls found Thorn deliciously eccentric, so totally unlike anyone else from their city existence. Sean started calling him Nature Boy, a nickname that seemed to please everyone.

Over the years Allison and Thorn had stayed vaguely in touch, bumping into each other once a year or so. And in all that time, she had never seen him in any clothes but shorts, T-shirt, and old tennis shoes. But today he was wearing white jeans, creased as stiff as sheet metal. A black-and-white checked cowboy shirt with black pearl buttons. He had on a pair of white-soled boat shoes that looked hastily and inexpertly polished.

Last spring Allison heard about Thorn's most recent loss. The woman he'd been living with had drowned in a diving accident. Since he had no phone, Allison called his best friend, Sugarman, to see how Thorn was doing. Not good, he told her. He's holed up in his house, hardly ever goes out, grieving. Depressed. But Thorn is always holed up, Allison said. No, not like this, Sugarman said. This is serious.

A few days later Allison drove down to Key Largo and dropped in on Thorn. She claimed she was looking for someone to fill in for her at Parrot Jungle while she was away at various conferences. Maybe a week out of each month for the next few months. Could he do it? The job involved cleaning cages, and helping to feed the primates and the hundreds of birds that were housed there.

A *job*? Thorn said. He'd never had one of those and didn't want to start so late in life.

Not even to help out an old friend?

They shared a bottle of wine out on his porch, gazed out at Blackwater Sound for a quiet half hour. Then he turned to her. You got twenty people you could ask to fill in for you, don't you, Allison? At least that many, she said. But you drove down here to ask me 'cause you heard I was housebound. That's right, she said. Your friends are worried about you. Well, we can't have that, can we,

Thorn said. Can't worry my friends. No, sir. And then to
her great surprise he said yes, okay, he'd help her out, just
as long as they didn't call it a job.

For years Thorn had had a mild interest in orangutans, ever since he'd steered Allison to that tawdry roadside zoo on Lower Matecumbe Key, where a one-year-old
orangutan had been caged in a cramped, unventilated plywood box. It was Allison's first success at rescuing an ape,
and Thorn had been with her at every step.

For the last few months, since he'd begun subbing
for her at Parrot Jungle, Allison had loaned Thorn books,
articles, magazine pieces on orangutans, fed him information every chance she got. In that short time he seemed to
have mastered the subject, and Allison suspected that by
now he knew almost as much about those apes as she did.

During the two weeks that Allison was in Borneo,
Thorn had brought his boat up to Miami, found a marina
a mile from Parrot Jungle. He'd even begun giving the ape
talk to park visitors. From what she'd heard, he'd done an
excellent job. Perhaps he was a little low on social skills
from years of living a hermit's life. Thorn didn't tolerate
fools. There had been a few incidents with park visitors,
she'd been told by Crystal Slayton, one of the park workers. Incidents? Allison asked. What kind? Well, let's just
say this, Crystal told her. Our friend Thorn is not real
good at taking random shit.

Allison watched as Thorn finished looking through
Kurt Franklin's pages and refolded them and put them in
his pocket. He glanced down at Kurt and gave a small
apologetic headshake. Then he looked out at the assembly, cleared his throat, but said nothing. A couple of
Harry's partners on the other side of the aisle mumbled to
each other.

Thorn glanced around the sanctuary as if he were
absorbing the cold grandeur of the room. He looked over
at the lawyers from Harry's firm, then at a few of the
stained-glass windows. He brought his gaze back to Sean
and Allison. He seemed comfortable with the silence he
was creating, more at ease than anyone else in the room.

One of Harry's partners coughed. Allison looked over. A couple of the younger ones were grinning at each other.

Thorn took a long breath and stared down at the podium.

"I knew Winslow since she was little," he said, with a blend of Georgia cracker and the languid vowels of the Caribbean. A Florida Keys drawl that let lots of space accumulate between the words.

"I watched her grow into a damn fine lady. Graceful, kind, very smart. She was a quiet woman. She watched, she listened. She paid attention. She learned to catch fish pretty well, too, knew how to stay alert to any twitch of her line. Same skill a photographer needs, I suppose. Knowing just the right second to react.

"What I'm saying is, I liked Winslow. Liked her a lot. Respected her. I think her family did a damn good job raising her. It's a horrible shame we're here now, doing what we're doing."

The electronic warble of a cellular phone sounded over in the lawyer's gallery. One of the young men drew a small unit from his breast pocket and began to murmur into it. He fiddled with the antenna and continued to talk. One of the older lawyers sitting behind him thumped him on the shoulder and shook his head sadly at the boy, but the young lawyer raised his hand helplessly, and kept on speaking into the phone.

"One more thing and I'll get down from here." Thorn looked at the young lawyer chatting on his phone. "Lately I been to more funerals than is good for a person. And it seems like at every one of them, sooner or later somebody gets up and says that thing about God working in mysterious ways."

Thorn took a long, peaceful drink of air.

"Well, in the last few years I've also had the bad luck of encountering one or two killers. And I can tell you this with some confidence. If there's a God up there that uses people like the ones I've met to kill people like Winslow

Farleigh, then take me off his damn mailing list. I don't want any part of that God's mysterious plan."

Reverend Ruark was staring up at the ceiling, as if he were carefully weighing Thorn's theological argument.

Thorn came off the dais and walked down the aisle. He stopped at a pew halfway down, leaned over a couple of lawyers, and twisted the phone away from the young man's ear. He held the small black phone in both hands, lifted his knee and banged the phone down against it, cracking the thing in half, then dumped the pieces in the young man's lap and walked down the aisle and out of the church.

Reverend Ruark came back to the podium, thanked the gentleman for his heartfelt words, and began to read another psalm as if he were trying to purge the air of Thorn's paganism.

Beside Allison, Sean was staring down at her lap, breathing hoarsely. Allison reached over and picked up her hand, and held it in her own. It was cool, lifeless. Sean kept her eyes down, and in a moment she drew her hand away.

Reverend Ruark was just starting his benediction when Sean came to her feet and called out that she wanted to say something too. He stopped mid-phrase and looked down at her.

Sean stood very straight, arms at her side. She was wearing a simple black sheath. No hat, no jewelry. Her body tense. Straw-blond hair parted on the side; her tan, a roasted almond. Legs with chiseled calves, arms alive with muscles. A pretty girl who'd never fussed about her looks. Thought of makeup as a major nuisance. Never seemed bothered that when the boys began to line up at the door, most of them were coming for Winslow. Sean had never shown much interest in flirting or romance. She had plenty of friends who were boys. But it was always Winslow who had the boyfriends.

For the last year she and Winslow roomed together in an apartment in Coconut Grove. Sean was studying for her LSAT's, working nights as a waitress in a health food restaurant in the Grove. Winslow doing her photographic work nine to five.

Sean stood for a moment, holding the silence around her. Then she stepped past Harry and moved out into the aisle. She looked around at the gathering, her eyes resting briefly on Allison, then moving on.

"We have no business being here," she said. "Winslow never liked churches."

Harry reached out for her, but she stepped away.

"And Winslow had no business being where she was, out in that jungle. That wasn't her crusade. She didn't care about monkeys, apes, any of that. She didn't care one goddamn bit."

Sean turned her head toward Harry and Allison, but kept her eyes focused on the distance.

"I miss my sister," she said. Her voice was cold and rigid. "I miss her very, very much. My life isn't ever going to be as good as it was when she was alive."

She looked around the room again, this time fixing her gaze on Allison. Holding her with such fury that Allison could not endure it and looked away. When she looked back, Sean had turned and was on her way out of the church.

Allison stood and struggled past Harry's knees, hobbling into the aisle, her ankle throbbing. She watched Sean march away, then she swung around to face the minister.

He sighed heavily.

"And you have something to add, Mrs. Farleigh?"

"Yes."

She heard Harry groan, and looked over. He'd bowed his head, covered his eyes with his right hand, a prayer to the god of professional embarrassment.

"I know who did this thing," she said. She heard a few gasps, the stir and muted babble of voices. "From the moment Winslow was shot, I've known. And I'm not waiting another second. I'm going after the son of a bitch."

Allison glanced again at Harry. He was staring at her,

unblinking, mouth sagging. She turned and limped after Sean, out toward the November light. Behind her the minister was trying to carry on with his benediction over the murmuring of the congregation.

Normally the orangutan slept from sundown to sunup. Every night in the jungle its mother made a new nest of branches and leaves. She even formed a primitive roof because orangutans disliked being wet. Her young son clung to her as she snapped branches loose and formed the fronds and twigs into a soft bed.

When it was dark they slept together. The young male was usually restless for a while, climbing up and down his mother's body, inspecting it, familiarizing himself with her strong toes, her long, hairy legs, her crotch full of rich smells.

When he finally grew sleepy, he would nestle close to her head. He had learned that if he slept at her breast she might turn over in the night and lay her weight uncomfortably against him. But near her head he was safe from her sleep movements. His mother used him as her pillow.

Usually when the sun rose, the two of them opened their eyes and lay around for another hour or so waking up. With the sun well over the horizon, his mother would begin foraging for food. This hunt would last all day. Sunup, rise. Sundown, sleep. A leisurely life, simple.

But since the men had taken him on the river and across the bumpy water by boat and put him in a cage with all the birds in other cages, and then the long, cold ride in the airplane, and then the new metal cage with the straw floor, where hardly any sunlight came through the windows, the orangutan with the silver streak was confused.

He no longer knew when to sleep or when to rise. He was always tired, always restless. He felt as he sometimes had when first rising with his mother, irritable, drowsy. Only now he felt this way all the time. Not hungry either, but weak from lack of food. Not thirsty, but his mouth and lips were cracking.

The ape lay in his straw, neither fully awake nor able
to sleep. He looked out of his cage, up at the light through
the windows. The sun was no longer where he was, shining only through those few bright squares. Outside, inside. Something new. Something he was learning about.
The sun outside, the orangutan inside.

He played with the straw, lifted up a handful, let it
fall on his belly. Lifted another handful, let it fall on his
belly. Burying himself in straw. Deeper and deeper till it
was nearly dark. Trying to sleep in that dark, but unable
to.

# C H A P T E R

## 7

Allison came to a halt in the red marble lobby of the Crandon Building. There was a long line of businessmen waiting to give their names to the check-in guard. Allison listened to the protocol. A phone call upstairs for each visitor. Mr. Jones to see Mrs. Smith. Yes, Mr. Jones is harmless, he can come up. The security guard scribbles Jones's name on a lapel badge and away he goes. Two dozen aggravated people in front of her. Easily a twenty-minute delay.

She hesitated for a moment at the end of the line, then headed for the front. A heavyset bald man in a blue pin-striped suit was just peeling away from the desk, sticking his badge in place beneath a red silk pocket kerchief. Allison slid her arm through his.

The large man turned his head and looked her over. He was in his middle forties, maybe a year or two older than Allison.

"I know you?"

"Sure," she said, and nudged him toward the narrow lane of the security checkpoint, a chrome turnstile. "Chicago, last spring. That little bar on Michigan Avenue."

"Never been to Chicago in my life."

"New York then," she said. "West Village. Bleecker and MacDougal. *That* little bar."

She almost choked on the fumes of his bitter after-shave.

"I been to New York exactly twice," he said. Dubious, but moving ahead. "And I sure don't remember you."

"You were drinking," Allison said. "Budweiser, I believe."

"I do drink Bud." The man looked at her, his smile at half-mast, not sure what brand of joke this was. Whether he was in on it or the butt of it.

Moving closer to the checkpoint, arm in arm, an awkward dance.

"How come you never called me again? Like you said you were going to do."

Allison had the sudden urge to bat her eyes, but fought it off. The security guard watched them approach. She tightened her grip on the man's arm, snuggled in. The man took another careful look at her, then smiled to himself.

"I guess I must've lost your phone number," the man said. "I'm pretty damn sure I would've called if I'd had it."

"I've got a new one now anyway."

The guard nodded at them as they passed through the turnstile, Allison first, her escort following.

"She's with me," the man said, and the guard nodded.

As they approached the elevator, Allison said, "What floor are you going to?"

"Twenty."

Safer now, on the inside, but with two beefy security men standing within earshot, arms crossed, watching them.

"I'm going to twenty-five," Allison said.

"Well, maybe I should just check out twenty-five too. We can talk some more about old times."

He pulled his handkerchief out of his breast pocket and dabbed at the sweat growing on his forehead.

"What kind of business you doing here?" the man said.

They waited for the elevator to arrive.

Allison turned to him, stepped close.

"My daughter was murdered in the jungles of Borneo. Right now I'm headed upstairs to confront the man who did it. He's an animal dealer."

The elevator arrived and Allison stepped aboard.

"Aren't you coming?" she said.

"I'll wait for the next one," the man said.

Allison nodded at him as the doors closed.

Joshua Bond's company, International Primates, had a suite on the twenty-fifth floor, just down the hall from the offices of Roy Rothstein, the attorney who'd been suing Allison on behalf of Bond for the last three years.

Tortious interference, an offense she willingly admitted to. Yes, Allison Farleigh had knowingly and willingly interfered with Mr. Bond's business practices. Her only regret was that she hadn't interfered with them more effectively.

Bond had been doing business in Miami for forty years, long before there were laws governing the animal trade, and in that time he'd established an excellent reputation for delivering healthy specimens in a timely fashion to clients all over the country. His customers were private research institutes, government testing labs, even a few Hollywood animal trainers. In those four decades Bond had grown rich and respectable from buying and selling chimps, gibbons, every kind of monkey and ape. Now he was the golf partner of federal judges and congressmen. His photo showed up in the society pages, his name floated as a candidate for political office. He'd visited the White House, slept over.

He first came to Allison's attention four years earlier, when on an unannounced USDA inspection of his warehouse Bond was cited for a long list of infractions. The government inspectors found his cages filthy and cramped, the garbage Dumpsters filled with rats, and several of his caged animals sick or malnourished. The list was extensive, but worse than any of these violations was the discovery of fifteen gorilla pelts, and the skulls of six orangutans. All fresh kills, a week, two weeks at most. Five of the skins were from babies, as were two of the skulls. Whether Bond murdered the animals himself or not, he most certainly was guilty of obtaining and importing them illegally. Encouraging their slaughter.

But there wasn't as much money in the skin trade as in the pet trade. A live orangutan was worth far more than the sum of its parts. But hunters couldn't always capture them alive. Often both mother and child were killed in the fall. For every live one captured, a half dozen died. So the hunters harvested the carcasses, got what they could in the skin trade.

After learning of the infractions at Joshua Bond's warehouse, Allison immediately went to work gathering a list of names of all companies doing business with International Primates. Then she began a letter-writing campaign, urging her members to bombard their congressmen, state senators, and local politicians with outcries over Bond's sordid dealings. Was this the kind of man who should be supplying animals to government laboratories? The kind of man who should be welcome in the White House?

Within a week after her first round of letters went out to his customers, Joshua Bond sued Allison Farleigh for six million dollars. An injunction was filed. Two days later, federal marshals showed up at the Gables house with subpoenas to seize all Allison's newsletters featuring stories about Bond. All her notes, the early snooping she'd done on the paper trail of the gorilla pelts, showing where they were bought, how they were knowingly misidentified as brown bear skins. Correspondence, faxes, or phone notes pertaining to her attempt to disrupt the commercial enterprises of the honorable Joshua Bond.

In the four years since she'd been at war with the man, she'd been able to document a dozen instances in which Mr. Bond knowingly bought and shipped to his Miami warehouse endangered wild-born primates.

Though she had only a small amount of hard evidence, she had numerous eyewitness accounts, photocopies of suspicious bills of sale, faxes to Malaysian suppliers that were clearly written in code, and a host of other incriminating information.

But no one was interested in her evidence. State's attorney, Fish and Wildlife, customs, USDA, the *Miami Herald,* all were very polite when she presented her stacks of information, but there was only silence afterward. A conspiracy of laziness.

She had severely angered the great man, smirched his reputation, left her claw marks on his flesh. He'd tried his best to shut her up, but had failed. Of all the men she'd exposed in the last seven years, Joshua Bond had the most to lose, and was the most bitterly pissed off. Six million dollars' worth. He wanted Allison silenced, had the means to accomplish it, and was just depraved enough to want to pull the trigger himself.

Without a clear idea of what she would do when she faced him, she rode the elevator to his floor, and headed down the hall.

A young woman entered Bond's office a few steps before her. Allison pushed through the office door a moment later, stood impatiently behind the girl, fighting the urge to barge past her and into Bond's office.

"I'm Gretchen Garcia," the young woman said, not noticing Allison. "From Flower Circus."

"Oh, yes," the secretary said. "I have Mrs. Bond's list right here."

Allison shifted her feet and watched as the stern, silver-haired secretary shuffled through the papers on her desk, found the one she wanted, and handed the slip to Gretchen. The young woman studied it for a moment and nodded several times.

"I realize it's short notice," the secretary said. "But the florist Mr. Bond usually does business with had a fire two days ago, and all their stock was destroyed."

Discreetly, Allison took a seat off to the side.

"This is a wedding?"

"Anniversary," the secretary said. "Time and address is at the bottom there."

Gretchen was in jeans, a white T-shirt, work shoes. Her ponytail was held by a red bandanna, and she gave off a loamy smell.

"We can handle it," she said, tucking the slip of paper into her back pocket. "No problem."

"You need a check?"

"Usually we get half up front, the rest on delivery. But since it's Mr. Bond, however you want to handle it is fine with us."

"Bill us, then. That would be easier."

"So if it starts at nine, I'd need to get started, say, five, six o'clock."

"I'll make sure they know you're coming."

Gretchen thanked her again, and without a glance in Allison's direction she left. Allison leafed through the magazine she was holding, set it aside.

"Can I help you, ma'am?"

Allison looked up. The secretary was eyeing her warily. Maybe a wanted poster on the walls of the coffee nook. Watch out for this one.

Allison said, "Is Mr. Bond still out of town?"

"Do you have an appointment, ma'am?"

"No, I'm sorry," Allison said. "I'm from the *Herald*. I'm finishing up a story on Mr. Bond."

The secretary made a polite smile.

"Well, if he's busy . . ."

"You're from the *Herald*?"

"Yes."

Smiling brightly, Allison glanced around the office.

"I should have called first. I mean, I wasn't even sure if he was back in the country."

Allison kept her eyes on a painting on the far wall.

"Yes, he's here, but he's busy."

"He must have been back for two or three days now?"

"Two or three, I suppose," she said grudgingly. "If

you'd like to wait, I'll ring him when his conference is over."

"Where was it Mr. Bond went? He told me, but I forget. Was it Borneo this time?"

Exasperated, the woman rolled her pencil between her hands.

"Djakarta, I think it was. Is that in Borneo?"

"Close enough."

Allison stood, came over to the desk. The secretary straightened.

"Mind if I take one of these?"

Allison reached out and plucked a business card from a small silver tray on the edge of the desk. Then she headed for the door.

"Ma'am?"

"Never mind," Allison said. "Don't bother the great man."

She sprinted the last fifteen yards, and jammed her hand into the closing doors of the elevator. Gretchen was standing in one corner of the car, a Metro-Dade policeman in the other.

"Shew!" Allison said as the car began to descend. "Nick of time."

The young woman stared blankly at her. Allison handed her Bond's card.

"I'm awfully sorry, Gretchen, but Mr. Bond told me to chase you down. I'm Julie, his private secretary. Mr. Bond's changed his mind about the party."

"Changed his mind? About his anniversary?"

"Well, he was called out of town. He forgot till just a minute ago. He's like that, Mr. Bond is. So he'll just have to call you when he gets back and reschedule the delivery then."

Gretchen gave her a careful look.

"Maybe I should go back up, talk to him."

The cop was peering at Allison as well.

"And look, here's something for your trouble."

Allison found three twenties in her wallet, folded them in half and handed them to Gretchen.

"I couldn't," she said.

"Please, it would make . . . Mr. Bond feel better."

With a grimace of thanks Gretchen took the bills.

"So if you could let me have that list."

"The list?"

"What he wanted you to do."

"Maybe I should hold on to it," she said. "For later."

"Mr. Bond said something about wanting to make some changes. So he'll need it back. He didn't keep a copy for himself."

Gretchen groaned and dug the page out of her back pocket, handed it to Allison.

The car stopped on the eighth floor, a man in a gray suit got on, abruptly Allison got off. The policeman stepped out behind her.

"Sorry, Gretchen." Allison waved through the closing doors.

"So, lady," the cop said, edging close. "Tell me something."

"Yes?"

"You in an acting class? This some kind of assignment?"

"What's that supposed to mean?"

" 'He's like that, Mr. Bond is. Here's something for your trouble.' The girl seemed to believe you, but that story, naw, it sounded phony as hell to me."

The cop slanted his head, studying her.

"There's just something about you doesn't feel a hundred percent kosher."

"Is this what's happening?" Allison said. "The police are running so low on work, you've started interrogating complete strangers? That's what this is? Out trolling for lawbreakers?"

He kept staring at her, a half-smile flickering on his lips, trying to place her.

She turned her back on him, and casually walked to the end of the hall. At the last door she glanced back, and the cop was watching her intently. Allison reached out, opened the door, and stepped into the office of Dr. Irving Sharp, urologist.

For ten minutes she dallied, fending off the questions of the receptionist and the stares of two uneasy men in the waiting room. When she finally got her nerve back and went out into the hallway again, the cop was gone.

# CHAPTER

# 8

It took Allison all Saturday morning to assemble the flowers Mrs. Joshua Bond wanted for her anniversary party. She hit three flower shops in the Gables, one in South Miami, nearly cleaned them out.

Just after lunch, while she was storing the bundles and bouquets inside the house, Harry confronted her in the downstairs hallway, asked her what the hell was happening to her, the way she was acting, it was damn strange. Lying in bed for a week grieving, then all of a sudden there she was, gunning all over town, her Jeep full of flowers. What in God's name were all those goddamn flowers for? And what the hell had she meant about knowing who killed Winslow?

"I know," she said.

With an armload of gladiolus, she pushed past him and entered the back bedroom, where she'd set the window air conditioner as low as it could go. The guest bed looked like a funeral pyre, a foot deep in roses, poppies, daisies, carnations. Bunches of tulips, baby's breath, decorative palm fronds and ferns.

Tagging along, Harry said, "You *know*, or you *suspect*? There's a big difference."

He was still in his golf clothes, damp, smelling of the locker room, a clear, bubbly drink with a slice of lime in one hand. The polite applause of golf on the TV.

She lay her armload of gladiolus on the bed and turned to face him.

"Have you called the police in Kuching, spoken to anybody over there lately? Is anyone doing anything about this?"

"I've called several times."

"And?"

"And nothing. No progress. But that doesn't mean you're suddenly empowered to pin on a badge and go off rounding up suspects, Allison."

"Well, thanks, Harry, for your legal opinion. Now if you'll excuse me, I've got to get dressed. I have a party tonight."

"Party? Jesus, what party?"

"I've asked you, Harry, I've pleaded with you to pull some of your famous strings with the State Department. Have our people in Malaysia put some pressure on the authorities over there. But I don't see you doing a thing, and no one over there is doing a thing either. No calls, no letters, nothing. Dead silence. So, Harry, I'm getting busy. I'm doing this myself. That's how it is. Legal, illegal, I don't give a damn."

"What's happening, Allison? This isn't you. You're acting so . . ."

"So what?"

"You're out of control. Wild-eyed."

"Am I, Harry? Wild-eyed and out of control. Is that what I am?"

"I think you need to see somebody. Talk to a professional."

"Maybe I like being wild-eyed. Maybe it's about time I went a little crazy. Maybe this *is* who I am, Harry. The real Allison."

He tried to turn away, but Allison ducked in front of him.

She peered into his eyes. Trying for a moment to recall the thing she'd seen there over twenty years ago. The twinkle, the wry spark that had been part of what convinced her she'd found a man as vibrant as her father. As full of fierce passions.

"I don't like it," Harry said quietly. "This isn't you."

"Oh, no, you're wrong. It *is* me."

He was staring back at her as though he, too, was searching her eyes, maybe looking for the sparkle that had aroused him long ago. The thing that made him, after thirty-eight years a bachelor, embrace the married life. Allison twenty, Harry thirty-eight. He'd been one of her father's many young friends. Part of his masculine entourage. Ivy League lawyers, outdoorsmen, poker players, bourbon drinkers, boaters, shooters of rifles and handguns.

Her father had been all those things to the end of his life. But little by little over the last ten years, Harry had abandoned it all. The boat was sold. Rods and reels corroding in the garage. The hunting rifles donated to auctions or given away. Those old tramping clothes thrown out. Decks of cards tucked in the unused drawers. He didn't even drink bourbon anymore. It was vodka now. Vodka gimlets, for god's sake.

Finally he took a deep breath, let go of her eyes. Looked away and then looked back. He seemed to gaze at her now from a great distance, as though he were on a ship departing for a remote continent.

"This is hard for me, too, you know. It's not your pain alone."

"I know, Harry. I know it's hard."

He licked his lips, eyes filling.

"Did you have a woman in Brunei?" she said it with a casual, almost indifferent curiosity.

Harry winced but recovered quickly. Years of diplomacy. He cleared his throat and demanded to know what the hell she was talking about now.

"A woman, Harry. Did you have a lover on your first tour of Brunei?"

He rattled the ice in his drink. Looked down into it.

"If I did, Allison, that was before we were married. Years before. I hadn't even met you then."

"Was she still there on your second tour? I always wondered. Is that why we went to Brunei, Harry? You took your wife and two teenage daughters to the Far East so you could be with her again?"

"What the hell are you talking about? That was years ago. Years."

Allison picked up a white rose from the bed, held it to her nose. No scent at all. Like smelling a chunk of plastic.

"It all changed for us that year," she said. "Before that we loved each other. I mean, maybe it wasn't ever as passionate as we would have liked, but it was love. Before that year in Brunei."

He looked at her for a long, unflinching moment.

"It was love all right."

"But then we stopped. I mean, it takes a while to tell what's happened. It leaks away so slowly. You don't register it immediately. Oh, I realized something wasn't right in Brunei, but I couldn't name it. I was lonely and depressed, but I thought I was just homesick, or maybe there was something wrong with me, something psychological.

"But eventually I figured it out. We'd stopped loving each other. You had your mistress in Brunei. All I had was the girls, and they were growing up, finding themselves, keeping me at arm's length. Sean with her sports; Winslow had photography. I didn't have you, and I was losing them. That's when I discovered the apes. A way to go on like nothing had happened. And that's what we've been doing since then. Seven years of going on."

"Why are you doing this, Allison? Why now?"

"I always hoped," she said. "I thought we'd find a way to get it back. What we had. But we haven't, have we? This is the way we are now. This is the only way it's going to be with us. Never any better than this."

He rattled his ice again. He licked his lips, looked at the wall behind her.

"So what party are you going to?" His voice was empty.

She conjured a weak smile.

"I'm crashing an orgy at Joshua Bond's."

"I should have known."

Allison set the white rose down, chose a yellow one. It had a syrupy scent that almost choked her.

"We did love each other, though. When the girls were young, that was love. Our version of love."

"It was," he said.

She looked at Harry, sucking down the last trickle of his drink, Adam's apple bobbing.

"Harry," she said.

"Yes?"

She forced a smile.

"Do you happen to know anything about flower arranging?"

He lowered his glass, looked at her for a second or two, then said no, he didn't know a goddamn thing about flower arranging.

"Damn," she said. "Neither do I."

She leaned close and kissed him on the cheek, tasted his golf sweat, inhaled the vodka fumes. And for half a second she was back there, the time before Brunei, on the fishing boat with Harry and the girls out in Biscayne Bay, watching Sean reeling in a barracuda. Allison's lips pressed against her husband's sun-scorched flesh, that same aura of sour sweat and whiskey, smelling so much like her own father, a thousand vivid incidents from her childhood collapsed into one, the fishing rod in her own hand then, her father, her mother, her whole family cheering as young Allison hauled in yet another fish. Her father's boozy kiss of praise.

Upstairs she showered, dried her hair, then dug through her closet until she found the dress she remembered, one she hadn't worn in years, tucked away near the back. A white embroidered sheath with a deep-dipping neckline, a sheer mesh bodice. Show them cleavage, they'll never notice your face.

She wriggled into it, got the zipper up; tight but

wearable. She went through Winslow's bathroom drawers, found some makeup from a decade ago. Dark blue eye shadow, carmine blush, a lipstick brighter than the reddest of the gladiolus. She located a pair of reading glasses Winslow had worn in high school. Black and square, like something from the PX. Fuzzed up her vision, but they certainly changed the shape of her face.

In her bathroom mirror she examined herself critically.

Half hooker, half librarian.

Friends might do a double take, but they'd recognize her. And Harry would, of course. But would a man who'd seen her only twice, both times across a tense courtroom? Doubtful.

The address was in Pinecrest, a woodsy neighborhood south of Miami, everything at least an acre. Allison loaded the car and was in the Bonds' neighborhood by five. She rang the bell at the gate, spoke into the box, told the female voice she was the flower lady.

"The who?"

"Flower Circus. Roses, tulips. Decorations for the party."

"Wait, please."

After three or four minutes' anxious delay, she watched the gates roll open. Allison drove up a hundred yards of white river rock, entering five acres of high-walled privacy. She parked next to the white-tiled Mediterranean monster of a house. Probably fifteen thousand square feet, all glass and stucco with jumbled angles. A scramble of windows and overhangs and cupolas and dormers. Chaos architecture.

A young Latina in a maid's black uniform opened the double front doors and told her to wait, she would go find Mrs. Bond.

Allison took a breath, tried to swallow away the lump of doubt that was building in her throat. She could hear an argument somewhere inside the house, a hoarse smoker's voice complaining to someone on the phone, or else a servant who was unable to answer back.

When Mrs. Bond appeared at the door, Allison took a half step back. She was a big woman, middle sixties, every inch as formidable as her husband. Thick-waisted, with a face as haphazardly designed as her house. Large, mannish mouth, a delicate nose, and dark, pretty eyes. She wore a black warm-up suit, which showed a lot more of her figure than was wise. But Allison sensed she was a woman proud of her bulk, enjoyed using it to intimidate her skinny foes.

"And now what?"

"I'm Gretchen," Allison said. "With Flower Circus." She motioned at her Cherokee and said, "Roses, tulips, glads. Like you ordered."

"The party's off. We don't need you."

"Off?"

"Off. You know, darling—kaput. No party. You can go now, enjoy your weekend."

"And what am I supposed to do with all these flowers?"

Mrs. Bond considered the question, pulling a gold cigarette case from her pants pocket. She tapped out a cigarette, then extracted a lighter the size of a half-dollar from the same pocket, and performed an intricate ritual that culminated in a long exhalation of smoke in Allison's direction.

"It seems to me," Allison said, "at a moment like this, your anniversary party called off, anger floating through the house, it's the perfect moment to surround yourself with flowers."

Mrs. Bond coughed out a raspy laugh. Then she observed Allison through the thick haze of smoke. She put the cigarette back to her lips and sucked the thing so hard, she might have been drawing on five cigarettes at once.

"Anger floating through my house?" she said in her braying New York voice, letting the smoke seep out around her words. "Wherever did you get an idea like that, darling?"

"I heard you on the phone."

Mrs. Bond thought for a moment, eyes thawing as she recalled.

"Oh, that. That's how we talk, my husband and I. There's no anger. He just got a better offer at the last minute, an invitation he's been after for a while, so we had to cancel the party. We'll try again next month."

"Still," Allison said. "I have all those roses, poppies, gladiolus."

"Well, aren't we persistent."

"Just wait till you smell them. Delicious."

"All right, all right. Come inside. I'll have Mercedes find some vases. Wouldn't hurt to sling some color around the old joint, I suppose. But let's try to get it done before Joshua gets home. He hates projects going on. Just wants his martini and neck rub. The TV on loud."

"I have that same husband," Allison said.

Mildred Bond watched as Allison arranged two vases of gladiolus. Working with Mercedes' pinking shears, she set the flowers in tiers, their pretty faces heading forward, backed by sprigs of baby's breath and two small palm fronds, nipping and tucking with great focus. But the arrangement was a botch. Clashing angles, chaotic mixtures of color and shape. Even Allison could see how wretched it looked.

"Have you been in the flower business long?"

"Years," Allison said, smiling, but feeling the sweat run cold down her ribs. "Why? Don't you like it?"

She stepped aside and Mildred hummed her disapproval.

"Oh," Allison said. "It's the new Japanese influence. It takes a while for the Western eye to catch on. Looks very jumbled at first, but believe me, Mrs. Bond, this is quite stylish, very chic. We do all of Gloria Estefan's arrangements. I'm at Madonna's house every other week. It's very New York au courant. Cutting edge."

"I thought you said it was Japanese."

"Japanese filtered through the New York style."

"Who are you trying to kid?"

"All right then," Allison said. "If you want, I can do a traditional arrangement. But I thought, living in a house like this, the fresh, modern architectural mode you've chosen, you would want to be as up-to-date in your flower decoration."

The woman peered at Allison for a moment, then stared dubiously at the flowers, moved the vase around for a different slant. She made a quiet hum.

"Well," she said. "I *do* try to stay up. But it's very hard. Things change so fast."

"It grows on you," Allison said. "A little brash at first, chaotic. But each trivial snip has a purpose. I can explain it to you if you like. The doctrine behind the arrangement."

"Maybe later," Mildred said. "And I'd also be interested in hearing about Madonna, what goes on over there."

"Of course. Whenever you want."

Mrs. Bond took another look at the flowers and left Allison alone in the large chrome kitchen with one parting blast of smoke and a see-you-later, I-have-things-to-do-now.

Mercedes ran out of vases with half the flowers left. She headed off to the garage storeroom to look for more, leaving Allison in the library. She could hear water running somewhere upstairs, which she took to be the protracted showering of Mrs. Joshua Bond.

Allison ducked her head out of the library, saw no one in the foyer or the long hallway. She judged she had twenty minutes, possibly more, before Mildred could towel off, redo her face and hair, and return downstairs. Time enough to prowl.

Carrying a handful of roses, she tried five rooms before locating Joshua Bond's office. With her heart tapping an unsteady rhythm, Allison shut the door behind her and headed for his desk.

It took her only a minute to discover that all his drawers were empty. Not even a speck of lint, a random paper clip. As though the large mahogany desk had only just arrived, still virginal. Nothing on the top, and no file cabinet. Three walls covered with fine oak shelving, the bookcases crammed with hardcovers, spines unblemished. Thousands and thousands of unread novels. The other wall held his photo gallery, an array of safari shots, Joshua Bond's leather jackboots on the necks of innumerable beasts, holding up his rifle du jour. Other photos showed Bond gripping fish or fowl by tail or throat. A few hundred kills on these walls alone.

Bond was unchanging over the years: a shaved head, handlebar mustache. Six-two, six-three, well over two hundred pounds. A thick-necked, deep-chested man, like the bass singer in a barbershop quartet, or one of those antique footballers who'd played the game in leather helmets. A man's man, dressing that way, grooming that way, sending every signal he could that Joshua Bond was a conqueror, a savage competitor who could, by God, overpower whatever the world could throw in his path.

And in the corner of the room was his glass-encased rifle rack. A dozen shotguns and big-scoped carbines. One of them might very well be the murder weapon, brought home, cleaned, dusted. Bond was the kind of man who would insist on using only his own rifles, the kind who'd find a way to transport weapons across international borders.

Allison shivered, put her hand on the edge of the rifle case, tested its balance. She tried to contain her anger. Here in the man's office, she wanted only to overturn things, rip down each of those trophy photographs, smash them all. Haul away an armload of rifles for ballistics testing. But no, she had to stay on track, be calm, not settle for petty sabotage, use this moment to achieve a larger injury.

Muffled voices sounded far off in the house. Perhaps another phone call, or maybe Mercedes discussing something with the lawn man.

Allison set the roses on his desk, took off Winslow's glasses, rubbed the focus back into her eyes. She circled the room, touching the bookshelves, the dictionary stand, the leaves of a silk plant, her heart sounding an alarm in her chest.

It was starting to look like she was wasting her time here, putting herself in jeopardy for absolutely no reason. This didn't even seem to be a functioning office. It was nothing more than a theatrical backdrop, a room full of props, an obligatory studio for a man who took no significant work home. She could imagine what Jeff Aronson, her attorney, would say if she were discovered in that room. I'm having a hard enough time fending off this tortious suit, Allison, without you adding a goddamn breaking and entering charge to the stew.

With her back to the door, Allison made one more careful circuit of the room, ticking off each item. She heard the voices again; this time she could tell clearly it was a man speaking, and the husky voice of Mrs. Bond answering.

And then Allison noticed it, a small black metal case, pebbled aluminum, no larger than a dictionary, sitting discreetly on one of the bookshelves behind the desk. A laptop computer, its lid shut, with two wires running from its rear.

She hurried over, flipped up the screen, found the switch in the rear and flicked it. As the machine whirred and cycled through its opening messages, she heard Mrs. Bond's voice calling out. *Hello, hello. Flower lady.*

Allison stared at the door for a moment; no lock, no dead bolt. She turned her eyes back to the machine. No expert with computers, she'd killed time once or twice fiddling with her own machine, exploring the half dozen programs that resided in its brain. But she'd acquired only scant knowledge beyond the one word-processing program she used to compose her newsletters.

Now she watched Bond's colorful screen settle into its opening menu. Quickly Allison ran her finger down a short list of directories. Work Orders, Customer/Vendor

File, Orders and Quotes. Inventory Entry. She started at the beginning. Used the arrow key to move to Work Orders, hit *enter,* and the screen went instantly to a submenu. A list several columns wide filled the screen. Some kind of shorthand, computer garbage she couldn't read. Randomly she chose one from the list.

The screen blinked and a work order form appeared. It took her a moment to read, but apparently it was a plan to enlarge the cages in Bond's warehouse. Cost estimated by a local welding company.

She exited the file, went hurriedly back to the main menu, tried Orders and Quotes this time. Same procedure, similar long list of gobbledygook. This time she picked the first item on the list and an order form filled the screen. Delta Laboratories, Westport, Connecticut. Twelve macaques, ordered in July the year before. Delta Labs did cosmetics research. Monkeys with eyeliner. Chimps with blush.

She'd visited their Connecticut facility, taken their PR tour, written a scathing article for the newsletter. According to the order form, Joshua Bond purchased the twelve macaques locally from another Miami animal dealer. White Brothers Imports. Raimondo and Orlando White. A couple of shabby snake dealers who had been trying to branch out in the last few years. Allison had gone after them in her newsletters last winter, had succeeded in getting the county attorney general interested in their case, had even aroused Fish and Wildlife to raid their warehouse.

Allison was surprised the White brothers had developed contacts to supply macaques. Interesting, but not what she was looking for. She sat down in Bond's chair, tried to consider this logically. She was certain this goddamn computer contained records that would uncloak dozens of crimes, but there was no time. Mrs. Bond was calling out for her, moving about the house.

Allison exited, went back to the menu, chose the last category, Inventory, tapped the *enter* key. The submenu appeared, offering a list of animals: chimps, gibbons, macaques, other. Feeling a small jiggle in her pulse, she selected *other,* and watched as the screen blinked, then showed a list of dates.

She chose the most recent, October 28, tapped *enter* again, and an invoice sent to Primates International filled the screen.

A bill for 240,000 Singapore dollars. Wang Son Bird Emporium, 1133 Chan Avenue, Djakarta. Invoice number 1323. Account paid in full. Item sold: *Six Orang.*

Allison took a deep breath. She scrolled down, read the next page, a shorthand note. *Hold in south Dade warehouse.* The six orangutans were to be FedExed Tuesday, November 8, to 15553 Hibiscus Way, Orlando, Florida.

Next Tuesday. Three days.

She sat back in the chair.

According to the document, the shipment arrived stateside last week, a few days after Winslow's murder. Bond could have shipped the six young apes down to Djakarta, where they'd been repackaged and labeled as birds or reptiles. He would have greased their way with dollars, picked them up at Miami International four days later. And no one questioned why an animal dealer who dealt in primates was importing birds. No one questioned Mr. Joshua Bond, felt any need to examine the contents of his box, this golf partner of senators, overnight guest at the White House.

Allison traced one of the wires leading from the computer to a small laser printer secreted behind a shelf of art books. She found the *print screen* command key, hit it, and the machine hummed to life.

Now a man's voice had joined the other, calling out for the flower lady. Allison heard doors opening and shutting on her hallway, the deep voice singing out for her as the printer chattered.

When the page was printed she folded it, tucked it into her bra, put on her glasses, and picked up the roses. As she was opening the door, the knob jerked out of her hand.

# CHAPTER

# 9

Allison forced a smile to her lips. With a half dozen roses in her left hand, she put out her right and reflexively the big man's hand rose to meet it. He took her hand into his ample paw and Allison gave him a firm shake.

"What a lovely house you have. I was taking a little unguided tour—I hope you don't mind—trying to get an idea just how to distribute the rest of the flowers. You know, you might consider putting in a standing order with Flower Circus, a weekly delivery, keep this place livened up with color."

Allison moved past him into the hallway. Joshua Bond studied her with befuddled curiosity while Allison continued her smokescreen of babble.

"It's amazing how a big house like this can seem drab and gloomy without the right kind of decorative plants. And we don't just do flowers either. We have palms, ferns, begonias, philodendrons, the full range of indoor potted plants. You really ought to have Mrs. Bond stop by our showroom and take a look. It's the best selection in the city. Now if you'll excuse me, sir, I suppose Mercedes has found more vases for me. I'll have to get back to work."

He stepped around her, blocked her path.

"Did you find what you were looking for, Allison?"

He was wearing a short-sleeved khaki shirt with epaulets, pants to match. Every day a safari for this man. She took off Winslow's glasses, held them in her free hand, and stared into the man's eyes. She had never been this close to Bond before, and now she saw something behind the glaze of anger and menace—a flat and stunted light. Around his eyes there was a fine tracery of wrinkles, but the eyes themselves seemed simple and young, as if he might be trapped in some unending boyhood. Doing today exactly what he had done fifty years ago, no more, no less.

"What the hell are you doing in my house, woman?"

Bond's wife approached down the hallway, and Allison could see in her careful step, the sag of her shoulders, that her authority over this house ended when Mr. Bond came home. Surely Mrs. Bond would be disciplined later for allowing this intruder inside the fortress.

"Let me ask you something, Joshua."

She watched for a moment as his wide chest swelled and shrank inside his shirt.

"Is there anything alive," she said, "you haven't killed?"

He snorted, and an ugly smile disfigured his face.

Mrs. Bond drew on her nervous cigarette and shifted her gaze from Allison to her husband, letting the smoke seep from her mouth. Bond glanced at his wife and his smile soured before he brought his gaze back to Allison.

"Let's just put it this way, Mrs. Farleigh," Bond said. "There isn't anything on earth I *wouldn't* kill."

Allison held out the half dozen roses to Mrs. Bond, who, after a moment's uncertainty, took them.

"Sprinkle a little sugar in the water," Allison said. "They last longer that way."

A curl of smoke rose from her cigarette and laced through the bright red blooms.

"Good luck, Mrs. Bond," Allison said, and walked past the two of them out of the house.

As soon as she got home, Allison faxed a note to Sidra Tindusiri in Borneo. Could Dr. Tindusiri confirm that a four- or five-year-old male orangutan living in the sector of the jungle where Winslow was murdered had a rare and distinctive silver patch of fur on its head? Urgently need an answer.

At five minutes past eight on Sunday morning, the fax rang in Allison's bedroom. She climbed from her sleepless bed and watched the paper inch from the machine.

Yes, Dr. Tindusiri could positively confirm that a young male orangutan with that very unique marking had lived in the sanctuary until just recently. Furthermore, she could state unequivocally that this young ape's mother had been the one that was shot at the same time and the same location where Winslow Farleigh's murder had taken place.

Allison spent all day Sunday phoning her local members. Told them what she'd learned. Could they help? Twenty-three calls earned twenty-three pledges of devotion.

Steady, keeping her voice quiet, measuring her breaths. Here was the plan. Monday afternoon. Monday at four. In time for the evening news. Monday at Joshua Bond's warehouse. They would find six orangutans, one of which was a young wild-born male with a streak of silver fur on its forehead. An orangutan with a very provable, very direct link to her daughter's murderer.

Most of her members had a friend, or a friend of a friend in the media. Twenty-three guarantees. The *Miami Herald* would be there, all four TV channels, several AM radio stations. Joshua Bond, man-about-town, was going to be charged with murder. You don't want to miss this. Monday at four, they'd converge on Bond's warehouse in south Dade county.

Once they had him on the orangutan-smuggling charge, the rest of it would fall into place. Place him in Kuching on the day Winslow was murdered, have Dr. Sidra Tindusiri confirm the identity of the orangutan, do ballistics tests on Bond's weapons, match them against whatever slugs the Malaysian police had found, use customs records to learn who Bond's traveling companions, his fellow hunters, were, interrogate them, offer plea bargains. When the mountain of circumstantial evidence reached critical mass, she was certain it would convert into irrefutable proof.

Late in the evening on Sunday, she got through to Bill Taylor, senior partner at Barker, Hoff, Taylor, and Stern, lied to him effortlessly, saying Harry urged her to get in touch. Would Bill be willing to use his considerable influence, make a call on the Farleighs' behalf? Because she'd obtained concrete evidence, a document from Joshua Bond's own secret files, proving he was the man behind Winslow's murder. Shocking, he said. Unbelievable. Believe it, she said. But why not proceed through normal channels, Allison? Turn it over to the D.A., get a grand jury working on it.

"Normal channels? Bill, you know Bond, the influence he has. If this isn't exposed in a very public way, the whole damn thing will disappear in some whitewashed back room and get nibbled away by lawyers, mitigated into oblivion."

"Those lawyers," Bill said, "those damn lawyers."

Finally Taylor agreed to make the call, inform his friend at the D.A.'s office of her allegations, strongly encourage him to meet with Allison at four tomorrow.

Next was Fish and Wildlife. It was their jurisdiction, six endangered animals smuggled illegally into the U.S. They should be elated to make a major bust like this one, the whole thing landing in their lap. The problem was, Allison had long ago converted Fish and Wildlife from allies to enemies.

Mrs. Farleigh, the agents called her now. Always so officially polite. Mrs. Farleigh, you must understand we're doing all we can. There simply aren't enough wildlife agents in the entire country to check every crate that comes through Miami International. Mrs. Farleigh, we appreciate your concern, your interest, your commitment, your energy, your research, your insightful observations, but there's only so much six officers can do against two hundred–plus animal dealers registered in South Florida, hundreds of shipments coming through the airport each week. Only so much we can do, only so much, so much.

Last spring, with the help of some of her local volunteers, Allison had run a survey on a typical month of Fish and Wildlife inspections, and printed the results in her August newsletter. In the month they studied, June, over ninety percent of the wildlife containers entering Miami International Airport got no visual inspection whatsoever. Not that the agents were lazy or derelict. They were simply overwhelmed, had to make choices on whose shipment to rip open, whose to pass through.

Crate after crate of boas, jaguar skins, sea turtle eggs, and tropical fish in the millions arrived every day from Peru, Costa Rica, Trinidad, Nigeria. Reptiles, birds, mammals. Skins, skulls, eggs, live animals. A great deluge of the world's exotic live animals or pelts, on their way to collectors all over America, was flowing steadily through the back room of the Miami airport every hour of every day with only those six agents at work, and the majority of their time was spent manning phones, reviewing documents, issuing export certificates, preparing investigative reports, and responding to calls at the passenger terminal or foreign-mail room.

For the ninety percent of wildlife cargo they couldn't eyeball, they had to trust documentation. If the paperwork claimed the crate held a hundred Grand Cayman iguanas, then more often than not it was approved. Grand Cayman iguanas were legal. What could they do, open every crate?

The Wildlife agents were good people. Smart, sincere, well-educated, badly underpaid. They cared about animals. Were knowledgeable and dedicated. But with Allison it was, "Thank you very much, Mrs. Farleigh, for your continued concern, but we secretly and politely and unofficially and unspokenly would like you just to fuck off and stay fucked off for as long and as far away as you can possibly manage it, thank you very much, Mrs. Farleigh, and please don't quote me in that goddamn libelous piece of shit newsletter of yours either."

She understood how they felt. Even sympathized. She could see herself from their eyes. Affluent, bossy housewife, always critical, badgering. A woman who didn't have to pay allegiance to handbooks of rules and official guidelines like they did.

And sure, she'd admit to that. On the other hand, if it weren't for all those folks with badgering ways, annoying cries from the sidelines, the great clunky machinery of status quo would never move at all. It would grind away as it always had, day after day, slowly replicating itself, slowly reproducing today the exact same results it had produced yesterday.

At ten-fifteen that Sunday night, Allison located the home phone number of Penny Richmond, the newest Fish and Wildlife agent. Just moved to Miami from Idaho a month before, perhaps still boggled, hadn't gotten the lay of the land yet. Maybe she didn't have the official scoop on Allison Farleigh yet either.

The phone rang a half dozen times before someone answered with a sleepy hello. Allison introduced herself as Gretchen Jones, saying she worked for a Mr. Joshua Bond. Was Penny familiar with Mr. Bond? She'd heard the name, she said. An animal dealer? That's right, the biggest one in the Southeast, third biggest in the country. What about him? Penny said, waking up now. Well, I hate to snitch on my boss, Allison said, I'm not a whistle-blower by nature, but what he's doing isn't right. What's that? Penny said. Orangutans, said Allison. He's holding them in his warehouse. Six wild-born orangs, no documentation. Is that right? Yes, Allison said, and listen, Penny, I know he's going to be at the warehouse at four tomorrow afternoon. Four o'clock? Yes, four o'clock precisely.

As Allison was setting the phone in the cradle, it rang in her hand.

"Christ, Allison, don't you have call waiting? Goddamn phone's been busy for hours. What if your attorney had an emergency, had to talk to you right away?"

She said hello to Jeff, told him he was on her list to call, that she was almost to him.

"Okay, now listen to me, Allison. A little while ago I had a very disturbing conversation. Roy Rothstein called me. You know who I mean? The man who represents Joshua Bond."

"Go on."

"Roy claims one of my clients broke into his client's home yesterday afternoon. Is this man nuts, Allison, or are you?"

"Broke in?" Allison said. "That's perhaps a bit strong. I finagled my way in."

"Finagled, broke. Any way you say it, it isn't good."

"Jeff," Allison said. "I want you to set up a meeting. We'll settle this. Suits, countersuits, breaking and entering, all of it. I have a deal to offer the man. Face-to-face."

"*You* have a deal? Now, that's rich, Allison. Hey, they're pressing charges against you. It took all my persuasive powers to keep them from sending the squad cars over to your place tonight. What deal could you offer him, for god's sake? You're the one that needs to cut a deal."

"Tomorrow at four, Jeff, a meeting with Bond. Can you arrange it? It has to be four o'clock, and it has to take place at his warehouse out near Krome Avenue. Okay?"

"Are you serious?"

"It's going to happen, Jeff. Either you set it up, or I'll have to find someone who will."

"What kind of meeting are we talking about here?"

"Four, okay? Four o'clock."

The attendance was excellent. A circus of police cars, and bland white government Fords, green pickups from Fish and Wildlife, television vans, one after the other rolling up the dusty road, a great pincer movement of press and law enforcement and concerned citizens. It was a credit to her organizational skills. Fifteen of her Wildlife

Protection League members attended, a couple from as far away as Jacksonville.

At exactly four o'clock Allison marched to the door of his warehouse, a hubbub of electronic media gathering behind her. People calling her name. Shoulder cams. Halogen lights. Microphones. Men with pads and pencils jostling other men with pads and pencils. Even Thorn was there in cutoff jeans and a T-shirt, looking uncomfortable. Jeff Aronson, in the back of the crowd, his shoulders slumped, shook his crew-cut head.

Allison hammered on the door. A second later, Mr. Bond swung it open, smiled into the bright lights. He crossed his arms over his chest, blocked the entrance.

"I hope you people brought a warrant. We're still using those little things, aren't we?"

"We want to see these." Allison handed him the invoice.

He stared at her for a moment, then took the paper, looked it over, sighed.

"All this effort, Allison, all these people? You break into my house and this is all you can manage? I'm disappointed in you, sweetheart."

"Show us, Mr. Bond."

He studied her for a moment, his ruddy face darkening. He took a slow breath, blew it out, and stood aside.

"Come on, Allison. In fact," he called out to the crowd, "why don't you all come in. Have a nice long look around."

During the next hour Joshua Bond allowed the group access to every cranny of his forty-thousand-square-foot structure.

"Rip it apart, if you like. I'll provide the hammers, the crowbars. Stay as long as you want."

There were no orangutans. None with silver markings, none whatsoever. Not in the cages, not in the bathrooms, the offices, behind the dropped-ceiling panels. There *were*, however, six matched orange-banded thrushes, which Joshua Bond had purchased in Djakarta last week as a gift for his daughter, whose wedding was next Friday in Orlando. He had all the documents for the thrushes, everything precisely in order.

*Six Orang,* the bill of lading read. The other information matching exactly that on Allison's printed page.

"They're songbirds, Allison. *Zoothera peronii,* found in the lowland deciduous forests of Wetar, Timor, also on the small islands of Romang, Damar, and the Babars. Anything else you want to know about them?"

*Six orang.*

Allison stared at the bill of lading: 240,000 Singapore dollars. Seeing now what she would not let herself see before. A faint period in the middle of the four zeros. Twelve hundred dollars.

"I'd invite you to my daughter's wedding, Allison," he said, the cameras rolling, the Fish and Wildlife agents glaring at her, "but I think you'll probably be otherwise occupied."

Allison's fiasco took up the first minute of the local six o'clock news. *Animal rights activist goes ape over songbirds.* Joshua Bond was interviewed. Smiling, speaking familiarly with the newswoman. Oh, no, Michelle, it was a simple error on Mrs. Farleigh's part. He held no grudge against her, gracious, no. The woman was grief stricken over her daughter's recent death. Though he had to admit, he couldn't quite understand Mrs. Farleigh's fanatical resolve to tarnish his good reputation. He guessed it was possible the woman's grief was distorting her judgment, causing her to flail about.

Harry and Allison watched the news together in their living room. They sat on opposite ends of the couch and didn't speak. Harry's impassive eyes were trained on the set. When the segment was done, the other local news beginning, Allison rose from her seat.

"Congratulations," Harry said quietly. "You shot your complete and absolute wad on this one, Allison. Nobody in their right mind is ever going to believe you again. You're done. Way to go, Allison; way to go, babe. This finishes it. You're going to have to find yourself a whole new hobby."

Allison went up to her bedroom, lay down. She watched the room darken. Watched a warm breeze stir the curtains into a ghostly dance. She felt a corset tighten around her middle, her breath coming hard and shallow. She watched the curtains move, and she wept.

# C H A P T E R

# 10

Just past eleven that night Allison used her key to open the steel gate on the west corner of Parrot Jungle. She stepped inside one of the narrow compartments and swung the big gate into motion. It squeaked, as it always did, and for a moment she was trapped inside its grid of bars until it rotated halfway around and she could step out freely into the park. A dozen years ago, when she used to bring her daughters to Parrot Jungle, they'd loved that heavy revolving gate. They'd played jail there, one the inmate, the other the jailkeeper. The jailer taunting the prisoner, the prisoner rattling the bars helplessly. Playing their game until another patron came along, ticket in hand, and forced them to go inside.

Parrot Jungle had been a tourist attraction for over fifty years; a bird show, smallish zoo, lush tropical gardens, pink flamingos, coral rock buildings. When it was built, Miami was a small town and Parrot Jungle was at its outer fringe. Now the park was surrounded by half-million-dollar homes, tennis clubs, churches, and busy roads. An oasis of wildness lingering at the city's core. The fifteen acres was covered by a complex network of twisty paths, hills and gardens, and artificial ponds that had been there so long they were no longer artificial. The shows had changed little in fifty years. Parrots riding miniature bicycles across tightropes, a petting zoo, jungle theater, alligator pond. The kind of quaint, no-tech place that had once seemed incredibly hokey to Allison but now resonated with a nostalgic authenticity. A last shred of old Florida still hanging on.

Allison walked toward Bronson's guard shack, guided by the radio noise. A talk show, Bronson's favorite, some manic female jabber. He was always making Allison stop and listen, have a taste of the radio queen's trashy jokes.

She ducked her head into the open doorway. Bronson looked up, took his feet off his desk. Smiled and pointed at the radio. She listened for a moment to the woman's raunchy lecture about PMS. The headaches, the cramps, the swollen breasts. Mocking men for their frailty. You don't get it, what we have to go through every month. You just don't get it. You'll never get it. You can't get it, because we got it and we're not giving it to you.

"Hell," Bronson said. "We don't want it."

Allison gave him a wave and started off. She was halfway down the stone path to the cages when Bronson hailed her. She waited for him, lifting her eyes to watch a small plane flying low overhead, lights blinking through the calm night. A parrot screeched, a macaw replied. With a flashlight lighting his way, Bronson hobbled down the stairs and joined her. He, in his usual overalls and white T-shirt; Allison wearing a long-sleeved denim shirt, white shorts, Keds.

"Meant to tell you, Miz Farleigh, Broom had another one of his bad days."

"What'd he do now?"

"Same as last week. Hid some food under his straw, then about two, three o'clock in the afternoon, he saw somebody in the crowd he didn't like, some kid making faces, and he slung two handfuls of tomatoes at him. Like to've started a stampede, people screaming, running off, falling all over each other. That damn Broom, he's been in a snit the last two weeks."

"Because I was away," she said. "I deserted him."

"Yes, um, that's how it seems. If it ain't the food, it's

his own manure. Got to keep the crowds back another ten feet to keep them from getting dirtied up."

"Well, I'm back now," she said. "He'll calm down."

"I hope so. I'm afraid he's getting so he enjoys it. Attached to it now, throwing stuff at the people."

"It's just a tantrum," she said. "It'll stop. But you know, Broom has to learn to adjust. I won't be around forever."

"Well, Miz Farleigh, maybe I should go along, stand around, make sure you're safe."

"Broom's not going to hurt me, Bronson. Don't worry."

Bronson shone the light on the path for Allison, kept it a step ahead of her till she'd rounded the tall flagstone wall. She found her way by moonlight to the orangutan cage. A thirty-foot-high, fifty-foot-square construction. Large enough to give Broom a chance to swing, climb, pace a square mile if he felt like it.

The orangutan was eight years old, weighed nearly two hundred pounds. He'd be lighter in the jungle, more fit, more agile. Despite his careful diet at the park, he was gaining weight. But better fat than a lot of other fates.

Allison found him seven years ago, her first year as a wildlife vigilante. Out of nowhere Thorn had phoned her, describing a shabby roadside zoo he'd seen operating on Lower Matecumbe Key. Heard she was in the wildlife protection business and thought she should come take a look, it just might interest her. What she found was a rickety tilt-a-whirl and merry-go-round, and inside a small tent a menagerie that included several alligators, a black bear, a mangy deer, and the star of the show, a baby orangutan, looking like a human toddler with drifts of flyaway red hair.

She and Thorn bought tickets for the show, watched with a carload of tourists from Mississippi. The owner was a tall, gaunt man with a perpetual cigarette stuck to his lip. He wore an orange clown nose and carried a broom handle that he waved like a baton throughout the show, and used as a prod or bat when the animals resisted his cues. The ape was emaciated, had weeping sores on its back and arms that looked a great deal like cigarette burns.

After that day in the Keys, it took Allison three months of arduous fund-raising, and four more visits to the roadside attraction, before she haggled the ape away from the man. Nine thousand dollars cash.

When the orangutan was safely strapped in Thorn's car, she went back into the carnival tent and asked the man if he would be willing to throw his broom handle into the bargain. With a flourish and a bow he presented it to her, and Allison drew it back and hammered the man's right arm, then hammered it again and again. Thorn had to separate the two of them, the man screaming that he would sue.

She named him Broom and erected a cage for him in back of her Coral Gables home, hidden from her neighbors and the code inspectors. During the day the orangutan had the run of the house, and even slept in her bed at night. When Harry was home on weekends, it stayed mostly in the outdoor cage.

She fed him vegetables and fruit and gradually nursed him back to a healthy weight. For two years Broom and Allison were together almost every hour of the day. She took him along on fund-raising speeches to women's clubs, Civitan, the chamber of commerce, held his hand while they walked up the front steps of the Fish and Wildlife office. Those were the days when the wildlife agents smiled when she came into the office, listened to her worries and complaints, indulged her, explaining the legal complexities that faced them in bringing animal smugglers to justice.

She bought Broom stuffed animals and balls and ropes and bells and windup toys. Gave him cherry Popsicles. He was her companion and friend. Her adopted child and her confidant. He listened to her, played games with her hands and fingers, studied her eyes, touched her hair, plucked off her reading glasses or her earrings to examine them more carefully. He wore a diaper in the house, and let her know with grunts and peeps when he was ready to be changed. He found her furniture and clothes endlessly absorbing.

But by the time he turned three, he had grown so powerful that the games they'd played just a year before were potentially lethal. In a moment of exuberance, he could easily snap Allison's forearm in half with one hand. She had seen Broom, with an almost casual gesture, tear a bedroom door off its hinges, smash a coffee table in two. In a fit of bad temper, he'd once picked up an ornamental ceramic pot filled with a hundred pounds of dirt and a ten-foot palm, and hurled it across the living room.

The thing had to be done. And though she could see the day coming from months away, it cost her more emotional pain than she'd known since her father died. She donated Broom to her friend, Dr. Sam Tremble, the owner of Parrot Jungle. And for months afterward, each day when she woke to the empty house her chest ached and she had to fight off another surge of tears.

Now she visited Broom only twice a week, and though the bond was not as powerful as it had once been, and though many orangutans and a host of other animals had passed through her life since she'd first found him, there was none she cherished like Broom.

Tonight, as she hauled up the canvas curtain covering the front of his cage, Broom sat up sleepily in his nest. It was perched atop a cross-hatching of pine logs, which was raised ten feet off the floor of the cage. It was like a huge four-legged table, on top of which Broom built his nightly nest from palm fronds and straw. Tomorrow morning one of the attendants would dismantle the nest so that Broom would have to reconstruct it tomorrow evening. They tried to mirror as closely as possible what his behavior would be in the wild.

She used her key to open the padlock on the cage. She shut and relocked the door, stood looking up at him. He would not meet her gaze. In the moonlight she could see he had clutched a green coconut in his hands, a projectile too large to make it through the bars of his cage. As she watched, Broom broke the coconut in half. His hands were so strong that with a nonchalant gesture he could accomplish what a normal man would require a hammer and chisel and a half hour of sweat to do.

Allison walked to a corner of the cage and sat on one of the quilted packing blankets thrown about the cage floor. She propped her back against the bars and watched Broom tear the meat from the coconut. He was pretending to ignore her.

She could smell his rich funk, the rank meaty odor of his flesh. She listened to him gobble the fruit, gurgling with pleasure over his midnight snack.

At first, after she'd gotten him from the carnival show, Allison had tried to return Broom to the wild. It was her first contact with Sidra Tindusiri, who ran the most famous of the rehabilitation programs in Borneo and Sumatra. Sidra worked with young apes, helping them relearn their forgotten survival skills with the hope of eventually releasing them into the jungle.

But the required blood tests showed that Broom was the offspring of mixed parentage. Father from Borneo, mother from Sumatra. Bred in captivity. Because the international zoo association was determined to keep the orangutan bloodline pure, Broom's mixed background made him unacceptable as either an official zoo animal or rehab material. So he had become Allison's.

As Broom finished the coconut he dropped the shells to the floor, then stretched his hairy arms out wide and chittered softly, drawing his gums back, showing his teeth to the moon.

Grunting, he took a grip on one of the logs and swung down, hanging by one long arm, his broad back to her. He released the log, dropped into the straw. Stood for a moment looking out into the dark patio, where in a few hours the tourists would gather again to snap their photographs.

Finally he turned around and faced Allison. She didn't move, made no sound. She watched him as he reached out with both hands and grabbed one of the four legs of his log perch and shook it fiercely. Allison had supervised the construction of his perch. She'd helped bolt each juncture with stainless steel hardware, was certain it could withstand the ferocity of a dozen angry men.

Broom grunted and shook the structure, rattling it. One minute passed, then two, the noise growing louder, until finally the leg Broom was holding cracked, gave way, broke free in his hands like some Tinkertoy stick. The entire framework tipped over and crashed.

Broom tossed the ten-foot log against the bars, brushed it aside as it bounced back at him.

"Hey! Hey, you okay, Miz Farleigh? I heard the commotion."

Panting hard, Bronson stood out in the dark viewing area, shining his flashlight into Broom's eyes.

"It's okay, Bronson. I'm fine. I'll handle this."

"I don't know, Miz Farleigh. He's mighty worked up tonight. The full moon and all."

"It's okay, Bronson. It's okay."

Broom hooted at the man as he turned to go. Hooted and gurgled until he was gone.

Allison hadn't moved. Back against the bars, the blanket scratchy against her bare legs, she watched the orangutan turn to her, settle his eyes on hers. He looked thinner now, less fierce; his face had a haggard expression, the anger all burned away.

He shuffled over to the corner where she sat, loomed between her and the moon, put her in the broad shadow of his body. She had never been frightened of Broom and was not now. If he wanted to kill her, he could accomplish it easily, leave her a bloodless corpse in thirty seconds.

He sat down in the straw across from her, looked into her eyes for a long moment, then extended his hand.

She took it in hers.

The ape's eyes calmed, a watery softness. With his big, cool hand gripping hers, Broom scooted through the heap of blankets till he was beside her.

He let go of her hand, then lifted his arm and lay it over her shoulders. He drew her to him, arm circling her, bringing Allison's head to rest against his chest, Broom's cheek settling onto the top of her head.

He shifted his body, correcting their alignment. Then he sighed. Allison sighed as well. And as it so often happened, she was no longer sure which of them was comforting the other.

It was a single bang with no echo. Could have been someone popping a paper sack, or a sewing needle touched to a party balloon. Allison sat straight up, felt the muscles in her back aching. The explosion woke Broom as well. The moon had moved west. It was well after midnight, the night much darker.

Parrot Jungle was quiet. A few hundred yards to the east, Red Road was quiet as well. For a moment she thought she'd dreamed the noise, but then she saw the flashlights bobbing down the pathway, waves of light skittering through the foliage. Then she heard the voices of men coming near. Voices she recognized.

Allison wriggled across the floor of the cage, flattened herself against the log Broom had broken free from his perch. She hauled a blanket over her body, tucked it around her.

Broom watched her curiously, then shuffled over beside her. Squatted near her head. He made a noise in his throat that she'd never heard from him before, a husky groan. Sensing her fear, perhaps, or feeling the danger himself, those strange voices at an unaccustomed hour, the beams of their flashlights. Broom continued his low warning growl.

She heard the rasp of the men's shoes on the pavement near the cage. Heard them whispering. Felt Broom shift his weight, tensing. She could hear her own breath inside the blanket, fast and staggered.

"Hey, Allison? Your friend out front said we could find you with the orangutan. Not that that's any big surprise. You in there?"

It was one of the voices from the jungle.

"All-iii-son. Come on out, honey dumpling." The

other voice was deeper, mocking. "We watched you on TV tonight, honey. Going after old Josh Bond. You looked real cute. Real delectable."

"That lump," the tenor voice said. "Behind the ape. Is that you, Allison? You hiding in there?"

"Why don't you go in and find out," the smart-ass voice said.

"Yeah, sure. I'm going in there with that hairy bastard."

"So shoot the ape, then go in and find out."

"I'm not shooting that thing, it's in a cage, for chrissake."

"Jesus, man. There's that liposuction thing again. Soft, soft, soft. Give me that goddamn gun, I'll do it."

Allison could hear the scuffle of their shoes moving around the perimeter of the cage. Feel Broom swiveling slowly to watch them, his quiet growl deepening.

She fought the urge to draw back the blanket, take a long look at their faces. At least to know in her last seconds who her killers were. But instead she pressed her stomach hard against the log, head tucked down. She listened but heard nothing for a while. Even Broom was quiet.

Minutes passed. From a few hundred yards away one of the peacocks cried mournfully, a long echoing call. She felt the muscles unknotting in her belly. She drew an easier breath. But still she waited.

Another few minutes and Broom shifted his bulk away from her, silently prowled the cage as if he was staring out into the dark to make certain the men had gone.

She heard the rumble of a heavy truck out on Red Road. Heard the chatter of palm fronds in a surge of breeze. And then she thought, by God, she'd had enough of cowering. Lying just as she had while Winslow was being murdered.

She flung off the blanket and scrambled to her feet. In the same instant she heard the harsh double clack of a weapon being cocked. Broom roared and threw himself at the bars of his cage, let go an air-splitting bellow.

Lunging toward the door of the cage, Allison heard the crack of a rifle. A man yelling.

"Shit! Shit, shit, shit."

She had the key out of her pocket, fumbled with it for a moment, gouged it at the lock, and managed to unfasten the thing. She was out the door, slamming it behind her, when another rifle shot sounded from nearby. She saw the glitter of sparks as the slug clanged the bars a yard from her head, and for a second she cut her eyes toward her attackers, long enough to see the small one wiping his face furiously with both hands. Trying to scrub it clean. Making a retching noise.

Broom had nailed him with a handful of his own feces.

"Jesus, shit! Jesus! Shit, shit, shit."

The other man was holding the rifle. He was tall, had white hair, or blond. Beyond that she could tell nothing. The gun was stretched out toward her, the barrel floating her way. Allison ducked her head and dove for the mass of philodendrons beside the cage, rolled through them and down a grassy bank that sloped to the pink-flamingo pond. She heard the men up the hill shouting, heard the bark of another shot, heard Broom bellow at them again.

She came to her feet at the edge of the pond, sprinted for the cluster of oaks on the western edge. Heard one more blast and the spurt of water a dozen feet behind her. Lousy shots. She churned into the shadows of the oaks, cut sharply to her right toward the exhibits of macaws and cockatoos, took a hidden maintenance footpath behind the gift shop and down an alleyway of fire bushes and golden dewdrops.

Eyes lashed blurry with branches, dodging the dagger thorns of the century plants, but getting a hard poke in the thigh anyway. She yelped, stumbled briefly, plucked out the spike, took a hard whistling breath and ran on toward Bronson's shack. Hearing his radio now, the same female DJ rattling on. Bronx accent, bullying one of her callers. His radio coming from the darkness like the beam of a lighthouse. Her man with a side arm.

All over the park the birds had erupted into wild squawks and squeals, as if feeding time and mating season and a lightning storm had combined. She heard Broom's roar louder than all the birds together, the dark air booming.

She jogged to Bronson's guardhouse, but he wasn't there. His phone was torn out of the wall. The radio blared on. She stared at his empty chair for a moment, spoke Bronson's name as she gaped at his small cubicle.

In a moment she heard the men's breathless voices coming quickly up the pathway. Allison turned and rushed toward the park's entrance amid a great clatter of wings, the brilliant screeches of a hundred parrots. She could hear the men coming to the crest of the hill beside Bronson's shack.

She threw herself against the gate, but it didn't budge. She heaved against it again, and then she saw him. Bronson was squatting down, wedged inside the metal cage of the revolving door, a single bullet hole through his forehead. Head flung back, eyes open as if he were gawking at the moon.

She drove forward, both hands against the door, all her panicked weight inching it around, finally breaking it loose, expelling Bronson's body inside the park as the revolving door spun. And Allison hurtled across the parking lot, hearing one more shot a long way behind her. Racing across Killian Drive and into the protective labyrinth of dark, expensive neighborhoods.

# CHAPTER

# 11

At dawn on Tuesday, the police took her statement in Bronson's shack at Parrot Jungle. Harry was there, standing silently in the doorway. Thorn arrived, got the news from Crystal Slayton, one of the park attendants. Allison nodded at him, then went back to staring at Bronson's radio, answering the half dozen questions she'd answered a half dozen times already.

Two men. One short. One tall; white hair or blond. The other one, she wasn't sure. He had his hands over his face, trying to scrape away ape shit. It was midnight, after all; she was terrified. What did they say? She told them, calling out her name, looking for her, the same as they had in Borneo. And what was she doing in the ape's cage in the first place? She had no answer for that, just looked across at Harry. She does that sometimes, Harry said. What? the lieutenant said, you mean she comes down here, goes into the ape's cage? Why? All the cops looking at each other, trying to hold back their grins.

Harry came forward. Told the lieutenant that his wife had been under a lot of stress lately. She might not be acting a hundred percent normal. So we gather, a beefy cop said. So, Mrs. Farleigh, you think this has something to do with Mr. Joshua Bond? one of them asked her. Someone snickered. She looked up at the cop. Of course it does, she said. The beefy one stepped in front of his junior partner, addressed Harry. So is your wife given to paranoid delusions? Everything happens, it's gotta have something to do with her. Like a regular mental cycle.

Allison said something short and angry. Thorn shouldered up to the door of the shack. Told the men to take it easy, goddamn it. This woman had lost a daughter; she wasn't crazy. If she said she was being shot at, then, by God, she was being shot at.

Somebody mind telling me who the hell this guy is? the cop said. He's nobody, Harry said. A friend, said Allison. The beefy cop asked Thorn to step back, this was no business of his. Any more outbursts, interference of any kind, he was going downtown.

They asked Allison the same half dozen questions again, but made it clear this was shadow play, the motions of an interrogation. Telling Harry that it seemed to them Bronson's murder was a robbery gone awry. The cash drawer in the gift shop had been rifled, the old man's wallet stolen. Somebody tried to pry open the safe in the main office, steal the day's receipts. Allison demanded police protection. A car outside her house until this was over. Everyone looked at her. Take her home, Mr. Farleigh, the beefy one said. See she gets some rest. And maybe you should see about some medication. My wife speaks highly of Xanax.

Five-thirty on that cool Tuesday afternoon. Thorn had planned on being back in Key Largo today, tying flies. Tying one on. Crack open that Herradura tequila that was sitting on his shelf for a few months, mix it with some Cointreau, lime juice.

He'd agreed to sub for Allison while she was in Borneo, ten days, maybe eleven. But for the twenty-first day in a row he was again at Parrot Jungle. Holding Pongo, the two-year-old orangutan.

Actually it was more the other way around, the ape hugging him, its arms very tight around Thorn's neck, right cheek pressed against his sternum, Pongo looking out at the dozen eleventh graders from Palmer Trinity, a ritzy private school. A biology field trip to Parrot Jungle. Thorn was just winding up his talk, letting them have a long look at the baby orangutan while a few feet behind Thorn, Broom lurked in his big cage.

Thorn still had the question-and-answer period, for ten, fifteen minutes max, then it was back to Snapper Creek Marina where he'd been living aboard his old wooden Chris-Craft thirty-footer. Maybe tonight he'd call a cab, go over and see how Allison was doing, offer to take her out on the Chris-Craft, anchor off Elliott Key, sleep out there in the laundered breezes, where the air still had some oxygen in it. That wouldn't cure her, but it was a damn good place to stay while she healed.

Thorn was ready to call it quits early, send this bunch of sour-faced teenagers on their way, when Sean came down the stone steps from the Asian parrot exhibit, heading toward the primates. Gray jeans, black shirt, running shoes, short blond hair glinting in the sun. Looking pretty, as usual, sexy, an athletic bounce in her walk, healthy, strong.

Looking better than she had four days before at the funeral. She was starting the long trip back from the airless canyons of her grief. Thorn knew the look. He'd hiked those gorges a few times himself lately, found himself stranded down there without map or compass. He could see it in her eyes. Still lost, but at least she was a few feet up the path, getting her confidence back. Gonna climb and climb till she could see the whole span of sky again.

Thorn looked back at the teenagers, shifting around, bored, the teacher giving Thorn another look. The guy had made Thorn as a derelict who'd wandered in here, clubbed the regular lecturer and was impersonating him for the day. Not far off, really.

Thorn rearranged Pongo in his arms and went on with the talk.

"A mother orangutan will hold her baby twenty-four hours a day for the first three years. Travel together in the treetops. Never let go, no matter what."

One of the boys, the tallest, in overalls and a backward baseball cap, kept taking pictures, three rolls so far. Leaning in close to Thorn and Pongo, getting the lens a foot away and snapping. Thorn lifted his eyes to Sean, standing at the back of the group, just behind the teacher, Mr. Ranks. She smiled at him, halfheartedly, but a smile.

"The males are completely solitary, and most of the time the females are too. But not long ago a researcher observed a mother and her daughter bumping into each other as they moved through the jungle. Because the researcher knew the movements of these two females, she knew they hadn't seen each other for years. Mother and daughter wound up traveling together for several days before they separated again.

"On the other hand, researchers have never seen unrelated females do the same thing. So what it looks like is, orangutans have a sense of family, even if it is very loosely structured."

One of the students stepped out in front of the others.

"Mr. Ranks told us orangutans were the only primates that commit rape."

Thorn brought his gaze to the girl who'd spoken. Around seventeen, chunky, hair shaved on the sides, a few inches of blond mop left on top. A silver staple in her nose. Looking at Thorn with a very pissed-off squint. Both parents probably doctors. A BMW in her future if she kept her grades up. She wore blue jeans, a shapeless green T-shirt, combat boots.

"Mr. Ranks told you that?"

"It's true, isn't it?" the teacher said. He was a young guy in a polo shirt and madras walking shorts, a gold hoop in his ear.

Hell, everybody was wearing an earring today. Everybody but Thorn and Pongo.

"Yeah, it's true," Thorn said. "But I wouldn't say it's the most important fact about orangutans."

"I never claimed it was the most important fact, I

simply thought it was a fascinating detail," the teacher said. "Primates that rape."

"Well, yeah." Thorn shifted his gaze back to the girl. "It's true. The young males sometimes have forcible sex with females. At twelve to fifteen years old, the males haven't developed their cheek pads. Those are the large red sacks on the side of the face that the adult males fill with air, like bellows, to amplify their mating calls."

The girl was staring at him, paying utter attention.

He said, "Most female orangutans are only attracted to males with large cheek pads. The bigger the cheek pads, the more attraction. Fact is, a lot of the females initiate sex with the most dominant males. Go up to them, slap them on the face, punch them, then turn around and present themselves. So the big cheek padders pretty much have their pick. But even when they're in heat, female orangutans ignore the subadult males. So those males get very frustrated seeing the females standing in line for a cheek padder. As a result sometimes the subadults resort to rape."

"And that makes it right?" the grunge girl said. "They get frustrated, so then it's okay? Listen to you, you're standing there trying to justify rape."

Thorn glanced helplessly at Sean. Her eyes fixed on him. Thorn took a breath, gave the grunge girl a patient smile.

"It's not fair," he said, "to compare animals to humans. Start doing that and there's a whole lot we can't defend in the way animals act. Your own dogs or cats, they don't behave the way we think would be decent for humans. But that doesn't mean we condemn them."

The grunge girl looked back at her preppy teacher.

"He's got a point," Mr. Ranks said coolly.

Pongo shifted in Thorn's arms, then stretched his long hands up to Thorn's hair and hauled himself up, the ape's hairy chest sliding across Thorn's face as he worked onto Thorn's shoulder. He sat sidesaddle there, the ape's warm belly against Thorn's ear, gripping his hair like reins.

"Which is smarter, a chimp or an orang?" one of the boys asked. Sounded like he had a bet with his buddy: twenty bucks says chimps.

"Well, first of all," Thorn said, "the word *orang* means 'person' in Malay. *Orangutan* means 'person of the forest.' So when you say *orang,* what you've really said is *person.*"

"Well, ex-cuuuse me."

The kid looked at the boy beside him and gave him a major eyeroll. Looked back at Thorn, and spoke with mocking respect.

"Okay, sir, which is smarter, a chimp or an orang-*utan*?"

"It's not easy to say." Thorn smiled. "IQ's tricky."

"Chimps are smarter," said the teacher, glancing around at his charges. "I've read the literature."

"Well," Thorn said, "I wouldn't say that."

"Oh, you wouldn't, would you?" A smirk.

The kids chuckled, looked at Thorn.

"Okay," Thorn said to the group. "Which are smarter, dogs or cats?"

A chorus of *dogs,* a sprinkling of *cats.*

"Why?"

One of the neatly dressed girls said, "Dogs do tricks. Fetch the ball, sit, roll over, that kind of thing."

"Yeah," another girl said. "Dogs listen to you."

"Dogs are pack animals," Thorn said. "To survive in the pack a dog has to be alert to signals of authority. They get it wrong, they could get their face torn off. That's why most of them respond to humans.

"And just because cats seem cold and distant, it doesn't mean they're dumb. It's only the way animals act when they live alone. They make their own rules, and don't give a damn what people think one way or the other.

"Dogs are like chimps, cats are like orangutans. Pack animals versus solitary. It has nothing to do with intelligence."

"My, my," the teacher said. "I guess he put me in my place, didn't he?"

Thorn looked at the man for a moment, then took a step in his direction. Mr. Ranks stiffened, brought his hands up for a little tae kwon do or something. Thorn smiled innocently, leaned just enough to his right to bring the small orangutan within striking distance. It took the ape a moment, but finally Pongo's hand darted out and he hooked a finger through the shiniest object in range, Mr. Ranks's earring.

The man clapped a hand to his ear, tried to pry himself free, but Pongo wouldn't let go.

"So," Thorn said, holding still, "orangutans have developed a very high intelligence because their food sources required them to. In the jungle they eat figs and other fruits. To sustain their huge bodies, they have to be very efficient at finding the fruit, or else they'll spend more energy searching than they take in eating it. And if they do that too often, they'll starve."

The teacher was motionless, eyes frozen, glaring at Thorn helplessly. Pongo was stretching the young man's earlobe. Not to the danger point yet, but that goddamn ear had to hurt.

Thorn said, "Orangutans keep a map in their heads of the fig trees and durians and other fruit trees within their range. They also keep close tabs on the state of ripeness of each tree. Orangutans prefer sour or slightly unripe fruit. If he arrives at a tree too early, the fruits don't have much nourishment. If he's too late, the gibbons, monkeys, squirrels, and birds will already have stolen it all.

"To keep track of so many trees and to know down to the exact day when each tree will be filled with edible fruit, the orangutan has evolved a very complex brain. He has a very large map and a very accurate calendar that coordinates with it. Every day he accomplishes by himself what it takes a whole pack of chimps to do."

Thorn reached out and carefully unhooked Pongo's finger from Mr. Ranks's earring. The teacher groaned, turned his back on the group, and rubbed the life back into his ear.

The grunge girl angled forward, looked like she was ready to leap on him.

"Rape is bad," she muttered. "If it's an animal that rapes or a human, it's still bad. I don't give a shit what you say."

Most of the kids groaned and looked away from her. Heard these outbursts a few times before. One of her girlfriends moved in close and patted her hard on the back, as if the grunge girl were choking on a bone.

"That's all for today," Thorn said. "You can go now."

Mr. Ranks swung back around. He looked at his watch.

"That's not right. You can't do that. Just cut us off like that when things don't go your way."

"Tour's over, folks. I have to put the animals away."

The kids grumbled, then started to peel away. The boy in overalls took a couple of last shots of Pongo playing with Thorn's hair, braiding it into a complicated tangle.

Rubbing his ear, Mr. Ranks gave Thorn a we'll-see-about-this stare and headed back up the stone steps.

The grunge girl stayed on for a moment more, glaring at Pongo as if he were the source of all her misery, then she turned and followed her classmates back to the parrot exhibits.

Sean stepped down to the viewing area. Thorn waited for her behind the waist-high fence.

"This is what I've been doing lately," he said.

"You're good at it."

"I listen to the shit coming out of my mouth and I can't believe it. I talk more in a day in this place than I talk at home in a year."

"It's probably good for you."

"I doubt it. But I like the animals."

Pongo peeped in his ear. Sean looked down at the sand, rubbed her open palm against the hip of her jeans as if trying to scrape away some sticky film. A nervous move. She looked up at him.

"I heard about Bronson," she said. "I couldn't believe it. I've known him all my life. Killed for a few dollars."

"He was one of the good ones."

She drew a breath and stared hard at him.

"Are you having an affair with my mother?"

"What!"

"Are you, Thorn?"

"Hell, no." He looked around the area. Just a couple of tourists wandering slowly through, cameras ready. "Absolutely not. Your mother is married."

"And you don't have affairs with married women?"

"Haven't so far."

She held his eyes for a long time, as if replaying his words, running them through some personal polygraph.

Pongo climbed down his leg and shuffled over to the gym set. He climbed the bars and went hand over hand across the top rail, then slid down the rope and pulled himself inside the Goodyear radial hanging there. He made noises to himself as he swung wider and wider arcs. Broom walked out to the edge of his cage to watch the young ape play.

Sean reached out a hand toward Thorn, as if she was going to caress his cheek. Then she stopped, seemed suddenly not to know what to do with her hand. It floated there, her fingers coming close to his face, but halting and drifting down, hanging.

Finally she crossed the three inches of air, touched him lightly on the front of his shirt, his chest. She patted him with her fingertips. Patted him on the sternum. A weak smile.

"I'm sorry."

"It's okay," he said. "Forget it."

"I'm upset, is all. I guess I'm just looking for someone to be mad at. Somebody to blame."

"You have a right."

She smiled halfheartedly, then turned away.

He watched her walk away up the stone steps past the macaws, the Asian parrots, the hornbills, into the purple shade of the bougainvillea.

# CHAPTER

# 12

"Yeah, we got an albino Burmese python. It goes for eleven." Orlon listened into the phone for a second and gave Ray a frazzled glance. He said, "No, eleven *hundred*. That's right, eleven hundred *dollars*. Jesus, I thought you knew snakes."

Shooting Ray a peeved look. See what the hell he had to put up with for the financial enrichment of the White brothers.

"Okay, now we got that straight," Orlon said. "Then you want two blond Burmese pythons, which it just so happens we also got in stock, at three hundred and fifty apiece. Yeah, yeah, that's right, *Python bivittatus*. Yeah, yeah. And a tangerine Honduran milk snake, *Lampropeltis hondrensis*. Yeah, we can get you that one too."

Orlon rolled his eyes, listening to Trakas talk.

"Yeah, yeah, I remember you very well. Yeah, uh-huh. You know we carry good product. Yeah, yeah." Repeating all this for Ray's benefit. Putting on a display to show Ray he was carrying his own weight around there.

Ray sat down behind his desk. It was Tuesday afternoon, twoish. He was just back from the warehouse, two thousand square feet of cages, the big room connected to their office by a narrow hallway. Ray closed his eyes and listened to his little brother taking the semibig snake order. He rubbed his thumbs in hard circles against his temples. Ray White was seriously depressed.

Three of the five goddamn orangutans were dead. Dehydration, shock, froze to death in the plane, shit, who could say for sure? But three were dead, and the siamang gibbon didn't look too good either; wouldn't eat, lying on its side, some yellow foamy drool coming from his mouth.

All three that died were the ones they'd packed upside down. Back in Singapore it seemed like the logical thing to do, just in case the moron luggage handlers ignored the message stenciled on the outside, THIS SIDE UP, and set it in the plane upside down. Three crammed in one way, three the other, at least there was a fifty-fifty chance half of them would be shipped right side up.

But they lost the three upside-down ones, plus one packed the other way didn't look so good, breathing hard, panting. Sure, they could chalk it up to the cost of doing business, but it was a hell of a cost, a hundred and twenty large.

Across the room Orlon was gripping his throat with a one-handed stranglehold. Apparently the guy he was talking to was another dick-brain who thought 'cause he'd been bit once or twice it made him some kind of bona fide snake connoisseur.

A lot of herpers were that way. Guys bragged about their bites like Vietnam vets about war wounds. "See that thumb. That was '72, a spectacled cobra. And that first knuckle missing on the left hand, that was a green eyelash viper, '84. See this zipper on my cheek, shit. That was one mean canebrake rattler, June of last year. Took such a goddamn hold, I had to pour kerosene on it, light it up to get that sucker off."

Like for some reason it made them heroes, being so dumb as to let a snake sink its fangs in their face.

Finally Orlon hung up the phone and came over to Ray's desk near the front window and dropped into the chair beside it. He took his time lighting up a Hava-Tampa. Then the two of them looked out the tinted window at the view across the parking lot/cul-de-sac of their small industrial park, looking at a Mazda repair shop across the way, and a rattan store owned by some Pakistani guy.

Next to the rattan store was another place without a name. All the windows were blackened and no mailbox outside. Either a drug drop, or an FBI field office. Bad guys, good guys, who could tell the difference anymore? They dressed alike, the talk was the same, same cars, women, their offices had escape hatches, six or seven phone lines, not much action going on during daylight hours.

It was comforting, though, that's how Ray thought of it. Whether it was FBI or some drug lord's cousin over there, what it meant was, the White brothers weren't the ones going to draw the gunfire in this neighborhood.

Miami was good that way. You didn't have to worry about getting busted for trivial shit. From running red lights to holding up a 7-Eleven, hey, the cops didn't have time for the dinky stuff, man, they're too busy bulldozing the bodies off Biscayne Boulevard, unloading the freighters full of heroin.

With all the heavy-duty crime going on around this town, nobody cared if the White brothers were trafficking in a few of the lower life forms. Scaly creatures with lidless eyes and forked tongues, or animals with their heads below their shoulders—who gave a shit if they were endangered or not? The only ones who got in an uproar about it were a bunch of lonely old ladies like Allison Farleigh and her gang of ape-kissers. Too much time on their hands, bored housewives who'd taken to trying to trip up good working people like the White boys.

"I gotta ride up there to Hialeah, deliver the guy his snakes. You wanna come?"

"No," Ray said. "First thing we gotta do is finish with Allison. Clean up that mess."

"Yeah, yeah," Orlon said. "Only now it's gonna be a lot harder. The lady's probably got full-time police protection."

"The cops didn't believe her," Ray said. " 'Robbery

at Parrot Jungle' is how the paper called it. If anybody bought her story, it would've been item number one. Ape lady target of botched murder attempt. But they don't take her seriously after what she did, going after Bond like that. No, the door's wide open for what we gotta do."

"Pretty Miss Allison Farleigh's gonna be on the wrong side of the lawn before the day's over," Orlon said. "Then afterward you'll help me with this Hialeah delivery, right?"

"You didn't need to kill that old guy last night, Orlon. There was no call for that. Absolutely unjustified."

"Here we go."

"I'm going to have to take your gun away again."

"Fuck you."

"There's no call for all this goddamn violence, Orlon. None at all. True, we got to do Allison. But that's self-protection. Pure and simple. Like if somebody draws on you, you got to shoot. But those other times, that was bad, Orlon. That was gratuitous."

"After you kill one person," Orlon said, "I don't see how it matters after that. One, two, three. They can only strap you in the chair one time."

"I'm not going to argue philosophy with you, Orlon. You know it matters. Two is worse than one. Three is worse than two. You gotta get a handle on this, Orlon. I'm worried about you, man."

Orlon blew out a lungful of smoke and tapped some cigar ash onto the floor.

"All right, you stated your case. But after we do Allison, you'll come along, help me deliver these snakes, right?"

"What? You're afraid of handling a couple of goddamn pythons?"

"Hell, no."

"Well? So what is it?"

"It's that goddamn motorcycle club again." He shifted his eyes out the window. "That guy in Hialeah. Trakas, that's who wants the snakes."

"The Hell's Vipers?"

Orlon nodded his head sadly.

"I mean, hey, I'm not nervous about Trakas himself. I could handle him fine. It's that whole fucking scene I don't like."

"Another chopper guy getting inducted?"

Orlon nodded again, a case of heebie-jeebies in his eyes.

The last time his little brother took an order up there, the Harley guys were in the middle of some kind of initiation rites. A couple of new greasy-haired fat slobs learning all the secret handshakes. In the middle of things, the group got a little rough with some of their snakes, killed five or six of them, using them like whips, giving lashes to the new members. And suddenly they needed replacements. Called the White brothers and said if they could make it up there pronto, there was a bonus in it. So Orlon went. And he walked into the middle of some kind of demented party: drugs, rattlers, branding irons. Thing made a Santeria goat sacrifice seem tame. Beyond that, Orlon wouldn't say anything, which was unusual because Orlon loved to tell tales.

But these cycle guys were a few notches too bad for him. Orlon stumbled back into the warehouse later on that afternoon, the tip of his nose hanging halfway off, blood pumping across his lips, down his chin, Orlon blowing blood-bubbles as he talked. Ray had to rush him to Larkin Hospital, have his nose stitched back on. He looked fine now, just a little seam down his nostril, but the whole adventure had shaken him up. He'd never admit it straight out to Ray, but those guys had tweaked him down in his gut strength.

"How much is the order for?"

Orlon looked down at the slip in his hand and said, "All added up, ninety-eight hundred, thirty-seven bucks."

"Screw 'em. We don't need their fucking money, a little order like that. You're still thinking like it's the old days, scratching for every penny. Man, you gotta start adjusting to our new condition. Start thinking like a winner,

Orlon. I'm surprised you'd even talk to those people again."

"So am I," Orlon said. "Guy just took me by surprise."

"You should've hung up on the son of a bitch."

"But I didn't. I took his order like nothing'd ever happened. Don't ask me why."

"Maybe we should go up there," Ray said, smiling to himself. "Take a sack of mambas, a couple of Mojave rattlers, pitch them through the window. See what these cowboys are made of."

"You just come along, Ray, that'll be enough. They wouldn't do anything, the both of us there."

Ray looked out the front window, watched the Mazda mechanic coming back from lunch. Pants all greasy, carrying a bag from McDonald's. His wife worked over there, too, running the cash register. Jesus, it was pathetic what some people had to do for their money, stick their heads into gasoline engines all day. Man, oh, man. Least Ray's job had an excitement element, no two days the same. Plus a major ecological component, too, in tune with the natural world. Not to mention the fact that his reflexes stayed razor quick from nabbing venomous snakes on a daily basis.

"Another one of those apes died," Ray said. "The last of the upside-down ones."

"Shit."

"And you just watch, any minute now that phone's going to ring, it'll be our esteemed colleague wanting his money. He's not going to believe three out of the five died."

Orlon was leaning forward, elbows on his knees, staring down at the floor. Still worried about those guys in Hialeah.

"Screw our esteemed colleague."

"He'll be pissed we don't get him the full amount. He's a stickler about money."

"Let him be pissed. He starts giving us any shit, we'll just mention that girl he shot."

Ray pointed a finger at his brother.

"We agreed we're not bringing that up with him unless it's absolutely necessary. I don't trust this guy one bit, but we gotta stay on good terms with him. That girl he shot, that's our backup plan—something goes sour with our business relationship, we're keeping that information as a last resort. Right?"

"Yeah, yeah."

Ray watched a car pull up to the rattan place. Young guy gets out. Short pants, tennis shirt, cute blond wife gets out in her matching outfit. Auditioning for the *Newlywed Game.*

Watching the two, Ray said, "I been thinking about that Borneo trip. Him calling us like that, we gotta run over, take him on a safari. I thought, yeah, okay, the guy's got a wild hair to go hunt, wants us to show him how. But then we get there, and it's all his show. Go here, go there, jerking us around. I mean, yeah, he's paying the light bills these days, putting us in a positive cash flow situation, but that doesn't mean he can just call up like that, make us jump over every little thing."

"Maybe he's having one of those mid-life crises. All of a sudden he's gotta do something to substantiate his manliness. So he wants to go hunting in the woods. Shoot things."

"Substantiate his manliness?" Ray said. "Jesus Christ, Orlon, whatta you been watching, the Mind Expansion Channel again?"

"Hey, now, don't patronize me."

"Oh, yeah, and by the way," Ray said, "I called that vet guy. Kurt Franklin. Asked him to come by, look at the last two orangs. See what he can do, nurse them back to health."

Orlon stubbed out the remains of his cigar in the green saucer he kept there for an ashtray.

Ray said, "We lose those two, we don't have a fucking thing to show for a fifteen-thousand-dollar vacation to the Far East."

He watched as the rattan salesman started hawking

one of his big throne chairs to the young marrieds. The guy tried out the throne, then his bride tried it. You could look at them, tell which one was going to use it more. The lady boss. Her personal chair, gonna run her kingdom from right there.

"Well," Orlon said. "Let's go terminate a woman."

He stood up, stretched his arms above his head, yawned.

"But this is the last time," Ray said. "We gotta make a solemn oath, Orlon. This is the last act of extreme violence we do. I don't like how this is going. The pretty girl in Borneo, the old guy at Parrot Jungle. I mean, yeah, we'll do the dance on Allison, but after that we put the guns away. Right? Put 'em away for good like mother would've wanted."

"Man, you been seeing that shrink too long, Ray. Everything's about our mother."

"Everything is *always* about your mother. Whether you think it is or not. It is. Always."

"Right, right. Whatever you say, big brother."

"We put the guns in the closet, lock the door. That's the end of it."

"You're the boss."

"Goddamn right I am."

Ray looked at the photo he kept on his desk. His mom in a frilly yellow dress, big horn-rimmed sunglasses, lipstick a mile wide. Outside in their shabby front yard, looking around the trunk of that jacaranda tree they had, mugging for one of her boyfriends, Ray couldn't remember which. It was a smile that would break your heart if you knew what was gonna happen to the woman a year or two down the road.

Orlon said, "Let's go get it over with. And this time I'm doing it. No more shooting at trees."

Harry at work, Allison in her nightgown sitting at her bedroom desk with a pile of wildlife newsletters in front of her. All morning she'd been setting them on fire, tossing the burning sheets into the metal trash can beside her desk, where they smoldered. Using the silver Zippo lighter her father, Julius, had used to light his huge Cuban cigars. That Zippo, one of the few things of her father's she still possessed.

Allison was burning the newsletters, years and years of them, a decade of work. Editing, proofing, cutting and pasting, printing, bundling, mailing. Briefly, she glanced through each one, then touched the flame to a corner of the page. Hundreds of smugglers, shady animal dealers, corrupt zoo officials. Articles, photos, photocopies of evidence, editorials.

Allison burned them, destroying that life, every trace of those years of compulsive work. Seven years of making enemies. Burning the photos of all the people she'd helped expose, dozens she'd testified against in court, some who'd even been sentenced and spent time in jail.

She stopped for a moment and studied the black-and-white photo of a tall, wolf-faced man in a tight white T-shirt. Seven years ago she'd printed the blurry snapshot on the front page of her newsletter. Crotch Meriwether. A hunting buddy of her father's, a swamp rat, moonshiner, hell-raiser, who was born and raised around the Ten Thousand Islands, lived there all his life, and made his dirt-poor living by killing gators, ibis, flamingos, selling plumes, skins, skulls, whatever. It was men like Meriwether who'd wiped out entire species of bright-crested birds from the Everglades. Men like him who'd passed on their skills and lore to the next generation of low-life poachers.

Allison skimmed through the article about Meriwether, feeling an old pang of guilt for her betrayal of one of her father's cronies. Meriwether had been her very first target, easy prey. She'd used his friendship with her family to set up a purchase of a dozen gator hides. She'd worn a wire, gotten Crotch to speak clearly into the mike, establishing his knowledge of wildlife laws and his clear intent to break them. "You know we could get ten years for this, Crotch, trading in endangered species." "And is that just now dawning on you, girl?"

That was all it took for Fish and Wildlife to make a case. Fifteen-hundred-dollar fine, sixteen-month jail term, eleven of which he served. She'd received dozens of vicious postcards from Raiford. Meriwether bragging to Allison in his crippled, twisted script that there wasn't a living thing that walked God's earth, white or black, two-legged or four, male or female, that he hadn't already skinned or was planning on skinning real soon.

Despite that one victory, prison time for men like Crotch was extremely rare. One of the worst frustrations of her work had always been that judges and juries had such a goddamn hard time sending men to prison for dealing in protected animals. The defense attorneys invariably played the same tune. With all the things wrong in the world, thirteen-year-olds murdering for basketball shoes, how could anyone see fit to send a hardworking businessman to jail for making a little technical slipup about which species of animal he'd trapped, or killed, or imported.

And, of course, the reptile cases were the hardest to make. Try to find a jury anywhere who had any sympathy for a diamondback rattler, gator, or iguana. The less snakes in the world, the better, she'd heard one attorney say. My client should be congratulated for bringing this snake to the brink of extinction. Never mind that the snake population was a cornerstone of the ecosystem. Try to explain the crucial biological importance of water moccasins, and the jury would be snickering at you.

All morning Allison had been burning the newsletters. Each and every page, stacks of them, the room choking with smoke despite the overhead fan set on high, all four windows flung wide. Burning every reminder, every relic from that life, that mindless crusade she'd been on for seven years. It had murdered her own daughter. Killed Bronson too.

Burning every one. Destroying it all.

Finally, when the last page twisted and warped into flame, curled into black smoke, she set the Zippo aside, closed her eyes, propped her forehead against her palm.

She was spent. Weary beyond anything she'd known. Across from her desk the blinds were drawn against a bright afternoon sun. She could hear the dull static of traffic from Coral Way two blocks off. The bedroom faced north toward the golf course, and caught a draft just then that rattled the venetian blinds, billowed the curtains.

Those first cool breezes of the fall. Temperatures finally drifting into the seventies. A time of year she usually loved, that energized her. Feeling the humidity dying back, a hint of Canadian pine in the air, that wash of blue-tinged arctic air. The first tourists beginning to trickle in.

She sat at her desk and listened to the distant traffic, felt a current of air pass across her. She listened to the mail truck making its stop-and-go tour of the neighborhood. She smelled the garlic and onions sautéing in Mrs. Casines's skillet next door. Inhaled the last blooms of confederate jasmine climbing the trellis on the north wall of the Farleighs' house.

Maybe if she gave herself over to her senses, drank in every whisper of scent, each sound vibrating through the air, let each new sensation replace the last, savoring each one, focused completely on the pastel light filtering through the jacaranda, the stumbling flight of a moth against the far wall, kept her mind sharp and utterly fixed on each second as it unfolded, then just maybe the images wouldn't resurface, she would not see Winslow's wounded face, feel her daughter's slender body growing cold in her arms, would not remember every second of the long night battling the creatures of the jungle. Maybe she wouldn't become mired again in the insufferable gloom.

In the distance she heard the squeal of tires, horns honking over on Alhambra, then with absolute clarity she heard the two-tone squeak of the hinges on the kitchen door downstairs. The door opening, and the soft click of its shutting.

She sat up straight.

Two-thirty in the afternoon, far too early for Harry to be home. And Allison had no friends who would think of entering without knocking first.

She listened as the intruder took several careful steps on the oak floor in the hallway, heading toward the front of the house. Then she lost track of their direction, the footsteps obscured by a passing car with its radio up full volume. A siren out on Coral Way, an aggravated blue jay in the jacaranda.

She heard Mrs. Casines's phone and then Mrs. Casines answering it, shouting in her half-deaf Spanish. Then heard, just beyond her bedroom door, the seventh step on the stairway. That old oak step crackled and screaked, the noise it had been making for almost twenty-five years. The seventh step up, seven to go.

# CHAPTER

# 13

Allison bolted the bathroom door and stood for a moment holding her breath, listening as someone squeaked open the door to her bedroom. She brought her eyes to the mirror above the sink and stared at herself as the intruder prowled the room. She was wearing a cotton nightgown, lace embroidering the collar. Her face was gaunt and had lost its color, dead flesh against bright red hair. It was not Allison in the mirror, but a papier-mâché likeness, a piñata filled with heavy vapor. The woman in the mirror no longer cared if she lived or died.

She pulled herself away. Stared at the doorknob. Someone was in her house, and the rage she felt freshening her blood had come unbidden. It had nothing to do with Winslow or Bronson. It was purely territorial. Someone was in her house.

Allison rubbed the focus back into her eyes, then turned and scoured the bathroom for a weapon. It only took a few seconds to see that that was futile. There was nothing sharp, nothing heavy.

Outside the door she thought she heard a voice, and then another replying, but she wasn't absolutely sure. It might've been someone passing by on the sidewalk, or even a random shred of conversation carried from the golf course by a gust of wind.

She could scream. Rape, fire. Though the only neighbor home during the day was deaf Senora Casines. In any case she doubted her voice would work. She was fairly certain the only noise she could produce would be a gargle, a strangled croak.

Outside the bathroom window was an oak, its largest branch sloping gently back to the main trunk. It was the tree Sean and Winslow had scaled as kids. Just below that window the two of them had constructed a tree house, and there with their cups and saucers they'd had tea parties. *Good Housekeeping, Redbook* in neat stacks. Allison standing in the bathroom, watching them play husband and wife. Hearing their sad reenactments of Harry and Allison.

She gripped the window frame and heaved upward, but it was sealed tight by layers and layers of paint. One more thing Harry had continually promised to fix.

She blew out an exasperated breath, then quietly turned from the window and opened the medicine cabinet, moved aside old pill containers, petroleum jelly, deodorant, searching for one of Harry's straight razors. The least she could do was come out slashing. Get in one good swipe before they took hold of her. But his razor was gone. A few months earlier Harry had moved all his things down the hall when they'd finally agreed to abandon the pretense, and had taken up new sleeping arrangements. Harry in the guest room now, Allison in the master, still using their old bed with all its bittersweet sags.

She heard the footsteps come to a halt outside the bathroom. She shut the cabinet, faced the door. The intruder tapped lightly. One time, two. Tried the knob. Paused.

Allison moved close to the door. She reached out, took hold of the bolt, made one last survey of the bathroom, seized the first thing she saw of any size, then turned back to the door, drew in a long breath, slid the bolt back, and yanked the door wide.

With a defiant scream she lunged out, and swung her half-filled bottle of mouthwash at her daughter's face.

\* \* \*

"So what the fuck, Rayon? We going in or not?"

Ray said, "Someone's visiting her."

"Yeah, and how the hell you know that? You having a psychic experience?"

"That car in the driveway," Ray said. "The Toyota Celica, it doesn't belong to the husband, it doesn't belong to Allison either."

They were parked a few feet off South Greenway on the rough of the golf course, the car idling in the shade of a banyan tree, some of the limb roots dangling to the windshield. Three or four houses to the east was the Farleighs' two-story Spanish-style home. A ritzy-titsy neighborhood in Coral Gables, right across from the country club. Red-tiled roofs, big lots—man, the houses had to start in the seven figures. Kind of neighborhood used to boggle young Ray White. He knew how goddamn hard his own mother worked, and look at the shithole they lived in. How in hell could anybody work hard enough to buy houses like those?

Now he knew the answer. One way or another, the people who lived in those houses stole that money. They'd found a way, legal or illegal, to fuck over their fellowman. They hired a hundred Darlene Annette Whites to do their stoop labor, paid them a nickel out of every dollar that crossed their desk, then they moved out of their own shitholes and alongside this golf course.

Orlon swiveled around in the bucket seat.

"Tell me, how is it you know what cars these people drive?"

"I've done my homework." Ray drummed his fingers on the glove compartment, stared out the windshield.

Orlon said, "Maybe what we should do, we should go on in there anyway, abduct them both, Allison and whoever's come to visit. If she's a friend of Allison's, she's gotta be another ape-kisser. We'll get two for the price of one."

"Listen to you, Orlon. Listen to what you're proposing here. Commit a home invasion, broad daylight, a double kidnapping, double murder."

"Oh, yeah, yeah," Orlon said. "I forgot. Ray's gone soft. Ray's a peacenik."

Ray turned his eyes to his brother, gave him the megawatt stare. Took only a second before Orlon had to look away, probably feeling his corneas crinkling up at the edges.

"Look, man," Orlon said, "we got to do this broad. That's all there is to it. No choice. She's heard us, seen us. We gotta do it now."

"I know that. You think I don't know that?"

Ray stared at the house.

He was sure the two of them looked pretty conspicuous out there on the edge of the golf course, in Orlon's '79 black Vette with flames coming off the front wheel wells, big blower and airscoop jutting out of the hood. This part of town was full of BMW's, Jap luxuries, Mercedes sedans. Neighborhood with some serious old money. Everybody looked so law-abiding, churchgoing. But then, Ray knew better than that.

One morning about a year ago, some woman called up White Brothers Imports saying to Ray in a very thick Spanish accent that her boss instructed her to get in touch. He'd acquired their names from a very reliable source. Seems the guy had woken up that very morning and decided he couldn't live another day without owning a chimpanzee.

"Chimps are endangered," Rayon told the secretary. Playing cautious, not sure who the hell he was talking to. Could be one of the ape-kissers trying to lure him into agreeing to something shady on the phone, get him on tape.

The guy's secretary said, "Senor Robales doesn't care about that. In fact, he prefers things which are dangerous."

" 'Endangered' is what I said, not 'dangerous.' "

"I know what you said. And what I am saying to you, Mr. White, it doesn't matter if this animal is endangered or not. My employer is not a man who is restrained by the pitiable laws of this country. Do I make myself clear?"

Ray loved that. A guy who wasn't restrained by the pitiable laws of the country. Welcome to America, stay as long as you like, do whatever the hell you feel like, and come back anytime.

"I'd need to know who recommended us. Check your guy's references."

"Of course."

"And I'd like to meet this Mr. Robales," Ray said.

"Senor Robales will meet you when you deliver the chimp."

Ray ordered the chimp by phone from Djakarta, guy had the thing ready and waiting in a cage in one of the back stalls at the Pramuka Market. No ape-kissers over there, at least none with any clout. A week later White Brothers Imports received the ape, documentation papers saying he was captive-born, the head Fish and Wildlife guy not liking it a bit, but there wasn't a thing he could prove. So Ray went on and delivered the chimp a stone's throw from where they were parked right now.

Two blocks away, at this very moment, there was a year-old chimp walking around in his diapers in this guy's two-million-dollar house. Mr. Robales, dealer in dubious pharmaceuticals, was probably letting the hairy thing crawl all over him at that very second.

The day he delivered the chimp, Ray was standing there, trying to have a conversation with this guy, ascertain the exact nature of Mr. Robales's evil.

The man started out being very cool, dark glasses, silk clothes, little slipper things on his feet. Not saying a thing, letting his secretary handle the money part. But then Ray released the chimp and it waddled right over to Robales, reached up and yanked off the guy's sunglasses and tried them on himself, and instantly the bad guy changed into a slobbering idiot. Cooing, baby-talking, stroking the hairy fucking thing. Never ceased to amaze Ray the way some people turned to mush when they were exposed to the lower life forms.

Of course, in most cases what happened next was, the chimp would grow up in a year or two, stop being a cuddly little thing, and move into adolescence. One day it has a tantrum about something and bites its master on the finger. Bites down to the fucking bone, spits out a knuckle or two. Cute little Bonzo's chewing away on human flesh. That's when the White brothers get the call. Come take this fucking ape back, it bit the shit out of me. No, sir, sorry. We don't do trade-ins. After that the ape either winds up wandering around in the Everglades, alligator bait, or takes a trip a couple of feet under Senor Robales's backyard.

Ray turned the air conditioner down and glanced over at his brother. Orlon was concentrating on that Toyota Celica like he was Superman trying to vaporize it.

"So tell me about this homework you been doing, Rayon. This is the first I heard of that."

"Nothing special," Ray said. "I made Allison a little hobby of mine, that's all. Weekends, evenings. I cruise by a few times, or park awhile, watch who's coming and going. I believe in acquainting myself with my enemies."

"Since when?"

"Since she took an interest in our comings and goings last winter."

"A couple of articles in her crummy newsletter—shit, that's nothing. That indigo snake case, hell. Nobody takes that woman seriously."

"I wanted to find out who she was, that's all."

"Well, I gotta say, Rayon, maybe you got more testicular energy than I been giving you credit for."

Ray watched a gang of golfers go by in their carts. Bunch was dressed up like a flock of amazon parrots. Man, if he were running things, he'd make it a federal crime to dress that way. Instruct the FBI to arrest anybody wearing madras of any kind, or white belts. Any clothing you can see from more than a hundred yards away.

Ray turned around, touched the gunnysack lying on the jump seat. The bag boiled and bumped. Pythons were getting more and more pissed the longer they had to stay knotted up like that looking at each other.

"Mary Astor," Orlon said. "I just thought who it was the dead girl looked like. Mary Astor with red hair."

"Mary Astor."

"That's right. Played Brigid O'Shaughnessy in *The Maltese Falcon*. Always out of breath because of John Huston, the director, running her up and down a flight of stairs before every take. To make her sound like she was lying, out of breath all the time. You know, tall, skinny, had that same blue-blooded face as Allison's little girl. A dead ringer." Orlon smiled, rubbed a hand over his bald head. "A red dinger."

"Let's go," Ray said. "Get the hell out of here."

"I always liked Sydney Greenstreet in that movie. Great part, laughing all the time. Fat Man, very jovial. Looked like Santa, but turns out he's Satan. I liked that guy. Felt a karmic harmony with him."

"Get going, Orlon. We'll come back later. Do what we have to do when there aren't so many people around."

Orlon slipped the car into gear.

"Santa, Satan," Orlon said. "You know, when you think about it, what if those two guys are really the same guy? Santa Claus and the devil. Guy spends his whole year in hell, gets to go out one night a year, like part of his plea bargain. He has to deliver presents to the poor kids."

"It's two different guys, Orlon."

"How do you know that for sure? Where's it written down it's gotta be two guys?"

"It's written down everywhere," Ray said. "Good's good. Bad's bad. Satan's the devil. Santa's a saint. You start mixing them up, you're fucked."

"Well, maybe I'm fucked then."

He revved the Corvette's big engine.

"Yeah, maybe you are, Orlon. Maybe you are."

The orangutan's cage was four feet square. Just enough room to make one swing before reaching the other end. Or hang from his toes and play with the straw on the floor of the cage. Also, he could force his nose between the grid of his cage and smell the feet of the sick orangutan in the cage next to him.

The sick one's feet didn't smell like the jungle anymore; they didn't smell like the orangutan's mother either. Now they smelled like the inside of the airplane cargo hold. They smelled like gasoline fumes and vomit.

Many years ago the orangutan's mother had been a captive herself. When she was only a year old, she was abducted from the jungles of Sumatra, and eventually sold to a small research center in Arizona.

A linguistics professor wanted an ape for his project in animal intelligence. He wanted an orangutan so badly, he was willing to overlook the suspicious paperwork that accompanied the animal. The papers stated that the orangutan was a captive-born animal raised in a wildlife refuge outside Kuala Lumpur. Because Appendix II of the CITES international treaty allowed for sale and shipment of captive-born animals but not wild ones, it had become common practice for poachers to create fictitious zoos or refuges in order to obtain the necessary documents to get the animals past customs.

For over a year the Arizona professor taught the young female orangutan sign language. She learned sixty-eight signs in thirteen months. But then, through an oversight, the professor was late in filing his grant applications and the federal money his facility had been surviving on for years was cut off. He was forced to shut down his lab, and all the research animals were put on the market.

The orangutan's mother was sold to a woman in Tucson who cared for primates on her ranch and tried to find good homes for them. After a few months, the Tucson lady sold the ape to a trucker and his wife from Texas. But when it bit the trucker's wife on the cheek, the couple contacted a man in Cincinnati who'd been advertising in a pet-trading magazine for months, seeking an orangutan or chimp. The man paid the Texas couple twenty-eight thousand dollars for the ape.

He owned a bar and poolroom along state highway 744 outside Cincinnati. To provide for his new attraction, he dug a pit in front of his bar, poured a concrete floor, put bars over the top, and then settled the orangutan inside.

The orangutan was a hit. It drew more drinkers to the bar. Some of the patrons got in the habit of stopping at the pit on the way in or out, where they amused themselves by offering the ape cigarettes and beer. After a while the mother orangutan developed a taste for Colt 45 and Marlboros. She ate the cigarettes.

Early one morning, seven months after the orangutan moved into the cage alongside state highway 744, an outraged animal-rights activist used a blowtorch to cut the bars of the cage. The young man freed the ape and drove it to a wildlife refuge in South Carolina. After a month of long-range legal battles with the bar owner, the woman who ran the South Carolina refuge agreed to pay an out-of-court cash settlement to the bar owner, and all criminal charges were dropped.

A month later the animal was shipped back to Borneo, where it spent the next four years in a rehab center in the Tanjung Puting rain forest. Gradually it was taught how to forage for food in its natural habitat, and reintroduced to its traditional behaviors. Eventually one morning it disappeared into the jungle.

The mother orangutan roamed the jungle for fifteen years before it was shot by the poachers. From its months in the research center in Arizona, the mother orangutan had retained a half dozen of the words the professor taught it. At the time of her death, she could still sign the words *tree, nest, fruit, sad, sleepy,* and her favorite word, *shit.*

The orangutan with the silver patch of hair had seen his mother use all six of these signs in the four years it had spent with her. And now, as the young orangutan hung upside down in its four-by-four cage and looked around at the stark warehouse, it made the sign for *fruit.*

Because it was hungry and bored, it made this sign again and again.

# CHAPTER

# 14

Allison charged from the bathroom, swinging her bottle of mouthwash. Sean ducked out of range, stumbled backward, then both of them froze for a second, absorbing the situation, the absurdity of it. Allison looked down at the bottle in her hand, and chuckled, then Sean joined in, and both of them let go, began to laugh in earnest. The first good laugh they'd shared in a while. God, such a release, it felt wonderful to Allison, flushing away all the accumulated poisons of grief and confusion.

But now the ludicrous moment was well past, and Allison was still laughing, her stomach cramped, eyes full of tears, knowing full well she was out of control, hysterical, that her laughter was rolling ahead on its own momentum, crossing a border into more serious emotional territory. But she couldn't stop, one flurry of chuckles after another, couldn't stop even though she saw the worry in Sean's eyes, the frown, knew that whatever had begun to heal between them was already being injured again.

Fighting it, Allison gasped, drew in a deep gulp of calming air, tried to bite back the next gush of air, but a trickle of laughter broke free, a suppressed giggle, a hiccup, several small bursts.

"All right, Mom. Quit it. Quit."

With a helpless smile fluttering on her lips, Allison

drew in a huge breath and expelled it harshly as though she were trying to blow down a cobweb.

"Goddamn it, stop!"

Allison kept her lips sealed against a great bubble of laughter growing in her throat.

"Okay, now listen," Sean said, and took a long breath. "I came over here because I wanted to know what you did about Dad."

"What?"

"Did you tell him yet?" Sean braced herself against the side of the bed, eyes wandering the room. "Did you tell him you were leaving?"

"No," she said. "Not yet."

"He's worried about you, Mom." Eyes coming back to her, gray-blue like warm steel. "He cares about you."

"Cares about me."

"That's right," Sean said. "And he's very upset about Winslow. Deeply upset. He tries not to show it, to be strong, but it's hurt him very bad. He's depressed. I can tell."

Allison felt the humor drain from her face, and the weight of gloom begin to seep in again, dragging at her eyes and mouth. She took a shaky step toward Sean, but her daughter stepped away, then assumed a stiff and distant perch on the edge of Allison's bed. Drew one leg up, hugged the knee. She glanced around at the disarray, the jumble of clothes on the floor, a bottle of red wine overturned on the rug in the corner, the wastebasket still smoking.

"What the hell've you been doing in here, anyway?"

Allison opened her mouth, but had nothing to say. Sean shifted her seat on the bed. She was wearing white jeans, an oversize blue button-down shirt, white and gold Nike running shoes. Comfortable clothes. But her face was shut up tight, all the animation held rigidly in check below the surface, as though her face were some brittle mask that might crumble from even the slightest twitch of emotion.

Allison looked away. She paced slowly around the

room from window to window, glancing into the branches. Gathering herself, feeling the chill return to her blood, the shiver she'd been battling since that afternoon two weeks ago.

"I came over here," Sean said, "to ask you a favor."

Allison heard a roar outside, and turned to the front window. Some idiot in a black Corvette was gunning along the edge of the golf course, tearing up the grass. The car swerved out onto the street, burning rubber, and peeled away. A couple of codgers in their golf carts yelled and shook their fists as it passed.

Allison could smell fresh bread baking. Poor Mrs. Casines next door. A widow for fifteen years, her children never visited, no friends. Cooked all day, set places every night for five people. Trying to lure the phantoms to her table, but they never showed. Always those wonderful smells wafting from her house. Cook, cook, cook, it was all the woman knew, all that kept her going. Roasts, arroz con pollo, cobblers, meat loaf. Three garbage cans on her sidewalk every Monday. Maybe that's how Allison would turn out, using orangutans instead of food. The crazy old lady down the street with her house full of orange apes.

"What is it, Sean?"

Sean let go of her knee, crossed her legs, a loose lotus.

"Go on."

"Just give it some more time, okay?"

"What?"

"I don't think now's the best time for you to be making major decisions. For Dad's sake, and for your own. Couldn't you just wait, think it through some more? Keep the family together."

Allison crossed her arms across her chest, tried to hug the shiver away. She took a slow breath.

"I've already thought it through, Sean. There's nothing more to consider."

"Mom." Sean swallowed. "You're under severe strain. You need to calm down, give yourself time to get your balance back. I'm worried about you, we're all worried about you. How you've been acting."

Allison shook her head to clear it.

"My balance? You mean my mental health?"

Sean glanced around Allison's room. Stared at the smoking wastepaper can, the wine bottle, the disarray. The room of a crazy lady.

"Mom, come on. Don't you see it? This isn't the best time to be making such decisions. Throwing away your marriage. That's all I'm saying. You've got enough stresses to deal with already."

"Well, yes," Allison said, trying for a smile, a light tone. "It is a little stressful to be shot at."

"See," Sean said. "That's what I mean."

"What?"

"Nobody's shooting at you, nobody's trying to kill you, Mom. Nobody."

"They aren't?"

"No, Mother, they aren't."

"And what about Winslow? What about Bronson?"

"Bronson was a robbery victim. And Borneo, that was just poachers. Winslow stumbled into their path, they killed her."

"They weren't poachers," Allison said. "They spoke English."

Sean stared at her blankly.

"What the hell does that mean?"

Allison turned away, stared out the window.

"They spoke English. Poachers don't speak English."

"What the hell does that mean?"

"It's complicated. You'd have to understand the animal trade."

"I've got a minute—why don't you explain it to me."

Allison heard the throaty rumble of Harry's Porsche in the drive. His new toy. For twenty years he'd driven blackwall Fords, bland government cars. Never flashy; not his clothes, cars, or personality. A requirement of the State Department; live a drab, circumspect life or find another line of work.

But since he'd returned to Miami he'd been transforming himself. Gaudy car, sharper suits, a new hairstyle. The last traces of the innocent country boy she'd married were disappearing behind his trendy sunglasses.

Allison heard the front door shut. Harry called out that he was home.

"Okay," Allison said. She took a breath, looked around the room. "There're levels. Like every business, animal smuggling has levels of workers. Animal trackers are the lowest. Poachers. In Borneo they're Ibans, Dayaks, villagers. They know the jungle, they know where the orangutans live, so they're the ones who shoot the mother apes, cage the babies in their villages, then, when they have enough of them, they transport them in a group downriver to the coastal cities, Kuching, Damai.

"The smugglers pick them up like smugglers everywhere—the same methods. Fast boats, night crossings, all that. They take the orangutans to storage pens in Singapore, Djakarta, Bangkok—bird shops, places like that. When the deals are made, it's the smugglers' job to forge paperwork, package the animals, walk them through customs.

"The smugglers ship them, and the dealers stay home in their offices, expensive suits, portable phones. They take delivery of the animals, house them for a few days till they find buyers. All they do is run the switchboard. Two here, three there.

"At every level it's different people. Separation of labor. And the ones my organization goes after are the people at the top, the large international dealers. Possibly an occasional smuggler when we get a tip, or if someone is discovered in the act. The dealers speak English. But not the poachers."

"But these poachers did," Sean said.

Allison was silent, wanting Sean to do this.

"So you're saying it wasn't a poacher out there at all, but a dealer trying to cut out both the middlemen?"

"Not likely," Allison said. "The poachers don't get paid enough. Smugglers make a little more, but it wouldn't be worth it for some dealer to fly in from Europe, the States, put himself at that kind of risk, stalking around the jungle, sweating, shooting a gun, all to save a few dollars."

Allison heard Harry speaking quietly to someone downstairs. In the bar, the sound of glasses, the clink of ice. Another man's laugh. The second voice sending a brisk flutter of recognition through her.

"Then why? If they weren't poachers, why were they in the jungle?"

"Maybe they weren't hunting orangutans."

Sean came off the bed, stood stiffly, peering at Allison.

Allison looked out the front window again, at an oak branch swaying, its shadow passing across the floor of her bedroom. She brought her gaze back to Sean.

"After they shot Winslow, they yelled my name."

"What!"

"They called it out over and over. Allison, Allison. Trying to scare me. Flush me out."

Allison lowered her head, pressed her thumb against one eyelid, her first finger against the other. Squeezed her fingers together at the bridge of her nose.

"Oh, come on, Mom."

"It's true, Sean."

"Wait just a damn minute. These guys bump into Winslow, this young American woman in the jungle, and instantly know she's Allison Farleigh's daughter? How in the hell could that be?"

Sean's mouth was set, her eyes fixed hard on Allison.

"They were hunting for me, Sean. They knew I was out there."

"Hunting for you!"

"There's no other explanation. They were Americans. I recognized their accents. It was somebody my organization was after. They were tracking me, looking for the right time to kill me. And Winslow just got in the way. If things had been a little different, all three of us would have been killed that afternoon."

Allison heard Harry's steps on the stairway. The low murmuring of male voices, the clitter of iced drinks.

She walked across to the half-open bedroom door and turned around. In the center of the room Sean stood with her arms at her sides, legs spread, shaking her head, the rigid mask beginning to crack at the edges.

"They were hunting me," Allison said. "That's what it was."

Sean stepped close, her face dark and twisting into a bitter scowl.

"Joshua Bond. Is that what you're saying? This is about Joshua Bond again."

"Maybe."

"Goddamn it, Mother. Listen to you. Just listen. It's like everything has to revolve around Allison Farleigh. Winslow is murdered, it's got to be because of how important Allison Farleigh is. How threatening she is to the big, bad animal traders. Bronson gets shot. It can't be a simple robbery. It's got to be because of Allison Farleigh again."

"I'm not paranoid. This is not some fantasy, Sean."

Sean's face colored, seemed to grow tight as if she were holding her breath.

"What I said in the church is true. Winslow had no business being where she was. That wasn't her fight. If it wasn't for you, if it wasn't for all this damn animal business, your obsession, I'd still have my sister. You did this, Mother. You did it."

Allison wrenched her head to the side as if she'd been slapped. And at that moment the door swung open behind her.

"Hey, everybody," Harry said. "Look who I've brought."

Allison turned. She had to wipe the blur from her sight, and for a second she didn't register anything but the man's eyes. The same steady gaze he'd had seven years before. A boy of seventeen, staring at Allison's teenage girls, contemplating them from afar.

"Aren't you going to say hello, Mrs. Farleigh?" Patrick said.

She murmured a greeting. He stepped forward, reached out, took hold of her hand, bowed his head, and brushed her knuckles with his lips.

Patrick Bendari Sagawan. Royalty once-removed. One of the sultan's nephews. The last time she'd seen him was in Singapore's Changi International Airport, the afternoon when she'd been riveted to the cages of monkeys in the back room at customs, pestering the officials about who the animals belonged to, where they were going, was this legal, had they been attended to, they looked so sad, so thirsty.

At that moment the Sultan of Brunei and his brother and young Patrick swept in with armloads of presents. Flew all the way from London to wish the Farleighs goodbye. Embraces all around. In the midst of the hubbub, Winslow and Patrick had stolen away, disappeared for fifteen minutes. She came back clinging to his hand. They kissed at the gate, the first and only time Allison had seen Winslow kiss a boy, a real kiss, deep and long. Inconsolable, Winslow cried for the first half of their long flight home.

"I was terribly sorry to hear about Winslow." Patrick stepped farther into the room, shifting his drink to his right hand. "Mrs. Farleigh, Sean, I don't know what to say. Your loss must be unbearable."

He held Allison's eye for a long moment, then she mumbled an apology for the mess the room was in, turned her back on them, and limped into the bathroom and shut the door.

# CHAPTER

# 15

"All you do is, you take the bag of snakes to the door, hand it to the motorcycle guy, wait for your money, then turn around and come back."

"He's gonna make me come inside. A guy like that, he's not gonna do business on his front porch."

"Now, look, Orlon, you gotta face your fear, man. Sooner or later you gotta stare right into its cold, bottomless eyes."

The Corvette was idling on the shoulder outside a yellow wooden house on a busy street in Hialeah. A few other houses just like it nearby, but mainly transmission shops, donut places. A couple of broken-down gas stations, a Farm Store, pawnshop.

Out in the dusty front yard of the yellow house, there were half a dozen Harley hogs neatly lined up. All the shades were drawn. No sign of anything weird going on.

But Orlon had his hand on the shift lever, revving the engine, looking straight out the windshield at the traffic streaming past, hadn't even taken a peek at the place yet. Seeing his brother that way, knowing his love of violence, Ray was getting a little spooked himself.

"I'm telling you, Orlon, you need to get past this. Just take the goddamn snakes in there, collect the cash, come back out, we can go eat supper somewhere. We'll do Denny's, have the rib eye, the cherry pie. Celebrate getting over your trepidation."

"You're not going in there with me."

"That's right. I'm sitting here and letting my little brother go up to that front door, stare down his demons."

Orlon fiddled with the shifter, rocking it side to side in neutral.

A woman was coming up the sidewalk toward them, a grandmother in her white organdy dress, a pink parasol in one hand. She got a little closer, took a better look at the White brothers in their Corvette, cut her eyes to the Hell's Vipers' clubhouse, scowled, then started on across the street, weaving through the cars stopped for the light.

"Face my fear, huh? Stare down my demons. That the way your shrink talks, is it? Bottomless eyes?"

"Don't start with that. You're just trying to distract yourself from the issue at hand."

"You pay that psychology doctor eighty an hour and all she tells you is you ought to face your fear? I mean, hey, for eighty bucks she should get out her whip, give you a few lashes."

"You going in there, man, or I gotta start looking around for a new brother?"

Orlon stared ahead out the windshield.

"All you want, Ray, you want somebody handles the dirty business. That's all I am to you. I do the real work, you kick back, add up the profits. Buffing your fingernails."

Ray wasn't going to trade insults. He was tired of this whole scene. Wanted to get home, knock down a few rumrunners, call the drugstore, see if those photographs were developed yet. That was where their future was, getting the dirt on their business partner. Not this pissant stuff, selling snakes to bikers. That was the old White brothers. The White brothers a year ago.

The grandmother was on the other side of the street, standing in the pink shade of her parasol, waiting next to the bus bench. Staring at the Corvette through all the rush hour traffic along Northwest 103rd Street. Must've been a slow afternoon in grandmotherland if the best entertainment the lady could find was to glare at the White brothers. Standing there like that, her parasol in one hand, the woman was starting to remind Ray of somebody, he wasn't sure who.

"The fuckers got illegal drugs in there."

"Now you're whining, Orlon. You're making me queasy listening to you."

"They got PCP, shit like that. Makes them ultraviolent. Smoking crack, drinking rattlesnake venom, hell, I come to the door, what if they're hallucinating, think I'm the cops? Blow my head out into the street?"

"They do that, then I'll go out into the street, pick it up, bring it back, and screw it on right this time."

"Shit."

"Just do it, get it the hell over with. Be a man."

Ray swiveled around, grabbed hold of the snake sack, plunked it down in his brother's lap.

Orlon sat for a minute more, the things squirming in the bag, hissing, then he opened his door, dragged himself out. Didn't say a word. Marched to the front door very stiff, like he was headed down the corridor to the gas chamber.

Ray opened the glove compartment, took out the Glock nine. Eyes on Orlon as he hammered at the front door, and it swung open instantly. Fat guy in a black T-shirt and a moth-eaten beard hanging down to his belly stood there and said something. Orlon paused, looked back over his shoulder, then went inside.

Ray waited, holding the weapon, finding a grip he liked.

Waited three, four minutes. Looked over, and there was the grandmother still standing guard across the street. A couple of buses came and went, and she was still there. Crime-watch poster girl.

Yeah, now Ray knew who it was. That old lady. About the same age his dear old mom would be if it wasn't for the breast cancer. Probably be just as hefty, too, the way she was packing it in the last few years of her life, cooking all that Cuban food. Pork loins, sausage, fried plantains, night after night. Turning herself into a Cuban, taking Spanish lessons, dressing Cuban, dying her hair that fake red color.

She'd even carried a frilly parasol a few times, mainly to church, but once or twice on the way to work, waiting out in the sun at the bus stop on Flagler and Seventeenth, going off every day to clean people's houses along the bay. Darlene Annette White. Saying how Miami was the perfect place for someone like her, a woman full of wanderlust but too poor to travel. The town was turning itself into a foreign city. All you had to do was stay put, watch it become Havana. Didn't cost you a nickel. Right at the end she even got herself a live-in Cuban boyfriend. Her own Ricky Ricardo. Jorge something or other, but it didn't last long, less than a year before she died.

The cancer got her when Ray and Orlon were in the eighth grade. Jorge moved his clothes out the same day, didn't even say adios. All of which started Ray and Orlon on their life of crime, lying, forging Darlene's signature so the school people wouldn't know she was dead. They kept on paying the rent, the light bills, stealing to do it. Breaking and entering. So they could stay in the same house, fulfill Ray's deathbed promise to Darlene to keep the family together.

At least that's what he thought she said, mumbling under her breath as she was dying, Ray with his ear close to her mouth. Keep together. Or something along those lines. Anyway, Ray was still trying to manage it. He and Orlon with bedrooms down the hall from each other, still stealing to get by.

Back then, eighth grade, it was no great life, but at least they didn't get shipped out to some foster home, no HRS shelter. Shit on that. Yeah, that's who the Cuban grandmother looked like. Darlene White, stay-at-home world traveler. Same parasol. Only yellow.

Ray put his hand on the door handle. Feeling dizzy all of a sudden, seeing his mother's double over there. A tickle of sweat down his ribs. Like a vision, a mirage of

Darlene Annette White, come back to tell Ray something, give him a message, or chastise him, slap him hard in the face like she did sometimes when he was bad. Raimondo, you're screwing up. Look at your little brother, what he's become. Raimondo, wake up, see what's going on.

Ray glanced at the clubhouse, picturing again the way Orlon looked with the tip of his nose flapping loose. Starting to think too much time had slipped by.

Ray opened his door. He was just stepping out of the car when he heard tires scream. He jerked around, and watched the whole goddamn thing unfold in sleepy half-speed. A black Camaro waiting to turn left at the light, some little red pickup truck speeding from the other direction, trying to make the last second of the yellow. Ray watching the light turn red, the guy in the Camaro not seeing the pickup, going on and making the turn, right into the path of the speeder. The pickup's brakes screamed as it slammed into the Camaro's passenger door, hurled it backward; the Camaro spun once, twice.

Ray saw what was about to happen, saw it like it was underwater; all he had to do was walk across 103rd, loaf over there in normal time, scoop up the grandmother and set her down ten feet to the left and she's okay, going to live to glare another day.

The Camaro made one 360, then another, dream-slow, tires screaming, horns going all over the place, somebody screamed, but the old woman with the pink parasol didn't see anything happening, 'cause she was staring into Ray's eyes as he stood across the empty street, Darlene Annette White, and Ray raised his hand to wave at her, wave her the hell away from that spot, the Camaro going right for her like it had all been planned out in advance, a bunch of engineers plotting out the angle of impact, number of rotations of the Camaro, an $X$ painted on the sidewalk where the grandmother should stand.

The Camaro whirled around one more time, then thudded against her, its right front fender catching her on the left hip, launching her backward into the air, the lady still holding the parasol. Mary Poppins. But this one not making a soft landing. This one going ass first, fifty feet, a hundred, losing the parasol, then smashing her spine against a four-legged mailbox, knocking it over, the lady going on some more, rolling down the sidewalk, her body all loose, a jumble of meat and bones. A sack of dead potatoes.

The red pickup came to a halt in the middle of the street, a few yards in front of Ray. Ray found himself walking over to it. Numb, caught up in the dream-trance now. Time stretching out all around him. A dead hush. Feeling the gun in his hand as he stepped up to the window. Looking in at the pimply kid behind the wheel, shaking the fuzz out of his head. Eighteen, nineteen years old, radio on superloud. *Boom boom yadda yadda.*

Ray ducked his head down to the window, reached across the kid and shut off the noise.

The boy stared up at him.

"You killed her, kid."

The boy gave Ray a nothing look.

"You a cop?"

"You're gonna wish I was a cop."

Ray raised the gun, pressed the barrel against the boy's neck.

"Now, you should say you're sorry, kid."

The boy opened his mouth. No sound came out.

"Apologize, you fucking cancer. You ran a red light, killed an old lady. Minding her own business."

The boy was starting to materialize in Ray's sight. Jorge, the last boyfriend. The one that walked out when his Anglo girlfriend died. Ricky Ricardo. Striking resemblance.

"I was late for work," the kid said. He took a hard breath, looked like he was strangling. "Now, lookit. My truck's totally fucked and I think I got a case of whiplash."

The boy tried to open the door, but Ray forced it shut.

"Not good enough," Ray said.

"Whatta you want me to say?"

"A simple apology would be a good start."

"I didn't do anything. I was just driving."

"Just driving. Is that right?"

"Hey, let me out of here. Let me out."

Like Jorge, just exactly like the guy. Walking out the door that day, bag of clothes in one hand, a toaster in the other. Not saying it out loud to the two kids he was leaving behind, but there it was, let me out of here. Let me out.

"Wrong answer," Ray said.

He squeezed off a round into the kid's shoulder.

And then Ray's trance was over and everything was back to normal time. Like somebody'd given the pendulum a bump and the cosmic clock was ticking again. The volume had turned back up, lots of noise all around him, voices, cars, sirens, people rushing, Spanish gobbledygook, radiator steam spewing out of the car.

Ray slid the Glock under his shirt, walked back to the Corvette. No one paying any attention to him. People coming out of their businesses, their houses, standing on their porches. People slamming their brakes. A crowd gathering all along the walk.

Then Orlon was there, hairless Orlon, standing beside him counting a wad of cash. Ray looked over at the lady's body, the people collected around her, nobody touching her. He watched the police arrive. Damn good response time, give 'em that.

Orlon said to him, "Don't you want to hear about it? What happened in there? You won't believe it, man, you won't fucking believe it."

Ray didn't answer. Just got into the Corvette, sat there, his eyes scanning the scene till he found the pink parasol, stuck on a low branch in an oak tree over there. Upside down. The traffic had already resumed on 103rd. Swinging out around the red pickup. A cop standing by the pimply kid's window, looking inside.

Orlon got in the car, slammed the door.

"Piece of cake, man, piece of lemon-frosted cake."
He started the car, juiced it up. "See, what I didn't realize

was, last year, that cut on the nose they gave me, it was like an induction thing, that cut made me an official Hell's Viper. Trakas told me. The fat guy at the door, the chapter president.

"Guy sat me down, explained I was a Viper from the second I got cut, said he told me about it last year. In fact, everybody wondered why I never came back. Says the guys like me, think I'm terminally weird.

"But hell, I don't remember anything about it. I guess I was so fucking discombobulated. I mean, can you believe it? I'm a Viper. I get regular club privileges. Full use of the clubhouse anytime I want. You and me, we could have a party up here, invite girls over, whatever. Be loud as we want."

Ray could count the exact number of rotations the Camaro had made. He watched in his head as the pink-parasoled Cuban grandmother flew. The mailbox, all of it.

"You okay, man?"

"That accident," Ray said. "An old lady. She had a parasol."

"You been listening to me? What I just told you?"

"You remember that parasol Mom had?"

"What the hell you talking about, man? A parasol."

"It was yellow," Ray said. "A yellow parasol."

Orlon put the car in gear, eased out into the street.

"You mean that umbrella doohickey? That thing? Twirling it all the time. Kicking up her legs like goddamn Ginger Rogers."

"A parasol is what it's called."

"Jesus, man. You coming down with something, or what? You look like you just got fucked by a ghost."

Sean's father was sixty-one. Tall and angular with a body kept hard by endless rounds of golf. A country club tan. That afternoon in her mother's bedroom, Harry was wearing a beige twill suit, a yellow Oxford shirt with a burgundy tie. He had bright green eyes that took slow, silent measure, missing little. He was not a talker, not a demonstrative man. Guarded, an excellent diplomat, and now a careful lawyer. Though Sean was over the regret, she still wished sometimes that her father had been the kind of man who'd swept his daughters off their feet for extravagant fatherly embraces, rollicking swings through the air, instead of the one who gave her cool pecks on the cheek, a light pat on her head.

After Allison shut herself in the bathroom, all three of them stood stiffly in the doorway, and after a moment's awkward pause, Patrick apologized for upsetting Allison.

"Oh, it's not your fault," Harry said.

Patrick stared at the bathroom door.

"I wish there was something I could do."

Harry led them out onto the landing, and shut the door.

"Aren't you going to say hello?" Sean held her hand out and Patrick smiled, took it lightly in his hand and pressed his lips to her knuckles, kept them there a second or two.

"So," Harry said. "What about that tour? Still want to take a look at the house?"

Patrick let her hand go, and gave her a steady stare as if he expected her to swoon away before him. Sean smiled back at him with amusement. He was probably just off his uncle's Concorde. Somebody needed to remind him which tarmac he'd touched down on—America, land of sexual democracy and pragmatic women. A place where hand kissing didn't have quite the sway he imagined.

Harry led them around the three other upstairs bedrooms, his own, Winslow's, finally Sean's. Patrick lingered there. He stared at a bookshelf where Sean's collection of stuffed animals was wedged tight. He picked up a framed photo of her in her cheerleader outfit. Back from Brunei just in time for her sophomore year, in time to do the splits for dear old Gables High. Patrick examined the photo closely, then set it back exactly in its place. Slowly he bent over and brushed his fingertips across Sean's teenage bed. For a moment his smile vanished, then resurfaced with a wistful edge.

"I always wondered," he said.

"And is it how you imagined?" Sean said.

"Oh, better, much better."

Harry glanced at Sean, then Patrick.

"Am I missing something?"

"Apparently Patrick used to fantasize about us, Harry. What our bedrooms were like, that kind of thing."

"Oh, yes," he said. "Boys do that."

"Well, some do anyway," Sean said.

They headed downstairs, visited the bar first, a chardonnay for Sean, freshened Dewar's on the rocks for the men.

Patrick wore a silk suit, apricot, an impeccable white shirt with a mandarin collar buttoned to the throat. His hair was glistening black, hanging in waves just past his collar. Sean could imagine it in a ponytail, drawn back tight to highlight his cheekbones. A roguish look.

As she followed them through the rest of Harry's tour, she examined this boy she remembered so vividly, now filled out in his young man's body. Unlike most men from that side of the world, Patrick was almost Harry's height. Slender hips, wide shoulders. He moved with a quiet poise that suggested a strength beyond his size.

She remembered Winslow saying Patrick's real father was English, his mother Malaysian, or vice versa. Part of the sultan's large extended family. But beyond that, Winslow knew nothing of them. With such pale skin, light blue eyes, and large bones, Patrick looked far more like one of the British royals than one of the Malaysian aristocracy.

In a vaguely American accent he told Harry how charming he found their house, the Moorish style, the thick, cool stucco walls, the terra-cotta floors, the skylights, a small mosaic of a tropical scene, parrots and banana trees, on the dining room wall. He said little else, but seemed to drink in every detail. In the living room he paused once more to examine a photograph of Sean and Winslow that sat on a side table. He picked it up, gazed at it silently for almost a minute, then put it down with a quiet sigh.

"It must be very hard for you. Your only sister."

Sean nodded but said nothing.

"Have the Sarawak police been helpful?"

Harry said, "The Sarawak police have been utterly goddamn useless. We have the impression they've given up on it already. I call them every other day but they're very vague. No leads, that sort of thing. I've tried to pull some strings over there, our people in Kuala Lumpur, but you know how complex that world is, how restrained everyone is by their goddamn rules of etiquette. Their mysterious protocol."

"Perhaps I could do something."

Harry shrugged.

"I don't know what anybody could do at this point."

He turned his back on Patrick and wandered outside to the patio beside the pool. They joined him there and the three of them stood for a quiet moment in the shade of an old banyan.

"Let's sit," Harry said. "Been on my feet all day."

They drew the patio chairs in a semicircle facing the pool, and Patrick stared at Sean, drinking her in, and shook his head in wonder.

"What's wrong?" she said.

"Oh, nothing."

"I know what it is," she said.

"Yes?"

"It's that we've all grown up. We're all big people now. Amazing how it happens."

He leaned forward in his chair to stare into the pool, elbows on his knees. He had a sip of his drink. Turned his head and smiled at Sean.

"You're wrong," he said. "I am still seventeen. I am a boy sitting on the porch of my father's house watching the vice consul's lovely daughters strolling down the sunny boulevard. Jalang Tasek. The mimosa trees are blooming, the alamandas. The American girls are swaying past in their bright summer dresses.

"And I am sitting out on my aunt's verandah listening to those same girls as they discuss world events with the adults, drink coffee, and laugh. I am sitting very still, hearing the cicadas chirr, and their calls are mingled with the sound of the Farleigh girls' beautiful laughter rising up into the dark like the fragrance of powerful incense."

Harry cleared his throat. He glanced up toward Allison's bedroom window, checked his watch.

"So, Sean," he said. "I'm taking Patrick to Mark's Place for dinner. Give him a chance to experience our famous Miami cuisine. If we promise not to talk business, are you free to join us?"

She watched the young man lean forward, his elbows on his knees as he stared into the clear swimming pool. His smile turning inward.

# C H A P T E R

# 16

The White brothers ate supper at a Denny's near the airport. Orlon ordering a double portion of ribs, two helpings of pie. Seemed to be celebrating conquering his fear.

Afterward they swung by the office. A half hour late for their meeting with Dr. Kurt Franklin. In the warehouse Ray took down the box of monkey chow from the shelf next to the elapid envenomization kit, fancy phrase for snakebite medicine. He checked the phone messages, nothing, then walked down the narrow corridor and pushed open the metal door into the primate area.

The air was pollinated with the rich stink of straw and piss, and the sweet funk of ape dander, a collection of smells Ray found strangely comforting, reminding him nearly every day he walked in of all those times his mother had taken Orlon and him into pet stores, standing before the garish birds, the snakes, iguanas, Darlene Annette cooing at all the animals, but always too poor to buy anything. Telling Ray and Orlon how this parrot or that Gila monster came from thousands of miles away, a desert that looked like the moon. Australia, the Belgian Congo, Persia, her eyes coming unfocused, hypnotizing herself as she chanted the names of those distant lands.

Ray found Orlon standing in front of the primate cages saying, "Shit, shit, shit, shit."

Another orang was lying on its belly, facedown in the straw, not breathing. Which left only one. And the siamang gibbon looked like shit, sitting up, stuffed into a corner of his cage, his eyes blank, yellow foam on his lips.

"It got dehydrated," Ray said. "Or something."

"Well, it's too late now."

Orlon turned and leaned in, getting up into Ray's face.

"Whatta you looking so sad about?"

" 'Cause it died, that's why."

"It's just a fucking animal," Orlon said. "Squirrel without a tail. Lower life form."

"I'm thinking about the goddamn money we just lost, is all. Leave me the hell alone."

Ray took out his keys, unlocked the cage, hauled out the dead orang, dropped its body in a heavy-duty garbage bag. Orlon stood nearby and began to chant a ditty he'd made up years ago. Liked to quote it at moments like this. He called it the animal dealer's national anthem.

"When in doubt, ship it out.
If it's sick, make it quick.
If it's dead . . . well,
Aw, shit, go ahead."

Ray opened the last orangutan's cage, sprinkled some monkey chow in the dish, filled his bowl with water. The thing was making noises, cheeping like a dime-store bird. It stared into Ray's eyes forlornly and didn't make a move toward its food, so Ray took it out, held it a minute, let it crawl over him.

He understood why people liked these things. Of course, it was partly because they were damn cute. But there was something more, something mystical about them. The little guy hugged Ray same as a baby would do, but at the same time his eyes were old. Older than old. Like he'd sat through this movie a few times already, accumulated a shitload of wisdom from being reborn over and over like the Buddhists believed, or was it the Hindus?

The hair on its head was all wild, permanently wind-blown like a redheaded Albert Einstein. Eyes with emotions flitting around in them: one minute sad, the next bored, the next worried, then excited—all kinds of looks. The orang raised his right hand to his forehead, scratched at that silver patch, then took a grip on his head and squeezed it hard, hunkered over like that bronze statue "The Thinker," like the little guy was working out some calculus problem.

When Ray finally went to put the orangutan back, the thing wouldn't let go of his wrist. He had to peel the fingers off one by one. Three or four years old and already the beast was nearly as strong as Ray.

Back in the cage, the orangutan picked up a fistful of straw in each hand and stared at Ray for a minute.

"Eat," he said. "Eat your chow, you little hair ball."

The orangutan studied Ray as he locked the cage door with his key. Then the ape dropped the straw, stared at Ray a few moments more, and turned to the dish and started scooping up the chow, gobbling it down. Slurped every drop of his water too. Ray waited till all of it was gone, then dumped more food in the dish, filled up his water bowl.

He found Orlon in the reptile-amphibian room feeding the creatures. Ray watched him going around the room, dropping white mice into the cages. The monitor lizard, Grand Cayman iguana, the skinks, the geckos, Surinam toads, bearded dragons, the owls, the eagle, the crocodiles, young gators, rat snakes, fox snakes, king snakes, rattlers, the albino cobras, the mamba, the racer, Cape puff adder and diamondbacks. Four dozen white mice gobbled down in twenty minutes. Five handfuls of crickets.

They were on the way out, Orlon locking the front door, when a taxi rolled slowly into the lot, parked next to the Vette. A guy climbed out of the back, came strolling over.

In his early forties, blond, sunburned, wearing khaki shorts and a blue work shirt. Looked like a surfer out for a stroll in the warehouse district.

"Help you?" Ray said.

"You the White brothers?"

"That's right."

"Dr. Franklin asked me to stop over. I'm his associate, Dr. Thorn."

A month ago Kurt Franklin showed up at the front door, said he was interested in purchasing a gorilla or an orangutan, heard the White brothers might be the people to talk to. Right away Ray was suspicious, thinking he was a spy from the ape-kissers, trying to trap them, though even for those people it seemed like a stupid-ass approach, a guy right in off the street.

Ray said they didn't deal in apes, never touched them, though the truth was they had a chimp caged in the back at the time, the thing throwing up every five minutes since he'd come in from Gambia. And the skinny man said, fine, okay, but if they ever came across either one, give him a call, he was in the market. And he handed Ray his business card, Franklin's Veterinary Clinic, an address in south Dade. Card had a picture of a chimp up in one corner of it. PRIMATE SPECIALISTS, it said below the chimp.

Ray said, whoa, there. You a doc?

I am, the guy said. Why?

Ray told him to wait right there a minute and went to find Orlon, run this past him. But Orlon wasn't anywhere around, so it was up to Ray to decide. He stood around in the warehouse for a minute considering it, looking over at the sick chimp, then went back up front.

Well, it just so happens, Ray said, I'm keeping a chimpanzee for a friend of mine who had to go out of town for a week, and the little bastard's been puking his guts out for the last few days. Mind taking a look at him?

Twenty minutes later the vet had it figured out, studying vomit specimens, asking Ray a bunch of questions. Wrong brand of monkey chow, simple as that. They were buying the cheap stuff, too much ash content, it was upsetting the ape's stomach. And they should've been supplementing the chow with a fig now and then, an apple even. Soaking the chow in warm apple juice to soften it up.

Ray gave him a hundred-dollar bill and told him he'd call him again if he ever heard about an orangutan for sale.

"I thought maybe you forgot our appointment," the blond guy said. "I came by earlier, but you weren't here. I was about to give up."

"Where's Franklin?"

"He's out of town on business. He asked me to come. I'm his associate."

"Well, it's too late," Ray said. "The sick orangutan got sicker and died. The one that was well is still well."

"Is the healthy one for sale?"

"It's spoken for," Orlon said.

The blond guy looked over at Orlon the way everybody did the first time they met him. Like hey, what the hell happened to this guy, completely hairless, he taking radioactive suppositories?

"Your orangutan may be healthy now, but you never know," the guy said, turning back to Ray. "Could have a bug of some kind, parasites. I should probably have a look while I'm here. Play it safe."

"I don't know about this guy," Orlon said.

"He's okay," said Ray. "Don't worry about it."

Orlon shook his head, but Ray budged past him and led Thorn back into the warehouse, let him take a look at the healthy orang. The ape crawled all over him. Thorn pried open the ape's mouth, peered inside, looked at his eyes, squeezed his joints.

Orlon stood on the side looking suspicious.

"He's dehydrated, but beyond that, he's in pretty fair shape. When'd he come in?"

"Come in?"

"When'd he arrive?"

"A week ago, ten days," Ray said. "Why?"

"Sumatra or Borneo?"

"What's with the questions?" Orlon said.

"He's captive-born," said Ray. "On his way to a zoo out West."

"Who're his parents?"

"How the hell should I know who his parents are?"

"If he's captive-born," the vet said, "he's listed in the stud book, the lady at the Smithsonian keeps it, tracks the bloodlines of every captive-born orangutan in America."

"Wait a fucking minute." Orlon stepped up, getting into Thorn's face, taking a stance. "You interrogating us? You making some wild, unsubstantiated claims here?"

Ray said, "Cool it, man. He's okay."

"Shit, Ray. This is fucked. I don't trust this guy."

Orlon was up in his face, but Thorn didn't budge.

"Back off, Orlando. Come on, back off."

"Who you calling Orlando?"

"I said back off, man."

Orlon kept glaring into Thorn's eyes, but he obeyed Ray, moved back a half step. It felt like the room was packed with steam, all the male hormones being discharged.

"Okay, if you want to know, we'll check tomorrow," Ray said. "See who his parents are, call you. That be okay?"

Thorn said yes, that would be fine.

"Hey, thanks for stopping by," Ray said, and maneuvered the big guy toward the hallway, getting out his billfold and finding a twenty for him. Which the guy looked at for a second or two, then took.

Ray led him on outside, over to his car. Orlon standing back at the front door looking like he was about to draw his hardware and open fire.

"You know," Thorn said. "That orangutan needs a lot of physical contact. It's only three or four years old, way too young to be separated from its mother. So you should pick it up, handle it on a very regular basis. They can die from emotional deprivation."

"Yeah," Orlon said. "Can't we all."

"Right, doc. I'll sure do that, play with the little hair ball, yes, sir."

"You should definitely do that."

The guy got back into the taxi and drove out of the parking lot. Ray went back to the front door where Orlon stood scowling.

"That guy's no vet. He's an ape-kisser. A fucking spy."

"Yeah? How the hell you know that?"

"There's ape stink on his breath."

"Bullshit, Orlon. Bullshit."

"I got a sixth sense about ape-kissers. I can spot them a mile off. Like Leonard Nimoy in the second *Invasion of the Body Snatchers*. It's the way he walks, way he twitches. Maybe you can't tell the difference, but I can. It's an intuitive thing."

"Yeah, a sixth sense," Ray said. "Only thing is, Orlon, you can't have a sixth sense till you get the first five."

"Fuck you."

"Not tonight. I got a headache."

The taxi driver was a New Yorker who gave Thorn his life story in the first ten blocks from Snapper Creek Marina. They'd run out of things to discuss a half hour ago, and were now seriously getting on each other's nerves. Guy wasn't used to spending more than a half hour at a time with anybody. Didn't have but thirty minutes' worth of bullshit. Long enough to get you from anyplace to anyplace else in Miami. Beyond that, the guy was out of material and started getting testy.

Thorn told the driver to pull into the parking lot of the Burger King. He told him exactly where to park, then they waited. The driver told him this was costing money, sitting like this. Costing the same as if they were driving. Thorn said fine.

He stared out at the avenue across from the Burger King, kept watching till the White brothers' black Corvette appeared. It stopped at the light, then when it turned green, the Vette burned a few seconds of rubber and fired out onto Bird Road.

Thorn told the taxi driver to follow the Corvette.

"What? Like in the movies? 'Follow that car.'"

"That's right," Thorn said. "Like in the movies."

"What're you, a cop?"

"I'm a veterinarian," Thorn said.

The taxi driver swung the Ford out into traffic, kept the Corvette in view.

"A vet?"

"That's right."

"Hey, I got a couple of toy poodles myself. Very smart little things. My wife's got them trimmed real nice. So tell me, you know anything about fleas?"

"Not really."

The taxi driver glanced in the rearview mirror.

"What kind of vet are you, you don't know about fleas?"

"I'm just a vet for tonight."

The New Yorker took a long look at Thorn in the mirror, then went back to following the Vette. Quiet now. Completely out of talk.

They didn't speak on the ride home. Ray was irritated, depressed. Orlon seemed pissed, probably from Ray pulling rank on him back there, calling him Orlando, having his way in front of the vet.

Orlon kept the Vette to the speed limit, which was unusual for him. Out the Palmetto till it emptied onto Dixie Highway, then pulling in behind the Publix at Suniland, Orlon tossing the orang into a Dumpster, then squealing down some backstreets, east over to Old Cutler. North to Gables by the Sea. Their half-million-dollar house on the bay, bought just last year with the profits from their new business partnership.

Orlon went straight into the living room, turned on the TV. Eleven o'clock news. Ray watched for a second or two till Orlon plunked a tape into the VCR and took a seat on the couch. The news blacked out, and some opening credits came floating onto the screen.

Ray went up to bed. Washed his face, flossed, brushed his teeth, put on his pajamas, then lay there and listened to the TV going downstairs. A gangster movie he and Orlon had sat through a half dozen times. Humphrey Bogart shoots his way out of prison, then starts running from the law, driving across the badlands, Death Valley, somewhere like that, cactus and sand. While Bogart and his gang were staying in some cheap motor court, he meets a crippled girl and her family.

Right away the girl turns Humphrey sappy. He winds up giving the girl's father a bunch of money he'd stolen. Gave it to him so the pretty daughter could have a leg operation, walk around normal like everybody else. Ray listened to bits and pieces of the dialogue as it floated up from the living room. He thought about the story as he was getting sleepy. A bad guy, tough and mean, prison hard, who'd machine-gunned bank guards without blinking. If he had to, Humphrey Bogart could chew the ears off somebody he was fighting, suck out an eyeball. But along comes a crippled girl with blond hair and big eyes, and the bad guy turns into Saint Bogart.

Ray didn't believe the story for a second. Typical moron drool leaking out of Hollywood. Didn't square with what Ray knew of bad people. A guy who'd spent most of his life robbing or killing, committing mayhem and assorted evil, he's not going to have a damn sentimental streak anymore. The bad just takes over, like cancer cells squeezing out all the decent cells. A man who'd devoted himself to decades of depravity wasn't going to get gushy over some cripple.

No, sir, Ray was sure of that. And he was sure it'd take a hell of a lot more than some pretty girl in a wheelchair to convert the White brothers. In fact, when he thought about it, Ray believed he and Orlon were already too far gone. Cancer spread everywhere. He couldn't imagine anything at this point in his life that could get them back on the fucking straight and narrow.

He lay there for a while and tried to think of something he hungered for so bad he might be willing to give up his crooked life for it. But he couldn't think what it would be. The more he thought, the sleepier he got, until finally he drifted away.

A little while later the cops started blasting their machine guns at Bogart hiding up in the rocks. Ray was dead asleep by then, the gunfire sounding to his dreamy mind like popcorn exploding in his mom's heavy black iron skillet.

Sometimes when the popcorn was done, their mother would pour it directly into a grocery sack, and the three of them would go off to the movies, sneak the greasy brown bag inside. Back then it was anything to save a quarter.

# CHAPTER

# 17

Close to eleven, Patrick was done with his second brandy. Sean was nursing a White Russian, while Harry stayed with gimlets, his fourth, fifth, who could say? He could feel himself smiling, looking at Sean, at Patrick, the two of them chatting easily, joking, laughing, telling stories about Brunei, that year, events Harry couldn't remember, parties he hadn't seen. Seven years ago and it felt like a different century. A different Harry.

All around them the restaurant was buzzing with quiet elegance. Updated art deco, chrome sconces, burnished steel sculptures like exploded pretzels, carpets and walls in muted grays and salmons. A rock star sat at a table nearby, somebody Sean recognized. Patrick had heard his music, but never imagined seeing him in person. Harry looked around. Everybody in the room seemed famous.

Harry sat in the glow of his vodka, a glorious twilight washing the room. Feeling a sweet remorse for this evening at Mark's Place, the bonhomie with his daughter and Patrick. It was a mood that had been overtaking Harry with greater and greater regularity lately, especially after three or four gimlets. A sappy Irish melancholy. Sean had once named the condition *prenostalgia*. Sadness for a moment that wasn't even over yet.

Harry saw his drink was low, started looking for their

waiter. All of them looked alike at Mark's Place. Slim young men, the same razor-cut hair, unpretentious manners. Great waiters really, always there but not there. All very skilled in food matters.

People raved about Mark's, but the food inevitably gave Harry heartburn. Knocked his digestive system out of whack for days. Blame it on his deprived childhood, never learned to stomach rich food. Hell, how could anybody develop a subtle palate after spending their first eighteen years eating West Virginia pork and beans?

As he searched for the waiter through the vodka blur, Harry had a quiet psychological revelation. A Stoli insight. All at once seeing the connection between his digestive tract and his character. How there were certain aspects of his personality that no amount of education or training could root out. Seven nights a week Harry could eat at Mark's Place, refine his palate all he wanted, learn the name of every sauce, but his goddamn small intestines were never going to adjust. He simply wasn't bred for the life he was leading. Would always be an impostor.

Harry floated back to the table as Sean said "Golf."

Both of them were looking at him. Harry smiled. A big, loose-lipped grin that felt slippery on his face.

"Golf?" Harry said.

"Patrick asked what you and I had in common. I said golf."

"Yes," Harry said. "We play together most every Sunday. She beats my pants off. Not literally, of course."

"I seem to recall an interest in hiking, camping, the outdoors," Patrick said.

"We stopped that," Sean said. "I got interested in sports, Mother started with the ape thing. Dad went with golf."

"I see," Patrick said. "And Winslow?"

"Photography."

"She was the artist in the family," Harry said.

It almost killed the conversation. Winslow's name sucking the air out of them. Everyone had a sip of their drink. Then Sean excused herself to go to the bathroom.

Harry and Patrick stood and watched her make her way across the room. Floral knit dress, short. Great legs. Like Harry's. Always proud of his legs, Harry was. Wore shorts all weekend to show them off. In his sixties now and the old legs were still damn shapely.

"Sean has become a fine woman," Patrick said as they sat. He touched a finger to the rim of his glass. "You must be extremely proud."

"She's a good girl. Stubborn sometimes, a real bull-dog. Favors Allison in that regard. But good, yes."

"Would you like to talk about Winslow, what happened?"

"No," Harry said. "I wouldn't. Not at all."

Harry flagged down the waiter and ordered another gimlet. When the young man was gone, Harry rattled the remaining ice, took a last small sip, pushed the drink aside.

"You have very good table manners," Harry said. "I've been watching you."

Patrick eyed him cautiously. Harry knew he was drunk, knew he shouldn't be trying to put two words together, but he was getting a rush of feeling, sitting here with Patrick and Sean, a wisdom flood, or at least it felt like wisdom.

Harry said, "The family I came from, I never saw my father use anything but a spoon. So what did I do? I went to Yale, for chrissake. I became a diplomat. I wound up eating with queens and sultans and princes. I learned the best table manners in the Western world. That's what I did. I followed my weaknesses. First you learn table manners, then you have dinner with the people who run the world, then later on you make lots of money doing favors for them."

Harry could see through the haze that Patrick wasn't paying attention. Listening, but with his eyes disengaged. Harry had learned to read the eyes. The eyes were everything. Little captions under the photograph telling you at every second what a person was thinking. Harry had played political poker with some of the best. He knew

Patrick was ticking off the seconds till Harry was through, looking for a space long enough to interrupt, say something, whatever he'd come twelve thousand miles to say.

In no hurry to hear what that was, Harry said, "Sean's granddad—now, there was a man with table manners of the highest caliber. The man who gave me my first job. Yes, sir, I worked in his little law firm here in Miami, served a year or two there, on the weekends I would play Daniel Boone with him and his cronies, hunting, fishing, booze. Shooting gators, for god's sake, bears, wild boars. Got to be very buddy-buddy with the old man. Even ran off with his daughter. God help me. I fooled old Julius Ravenel, I fooled him and I've been fooling all the other Julius Ravenels for years to come."

Patrick pushed his drink aside.

"Harry, we're running out of time."

"We are?"

"With De Novo. It's not moving on schedule. We're weeks off the target date."

Harry had a sip of the gimlet, put it down.

"Look," he said. "Good work takes time. Yeah, there've been some hitches, but basically, as these projects go, things on this scale, we're staying pretty close to schedule."

"Not close enough, Harry. I don't like it. The sultan won't like it either when he learns of it."

"Hey, there're some things even the richest man in the world can't change."

Patrick smiled delicately.

"Then it would be the first time," he said.

The young man picked up his unused spoon, drew a curving line in the tablecloth, concentrating on his work. Then he set the spoon aside, looked back at Harry.

"What are you going to do to speed things up, Harry? Tell me specifically, what will you do to motivate Rantel?"

Harry Farleigh had been doing business with Patrick for two years now, but damned if he wasn't having a hard time just now seeing Patrick as an adult. The other image was still too strong, that boyish face from Harry's last tour of Brunei. The seventeen-year-old kid who'd had a few thousand girls in Brunei mooning over him, but had ignored them all so he could moon over Harry's daughters.

Harry glanced up as the waiter set the fresh gimlet on the table. He picked the old one up, but Harry nabbed it from him, polished it off, then handed it back.

"Don't worry, son. I'll call them first thing tomorrow, crack the whip. Raise some hell."

Harry saw Sean stopping to speak with someone at a table across the room. A couple her age. Patrick brushed a crumb from the white tablecloth, held his tongue till the waiter was gone.

"Harry," Patrick said. "Are you prepared to lose the De Novo project?"

Harry bumped his glass, slopped some booze onto the linen tablecloth. Patrick watched the stain spread.

"Now, wait a goddamn second."

"You wait a second, Harry. I've spoken to you repeatedly about this, but things are not moving. Not moving fast enough. And as you know, Harry, the sultan is to select his new Minister of Finance and Economic Development in January. Two months from now. I want that job, Harry. And I would find it most embarrassing to explain to his Majesty that phase one of the De Novo project is far behind schedule."

"Look, I'll do what I can."

"I've heard that before, Harry. It's not good enough anymore. I am very close to pulling the plug on Rantel, handing the project to the French. At least then, his Majesty will have evidence of my decisiveness."

"Look here," Harry said, leaning forward across the table, trying to bring Patrick into focus. "Rantel is eighty million dollars past the design phase: architects; drawings; foundations being poured. Christ, there's a contract. Everyone's already signed off on De Novo."

"Is that right, Harry? Is that what the partners in your prestigious law firm believe? Do they think they wrote an ironclad contract?"

"The sultan wouldn't do that."

"The sultan doesn't deal with details like these anymore. It's strictly my call, Harry. I picked Rantel, I can choose another firm to replace them."

Now Sean was coming slowly across the room. Patrick had his eyes on her. Sean was walking like she knew she was being watched. A womanly sway, the hint of coquettishness. Something Harry had never seen before from her. Something he didn't even know Sean could do.

"De Novo translates to over three billion dollars for your nation's economy, Harry. Ten years of steady work for Rantel. Ten years of fat retainer fees for you. And you are willing to lose all that?"

Harry stared at Patrick for a moment. Hard eyes, a glaze of indifference. Not bluffing. Perfectly willing to dump Harry. An icy-hearted bastard, exactly the skill required to do business on the scale he did.

Patrick leaned close, lowered his voice.

"You have two weeks to show me that I have not made a mistake with you, Harry. I am returning to Brunei and I will watch carefully what Rantel accomplishes in this two-week period. If there is not an immediate and dramatic surge in construction, then it's over for you, Harry. It's finished."

Patrick glanced up as Sean approached and his scowl dissolved smoothly into a smile. He pushed his chair back and stood up. He drew back Sean's chair and she sat.

Harry watched them look at each other. And in a sudden moment of recognition Harry Farleigh remembered how as a child he had often been so hungry, so utterly famished that he had gone outside into the snow, kneeled down and scraped away the black crust of coal soot, then eaten scoop after scoop of the white, lifeless stuff. He remembered the feeling now as he looked at his daughter and Patrick Sagawan sharing their smile. A cold, sickly emptiness in his gut.

It was after midnight, the moon directly overhead. Three-quarters full, giving the beach a powdery luminescence. On Ocean Drive the traffic was at a standstill, the garish parade of gender-benders just getting under way. From where Sean and Patrick stood, their backs to the surf, the neon from the art deco hotels was creating a feeble halo that filtered out to the beach, penetrated the first row of palms then dwindled finally to darkness.

They sent Harry home in a cab, then took the Porsche for a cruise, Patrick driving, and wound up here. Only a few words along the way, the silence okay with Sean. Nothing uncomfortable about Patrick. He'd glanced at her a few times on the causeway over. She'd held his eye once and they'd smiled like old pals sharing a delicious secret.

Now they carried their shoes, Patrick with his cuffs wet, taking deep breaths of the night air. Finally it had cooled. Seventies again, a weak cold front the night before had eased the temperature back ten degrees. Dried out the air.

"It smells like neon," he said.

"What does?"

"The breeze."

"I don't think neon has a scent."

"But if it did," Patrick said, "if green and pink were blended in equal parts, a dash of blue, it would smell like this."

Sean looked out at a passing yacht. Maybe a mile offshore, the sky choked with stars. The mild splash of the surf. Patrick turned away from the hotels, stared out into the dark with her.

"Do people swim in this ocean?"

His shoulder brushed hers.

"Yes, of course. They do everything in it."

"Everything?"

She smiled.

"Everything," she said.

A couple passed them, speed-walking, disappearing quickly into the dark. Patrick and she began to walk, heading north out of the range of the streetlights of South

Beach, moving into the heavy shadows behind the last few derelict hotels.

New money had continued to flood into South Beach. If it lasted a little while longer, every single building out there would be refurbished soon. But someday not far off, Sean was certain the boom would finally die. The trendies would roller-skate off to the next fair-weather spot, and the beach would once again be on its own, and would have to coast for another forty years on the momentum of all this hoopla. Probably drift back finally into comfortable shabbiness, all the neon fizzing out, the lawn chairs reappearing on the front porches of the hotels, congregations of grandmothers hobbling out to take back their seats in the sun.

Patrick halted, faced the sea.

"Shall we see how far we can swim? Beyond the horizon perhaps."

"I don't think so."

"But you are a swimmer, aren't you? Why not?"

"This dress is why not."

"I'm going," he said. "I want to swim in the neon sea."

He dropped his shoes and waded into the surf, kept going, not shedding his jacket or shirt. As he moved into chest-high water, he called out for her to join him.

He began to swim, a good stroke from what she could tell, strong and even, perhaps a little stylized, taught to him by someone more concerned with form than function. She saw him stop and wriggle out of his jacket and toss it aside. Watched the current carry it north. Sean felt herself walk into the water, drawn by Patrick's rashness, his childish pleasure.

Sean unzipped her dress, stepped out of it. Balled it up and tossed it back on the beach. Black panties and matching push-up bra. She waded out, to her knees, her waist, felt the cold slap of water against her flesh, had to duck her head beneath the curl of a sudden wave.

When she resurfaced, swimming now, she could barely make out Patrick treading water fifty yards ahead, a path of moonlight lay before him like a golden highway that circled the earth.

She swam toward him, head up, keeping him in view. When she'd closed in to twenty yards, he turned and resumed his stroke, leading her farther out, into the deeper rollers, the black sea.

She followed, gaining on him, a yard, another yard. He was faster than she'd thought, but not as fast as she was. She'd trained for this, had put in her weekly miles at the university pool. Could swim for an hour at this pace if she needed to.

She seized his ankle, held on against his flutter kick. Hauled him to a stop. He sputtered and treaded water in front of her, then both of them looked back for a moment in silence at the beach. Riding up and down on the smooth waves, losing sight of land, then seeing again the vague pastel lights of the hotels, the headlights, but little else.

"It's beautiful out here, isn't it?"

"Spooky too. A boat could come along, *bam*."

"Is that who you are, Sean? Who you've become?"

"What's that mean?"

"Are you frightened of things?"

"Some things, yes. Boats that can't see you."

"Are you afraid of me?"

"Should I be?"

His teeth were moon-white, hair a dark sparkle.

"You should be terrified," he said. "Absolutely terrified."

She swiveled around, started a slow breaststroke toward shore. Patrick swam alongside her.

"Have you ever done this before? A midnight swim."

"No," she said. "Have you?"

"Oh, no. I have been saving it."

She was silent, feeling him stirring the water beside her.

"Do people make love in this ocean?"

She stopped swimming. Treaded beside him.

"Yes, I suppose so. The ones who are ready to make love."

She began her breaststroke again. He was quiet, swimming beside her. She glanced over but couldn't make out his expression.

On shore, she found her dress and stepped into it, clammy against her skin. Patrick put on his shoes, tucked in his shirt. He came over to her, stood quietly beside her, looking up at the neon hotels with a sheepish look.

"You live in a beautiful place. So full of life."

"Brunei is beautiful too," she said. "Better than this."

"Do you think so?"

He looked closely at her.

"Do you think of Brunei often?"

"Yes," she said. "All the time."

"I'm glad," he said. "That was a very special year, a glorious season in my life."

"We were young. No one had died yet," she said.

"True," he said. "No one had died."

She searched for a clear view of his eyes, but could see nothing through the slab of shadow he'd stepped into. Finally, she stepped close to him, reached out and took hold of his chin and guided his mouth down to hers. As she kissed him, he stepped close and his arms rose up slowly to hold her.

She meant it to be a perfunctory kiss. A friendly thanks for a memorable night. But the kiss went on, much softer than she'd imagined, more inquisitive than assertive. Sean felt her stiffness and restraint begin to sink away, felt her eyes go slowly blind behind her lids.

And she pictured again with perfect clarity Winslow's mysterious smile that day at Singapore's Changi International Airport when she'd returned from her farewell rendezvous with Patrick. Now it was Sean's turn. She was kissing that same boy her sister had kissed, the one who'd turned into this man. Sharing with Winslow her long-ago secret, feeling a communion with her across the wide gulf of silence between them.

She kissed Patrick, kissed him till she almost lost the strength to stand.

The orangutan spent Tuesday night trying to pick the lock on his cage. He used a piece of straw, reaching his hand out the bars, and crooking it around so the straw entered the lock mechanism in the same way that his keeper had used a key.

He spent an hour, then another hour, working at the lock. The warehouse was very quiet. Sometimes a noise came from the back room where the owl was, or the mice would scrabble through their sawdust, burrowing down.

The air conditioner turned on for half an hour at a time, and when the temperature in the warehouse dropped to eighty, it would shut off. At eighty-six it would turn itself on again.

The orangutan was very patient. He was full of food and water now, and the gibbon in the cage above him had finally died, which meant there was no more of his drool or feces dripping down through the bars of the cages, soiling the orangutan.

When he stuck the stalks of straw into the lock, each of them bent. So the orangutan spent some time searching through his bed for a stronger piece. He couldn't find anything that seemed right, so he reached through the bars of the cage and tore free the ID tag that was wired to the door.

He sat in the corner of his cage and uncoiled the wire, then straightened it. He bent the wire in half, doubling it side by side, then twisted it till it was straight and much stronger than a stalk of straw.

He reached through the bars again and inserted the wire into the lock and poked. There was a noise inside the lock but the cage door stayed shut.

For most of the night while the orangutan worked on the lock, the air conditioner made a bad noise, straining. As the sun finally began to shine through the dirty windows of the warehouse, the motor gasped loudly and began to smoke.

The orangutan slept for a while, then woke and began to work with the twisted wire again. By three in the morning he was growing very thirsty. He made the sign for *fruit* a few times.

It was almost dawn when the lock made another noise. The orangutan became very still, working the wire carefully until finally his cage swung open.

As if to celebrate, he extracted the diamond ring from the pocket of his cheek and examined it for a long while before replacing it in his mouth. Then he pushed open the door to his cage and jumped down to the floor.

# CHAPTER

# 18

Wednesday at ten-thirty Ray went for his weekly visit to his shrink, a pretty, auburn-haired woman with an office on Red Road. There were dentists on both sides of the shrink's office—oral surgeons, they called themselves. Each week Ray sat in the lady psychotherapist's darkened office, sunk deep in a comfortable chair with drills grinding away through both walls. Sometimes, from just sitting there, he got a sympathetic toothache.

The shrink, Tricia Capoletti, sat in a green leather chair across from him. This week she wore jeans and a man's blue denim work shirt with a string tie and a brown corduroy jacket. A few weeks back she'd let it slip that she was just a year out of psychology school, so Ray figured she hadn't learned yet how to dress like a professional, still thought of herself as a college student.

Ray liked her. Liked looking at her in the shadowy room, talking to her. This was Ray White's one and only opportunity to speak with an intelligent woman, even if he did have to pay eighty bucks an hour for the privilege. Christ, he'd paid a lot more for a lot less.

Ray was wearing khaki Dockers with the pleated fronts, blue-and-white striped shirt, red suspenders, Weejuns. He'd considered wearing a bow tie, but thought better of it. Intelligent women liked preppy clothes, L.L. Bean apparel. Personally Ray leaned more toward Italian styles, silver shirts with geometric patterns, black-and-gray checked pants, pointy loafers with tassels. Racetrack attire, he called it. But, hell, he was willing to accept a few compromises in the clothing area to make a good impression on Tricia.

Ray was saying, "Every morning he wakes up, goes into the bathroom, spends a couple of hours on it. He shaves all his body hair, plucks out his eyebrows, his goddamn eyelashes, the hair on his toes and knuckles. It's a fetish, I think."

"And this has been bothering you."

"Bothering me, yeah. I guess you could say that. But mainly I'm trying to figure out why he's that way. See if I can do anything, nudge him back to mental sanity."

"Can you tell me why your brother's hygiene practices should be a problem for you?"

"Hey. It's not my problem, it's my brother's problem. I got my own set of issues. But body hair isn't one of them."

"Your brother seems to derive some satisfaction and pleasure from this activity. Is that what disturbs you? Do you feel uneasy when he experiences happiness?"

"You put a rinse on your hair, Doc?"

"I told you, Ray. I'm not a doctor. I have an MSW."

"Yeah, I know," Ray said. "It's just that I think of you as my doctor."

Tricia didn't say anything for a few seconds. Uncrossed her legs, recrossed them the other way. Right hand rising up to touch her hair, then dropping away. Didn't wear a wedding ring.

"Why do you ask about my hair, Ray?"

"If you have it done professionally, you should stick with that guy. Color's very natural-looking. And if you don't dye it, that's fine, it's just the right color for your skin tone. And this is something I've made a thorough study of; I take an interest in such things—women's hair color. I consider myself something of a pundit on these matters."

"You were talking about your problem with your brother."

"It's not my problem, I told you. It's *his* problem. I think we should get that straight. I don't pluck my hair. I mean, yeah, I shave my face, but that's it. I'm a normal guy."

"Is that important for you, Ray? To be normal?"

Ray White considered telling her about the kid he'd shot yesterday, left bleeding in his pickup. He'd seen in the paper this morning that the old lady had died on the scene. The kid was in serious but stable condition. Still alive at Jackson Memorial, hooked up to their machines. But before Rayon could tell Tricia about shooting somebody, he believed he needed to get to know her better. You couldn't spring something like that on a woman unless the foundation was strong. Anyway, he wasn't absolutely sure about shrinks, if it was the same as priests and lawyers, tell them anything, they had to keep it confidential.

Maybe next week.

"I'm a normal guy," Ray said. "I don't go out of my way to be normal. I don't worry about it. That's just how I am."

"So why do you need my help, Ray? If you're so normal. Why do you come to see me every week?"

He looked at her over in the shadows. Pretty woman, blue eyes, freckles. She could ask good questions, too, like that last one. She could tie him up in knots when she tried.

"I don't want you to waste your money, Ray, if there's nothing serious bothering you."

That's how it was to talk to an intelligent woman. They didn't let you get by with bullshit. They nailed you.

"Doc," said Ray. "I truly believe I'm getting my money's worth seeing you. Believe me, I feel better and better, week after week coming here. Trust me, you're helping."

\* \* \*

After his session Ray drove to the drugstore on Red and Sunset, got his photographs, took the packet back out to the Volvo without opening them up. Started the car, let the air conditioner run. Sitting in the parking lot of Ace Hardware, cooling off the interior.

It was an eight-year-old black Volvo. Zero to sixty in five minutes, give or take. Ray didn't require the G-force that Orlon thrived on. Hell, Orlon would never own a car that couldn't slam his skull against the headrest and keep it pinned there while he worked through the gears. For Orlon, Detroit died the day they slipped below four hundred horses.

Ray just sat for a minute or two, letting his heart throttle down. Out his windshield there were the usual throngs of thirty-year-old mothers coming and going, dragging their blond kids with them, the young and the breastless. Going into the hair salon, health food store, tennis store. Ray watched them pass. Out in the Wednesday sunshine running their errands, everybody in their track shoes, their jogging shorts. All of them healthy, tanned, no fatties.

Ray felt like he did every Wednesday after he left the redheaded shrink. He liked to sit in his car and imagine he had a wife like her, somebody to give him towheaded kids he could take to soccer practice on Saturday morning, a woman who'd go with him to Ace Hardware afterward, the two of them could pick out a new trash can, bring it home, they'd stand around and look at it and say, hey, that's nice. Good wheels on it. Can't wait to fill it with all our happy-family garbage.

But then he'd think of Orlon, what would happen to him if Ray found a woman, got married, all that. And when he started considering the reality of it, moving out, leaving Orlon on his own, the fantasy soured, left a greasy lump in the pit of his belly.

Ray pulled open the packet of photographs. He could feel his heart thumping. A roll of thirty-six. Nice sharp color. Ray took his time, looking at each one. Wanting to hurry, but holding back. First ones were a couple of mosques, just like Orlon predicted. One or two after that of the swimming pool at the Holiday Inn in Kuching. Ray recognized it, having stayed there once on his first trip over, making connections with the local trappers. In the Holiday Inn pool a twenty-year-old girl was waist high in the water looking up at the camera, fingers pulling at the corners of her mouth, sticking her tongue out, mugging. Short blond hair, same length as Ray's. Good tight body inside a black tank suit. Nice round breasts, nipples at attention. Resemblance to Allison around the mouth, the eyes, too, so Ray assumed it was the dead girl's sister.

The two photos after that were wide-angle shots of a longhouse, one of those huge Borneo wooden shacks built on stilts over the swamp. Like a cheap, slapped-together apartment building, even worse than the projects in America. Twenty, thirty families sharing the place, dingy building but with very bright clothes hanging out on the porch.

He set the tourist shots on the passenger seat. Dealt off the next one, the one after that. Chinese herbal shops, then more snapshots of the open-air market in Kuching, stalls of fruit, sides of beef hanging out in the sun, fish and clams and oysters lying in their wood boxes, no refrigeration, no ice. Botulism central. Christ, just walking through those markets made Ray's sphincter muscles loosen.

The photos were a cut or two above your average tourist shots, arty in what she'd focused on, an old woman with black teeth, smiling, pointing at her wooden tray full of gleaming white beads. Black, white. Teeth, beads. Ray could see what the dead girl was driving at. Some kind of contrast, irony or whatever it was called. Same as with the longhouses, rundown buildings with colorful clothes outside. Interesting.

He worked his way through thirty of them, forming an idea of the woman they'd killed, finding he connected with her a little, the way she saw things. But at the same time starting to get a sinking feeling, 'cause there was nothing in the photos he was looking for. No jungle shots at all. Just places around town, people, marketplace, some narrow, sandy road with shadows on it that looked like bayonets. Ray moved through the pile, came down to the last couple, and then *bing, bong, boom,* there it was.

Two sets of rifle barrels pointed upward, gleaming, but a palm frond hid the faces of the hunters. And the last one, the one on the very bottom of the stack, by God—there was the one he'd been hoping for. The dead girl had edged to her right around the palm, and gotten a clear angle on the shooters. There was Ray in profile and beside him was their business partner. Their esteemed colleague, in sharp focus.

Ray switched off the Volvo, went back to the drugstore. He stood in line behind some old lady who was angry none of her pictures had come out.

"You probably forgot to take your lens cap off," said the kid behind the counter. "That's how it looks to me."

"That was my fiftieth wedding anniversary," the woman said. "Can't you do something to fix these?"

When it finally came Ray's turn, he stepped up and said, "You guys do blowups?"

"Enlargements, you mean," the kid said. "That's what they're called."

"I don't care what the fuck you call them. I want one."

"It'll be ready Saturday," Ray said to Orlon. "A blowup."

"Blowup." Orlon smiled, smacked the side of his head with an open palm. "Christ, I been trying to remember that. The name of that English movie. *Blow-Up.* A guy in Hyde Park or somewhere, he's taking pictures, catches something on film he didn't see at the time, a murder, I think. Anyway, I remember them playing tennis without the ball at the end. Out there swatting at the empty air with their rackets. Lot of good skin in that movie. Good old British nudity. We should see if it's on video, rent it for tonight. Smoke some dope, have us some heavy-duty hippie flashbacks."

Orlon was naked, floating on a raft in their lagoon

swimming pool, hidden from their neighbors by tall ole-
ander bushes. Orlon's latest dickthrob, buxom Betty Penski, floated naked beside him, faceup. Big, bristly patch of
blond pubic hair on display.

A few weeks before they left for their Far East trip,
Betty had waited on Orlon and Ray at the International
House of Pancakes over on Bird Road. Buxom Betty
brought their pancakes and flirted with both of them
pretty much equally. But as usual, Orlon wound up being
the one to take a dip in her maple syrup.

"I need to talk to you about something important."

"You can talk in front of Betty. Can't he, Betty?"

"Ray can do anything in front of me," she said.

"And behind you, too, I bet," said Orlon.

"That's right. Either side. Either one of you."

"Over easy," Orlon said. "Right, Betty? You'll take
two over easy?"

"I'm always ready to take your order, sir."

The two of them laughed together. Betty wasn't
twenty yet. Just Orlon's type: big breasts, laughed real
easy, a few crucial wires loose in her cortex.

"Come inside when you're ready to discuss this." Ray
turned his back on them and went back into the house.
Waited ten minutes in the living room till Orlon came in.
Hadn't bothered to put his suit on. Standing there slick as
a seal.

"What's eating your ass, man?"

Ray opened the photo packet and held up the photograph. Orlon came over, took it out of his hand and carried it over to the living room window. He held it up to
the sunlight.

"Not bad, not bad. Makes you look kind of like that
guy, you know, that hunter guy, *Ramar of the Jungle.* You
remember? Those reruns, when we were little, on TV."

"We need to talk about this," said Ray. "Serious
talk."

Orlon came back over and sat down on the couch
opposite him. When they bought this house three years
before, they'd hired a decorator to choose the couch,

rugs, drapes, wallpaper, everything. Orlon insisted on a young homosexual to do the work, 'cause he said those people had the best taste of anybody on the planet. The house was done up in eclectic traditional. That's what the gay guy called it anyway. A few antiques, English primitives, some Shaker stuff. Quilts hanging on the walls, slipcovers burgundy and hunter green. The walls painted some kind of dull pinkish color. Straw baskets, dried flowers, some art deco pieces thrown in here and there, a pink neon sculpture of a flamingo that stayed lit day and night.

All in all, it was a living room you could bring a girl's mother over and show her, and the mother would say yeah, sure, go ahead, take my daughter if you want her. Trouble was, the White brothers never got that far, to the mother stage.

Orlon said, "So this is the photo you're so excited about? Man, I hate to be the one to break it to you, Rayon, but this is bullshit. The guy's aiming his goddamn gun up at the trees, that's all this is."

"Tell me something, Big O. What's that thing tied to his belt? You see that thing? Behind the frond there."

Orlon took another look. Squinted.

"An orangutan."

"That's right. A severely endangered animal. Our guy is out there in the woods shooting his gun, with a woolly ape tied to his belt. We get this photo enlarged, I think this would be a major source of embarrassment for our friend if it was showed in the right circles. Might even create some minor legal traumas. Could cause him to completely lose his station in life."

"I don't know. It's just a picture. And anyway, what's the goddamn hurry, man? This'll wait. This is my day to bop Betty. Her day off, my day on."

Ray took the photo back, sat down on the couch opposite Orlon. A long pine coffee table between them.

Ray said, "I guess you didn't listen to the answering machine this morning, did you, little brother? Didn't notice the red light flashing when you walked by?"

"No, I had a couple of other things on my mind."

"Yeah, that bimbo."

"Hey, that's a very smart young lady. And she's a hundred percent liberated feminist too. Burned her training bra and never bought another one, had a year of junior college, studying to be a nurse. And man, let me tell you, that young lady has already developed herself some very fine nursing skills."

"I don't want to hear about it."

"You know, Ray, you really should go out, find some mud for your turtle. Get your glands drained, maybe your Jockey shorts would loosen up. You'd calm down."

"Our man called us on the phone," said Ray. "He wanted a meeting. Sounded very ominous to me."

"So?"

"Now look, I've thought about this. And I've decided."

"Yeah? You have, huh?"

Buxom Betty was standing naked outside the sliding door. She looked at her reflection for a second and primped her hair. Then, smiling at Ray, she leaned forward and very slowly smushed her breasts flat against the glass and gave the White boys a big House of Pancakes wink.

Then she turned around, peeling her buttocks apart, and pressed her prodigious rear against the glass.

"Hey, tell me, Ray, do I know how to pick my women, or what?"

"Listen, man. You gotta concentrate here. You gotta stay on the same channel with me. This is serious business we're entering into. We have to talk this through, make contingency plans, blueprint it all out."

Orlon was watching Betty spread her cheeks, press them hard against the glass. She was looking over her shoulder at the effect she was having. Orlon touching his crotch in answer.

"Get rid of her," Ray said. "Get that monstrosity out of here."

"Hell, no, I'm not getting rid of her. Look at that.

That's the sun and moon and stars above. That, Rayon, is the ass that passeth all understanding."

Ray got up, walked over to the sliding glass door. He reached up and yanked the curtain cord and the Laura Ashley flowered drapes zipped across the window. He put his hand behind the curtains, made sure the lock was set.

He turned around, glared at his brother.

"So let me guess," Orlon said. "You want to use this photograph to blackmail our guy?"

"No."

"Hey, why not? Shit, we could leapfrog from fairly well off to totally rich in one jump. Burn our bridges with this guy. I never did like him anyway."

"Burn our bridges with us still standing on them is more like it," Ray said.

Orlon looked at the Laura Ashley curtains. Betty was out there knocking on the glass. Knocking without letup.

"Look," Ray said. "What we're going to do, we're going to keep this photo to ourselves. It's our kryptonite. We see we're in trouble with this guy, he starts making threatening noises of some kind, then we bring it out, use it to save our asses. But no blackmail. Nothing like that."

"Kryptonite," Orlon said. "I like that. Hey, I may finally be making some headway with you, big brother. Getting you to look at the world with a more cinematic perspective."

The orangutan stood in front of the open refrigerator cooling himself. There were several bottles of Miller beer inside the old Kenmore, several more broken on the concrete floor. The orangutan had licked up all the beer, and taken a small cut on his foot from the glass.

Now he stood before the cool box and looked around the warehouse. The oak desk was upside down, books and magazines flung across the floor. The first-aid box and the snakebite kit lay open, their contents scattered from one end of the office to the other. Band-Aids, gauze, adhesive tape, iodine, scissors, wooden sticks, and cotton balls.

The orangutan had ripped open a large Band-Aid package and one flesh-colored strip had become snarled in the hair on his leg. In the far corner of the room the watercooler was on its side, the plastic container lying nearby, a pool of water leaking around it.

Leaving bloody footprints as he went, the young ape walked across to the film of water, bent his head down and licked it. He continued until it was gone. Then he rose and walked to the bathroom, looked around, touched the toilet paper roll, spun it around, a yard or two of paper coming off, then he ripped the roll off its holder and dropped it in the toilet.

He leaned down and looked at it, then pulled the soggy mass out and let it drop on the floor. He stepped on it, squished it beneath his cut foot, then picked it up, brought it to his nose, sniffed, then slung it at the wall.

Back in the office, the orangutan climbed up onto the desk and looked around. Papers and pens and pencils lay on the floor. The computer had tumbled onto its side and electricity frizzed inside it every few seconds. Each time the current sputtered, the orangutan jerked his head up and listened.

Peeing as he went, he shuffled down the narrow hallway to the reptile-amphibian room. Worked for a while with the doorknob till the door came open. He went inside.

The snake cages had doors made of Peg-Board. A few hundred holes for the snake to see out, while the orangutan was unable to see in. He explored the room, pushing on the legs of the cages, testing their balance. Then climbing on top of one and reaching up for the water pipes that ran along the ceiling.

He hung from a water pipe, then hand over hand he crossed the length of the room. He let himself go, dropping down on the Peg-Board lid of the albino python's cage. A diamondback in the cage beside it struck at the lid of his cage, then thumped it again and again.

The orangutan paused, bent over, and studied the rattler's cage. Then he hopped back onto the floor and brought his eye close to a small hole in the Peg-Board. The diamondback struck at the ape's eye, and the orang-utan jumped back.

He stood in the middle of the room for a minute and looked at the cages. There were hissing noises, rattles, more thumps.

The orangutan turned and went to the door, opened it wide. Then he moved back to the cages and one by one he tipped them over. He stood for a moment looking at the snakes coiling out of the debris, then he shuffled back down the narrow hallway.

Again he climbed onto the overturned desk. He stared up at the water lines running along the ceiling. He jumped up and gripped them both, cold and hot. He squealed and immediately let go. He landed on the desk, and cheeped to himself, rubbing at his burned hand. Two hurt hands now. One with several broken fingers, now this one with a bad burn.

As he rubbed his blistered hand against his stomach, he watched an albino cobra glide down the hallway.

# C H A P T E R

# 19

Wednesday morning Allison waited till Harry left for the office before rising from bed. In the kitchen she made coffee, rinsed the huge pile of dishes Harry had stacked in the sink, put them in the dishwasher, wiped down all the counters, swept the floor, straightened, carried out three sacks of garbage. It took her just over an hour to undo weeks of accumulated neglect. She went back upstairs, showered, dressed in the first outfit she laid hands on: faded blue jeans, a green-and-red checked shirt, white Keds.

By noon she was driving her red Jeep Cherokee west out Coral Way. She cut north to Tamiami Trail, and by the time she was entering the eastern fringes of the Everglades, she had to roll up her windows, turn on the air.

A clear hot morning, the moderating effects of the cool front had vanished already, and now the sticky subtropical flow had returned. There was some cumulus build-up in the west, the tops of the clouds blowing off to the south, mare's tails, indicating a shift in the winds of the upper atmosphere. Like the winds shifting in her.

Everything seemed symbolic today, full of portent, all of it exceedingly clear, a perfect match for her inner landscape. No doubt, no confusion anymore. All decisions made, a calm finality. Just a few last details to settle, a few more hours to pass. Methodical, focused.

Thirty miles west of the city limits, Allison pulled off on an unmarked side road beside Joe Tiger's Authentic Miccosukee Indian Village, followed the road south as it turned to gravel, went further south till it became a tricky blend of sand and muck, and began to head west.

Surprisingly, the ten-foot chain-link gates were still closed and locked, no tire tracks in the soft sand of her drive. Over a month since she'd been out there and not a single forced entry. That was an all-time record. Usually on the weekends the three-wheelers came in swarms. They'd crowbar open the lock, race around her ten acres, jumping some small hammocks, chew up the mucky ground on the western edge of the property. They must go home covered in black mud. Indian kids, not malicious, never vandalized anything, never broke into the house, or tried to make off with her fax or copiers. The worst you could say about them, they didn't have much respect for fences.

Allison let herself in, looked around. It was a nothing house. Not the least bit of charm. Her father had built the place in the twenties, when Miami was still a town of only a few dozen paved streets. The structure was just a wooden box divided into four rooms, with an asbestos shingle roof, oak floor. The windows were barred to keep out the vandals, the glass full of hairline cracks. In Allison's family it had been nicknamed the Shack.

All through her childhood, her father had brought the male members of the Ravenel family and favored male guests out there for legendary weekends of hunting and whiskey and good Christian debauchery. The Ravenel girls were never invited, for, as Allison was told many times, there were no ladylike activities in such a place, no badminton, croquet, and it would certainly put a crimp in the men's frolic to have womenfolk around. Bunch of females complaining about the cigar smoke, the bugs, the dirty jokes, the energetic passing of gas.

As a teenager Allison had yearned to visit the Shack, glimpsing it only in an occasional snapshot, then later in a couple of those twitchy super-8 movies, the men with ci-

gar stubs in the corners of their mouths, dirty and un-
shaven, holding up strings of fish, a gator, snake, an infre-
quent deer. Once or twice a panther. Shirtless bucks
liquored up, apparently talking filthy into the soundless
camera, smiling, laughing.

To Allison's absolute amazement and to the shock of
all her male cousins, her father, Julius, bequeathed the
Shack to her. Apparently he'd glimpsed something in Allison she'd only half sensed herself.

Shortly after the will reading she'd gone out there,
escorted by her gloomy uncle Dan. Allison still remembered the reverential excitement she'd felt on the drive
out, the flutter in her breast as they crossed the last hundred yards, swung around the final muddy turn. And
there it was.

Allison was aghast. The place was a dump. Worse
than a dump. Four walls and a leaky roof, bars on the
windows, the glass broken out. A ratty yard full of metal
trash, hubcaps, beer cans, fifty-gallon barrels discarded
here and there. The insides stank of rot and dead animals,
mildew and fermenting beer. The toilet was stained and
terminally clogged, the appliances coated with yellow
grease, the walls defaced with the coarse hieroglyphics of
manhood.

Deeply let down, she drove away that day with the
intention of never returning. And for twenty years she did
not. Dutifully she paid the meager property taxes each
year, and even hired a lawyer once to fight a Department
of Interior attempt to absorb the land into Everglades
National Park. But it wasn't until the idea began to flower
in her to organize a group to fight the illegal trade of
animals that Allison thought again of the Shack as a place
she might inhabit.

It soon became her refuge. In some ways more her
home than the house in the Gables where she'd raised her
family. Indeed, Allison had come to see the Shack as her
singular heritage, all she had received from her own family, all she could pass on. The only true thing she owned.

First she'd won permission to tap into her friend Joe

Tiger's electricity, his water line. Then over the seven years that she'd been using it as the headquarters for the Wildlife Protection League, she'd cleaned and repaired and gradually softened the feel of the place. She'd committed feminine sacrilege upon it. Hung curtains, laid out rugs, painted the rough cement walls in beiges and yellows, filled it with garage-sale chairs and lamps, a lumpy double bed. A rolltop desk, several long folding tables where each month she collated and stapled together her newsletter, bundled them up for the post office. One newsletter for each of her fifteen thousand dues-paying members.

It was ten to two by the time Allison entered the Shack. She went to the broom closet and pulled out a wad of dust rags, the broom, dustpan. Continuing her fit of compulsive cleaning, Allison dusted and swept the living room, wiped down cobwebs. She threw open the windows, chancing mosquitoes so she could get the dank air moving again. She shifted the box of mail out of her way once, then another time. She took a dozen pages from the fax machine, and without a look she set them neatly on her desk.

In the bathroom and kitchen she wiped down the counters and shelves and finally she was left with the small room on the west corner she'd designated as her bedroom. With her broom in her hand she halted in the doorway of the room, looked back at the rest of the house, but could invent no more work to distract her.

On the chest of drawers in the bedroom was her complete collection of family photographs. She had realized for some time that she would have to look at them again, see Winslow in her prom dress, various bikinis, her tennis clothes. The tragic trajectory of her daughter's history.

Mustering her nerve, Allison sat for a few minutes on the edge of her bed. She drank a can of iced tea that had been in the fridge for months, wiped the sweat from her face. Finally she got up, took the framed photos off the bureau, carried them to the bed and lay down with them.

Although she'd planned for this moment, measured out some last reserve of strength, knowing she would have to confront the photos, still she wept. Wept for herself this time, for failing to find a way to lure either of her daughters out to the Shack, to interest them in this place that had given her such peace and inspiration. Wept for her total isolation from Harry and from Sean, for the string of choices she'd made that lead inexorably to Winslow's death.

When she'd pulled herself together again, she walked back into the living room, gazed around at the familiar objects she'd collected over the last decade. Aimlessly, she read one of the faxes, a submission from one of her members. It was a newspaper article from a Texas paper about a Mexican zoo owner's shopping list for illegal animals. The list had been intercepted on its way to a Thai animal dealer by a woman who worked as a secretary in the zoo. The zoo owner wanted one white tiger, one pygmy hippo, one Asian elephant, an orangutan, and a gorilla, among a list of twenty other endangered animals. He was willing to pay what he called "the very top dollar."

On a normal afternoon Allison would have fumed for an hour after reading such a piece, then she would've put the zoo man's wish list on the front page of her next newsletter and started a letter-writing campaign to the board of directors of his zoo, to the Mexican agricultural department, to expose this cretin to whatever public scorn she could whip up.

But today she simply set the letter aside.

All the busywork was done, the room alphabetized and orderly again, and Allison eased down in a rocker near the front window and let its rhythm lull her for a while. As she rocked, she found herself hearing again those bullying taunts, those bastards yelling out her name in the Borneo rain forest and again on Monday night at Parrot Jungle. She could recall the exact sounds of their voices, their accents, intonations. Still feel the faint tug of recognition, almost certain they were voices she had heard before.

But she could not place them. And now it no longer mattered. She was finished with all of it, even felt revolted at the memory of that other Allison Farleigh, the one who would have plunged in, investigated, hunted, pursued and pursued. The Allison whose relentless obsessions had driven her so far from her own family, had stubbed out the last ember of passion between Harry and her. No, that woman had died in the jungles of Borneo with her dead daughter cradled in her arms.

Allison rose, and found in the refrigerator, tucked behind a six-pack of diet Cokes, a single Budweiser. She opened it and took it out to the front porch. She dropped into one of the teak Adirondack chairs, sipped the cold beer and watched the sun mire itself in the saw grass and palmetto. Watched its blood seep into the slick of water that covered the earth in every direction. Watched the leisurely arcs of red-tailed hawks and the skittering of swallows. Dark silhouettes of other birds raced past, black cutouts against that savage red sky.

Over and again she had heard how this land paled in comparison to its earlier incarnation. She should have seen it thirty years ago, forty. Dozens of species had disappeared during her lifetime. They were surely disappearing tonight as she swilled her beer. It was only a fraction as lush as it had once been, with only a vague, pathetic resemblance to its early days.

All that might be true, but still it was a wild and gorgeous place, nearly as prehistoric as Borneo. Creatures owned it. Men were still strangers here. They blundered about, and only with the greatest difficulty could they penetrate the maze of saw grass and hammock. It was still so pristine that every human incursion, no matter how brief, fouled the place. Left the contaminated footprints, the stink of civilization behind.

Of course, Allison was as guilty as any of them, bringing her fax, her phone, into the center of this world, taking advantage of her father's pioneer status, the succession of leases to remain here. But it was a guilt she could abide. In some ways it was even a guilt she had relished, for she was living out her father's unspoken wish for her. To carry on the Ravenel way, yield to the pull of the wild, come out into the dark core of the swamp, breathe its sulfurous fumes, take strength from its strength.

Sooner or later, whenever she came out here, she recalled her father. Speculated again on what prompted him to pass the place to her. Thinking sometimes that he must have believed Allison would bring a different outlook here, a needed change. That she would not feel compelled to engage in raucous sport, to hunt and kill, to try to dominate the land. Perhaps he saw in her a willingness to give this house and land a feminine tilt, a milder, quieter reverence than any of the male Ravenels were capable of.

She hoped that was his reason. That he had decided she alone might know best how to live in this wild place in accordance with its simple cadences, its silence, its rapture. That Allison just might be the one to discover the secrets that she suspected he himself had discovered here, the lovely scents and colors, the sweet angles of light, those calm, hushed pleasures that because he was a man he could never openly admit to.

When it was completely dark and the mosquitoes began to attack her ankles and sing in her ears, Allison Farleigh went back inside, shut the windows, switched on a couple of lights. She listened to an owl in the pine outside the living room window, heard thunder rumbling in the west.

She went to the kitchen, took the flashlight out of a drawer beside the refrigerator, and limped outside to the storage shed. There she found the two five-gallon cans of gasoline, one of them full, the other only half. Fuel for her Honda generator, which she used almost weekly during the summer when the thunderstorms regularly knocked out her power. She hauled the cans one at a time back to the house, set them side by side on the porch.

She was focused now, seeing it all with vivid clarity. Not in some desperate frenzy, not trying to speed through this to keep from wavering. She simply went about her

work with a steady cadence as though she had uncon-
sciously rehearsed this ritual for years, smoothing out every detail, the precise mechanics of this night.

Out on the porch she walked down the stairs, out
into the dark. With great care, she poured the gasoline in
a wavering path around the entire base of the house, stopping several times to splash the walls. Then back at the
front door, she doused the porch with an extra portion,
ran a trail of gasoline around her chair. She slung the
empty cans into the yard.

After a moment staring into the darkness, listening to
the warble of frogs, the night birds trilling, she sat down,
reached into the pocket of her jeans and took out the
Zippo. She opened it, hearing the precise click of its latch,
the sweet metallic ring it made when it closed, like a tiny
guillotine slashing shut.

She opened it again, snapped it closed. Just as Julius
had done, her father fidgeting with his lighter while he
chewed his big Cuban cigars into submission.

Allison opened the lid again, and this time she poised
her thumb hard against the roughened wheel.

# CHAPTER

# 20

Allison held the Zippo motionless and watched a cluster of shredded clouds coast past the three-quarter moon. A gray light clung to the distant oaks like a mist of static electricity. Two hundred yards away in the marshy lowlands, the perfect sheen of the Glades was fractured by saw grass and palmetto into a thousand jagged mirrors, each replaying a piece of the action in the sky. Countless moons and clouds skated helter-skelter across the land.

She listened to a quiet rumble growing in the darkness. For a hazy moment she thought it was her own body she was hearing, the thud and rush of her blood. But slowly, as Allison peered into the dark, the noise rose and clarified until she could tell it was a straining engine, the snarl of a car's transmission laboring along the treacherous, sandy road.

The headlights made sudden silhouettes of the cypress and oaks as the car rounded the sweeping left turn and bumped along the rutted entrance road. Brightness flooded through the cabbage palms and sabals, passed briefly across her cabin.

Standing up, she snapped the Zippo shut and set it on the wicker table. She moved out to the edge of the porch, listened to the crunch of tires across her gravel drive. Strained to see through the gloom.

The driver shut off his lights and engine simultaneously and one of the rear doors swung open. A man's shadow emerged from the car. The first time anyone had ever come calling. For she'd made a point of keeping the Shack's location a secret, using a Miami postal box for her mailing address, keeping phone and fax unlisted. Given the people she harassed, it was only prudent to shield herself behind a layer or two of camouflage. Harry had been to the Shack with her father a few times before Julius died, but he'd never visited Allison there. After all these years she doubted he even remembered the way.

Whoever was standing out in the dark just now had ignored the half dozen NO TRESPASSING signs posted along the entrance road, and without anyone's permission had unlatched her gate, driven past the hand-lettered PRIVATE PROPERTY, NO ENTRY sign.

The large man hesitated in the shadows, then he moved cautiously past the soft gleam of the car's grille. She made a quick step to the door, eased halfway inside, a hand reaching up for the Remington, when the man swung around, turned his back on the cabin and took a long look at the expanse of darkness, lifted his hand, brushed aside his hair. And simply from that casual act, the language of his gesture, she knew it was Thorn.

She took a calming breath, closed the screen door behind her, sat down again in the chair and watched him. It came as a mild shock that somehow without being aware of it, she had acquired such knowledge of this man, had become so intimate with his movements and posture that she could recognize him in the dark. Hell, she doubted she could identify Harry so easily.

The car started, headlights flared on, and it carved a wide, slow circle in the yard and headed away down the gravel road. It was then she noticed the dim lights on its roof. A taxi.

Without a word of greeting Thorn mounted the porch, took a seat in the rocker beside her. In the weak moonlight she could see he was wearing khaki shorts and a work shirt, his boat shoes.

He reached over, lifted her left hand from the arm of her rocker, gave it short squeeze and released it.

"I found the guys."

"What guys?"

"Ones who imported the orangutans."

Allison opened her mouth but didn't speak.

"It was Kurt Franklin's doing," said Thorn. "He dropped by the marina, asked if I'd go check these guys out, pretend I was a vet, say I was there to examine a sick orangutan. Apparently he'd done business with these animal dealers in the past. I had the evening free, so I went."

"What in hell is Kurt Franklin doing playing around with animal dealers?"

"Apparently he'd been trying to help you. Doing some freelance undercover work for you. Wanted to impress his future mother-in-law. That's what it sounded like. He's been going around to different dealers around the area, pretending he was in the market for illegal animals. He'd leave one of his business cards, see who called. But now he's decided to drop it all. After Winslow and Bronson, he's scared. That's how he acted."

Allison shook her head. Good Christ, this is what she'd wrought with her warmongering against the animal trade, inspiring the Kurt Franklins of the world to put themselves in harm's way. Her own daughter. Innocents.

"But the point is, these guys have a young orangutan in their warehouse. I saw it."

"That doesn't mean a thing. It could've come from anywhere."

"It just arrived last week. And, Allison, it has a silver mark on its forehead."

She drew a breath, stared out into the night, felt as though her heart were taking a slow swan dive off the airless cliffs inside her. Then, from a great distance away, she heard herself ask, "Is it Joshua Bond?"

"No," Thorn said. "White Brothers Imports."

She turned her head, peered at him for a moment.

"Raimondo and Orlando White?"

"Yeah, a tall one and a short one. The small one's

bald, no eyebrows. Creepy little guy. The other guy is tall and blond, handsome in a slick sort of way, like a Miami Beach gigolo."

"That's ridiculous," she said. "The White brothers are snake dealers. Small-timers. Reptiles, a few birds, that's all. They don't even deal in primates."

"They do now. They have an orangutan in their warehouse. Three years old, four. With a silver patch."

Abruptly she rose from the chair, stood for a moment, then marched into the Shack, switched on several lights. She began to search the litter of newsletters on her desk, digging through the pile till she found the ones from last summer, a couple of articles on Orlando and Raimondo White. Feeling the shiver rise inside her as she turned the pages, a growing certainty even before she looked at their photos, recalling their voices speaking up in court, their paltry defense. They hadn't known indigo snakes were on the endangered list. In their warehouse they had a dozen of them. Six thousand dollars' worth. The White brothers were caught on a routine permit inspection by Fish and Wildlife. Allison recalled the little one, his courtroom whine.

"Hey, give us a break, we're just simple businessmen trying to make an honest living. Don'tcha have bigger fish you should be going after? The real bad guys. Dope dealers or something."

Replaying their voices in her head, she could recall their accents had the same colorless, generic vowels of Miami natives. The slightest tang of redneck mingled with a bland Midwestern flatness.

She located the newsletters, spread them open, stared at the photos she had snapped of the White brothers as they left federal court back in June, guilty, but despite a massive letter-writing campaign to Judge Hildreth, they'd received a suspended sentence. The photo was taken on a cloudy day, windy. The tall, blond one was making blinders of his hands to conceal his face, the short, hairless one was smiling insanely and shooting a bird directly into the camera.

"Is it them?"

She looked up.

"How did you find me, Thorn? How did you know where to come?"

He hesitated a moment, standing in the center of the small living room, glancing at the walls, the shelves of old leather books, photographs of Winslow and Sean. Fading black-and-whites of Julius Ravenel and his scruffy band of hunters squatting around their kill of the day. The oak tavern mirror with one of Julius's green felt hats still hanging from a peg, two wrought-iron lamps, a cherry drop-leaf table surrounded by four spindle-back chairs, one of her grandmother's forest quilts hanging from the west wall. Thorn's face softened.

"I went by your house," he said, bringing his eyes to her. "After I got off Parrot Jungle, I went over there and Harry said you were probably out here."

"And he told you how to get here?"

"No, *you* told me. A few years ago you described the place, which roads to take, all of it."

"I did?"

"You don't remember? You and me and Winslow, fishing the flats off Islamorada, two years ago, three maybe. She was still in college. It was spring break, I think. You caught a snook, a half dozen reds. Winslow and I were skunked. Beautiful day, though, glassy calm. One of those scrubbed-clean skies."

"Why did I give you directions?"

"You were going on about the Shack. I said it sounded like the kind of place I like. You gave me directions, invited me out for a visit. It took three years, but here I am."

"And you remembered something trivial like that, all this time? This road, that road, left, right."

"I didn't consider it trivial."

She looked at him carefully, this simple man who always seemed slightly cranky unless he was in a boat, out of sight of land. But not so uncomfortable now. Glancing around her cabin, liking what he saw. Shoulders relaxed.

A plain, almost ascetic man who had reduced his life to a handful of truths, a few things he loved. Fishing, tying his lures, his few close friends, his books, tinkering with his boats, endless repairs on his house beside the bay.

Winslow and Sean called him Nature Boy. And that was an easy mistake to make, for he often acted like a guileless adolescent. He was artless, with a silly Eagle Scout view of politics and women, totally out of synch with the jigs and jogs of current events, the MTV throb of the moment.

But even as a child, Thorn had seemed to Allison to have haunted depths. Struggles he didn't reveal, inner grapplings that never made it past the spartan surface. He was no saint. She'd seen him lose his Zen placidness more than once. But he was fierce in his loyalty to his friends and his quirky code, and just as resolute at keeping the rest of the world's troubles and modern ideas at bay. Nature Boy, yes. And he could be childish too. But as Allison had come to see over the years, Thorn was far more difficult to fathom, a man of more parts than he first appeared.

"So is it them? The White brothers. These are the guys from Borneo?"

She looked down at the pictures again.

"Yes, it's them. I'm pretty sure anyway."

"Good," he said. "So what're we going to do?"

She stared at him, felt a tingling behind her eyes as if tears were mounting again. Never any doubt from him that she was sane, that these men were after her. Might even be out in the dark right now, fixing their aim.

She said, "The first thing I'm going to do is talk to them."

Thorn took a seat on the rattan couch, with its faded cover of burgundy and gold flowers. Forty years out of style. Thrift-shop decor. Thorn looked entirely at home there.

"Talk?" Thorn said. "They don't strike me as big talkers."

"I didn't actually see them in Borneo," she said. "But

I remember their voices. So I need to hear how they sound. I need to be absolutely sure."

"And then?"

"They didn't do this alone," she said. "There's somebody pulling their strings."

"You're sure of that?"

"They have no reason to kill me. I went after them in June, it was a little case. They got off, suspended sentence, not even a stern warning from the judge. Where the hell's their motivation?"

"Maybe they took it more personally than that. Or maybe these two don't need a lot of motivation to get violent. That's how they seem to me, touchy, stretched a little tight. One foot standing on the brake, the other mashing the accelerator."

"There's more to it, Thorn. Believe me. Something else is going on here. It isn't about indigo snakes, a trivial court case."

Allison stood in front of the couch, rubbing at the groove where her wedding ring had been. Massaging that finger as if she were trying to bring blood back to a withered limb. Then following Thorn's eyes, looking down at her hands, seeing what she was doing, a gesture she recognized had become a habit.

"Are you okay, Allison?"

The varnished lamp shade behind the couch put Thorn in a pale golden halo. She dropped her hands to her sides.

"I'm fine," she said. "Getting my second wind."

He held her eyes for a moment, his gaze growing serious, then moving beyond that. Probing her eyes as though he were searching for something hidden inside her.

"Tell me something, Allison."

"Yes?"

Thorn showed the edge of a smile.

"Do you smell gasoline?"

She sighed, came over to the rattan couch, sat down, leaving a space between them. Looked at him straightforwardly. Then she admitted it with her eyes, what she'd been intending to do. And Thorn, without a nod or shrug, somehow acknowledged the confession.

"Been a hard time," he said. "You've been strained to the limits."

"*Hard,*" she said. "*Hard* isn't the half of it."

He smiled, brushed the coarse yellow hair from his forehead, resettled himself on the cushion, coming halfway around toward her, right arm up on the back of the couch.

"But not suicide," Allison said. "I was just going to get rid of this place. Be done with it. That part of my life."

He nodded.

"Because of what you did here, all those newsletters. You got people angry at you. This is where it all started."

"Yes," she said. "Exactly."

Thorn looked around at the room.

"Well, I'm glad I got to see it once before you torched it."

In the corner of the room the fax machine emitted a single ring. Thorn stared across at it.

"One of the members," she said, dismissing it with a wave. "The machine's out of paper, but it'll store the message. I've got it hooked through the computer's buffer memory. It can store a month of messages if it needs to."

"What the *hell* is that thing?"

She looked at him.

"It's a fax machine, Thorn."

"Oh," he said. And then a moment later, "I've heard about them."

She smiled uncertainly. It might be a joke, might not. With Thorn you couldn't tell. Living without hot water, radio, television, or phone, in a Key Largo stilthouse he built out of scrap lumber, Thorn considered it a major concession even to have wired the place for electricity. It wasn't so much that he disliked modern conveniences, but rather that he found the primitive way he lived to be sufficiently convenient already.

His gaze was wandering the room again, touching

everything, then lingering on the Remington beside the front door.

"You're my first guest," she said. "It feels very strange."

He turned his eyes on her. They were a greenish blue, the color of the ocean over white sand shallows.

He studied her as if he was searching for a way to begin, tapping his finger against the flowered cushion between them, his hand close to her shoulder. Allison felt a hard jiggle in her pulse, felt the two of them teetering unexpectedly on a critical moment neither had calculated or wanted. Then she saw his earnest expression slowly back down, dissolve to a drowsy grin.

"If I'm your first guest," he said at last, "that probably explains why you've forgotten your manners and not offered me anything to drink."

For a late-night snack they shared the last of a jar of crunchy peanut butter, with glops of raspberry preserves spread over stale Triscuits and Melba Toast, and washed the choking mess down with an Oregon pinot noir she found in one of the high cabinets, drank it from tea glasses with wicker sleeves. It was an absurd and wonderful feast, Allison finding herself suddenly famished from her voyage into the dark outlands of depression.

"I never should have gotten you involved," she said, at the round cherry table covered with the remains of their splurge.

"I'm glad you did," he said. "I like the orangutans. It's not like anything I've ever done before, holding them, talking about them to strangers. But it feels good. Like I'm stretching, finding some new muscles. I appreciate your coming to get me like that, dragging me out of the house, out of my navel gazing."

"You're welcome," she said.

"I'd probably still be in there. Drinking tequila, feeling sorry for my idiot self."

"I'm giving it up," she said. "The Wildlife Protection League, all of it. Going to start spending more time with

Sean and Harry. Learn how to be a mother again, a wife. Just forget the White brothers. Tell the police what I know and then just let it all go."

"And if the police don't do anything?"

"They won't. But that doesn't matter. I'm through with it, exhausted. Everything I've been doing, look what it's caused. Look at the horrible, shitty mess I've made."

Thorn nodded.

She said, "You're not going to try to talk me out of it?"

"Out of which part?"

"Any of it."

He said nothing, a sad smile rearranging his face. The man used silence like a second language. More honest eloquence in that one pained squint than Harry was capable of in a year of gilded talk.

"This guilt," she said, thumping a fist between her breasts. "I've tried to keep going, ignore it, outrun it."

"But the little bastard is tenacious, isn't he?"

He smiled, had a sip of his wine.

"Like one of those viruses that never dies," she said. "It gets into you, finds a place to hibernate. From then on it can pop up whenever it gets hungry again. Nothing you can do about it. It feels like it's going to be there forever."

Thorn brushed some crumbs off the edge of the table into his hand, then dusted them into his plate.

"Lately I've developed some fondness for the things I can't do anything about," he said. "It's all the other god-damn things that still give me trouble."

She made a bed for him on the rattan couch. Set up an old black oscillating fan on the dining table, aimed it his way. There was an awkward moment as she was heading for her room, about to bid him good night, a clumsy dance, he in her way, she in his.

He reached out, put a hand on her forearm, drew them out of their bumbling orbit. She faced him, swept her free hand through her hair. He seemed reluctant to let her go.

"It doesn't matter to me," he said. "If you don't want

to pursue this thing with the White brothers, drop it right here, that's fine by me. Don't feel like I'm pressuring you one way or the other."

"I'll sleep on it," she said. "Decide tomorrow."

He told her good night and stepped forward, pressed a kiss to her cheek. Not the least bit brotherly, but not pushing for more either.

She didn't know why, but the words came into her throat, thrummed her vocal cords and were spoken before Thorn's kiss vanished from her cheek.

"I've been planning to leave Harry for months, but now I don't know. I'm confused. Sean pleaded with me to stay with him, to try to make it work out. Maybe she's right."

"Maybe she is."

She stepped back from him.

"But I don't know," Allison said. "Sometimes I think I'd be better off by myself. Live alone, like you do."

She found herself massaging the finger again and pulled her hands apart, let them hang at her side. A long roll of thunder grumbled in the west.

"You've seen those pictures," Thorn said. "A row of chimps squatting down, three or four, each one's picking lice off the one beside it. Working together, the common good. I see that, and then I think about orangutans. You know, how they'll swing down out of the trees to mate for a few days, but otherwise they're by themselves. Up in the canopy, fifty years, sixty, hardly ever seeing another one of their kind. Nobody to pick their lice."

A breeze sifted through the house, a spicy hint of approaching rain.

"And who picks them off you, Thorn?"

He smiled, drew a breath.

"Oh, I've learned to get most of them myself. Now and then I stumble on somebody willing to trade off. But it isn't easy. It's not the life I would've chosen. Up in the trees."

"Do we get to choose?" she said.

He bowed his head slightly, considered it a moment.

"Maybe not," he said. "Maybe not."

She was silent. Thorn raised his eyes, looked intently into hers, observing her in a way no one had for years. As though he were seeing someone Allison had left behind long ago. Seeing her with a raw completeness, undistracted by her various aliases. Not Allison the wife, the mother. Not Allison the wildlife vigilante, the social activist.

Seeing instead Allison Ravenel. A thirteen-year-old girl fishing with her father alongside Thorn and Kate Truman thirty years ago. And seeing Allison Farleigh. A grown woman, vigorous, standing now in a cabin in the center of a stark and empty land. As if Thorn were looking at a person Allison had gradually abandoned in the countless qualifiers of growing older. Like a great river whose strength has dwindled as it wanders down a thousand lesser tributaries.

She stepped forward and returned his kiss. Briefly drew in his scent of sun and sweat, and the faint sweet pungency of Pongo, the orangutan he had held in his arms all day.

Abruptly she told him good night, made it to her room, shut the door. Looked across at the bars on her window, the perfect darkness beyond the screens. And this moment felt to her like the conclusion of something long and complicated and very sad. The beginning of something else entirely.

"Do you have to go?"

"Sean, we can't stay in bed forever."

"Why not?" she said. "I'm not tired, are you?"

"Not tired," he said. "Raw."

Patrick, standing at the mirror in Sean's bathroom smiled over at her, then went back to drying his hair with a towel. His skin glowed from the hot shower. Just beyond the open door she lay on her stomach in the bed, giving him a loose, drugged smile as if she were tranquilized on some deep chemical level.

"It's business," he said. "I won't be long. I promise."

"It's two in the morning, Patrick. What kind of business?"

"On this side of the world it's two in the morning," he said. "But my business is more wide-ranging than that."

Patrick smiled again, and after a reluctant moment she smiled back.

He was dressed in a pair of baggy jeans he'd found in Sean's closet. A red flannel shirt. Her clothes, he assumed. Another depressing American custom, the sexes dressing alike.

Finished with his hair, Patrick came back into the bedroom, sat down beside her, leaned over and kissed her on the forehead.

"I won't be long, lover."

She chuckled. Closed her eyes, let her head sink back into the pillow.

"That's what we are now, isn't it? Patrick and Sean. Lovers."

"Yes. We most certainly are that."

"Strange," she said. "Strange how it happened."

"Not so strange, really," he said. "Inevitable."

"Was it?"

"Yes," he said. "Predestined. Written in the heavens."

"You seduced me, didn't you? You had this whole thing planned out. You came all the way over here to seduce me. You planned it for years, to get me into bed."

"We seduced each other," he said. "That's how it happened."

"I don't like being tricked," she said, a pout in her voice.

"It happened," he said, "because we both wanted it. I didn't trick you any more than you tricked me. It was mutual."

He bent down again and kissed her frown away. Their lips lingered, tongues touched, his blood beginning to smolder, Patrick about to tumble forward into bed for a few more hours. But he pulled away.

Sean was breathing hard, her nipples wrinkled tight. White dust on her cheek, their accumulated sweat leaving its powdery crust. Twenty-four hours of continuous sex. Coming back to her apartment after their swim at the beach. Both of them with the same insatiable urge. Pushing Patrick's limits beyond anything he'd known. An entire day without sleep. Driven by years of lust for her, years of yearning. The American girls, the beautiful, dreamy Farleigh sisters.

Damp, knotted sheets. Moving around her apartment, finding new positions, new angles of pleasure. Arrangements of flesh Patrick had only imagined. She was so limber, so athletic, so hungry for him. Almost as much as he was for her.

Pushing himself beyond any limits he'd known. She said she'd never done this before. Never this long, this sleepless craving. She said she had no idea that all this was inside her. She said she was usually so rational, so clearheaded. What had he done, drugged her? The sweet funk of sex blossoming in the air.

Now Patrick touched a finger to Sean's cheek and told her he would be back as soon as humanly possible.

"You'd better be," she said.

He took his rented Cadillac west on Tigertail, got lost almost immediately in the center of the Grove, found himself in a black ghetto, stopped at a red light, groups of men on corners staring at him, one of them drifting away from his friends, heading Patrick's way.

He flattened the accelerator, ran the red light, squealed onto Douglas Road and in a mild panic raced south.

At last he found the traffic circle, and took the second shadowy spoke-road off it. Doing this from memory, from an hour of studying the Miami street map on the Concorde over. Driving south through a tunnel of banyans, fifteen minutes watching the houses grow larger, the lots deeper, until the mansions disappeared altogether behind stone walls, tall manicured hedges.

Then three more turns and he drew into a circular drive.

He checked the address on the business card. Then he looked at himself in the rearview mirror, combed back a strand of hair. His face smooth, flushed from the continuous fucking. Feeling more relaxed, more composed than he had ever felt.

He got out, went to the big double doors. Rang the bell.

In less than a minute the porch light came on, and the door swung open. The man in shorty pajamas said nothing for a moment, staring out at Patrick on the porch.

Then he said, "Jesus, will you look who's here."

A second later his taller, slightly smarter brother appeared behind him in matching pajamas. A ghastly expression coming to his face.

"Well, hello there," Ray White said at last. "Partner."

Patrick smiled at their discomfort.

"Did I catch you boys at a bad time?"

# CHAPTER

# 21

Allison lay still for a long while, forcing herself to think rationally, to bring her focus to the White brothers, the logical next step, what to do tomorrow.

"I heard their voices," she could tell the police.

"You heard their voices, but you didn't see them?"

"That's right, but I have a very good ear for voices."

"A very good ear, Your Honor. Yes, Allison Farleigh is a woman with a very good ear for voices. She remembers exactly what her daughter's killers sounded like over there in Borneo. What's that, Your Honor? No, sir. No, I have no idea whose jurisdiction Borneo is. I don't even have any idea where the fuck the place is located."

Or go back one more time to Fish and Wildlife.

Sure.

"So you are claiming that one of these gentlemen, Mr. Raimondo White or possibly Mr. Orlando White, shot your daughter. And furthermore, you're claiming that the Whites now have in their possession a wild-born orangutan illegally obtained from the very jungle where your daughter was murdered. All right, then, let's assume that this is all true. Then please help us out with this, Mrs. Farleigh, how is the presence of an orangutan in the White brothers' warehouse proof of murder? What is it, exactly, Fish and Wildlife are supposed to do? Interview the orangutan, see if we can get it to corroborate your story? Is that what you're asking us to do? Interview an ape? Oh, yes, and by any chance is this the same ape, Mrs. Farleigh, that told you about Joshua Bond?"

As the first gray moments of sleep began to take her, she had a brief vision of her father. He was lying on his bed upstairs in the Coconut Grove house, the room darkened. A doctor in one corner, Allison's mother weeping downstairs. Allison was nineteen. She kissed him on the forehead, brought her ear close to his lips. "I'm thirsty," he said.

No wisdom sent back from the brink of eternity. No final blessing or admonition. Not even an I-love-you. Just that: I'm thirsty. Smacking his withered lips.

Nine months later she was married to Harry Farleigh.

"Key deer," Patrick said, and looked up from his typed sheet. All business, giving Ray one of those impatient looks, like he was doing three or four other things in his head at the same time, using only a little fraction of his brain to deal with the White brothers.

Ray's way of dealing with people like him was to slow way down, drag things out, make the guy adjust to his rhythms, not the other way around. A cornerstone of bargaining. Whoever controls the metronome wins.

"Okay, yeah, the best count we got on key deer is, there's two hundred and fifty to three hundred left in the world," Ray said. "All those are down on Big Pine Key, couple of hours south of here. We got a guy down there working on it. Old-time trapper. And what he's telling us is, it's not going to be all that easy, everyone is so Bambi-happy these days. He's got to go out in the woods in the dark, dodge the tree-huggers, nab that deer—which even by itself is a hard enough job, the thing is so spooky. So all in all, it's gonna run ten thousand for his trouble."

"Male and female," Patrick said.

"Right," Ray said. "That'll be twenty thousand."

Patrick didn't flinch at the amounts, just looked over at Betty again, lying there on the couch, stomach down, the green silk kimono riding up to expose half her naked butt. Her flesh was glowing red from all the weekend sun. As far as Ray could tell, Betty didn't wear any clothes except for her House of Pancakes uniform and that kimono.

Sometime yesterday Orlon had convinced her to shave herself, and now her crotch was as slick as his. She still had her mane of blond hair, but Ray wouldn't be surprised to find her bald any minute now. Man, it was time to send this one back to the dumb-blonde factory, solder in some fresh silicone chips, have the technicians dial back her nymphomania a few notches. The two of them, Betty and Orlon, were rubbing their parts together so much they were becoming a goddamn fire hazard.

Still staring at Betty's rear, Patrick said, "And the West Indian manatee?"

"Yes, sir," Ray said. "We've captured one of the last two thousand in existence down there in Key Largo. That one's a male, I believe."

"No, it's a female," Orlon said. "Pregnant female manatee."

Orlon rearranged his balls inside his pajama bottoms. Ray was feeling a little foolish doing business with both of them sitting there in matching knee-length pj's. Green-and-red candystriped patterns on a white background. The pajamas were one of Ray's Christmas presents to Orlon last year. He always gave Orlon practical things, socks and underwear, even though Orlon inevitably groaned and fussed when he opened the boxes.

Ray said, "So that'll be seventeen thousand dollars on the girl manatee. Twelve grand for the boy—that is, when our lady friend down there catches the male. But that shouldn't take too long. The idiots swim right up to her dock every day for lettuce and a drink from her hose, so it's just a matter of picking which manatee looks right, lure it over into the cage."

"And that brings us up to two hundred and forty-one thousand dollars," Orlon said, scratching on his yellow legal pad. "Not including shipping costs."

"Tell me something," Patrick said. "Just where in

hell do you come up with these amounts? You pull them from the air?"

"We're professionals," Ray said. "This is our stock-in-trade. We know the numbers. We know value. That's why you're working with us."

"The reason I'm working with you," Patrick said, "is because I was convinced that you were capable of delivering the animals I wanted, protected or not. Legal or illegal."

"Yeah, and *who* was that anyway? I never do remember you mentioning who referred you to us."

Betty turned over, fluffed the couch pillow, and lay herself out flat for all to see, giving a little halfhearted tug on the bottom of the kimono, but it rode right back up, showing everything, her new hairless self. Patrick shook his head in distaste, but couldn't seem to pull his gaze away.

Ray locked his eyes on Betty's, giving her an ugly stare, though it didn't seem to have any effect.

Patrick cleared his throat and Ray looked his way. The man gave Ray a hollow smile and said, "You *were* planning to subtract one hundred thousand for my share of the orangutans, weren't you, boys?"

Orlon looked over at Ray, waiting for him to jump in, say something about having that incriminating photo. But Ray just gave his brother a little head shake and looked away. No, this was not a situation for kryptonite.

"Sure, we hadn't forgot about that," Ray said. Orlon coughed loudly, and out of Ray's peripheral vision he saw him shifting around in his chair, but Ray didn't look over, just kept smiling at their esteemed colleague.

Patrick got back to his list and they ran through the rest of it. Roseate tern, wood stork, ivory-billed woodpecker, Bachman's warbler, Kirtland's warbler, Cape Sable seaside sparrow, condor, bald eagle, sandhill crane, whooping crane, blue-tailed mole skink, sand skink, American croc and alligator, loggerhead turtle, leatherback turtle, gray bat, Florida panther.

Ray said, "I told you last time, that damn Florida

panther is going to be a bitch. Maybe impossible. We deal with a lot of trappers around the state, and I can tell you, there aren't any of them willing to go out there in the Everglades and trap one of those big cats, risk spending the next sixty years eating jail slop. Fish and Wildlife guys are big-time serious about panthers.

"Hell, they even got video cameras set up in the underpasses out in the Everglades, those things running twenty-four hours a day, so if a panther crosses from one side of the highway to the other, it's gotta go through that underpass, and its picture is on that film. Those guys know where just about every last one of them is, got agents out watching all the time. Some of the panthers even have transmitter implants sending out radio signals."

"Once again," Patrick said, like he hadn't been listening. "I want the male and the female. If you can't manage it, let me know now and I'll use one of my other people to do it. You don't think you're the only ones working for me, do you?"

"Hell, we can do it," Orlon said. "No sweat. Rayon's just a goddamn mother-hen worrywart. Haven't we got you everything else you wanted? Those Sumatra rhinos, for chrissake. Shit, anything you can name, we can get you."

"Little blue macaw."

Ray looked at his copy of the list, ran his finger down it.

"This a new addition?"

"Yes," Patrick said. "My bird people tell me there are only a few individuals left. On the edge of extinction."

"Where's it from?"

"Northeast Brazil."

"Jesus," Ray said. "We know anybody in Brazil, Orlon?"

"Not at the moment."

"Can you do it or not?"

"Little blue macaw," Ray said. "Yeah, yeah, sure. We'll get on the phone, talk to our Latin associates. No problem."

"All right, then," Patrick said. "That leaves us with only the unfinished business from our last meeting."

"What?" Orlon said. "Our little jungle soiree?"

Ray took a breath and looked down at the coffee table.

"But before we talk, we need to get rid of her." Patrick waved at Betty, lying there on her back, pillow over her face, making a snoring sound.

"Oh, don't worry about her," Orlon said. "She's deaf and dumb. She can't even read lips."

Patrick glanced at Ray, but Ray kept his face neutral. "Deaf and dumb?"

"That's right. Lost her hearing as a kid, poor thing. Had a hippie mother took her along to too many rock concerts."

Patrick scowled at Orlon, then reached into his pants pocket and came out with a pearl-handled .25, fit-in-your-palm special.

Ray stood up.

"Hey, man. None of that bullshit. Put that fucking thing away."

Patrick aimed the .25 up at the popcorn ceiling.

"Deaf and dumb?" he said.

"Hell," Orlon said. "Go on, test her out, see for yourself."

"Put it away," Ray said. "Put the thing down, right now."

Patrick looked at Ray, hesitated a moment, his hand wavering. Finally, his expression hardened, and he fired the pistol.

A large chunk of plaster crashed onto the rug. Ray jumped to the side, but Betty didn't so much as juke a muscle. Probably so zonked from her days of sex with Orlon that she was in some kind of subterranean alpha state.

"See," Orlon said, smiling. "Like I said, if you got things to discuss, then go right on and discuss them."

"And no more goddamn gunfire in our house. You got that?" Ray took his seat again.

Patrick slid the pistol back into his pants pocket.

"Jesus Christ." Ray stared up at the gash in the ceiling. "Mary, mother of Christ. What kind of crazy fucking person are you, shooting a gun off like that in a civilized person's house?"

Patrick washed his hands against each other, then set them in his lap. Untroubled, he looked over at Ray.

"I want to know why she's still alive."

"We're picking our moment," Orlon said. "You can't just go do the last tango on somebody willy-nilly."

"It's next on our list," Ray said. "Don't worry. Top priority."

"I don't know what the fucking hurry is," Orlon said. "If the woman had seen it was us over there in Borneo, the police would've been at the door already. She didn't see us, that's pretty clear."

"Don't worry, Patrick. We're doing her. Tomorrow."

Patrick slid his cold eyes slowly to Ray. The man had an aura about him. Gave off a spooky heat that Ray had only felt once or twice before. Like charisma, or whatever the hell it was called. Dominant dog in the pack. Eyes that could harden into black ice. The kind of guy, if you had a hundred just like him, you could set yourself up as a dictator of some little island country, rule forever.

Staring back into those empty eyes, Ray said, "That's the real reason we were over there in the first place, isn't it, in Borneo? You dragged me and my brother off the rhino hunt just to shoot that lady. You damn well knew she was going to be there. That's what it was all about. You didn't care about hunting any orangutans over there. That was just your cover story. What you were doing, you were trying to get us to do your dirty work."

Patrick smiled.

Ray had wrestled with the issue for days. Why the hell Patrick wanted to go hunt orangs. Then a second ago, all of a sudden he understood it, in a flash. Seeing what had happened, him and Orlon getting snookered into this situation.

"Well, it certainly took you long enough to figure it out."

"What I want to know is, why?" Ray said. "Why do you personally give a flying fuck about Allison Farleigh?"

"It came to my attention," he said, "that she was attempting to put you two in jail. And, you see, if that happened, where would I get these difficult-to-locate animals?"

"Bullshit," Ray said.

"Yeah, double that. Two bullshits," Orlon said.

Ray said, "You don't care if the White brothers go to jail or not. You just said you had other people working for you. They could pick up the slack easy enough. You wanted her dead for your own personal reasons."

"Is that right, Ray? Then tell me, why don't you. What were my real reasons?"

Ray swallowed a breath of air, let it out.

"Maybe you were worried, since she'd gotten interested in us, she might stumble across your name along the way, find out what the hell you're up to. And you're the kind of guy goes around in nice, fresh clothes, manicured nails, kind that doesn't like fecal matter splattered on your white suede shoes. So the woman had to die. That's it, isn't it? She was getting close to us, and you started feeling a bull's-eye growing on your forehead."

Patrick's lips formed a razor-thin smile.

"Let's put it this way," he said. "In my part of the world, a man of my stature does not associate with people like the White brothers. It would not enhance his career possibilities."

"If you'd just told us the truth, we would've disposed of Allison right here in Miami. I don't get it, why we had to go over there to do it."

Patrick leaned forward, gave Ray a careful look.

"Let me ask you something, Ray. You're a smart man. Now, here's a woman who is a threat to your careers, yet you did nothing about her. If I hadn't motivated you, would you have ever thought of removing that woman on your own?"

"Maybe," he said. "Maybe not. I didn't think she was that much of a threat. I still don't."

"Well, there it is. That's exactly why I felt I had to commit my little subterfuge with you."

"And shooting the orangutans, that was just a bonus?"

"Exactly," Patrick said. "As long as we were there, why not?"

"Okay, okay, all right," Orlon said. "So we kill the bitch. Do this favor for you. What the hell's in it for us?"

Patrick kept on smiling, his eyes working on Ray.

"What's in it for you?"

"Yeah, that's right."

"My continued good cheer," Patrick said.

"His continued good cheer," Orlon said. "Oh, boy."

Ray had to pull his eyes away from the man's smile. Felt like he was being possessed.

"Allison's on our plate. We'll clean her up for you. You don't have to worry about fecal matter anymore."

"I'm glad to hear it, Ray. I'm very glad to hear it."

He turned his head and smiled at Orlon, then got up to go, making a sly move to his pocket, touching his .25 through his pants, a little reminder.

"And I don't want to hear another goddamn word about your problems acquiring these animals. If you don't start moving faster on the deliveries, I'll be forced to give the work out to those who can."

"Not to worry," Ray said. "Twenty years of animal dealing, we haven't had a dissatisfied customer yet."

"Tell the truth, Ray," Orlon said. "We *did* have a couple of dissatisfied customers, but they didn't live to talk about it."

Patrick studied Orlon for a moment. Inspecting him like he was searching for a fleshy spot where he could sink his teeth, take a deep guzzle of Orlon's blood.

"I have to tell you," Patrick said at the door. "You two will appreciate the irony of this."

"What irony is that?"

"Right now I'm going back to sleep with the daughter of the woman you are going to kill."

"What?"

"She's my lover now. Another youthful fantasy fulfilled."

Ray shook his head. Stared at this man in their doorway. Dark-haired with those bright blue eyes. Grinning at the White brothers like a man who'd just told a dirty joke.

"You murdered one daughter and you're screwing the other?"

"Crudely put, but correct."

Orlon smiled.

"Man, I like this guy. He's got the morals of Cagney in *White Heat.* One sadistic son of a bitch."

"Good night, gentlemen. I expect the animals within a week."

Ray shut the front door behind Patrick, and he and Orlon went back into the living room. Betty pushed the pillow off her face and sat up.

"Holy shit," she said. "You guys are killers?"

"Not as a full-time activity, no," Ray said.

"Mainly we specialize in animals," Orlon said. "But humans seem to be the new cash crop."

Orlon sat down on the red-and-black Ralph Lauren couch, Ray sat across from him on a matching chair.

Betty said, "You all see what's going on here, don't you?"

They both looked over at her.

"I mean that story he gave you, that's a load of bullshit."

"Hey, Orlon. Take her upstairs, shut her in a closet, would you? Nail it shut."

Betty said, "You didn't manage to kill this Allison person over there in the jungle, right?"

"Yeah," Orlon said. "That's right. Her daughter got herself killed, but the mother escaped."

"Okay," Betty said, sitting up now, tightening the belt on her kimono, crossing her legs carefully, looking almost prim. "So what would've happened, do you think, if you'd actually killed her?"

"Nothing would've happened," Orlon said. "She'd've been dead, is all."

Ray was staring at her, all at once getting a glimpse of where she was headed. He felt the hairs rise on his neck, his arms. Hairs standing straight up. His questions getting answered, the ones he'd only been half asking himself.

Betty said, "If this guy's so concerned about his goddamn reputation, you think he's going to go out there in the jungle with you guys, kill a few women, then just let you walk away, the both of you knowing what transpired? He the kind of guy to trust that none of it'll ever come back to haunt him?"

"She's right," Ray said.

Betty said, "He was going to kill you guys. Except this Allison lady got away and then he thought better of it. Thought he should keep you alive, have you finish up the job, get you to murder her back in Miami, then he'll either turn you in to the cops or whack you himself. That's how I read the guy."

"She's right," said Ray. Hair on his arms trying to pull free, get the hell out of there. "We're in a flood of shit."

"He's not going to kill us," Orlon said. "He needs us."

"No, he doesn't," Betty said. "You heard him. There's plenty of people providing him with all those animals he wants. You guys are disposable."

"Christ, Betty," Ray said. "I didn't know you were so smart."

Betty smiled at the two of them, first Ray, then Orlon.

"Sure I'm smart, hon. Why else would I have picked your brother from all the other morons hitting on me?"

Orlon didn't smile. He stepped over in front of her.

"Why don't you go upstairs, get your clothes, Betty, go on back where you came from."

"What?"

"You heard me," Orlon said. "I'm tired of you. Get out."

"Is he kidding with me?" She was looking at Ray.

"No, I'm afraid he isn't," Ray said. "He's got a thing about women who're smarter than he is. They scare him."

"Well, hell," she said, standing up. "That narrows down the field considerably, doesn't it?"

"Get out of here, Betty," Orlon said. "Go on back to the pancake house, sit on the griddle and cool your butt off."

"Sorry," Ray said. "He gets like this."

"No problem." She started for the stairs. "Hell, I was starting to feel my IQ slip into the single digits from being around the guy."

Betty left, and Orlon sat down on the couch across from Ray and stared up at the ceiling and listened as she started to bang around up there.

"Shit," he said. "I was just getting to like the bitch."

Upstairs Betty slammed a door. Some glass broke.

Quietly Orlon said, "Now I got to put her under."

"What?"

"She knows who we are, man, what we do. We can't let her go waltzing out of here. The only question is, do I do the job upstairs or down here?"

"Oh, Jesus."

Orlon stood up. He brushed his right hand against his pajama leg like he was dusting it off, eyes on the ceiling.

"You just stay put, Ray. Watch some TV. Don't worry yourself. I'll handle the dirty work, as usual."

When Orlon had rounded the corner and was on the stairs, Ray found the TV zapper and switched the set on. The VCR too. And there was the tail end of the movie Orlon had been watching the other night. Humphrey Bogart still playing a gangster, up in the rocks having a shoot-out with the hick cops. Humphrey grimacing, firing his big tommy gun until it was empty and then throwing it down at the advancing men, and pulling out a six-shooter. Bullets zinging off the rocks around him.

Ray pointed the zapper and cranked the sound all the way up. Made it so loud there was nothing in his head but that noise. The *pop pop pop* of Hollywood guns. Humphrey firing slow and methodical. One, two, three, four, five, and six. Then standing up from behind the rock and hurling that pistol down at the posse. Snarling at the men, he catches a bullet in his chest, another one in the shoulder, and another one and one after that. Thrown to the side against a boulder, lying there, but still not dead, eyes open, his grimace getting meaner as more bullets strike him.

Ray watched Bogart's last seconds alive, his body shredded by lead. Ray was intent on the TV screen, on the racket coming from the set. Getting a little glimpse of what it must be like to be Orlon, feeling that movie replacing everything in Ray's head for those few minutes, squeezing out all the rest of it like a headache so brutal it wouldn't let you think.

# C H A P T E R

# 22

At six-thirty on Thursday morning, when she came out of the bedroom, Allison found Thorn sitting on the couch, reading one of the old newsletters. They exchanged good mornings and she went into the kitchen, made coffee. When it was ready, she and Thorn walked out to the porch, sat in the Adirondack chairs and faced the sunrise.

Discreetly she palmed the Zippo from the side table, slid it into the pocket of her faded gray jeans. She'd put on a long-sleeved cotton polo shirt, pumpkin colored, collar turned up, an old thing, soft and shapeless from a hundred washings. The right color for today, a tone that would blend with the parched browns and grays of the autumn Everglades, camouflage her approach. A pair of dirty Adidas tennis shoes, her black-framed aviator sunglasses propped up in her hair. No jewelry, nothing to catch the sun and flash a warning.

When her coffee grew cool, she set it aside and cleared her throat. Thorn looked over, and Allison began to explain what she wanted to do, the plan she'd conceived in the long empty hours last night. He listened without interrupting, nodding his head as she finished.

"A tea party," Thorn said. "Invite them over, everybody sits down, we all have a nice cup of chamomile and the White brothers just spill their guts."

She gave him a stern look.

"Look, Thorn, I need to be absolutely sure it was them, hear it from their own mouths. And I have to un- derstand why it happened. Why Winslow had to die."

"These guys aren't tea sippers, Allison."

"If we have the upper hand, I think we can convince them to tell us. Make a deal with them. We want their boss. We want to know what's going on. They can walk, as far as I'm concerned. They're nothing. Without some- body propping those two up, they'll turn into the same losers they were a year ago."

"The upper hand," he said. "What does that mean exactly? That I hold the Remington? That's how you see it?"

"Yes."

"And what if they struggle? What if it's not neat?"

She gazed out to the south, at the hammock of pines and cypress. A lone snowy egret was fastened to the high branches of one of the pines like some rare flower that had shut its petals.

"Well, anyway, one thing's for damn sure," Thorn said. "They're not very smart. I mean, if they fell for my vet impersonation, how sharp could they be?"

"I'm counting on that."

They watched a large red-shouldered hawk coast in and land nearby in the naked branches of a slash pine. Three kestrels followed it, and began dive-bombing the big bird, but it held its place and seemed to ignore their cries.

"And this guy Crotch Meriwether, you're sure he'll help?"

"He might, if I put it to him the right way."

"Crotch?" Thorn said. "That's the guy's real name?"

"It's the only name I've ever heard," Allison said.

"Crotch like in *crotchety*?"

Allison glanced over at him.

"Think lower," she said. "Below the belt."

"Oh."

"I understand he was considered a lady's man in his

younger days. I suppose that's where he got the name.
Though now that he's in his seventies, *crotchety* might fit
better."

For the first few years after moving her headquarters
to the Shack, Allison had been full of self-congratulation
for living in such isolation. She thought she'd penetrated
as deeply into the rich secret heart of the wilderness as it
was possible to go. Then she met Meriwether, a man who
had hacked his way far deeper, living as remote from human contact as was possible to get in the state of Florida.
And it was not just the miles themselves that separated
him from civilization, it was the nearly impenetrable tangle of vegetation that filled those miles. His isolation was
absolute. Any ordinary person trying to locate Meriwether's cabin would have to take along a week's provisions, a half dozen sharp machetes, a stack of snakebite
kits, and leave a thick trail of inedible bread crumbs going
in.

"Oh, yeah, Winslow told me about this one. The guy
you put in Raiford. Your first big win."

She mumbled in the affirmative.

"Mr. Extinction."

"That's right."

"Almost single-handedly responsible for eliminating
half a dozen species."

"Well, not quite that many."

Thorn stood up. He studied the kestrels hounding
the hawk. His work shirt was badly rumpled, hair un-
combed.

"This the same guy wrote you the postcards? Described in detail what he was going to do to you?"

"I didn't realize Winslow knew about it."

"Why him, Allison? The man hates you. He's not
going to cooperate, help you trap the White brothers."

"That's exactly the point, Thorn. He's the last person
they'd suspect of collaborating with me. They'll never see
it coming if it comes from Crotch Meriwether."

"But why would he help you?"

"I have reason to believe he may hate the White brothers even more than he hates me."

The hawk opened its wings, lifted up off the branch, then settled back in the same roost, shooing away the pestering birds. Looking very stately up there, surveying the distances. But the smaller birds weren't giving up, determined to drive this predator out of their feeding area. Diving, squawking.

"Now, look, Thorn," she said. "I'm going to have to do this first part alone. You can wait here till I get back."

"Hell with that."

"If it's just me, unarmed, coming into Meriwether's territory, very submissive, nothing will happen. But if he sees a man with me, it'll threaten him, get his blood going."

"This is a man who promised to kill you, Allison."

"That was a long time ago. I haven't heard from him in years. It's all cooled down by now, I'm sure it has."

"I'm going." He took a couple of steps forward, and put her in his shadow.

"No," she said. "I'm sorry, Thorn. But this is my problem."

"I'll make it easy for you, Allison." He looked out at the gathering daylight, the hum of the Everglades beginning to rise. "Either I go with you, or you don't go at all."

She gave him a long look, shrugged, then went back inside. She washed the coffee cups and plates from last night. Thorn used the bathroom, came out whistling a Beatles song. She had to work for a moment to remember its name. "Hey, Jude."

Hands in the dishwater, she lifted her head to listen to the tune, a dizzy sensation sweeping through her, feeling ancient and youthful at once. She watched Thorn walk onto the porch, whistling his simple-hearted song out at the wilderness.

Allison finished the dishes, and while Thorn waited for her at the Jeep, she put paper in the fax machine. She shut the front door, locked it, and as she was stepping off

the porch she heard the machine begin to crank out its
first stored message.

Thorn and Allison sped through the grassy marsh-
lands of the Everglades, water gleaming in all directions,
unusually high for this time of year, catching the reflection
of the slow-moving stratus clouds. It brimmed to the highway in places, and Allison could see her Cherokee rippling along, the aluminum jon boat lashed to the roof
rack.

She told Thorn what she knew about Meriwether. A
trapper for fifty years: gators, ratsnakes and rattlers, crocs.
He sold the hides to Texas boot makers, the meat to some
north Florida restaurants, and he even located a ghoulish
tourist shop that would pay him for each cleaned-up gator
skull.

Over the years Crotch had also served time as a commercial fisherman, stone crabber, charter boat captain,
and full-time drunk. Twenty years ago, when the pom-
pano and mullet started thinning out, and the crab and
lobster and shrimp supplies were nearly depleted, Crotch
had even taken a turn at smuggling pot.

But mainly he was a hunter. He'd been shooting cur-
lew for fifty years, ibis, spoonbills, even confessed to Allison that he'd killed manatees a few times, lured them to
the surface and shotgunned them. Killed them and grilled
them. Told her they tasted somewhere between pork and
beef.

"Jesus," Thorn said. "Manatee."

Allison looked out her window at the ghostly replica
of her Jeep traveling along beside them in the dark water.

"On the one hand, Crotch is a low-life trafficker in
illegal game, pelts, meat, even skulls. He's a poacher with
no regard for bag limits, or harvesting bans. He knows
which animals are protected and which aren't, but he
doesn't give a damn. He's been going into the park for
forty years, taking whatever game he wants. He's shot at
wildlife officers, set fires to keep his favorite deer-hunting
areas clear. The man's an outlaw, pure and simple.

"But on the other hand, you could argue that he's nothing more than an old coot who's simply behaving exactly as he always has, living a tough life, surviving off the land. Only problem is, the land got fragile all around him."

"Well," Thorn said. "Maybe he's one of the reasons it got so fragile."

"True, true."

"Sounds like you approve of the guy."

"I don't know. I guess I do feel somewhat kindly toward him now. I understand him better now than I did seven years ago. And somehow he's just not as bad as the young ones. The ones who should know better. The ones who could go into any business."

"He ate manatee, for chrissake."

"It was to survive, Thorn."

"That's probably the same thing the White brothers and Joshua Bond and all the other ones say. They're just trying to survive."

"It's different."

She shook her head, kept her eyes on the road, and was silent.

"Living off the land is one thing," Thorn said. "Ripping off the land is another."

Allison cut a look his way, saw the clench of his jaw. She looked back at the road, into the rearview mirror, and slowed to let a transfer truck blow past.

"Crotch was a pioneer," she said. "His only problem is he's lived a few years too long."

"You put him in jail. He made threats on your life. But you don't hate him."

She watched three great white herons drift low over a distant mahogany hammock. Wing tip to wing tip, they cruised like a squadron of angels coming down to escort another soul from this mortal plain.

"Thirty years ago," she said, "when I was a kid, Crotch Meriwether used to go to the Shack and take the Ravenel men hunting—my father, my uncles. I remember seeing pictures of him in my family album, a tall, sunken-faced man with long dark hair standing in the background looking shy. The other men were all excited, flushed and smiling, gathered around the kill. But I could see who the real hunter was from looking at his eyes. How serious he was, how intent, staring awkwardly into the camera.

"Then when I began the protection league, started looking around for bad guys to go after, Crotch occurred to me. I found out where he lived from some of the Miccosukees who knew Julius. I trekked out to his house. Because of who I was, Crotch trusted me. It took some wheedling, but I got him to agree to sell me a dozen gator skins. They were on the federal endangered list at the time.

"A few weeks later I came back to his place all wired up, and I got the whole transaction on tape. After that I only saw him once more, his afternoon in court. He wouldn't look at me.

"But now, from this vantage point, when I think about what I did, using his loyalty to my father like that to trap him, I feel guilty as hell. I betrayed a friendship and a trust Julius had worked hard to build. My father was a wealthy man, and the Crotch Meriwethers of the world usually stayed clear of men like him. But Meriwether and my dad got to respect each other. There was a kinship. I could tell from the way my father used to talk about him, and I could hear it in Crotch's voice when he recollected my dad that first time we met.

"So yeah, it's true, when he was in Raiford he threatened me, and I believe he meant it. But looking back on who I was back then, the hurt I must have given that man, threatening to kill me seems like a reasonable thing. Maybe even an honorable thing."

"Oh, come on."

"And think about it," Allison said, giving Thorn a difficult smile. "If he'd actually succeeded, Winslow would be alive today."

Fifty years back, Crotch Meriwether hauled the coral stones out into the saw grass marsh by shrimp trawler, making the arduous trip from Everglades City, navigating across the dangerous oyster beds of the Ten Thousand Islands, going up Chatham River till he ran aground and could go no further. Then he and his mules would slog the last twenty miles through streams and sloughs, water to his hips. Mosquitoes so thick, he had to breathe through a handkerchief.

He built his stone house big, like a national monument to hermits. One very large room, probably six hundred feet square. Tall windows placed high on the walls, rough cedar floors. And in the dead center of all that open space was a magnificent spiral stairway that twirled up to a loft where Crotch kept his cot. He'd salvaged the iron stairway from the debris of the Cape Hendry lighthouse after the hurricane of '36 reduced it to rubble. And now, more than fifty years later, that polished metal still gave off the faint glow of long-gone craftsmanship.

On Allison's first visit, the place had revolted her. It was an oppressive and tawdry museum of the trapper's trade, and going inside the house was as abhorrent to her as if she'd entered the unholiest inner sanctum of Lucifer himself.

The walls were covered with gator skins and the pelts of deer and raccoons, bears, panthers, and nearly every snake that flourished in those parts. There were skulls, too, and a few trophy heads, a wild boar, a bear cub, an eight-point buck. He'd also hung up his collection of vicious, sharp-toothed traps. And there were boiling tubs, awls and scoops and ladles and needles, the sinister gadgets he used in the crude surgery of animal skinning. She remembered the air in that big room, choked with carbolic acid and the stench of decaying fur.

And she recalled vividly his assortment of pistols and rifles, his array of knives, and his prized collection of hand-forged, razor-edged machetes.

# CHAPTER

# 23

Fifteen miles past Monroe Station, Allison wheeled off Tamiami Trail and circled behind an abandoned souvenir shop. She headed south along a narrow gravel road, and fifty yards from the highway, behind the gutted remnants of a storage shed, she located the jeep trail the park service maintained for their firefighters. She swung onto it, heading now into the heartland of the Glades. She shifted into four-wheel drive and bumped across the ditches and potholes, hard-packed corrugated stretches, keeping them moving steadily south. Branches clawed at the sides of the Cherokee, the dense canopy putting them in a dusty twilight, continuing for three quarters of an hour, till the road dead-ended at a thicket of vines, mahogany, and fiddlewood.

They got out, unloaded the jon boat, sprayed each other front and back with insect repellent, then lifted the aluminum skiff above their heads, Allison in front, and began to portage into the dense tangle of branches. She held to a southerly course, fighting through the lashing branches, the snarls of vine and thick spiderwebs. Around them the trunks of the trees were covered with peeling gray lichens, their branches decorated with bromeliads, Virginia creepers, bright yellow snails, and an occasional cottonmouth.

Silently, Thorn took more than his half of the jon

boat's weight. Along the trail, limestone outcroppings alternated with mushy earth, making every step a new adjustment. Allison stumbled over the marl and rocks; still, she managed to keep a brisk pace, Thorn breathing quietly behind her.

Though it was early still, nine-thirty, in only an hour or two, when the sun was higher, the air would clot with humidity and every movement would cost twice as much effort. It was punishing enough now, but the return trip would be hellish.

They forded small streams flowing dark with tannin-stained water. They struggled across brackish marshes that opened up to the enormous sky, splashing through water to their ankles, the noise of their approach flushing cormorants and great white herons, causing redbelly turtles to dive for cover.

On the high ground alongside another marsh, they rested briefly and watched a reddish egret standing a few feet away, poised, its neck cocked like a drawn bow, its huge wings spread to throw a shadow across the surface of the water so it could better select its prey. They waited until it struck, coming out of the water with a small bluegill in its beak.

"So you know where we are?"

"Roughly," she said.

"Roughly?" Thorn smiled through his sweat. "How roughly?"

"We're about ninety miles north of Cuba."

"Well, good," Thorn said. "As long as we're not lost."

By eleven the invisible steam had begun to rise around them. Breathe too hard and fast, you could drown in that air. Allison halted on the bank of a narrow creek. They set the jon boat down. Thorn wiped the sweat from his face. Allison sprayed more repellent into her hands, bathed it across her cheeks and forehead, coated her ears. She offered the can to Thorn but he waved it off.

"From here, it's just another three or four miles. Down that way."

She motioned at the creek. A hundred yards downstream it doglegged to the right and disappeared into a dark mesh of mangroves and loblollies.

"Is it passable?"

"It was the last time I was here. Barely."

"Seven years ago."

She nodded.

Thorn poled the jon boat for half an hour, sliding them across the clear, still water. The twisty creek was nearly blocked with mangroves at several spots, branches whacking them in the face as they snaked around bends. Twice they were forced to tip the skiff halfway out of the water to wedge through narrow passages.

"You did this by yourself last time," Thorn said.

"That's right."

"And you could manage it this time too. You don't need me."

She looked at his smile, half serious.

"I could manage," she said. "But I don't mind the company."

The silence was a solemn weight in the air, as though some great suppressing presence was stalking in the nearby woods, and all the noisy creatures were aware of him and had stifled themselves, hunkering down till he passed. Not even a single gator floated in the stream, none along the banks.

With her jeans soaked to the knees, the Ace bandage on her ankle turned to a soggy mess. She peeled it off, used it as a pad as she kneeled in the front of the boat. Thorn poled from the rear, leaning his weight into the long fiberglass rod, sweating profusely, only the deep rasp of his breath audible now. Allison stayed low in the bow, parrying the swipes of twigs and limbs.

At the tributaries, the current boiled. Big fish hung under shadowy crags. Off to the east she caught glimpses through the mangroves and stunted oaks of the wide, sunny prairie beyond. Thorn groaned softly with each thrust of the pole. No doubt his hands were blistered, his back stiffening up. They crept deeper into the Glades, and with each mile the gloomy silence hardened around them.

Several times they lost their way in the maze of islands and diverging streams, coming around the same bend, seeing the same lightning-scorched pine three different times. It was almost noon when they emerged into a small pond surrounded by sabal palms and palmetto, a thick stand of saw grass, and Allison sighed and pronounced that they'd arrived.

Twenty yards south of the pond, the back side of Meriwether's great stone house was barely visible behind a dense stand of mahogany and magnolia, cabbage palms and shrubs of every kind.

Thorn waded through the water, hauling the skiff onto high ground, peering at the house as he worked. Allison sat down beside the boat and massaged her aching ankle.

"Intriguing architecture," Thorn said. "Early crematorium."

"Unfortunately, Mr. Meriwether is not at home."

"How do you know?"

"He would have been out here by now. In fact, I've been expecting him to appear any second for the last half hour. I don't know what his technique is, but he's got some kind of brain-wave radar, anyone comes poling down Matheson Creek like we did, Crotch Meriwether knows about it miles upstream."

"He's probably out slaughtering a few manatees for supper."

Allison sat down on the overturned jon boat and scanned the surrounding woods. Something wasn't right. The silence that had followed them downstream was now a freakish hush. No bird calls, no rattle of underbrush, no heavy flap of wing. Not even a pulse of wind to stir the dry leaves. It was beginning to unnerve her. Beginning to make her doubt her plan, the whole misguided day.

When it happened, Allison was lost in the layers of her meditation, but somehow she heard it all, every brutal nuance, and could replay the moment, parse it into microseconds, each awful sound. The groan of a man straining, a blade's quiet whistle as it sliced the air in half, the nauseating crunch of human flesh and bone, followed instantly by the whanging double note of a whipsaw. And in the second it took to swing around, Allison felt all her confidence collapse, a frail old building imploding inside her, falling into itself, dust and chaos.

Somehow Crotch Meriwether had materialized from the open field and clubbed Thorn to the ground, and now as Allison whirled and screamed, the tall man raised his bright machete over Thorn's fallen body for a second blow.

Thorn lay facedown in the grass, the tall man's brogan planted squarely on the back of his neck. Though his face was smashed sideways into the dirt and weeds, Thorn managed to bark out a muffled threat as he clawed the ground, trying to push himself up.

Before Allison could rise, Meriwether chopped the machete down, a glancing blow against the side of Thorn's skull. Blood erupted through his thick blond hair, and began to leak down his right cheek. His body went limp.

Meriwether hopped back from him, glared across at Allison, and held up the long blade and twisted it in the light to show her he'd used the flat, unsharpened side.

"Don't want to dull my blade just yet," he said, and smiled at her. "Might need it later."

Allison wailed, and hurled herself at the man, but he dodged a half step to his left, snapped out a bony forearm and cracked her across the bridge of her nose.

She staggered backward, her head thrown up, face tilted to the sky, and she watched an asteroid shower explode, bright crimson comets etched against the black heavens. Then her body tottered, and she felt herself step forward off a ledge. And she dropped—a slow, pleasant free fall through miles of empty space.

Thursday, Orlon and Rayon slept late. It wasn't till eleven that they arrived at the warehouse. Wearing matching Nike warm-ups, Orlon in dark blue, Ray in white with red striping. While Ray unlocked the office door, Orlon stood behind him, buzzing his cordless razor over his slick head, scraping away some last neurotic stubble.

Ray got the door open and stepped a foot inside the front office, and stopped short. Speechless, he stared at the overturned desk, the shattered computer, fluorescent lights dangling, shelves pulled over, books and magazines and papers strewn everywhere, an electric sputter coming from somewhere. Then he saw the snakes. Goddamn snakes slithering through all the debris.

For a moment he thought he should go back outside, shut the door, take a deep breath, open it again and maybe everything would be back in place.

"Would you fucking look at this," Orlon said. "The entire Mormon Tabernacle Choir's been in here having an orgy."

Ray stepped over the broken watercooler, took a look down the hallway toward the warehouse. Back there, standing in a swath of sunlight, he saw the orangutan squatting over some papers on the floor, taking a dump.

Orlon banged his razor down, pushed past Ray, stalked down the hall, grabbed the ape by the scruff of the neck, hauled it over to its cage and flung it inside. He told Ray he was gonna kill the damn thing, throw one of the diamondbacks or the mamba into its cage, see which one came out alive. Look what the little bastard did, all the iguanas loose, the snakes going crazy feeding on all those white mice. Little dabs of white scrabbling everywhere.

"That ape is worth forty thousand bucks. You aren't going to kill it, man."

"So deduct it from my next paycheck, 'cause I'm strangling the little son of a bitch right now."

"We don't even know he did this."

"Hey, Rayon, look around you, the place is locked up tight. You don't see any windows broken, do you? The alarm's not ringing. And right over there, the ape's cage is standing wide open. Who you think did it? The mice? The fucking iguanas?"

"Cool down, now. Your blood pressure's about to detonate out your ears."

Orlon stayed put, kept glaring in at the ape.

"Listen," Ray said, "why don't you go over to the airport, see about the Bangkok shipment. It was supposed to be in last night. Calm yourself down, and I'll straighten up around here."

Orlon cursed the ape a couple more times, bringing his face close to the bars, the orangutan rolling over on its back, kicking its feet playfully at Orlon.

"Go on, man. When you get back, things'll be normal again."

Orlon stalked off toward the front door, muttering to himself as he went.

The shipment at the airport was nothing major. Just some animals they'd ordered a few weeks back, unrelated to the exotic ones they were assembling for Patrick. It was Ray's idea, invest some of that extra loot they'd been making lately to build up their stock. Made smart business sense. Don't let all this cash slide through their fingers.

Back in September they'd faxed their man in Bangkok a list of legal things they wanted, mainly snakes, some turtles, tarantulas, and toads. Though the unwritten agreement was that the guy would ship an extra surprise or two that wasn't listed on the shipping receipt—then bill them a few weeks later by fax.

That's how they did it sometimes, showing up to take charge of a legitimate order, lizards, iguanas, then if the Fish and Wildlife turdbrains were there holding the shipment, ready to throw them in jail for the illegal macaques or chimp or baby gibbons in the same crate, Ray and Orlon would get all shocked. "What the hell? We didn't order that. That's an endangered, illegal animal protected by international treaty. This is obviously some kind of stupid fuckup, that asshole in Bangkok can't read goddamn English. I mean, hey, officer, you see a chimp or a macaque on the shipping manifest anywhere? On our order forms? No? Well, see, there you go, it's that fucking guy in Bangkok did this, not us."

"Yeah," the wildlife guy would say. "That same ass-hole in Bangkok made that same mistake last month and the month before that and before that. His English isn't getting any better."

But what the hell could they do? Oh, yeah, sure, they'd confiscate the animal, register another complaint against the White brothers, but if they tried to make a case out of it, the state's attorney would drop it in a half second. Why bother a couple of legitimate entrepreneurs just because some illiterate Asian twelve thousand miles away screwed up?

While Orlon was away at the airport, Ray attacked the mess. He set things upright. Swept up the broken glass. Then he spent a while just locating all the animals, snatching them up, dumping them back in their pens. An hour into it, he found a couple of cobras burrowed be-hind the bathroom wallboard, already starting to build nests out of the insulation.

By one-thirty the stuff that wasn't broken was back in its place, the other shit was out in the Dumpster. Ray went back to see the orangutan, and right away the little hair ball started peeping, all excited. Ray unlocked his cage, and before he could stop him, the ape pulled himself up into Ray's arms, and glued its wet mouth to his face. He gripped Ray's head so hard, hugging him, Ray couldn't move. The ape sucked away, his tongue probing inside Ray's nostrils. Hell, if the thing decided to chew the nose right off his face, there wasn't much Ray could do about it, fucking ape was so strong.

Ray reached up and tickled the orangutan on its cheeks, under its arms, along the inside of its thighs, and finally the thing rolled its lips back, squealing, and broke its hold. Ray could feel his nose swelling from all that suction, but at least the ape had been careful not to draw blood.

Ray let the orangutan wander around while he made a phone call to a guy who lived on a ranch outside of West Palm. The guy said yeah, his boss was still interested in an orangutan, but he'd need to see the ape before any money changed positions.

"You want my address down here, where I'm located?"

The guy said no, Ray should come up to West Palm.

"And if your boss doesn't like my ape for some reason, I made a hundred mile trip for nothing."

"Hell, you'll get to meet Brad Randolph. Lot of people would drive more than a hundred miles for that."

"I'm not a movie fan," Ray said.

"Maybe you've seen him on the new Wheaties box."

"No," Ray said. "I'm not a breakfast person either. So, see, it'd still be a wasted fucking trip."

"Well, Mr. Randolph sure as hell isn't coming down to Miami to look over some ape. Maybe we should just forget this whole deal."

"I'll be there by four. I need directions."

"Give me your fax number, I'll zap 'em down."

"And remember, this is a cash transaction. Forty-five thou."

The guy paused a moment, then came back, his voice down an octave.

"Last time we talked you said forty."

"Since our last discussion the supply of orangutans has seriously dwindled. Add to that the fact that demand increased, so at this moment, the market value is forty-five."

The man was quiet on the line.

Ray loved negotiating with these civilians. Hell, even lifelong animal people didn't know from day to day what the damn beasts were worth. You couldn't flip open your Blue Book and run your finger down the page, find your year and model. That was one of the things he liked about this business. Every living creature on earth had a price tag on it. Somebody somewhere wanted it. Once you had your supply lines established—all those Indonesian hunters with their blowguns, their nets, the African spear hurlers, Georgia crackers driving down to snatch snakes out of the Everglades, El Paso boys gunning their four-wheel-

ers across the desert, scanning for Gila monsters—then all
Ray had to do was keep his inventory lists circulating in
the mail, and every day another buyer called the 800 number and the haggling started.

Ray watched the ape take hold of the handle of a file
cabinet. Carrying the aerial phone, Ray got up, went over,
and dragged the orangutan away, took him over to the
bathroom, flushed the toilet, got him interested in the
water swirling down the drain. The ape stuck his hand in
the water and chittered.

"Okay, Brad will go forty-five," the guy said. "But
don't come in here and tell us the supply dropped suddenly while you were driving up I-95. You got that?"

"Understood."

"You bring all the papers with you too."

"Papers?"

"Shots, and all that shit."

"Hey, whatta you think, this is some kind of docu-
mented legal alien? Like he's got a fucking green card?
Man, think again. This creature, just a week ago he was
hanging in the branches, shitting from two hundred feet
up."

"No papers?"

"That's right. But he's healthy. Smart, strong, a real
funny little critter. Burt should love him."

"Brad," the guy said.

"Yeah, yeah, Brad. Man on the Wheaties box."

"One other thing," the guy said. "Wear something
decent when you come. Mr. Randolph is getting married
this evening. He doesn't want a lot of slobs walking
around the premises. Is that clear?"

"What? Like a tux?"

"It's an Old West wedding theme. Related to the
movie he's making at the moment. Blue jeans, a plaid shirt
would do fine. Boots, if you have them. String tie, like
that."

"Come as a cattle rustler, you mean. Bring my branding iron."

"The wedding starts at sunset. Mr. Randolph will

only be able to see you for a few minutes. So be here promptly at four, or the whole thing's off. Is that clear?"

"Lucid as beer piss."

"And does the ape have anything to wear?"

"What?"

"You know—a cowboy getup, a little Stetson or whatever."

"Shit, no. It's got fur, is all. The thing's covered in it."

"It'd be cute, you know, if the thing was dressed up like the rest of the guests. See what I'm saying?"

"Then I guess you better go do some shopping, fella. Our animals don't come with wardrobes. They're naked. Every single one of them."

A few minutes later Ray got the fax with the directions and looked it over. He had an hour or two to kill before he went up there. Maybe he'd telephone Tricia, see if she was free, maybe she'd like to go for a drive, watch a movie star get married.

# C H A P T E R

# 24

Allison found herself lying on a hard pallet lodged in a shadowy corner of Meriwether's living room. The same stifling air that she remembered, a potent brew of solvents and sour animal fluids. She lifted her head and saw Crotch Meriwether across the room bent over a long workbench. In the open kitchen area a young Seminole girl stood at the chopping block. She was under twenty, possibly as young as fifteen. The girl was mincing onions with a heavy knife, glancing across at Allison every few seconds.

A gloomy twilight filled the room. It was lit only by the high windows that sent a half dozen planks of dull daylight across the wood floor. No electricity this far out, just one huge round candelabra suspended from the ceiling, a wagon wheel studded with unlit candles.

Thorn was nowhere in sight.

She lay her head back down and reached a hand up to her throbbing face and gingerly probed her nose. The cartilage felt mushy and crackled under her touch like pulpy gristle. Her nostrils were caked with blood. With a groan she sat up, put her feet on the floor.

"Your boyfriend's still alive," Meriwether said, hunched over the bench. "Didn't want to finish him off till I'd checked you over for wires and tape recorders."

Allison glanced down and saw her pants unzipped, the top button open.

"Where is he?"

She tugged her zipper up, slipped the button in its slot.

Crotch swung around and faced her. He wore gray dungarees, heavy black shoes, a tattered white T-shirt. His hair was drawn back into a long ponytail. Unnaturally youthful, it was black with a lacquered shine like the hair of an Iroquois warrior. His mouth was full of misshapen teeth, cheeks hollow, his humid eyes sunken even deeper into his skull than when last she'd seen him. His skin had turned to rancid wax. The diseased pallor of a man who'd spent a lifetime sucking greedily on unfiltered cigarettes.

His eyes, however, belonged to a different person. A clear, deep blue, they were lit with an intensity that seemed grotesquely unnatural in one so shriveled. As if the dregs of Crotch Meriwether's vast virility and drive had taken refuge there.

"Dermestid beetles," he said. "Ever see them work before?"

He held up a glass terrarium the size of a toaster. Inside it was a white oblong that she couldn't make out. Crotch came a step closer, held the glass case out into a dusty slant of daylight.

Perched in the middle of a bed of straw was the skull of a medium-size gator or crocodile. She wasn't certain which it was, because the white bone was deformed by a layer of black shiny insects, wriggling furiously.

"Flesh eaters," he said. "Damn bugs come from Africa and they'll gnaw a skull clean in just over a week. What you do, you drill a hole through the brain pan, another one back of the mandible, so these boys can get in there and chew off that hard-to-reach meat. Shake them up from time to time, get them moving again. Saves a lot of effort, though you gotta stay downwind of the cleaning box for the first few days. That is, unless you happen to like the smell of putrefying flesh."

Crotch lowered his head to the brim of the terrarium and took a deep drag of the air. He bobbed back up and smiled like a man who'd just savored a fine cigar.

"I should clear a hundred and fifty dollars for this one," he said. "Soon as I clean that skull up with a little bleach, scrape out those last few crannies even the dermestids can't get to. Should be enough money to get me and the girl through the end of the year.

"But, you know something, Mrs. Allison Farleigh? I always been real curious about whether or not these beetles would eat meat that's still alive. Or are they just vultures, they'll only feast on the dead?

"I been wondering about that for a long time now. Got so curious once or twice, I about put my hand in there with 'em, see what they'd do, but then I thought, no, I might still have some use for that hand one day. Now all of a sudden it looks like the good Lord has provided me with a couple of top-notch experimental subjects might just answer that question once and for all."

"Goddamn you, old man, where's Thorn?"

"Your friend," he said, "is resting outside. For now."

"He needs medical attention. He'll bleed to death from that wound."

"Brenda Cougar sutured him. My redskin Florence Nightingale."

She lifted her head at the mention of her name, but kept on mincing.

"Don't lie to me, Crotch. I want to see him."

"Well, listen to that," he said. "Look who's calling who a liar."

Woozily Allison tried to stand, but an invisible hand stuffed her back. Brenda Cougar put down her knife and came over. The girl was thick-waisted with a broad, indifferent face. She wore jeans and a bright yellow T-shirt that advertised a Chinese beer. She extended her hand, and helped Allison to her feet. With Crotch taking sidelong looks from his workbench, Brenda led her unsteadily across the room and outside.

Twenty yards to the east of the house were four rectangular holes, seven, eight feet deep, like rough-hewn gravesites hacked out of the limestone. The first two were empty, the next held a large hog that seemed to be drowsing. Cozy and warm in his little block of sun. A scattering of half-eaten corn cobs and rotting vegetables lay near his tusked snout.

In the last pit Thorn was slouched in the corner, several turns of silver plumbing tape twisted around his ankles and wrists. A turban of gauze on his head. At the crown of the bandage a bloody Rorschach had seeped through. His eyes were murky as he stared up at her.

In a shaky voice he asked if she was okay.

"I'm all right. Are you?"

"Can't seem to focus," he said. "But I'll make it."

"Everything's fine, Thorn. Just rest. I'll deal with Crotch. We'll be out of here soon. I promise."

She glanced at Brenda Cougar for some kind of confirmation, but the girl dodged her eyes, bowed her head in silence.

Allison turned back to Thorn, held his gaze for another moment, then she whirled around and marched back into the house, Brenda Cougar hurrying behind.

She walked directly to Crotch's workbench, drew back her fist, and hammered the man between the shoulder blades.

He grunted, fell forward, bent at the waist across his bench, and he stayed there, his head down, holding that pose for a long moment while he gathered himself. Then he pushed his body up, turned slowly to face her. Gave her a wretched smile.

"So, did you meet my feral hog?"

"You son of a bitch."

"I just captured the little bastard last week. Been after him for the last two months. They're dangerous, you know, feral hogs. Used to be domesticated, living the nice easy farm life. But when one gets loose, wanders off, has to learn how to fend for itself, it turns mean. Nobody pitching it bushels of corn anymore. Has to root, has to learn to kill. A thing that was civilized once, but it's gone wild, that's the worst thing you'll ever want to meet in the woods. It remembers how it used to be, the sweet peaceful times. And that just makes it all the angrier. Those hogs are insane. Worse killers than a wounded gator. One gets you down on your back, it'll tear out your goddamn throat in two seconds."

Allison stared at the beetles cleaning that skull and said quietly, "Thorn's probably got a concussion. He needs a doctor."

"He'll live."

"Come on, Crotch, be reasonable."

"Reasonable! Now listen to me, woman." His voice filled with a hateful hiss. "You're the one who snatched a year right out of my life. Got me sealed up in a cage, solid concrete walls between me and the sky. A man who's lived out in the open every day of his life.

"And you think you can come light-footing in here like we was old friends, just had a slight disagreement? Kiss and make up? No, ma'am. That's not how it works out in these woods. Only goddamn reason I didn't kill you on sight, Mrs. Allison Farleigh, is because I thought I'd like to study for a bit on the most enjoyable way to go about it."

"I need you, Crotch. I came out here 'cause I need your help."

For a second he was taken aback, then he sputtered out a bitter laugh, and that choked him, and sent him off into a hacking cough. He turned his back on her, gagging. Hands flat on his workbench till his body calmed.

She spoke to his back.

"I want you to help me set somebody up."

He came around, short of breath, a hand against his hollow chest.

"Now, why in fuck's name would I want to do that?"

"I think they killed my daughter."

"You think I give a shit about your goddamn family? Fuck your family."

"It's the White brothers I'm after," she said. "Raimondo and Orlando."

He peered at her. She heard Brenda Cougar stop slicing.

"Whatta you want with those shitfaces?"

Allison felt the muscles in her back relax, relief begin to trickle into her veins. Joe Tiger, who ran the Miccosukee village near the Shack, told her the story a year or two before. She'd been gambling her life and Thorn's it was true.

"Those are the assholes I told you about," Meriwether said to Brenda Cougar. "Rayon and Orlon. Orlon and Rayon."

Brenda looked his way, then went back to her work, chopping a carrot into orange coins.

Crotch picked up the terrarium again, peered down into it. Even from six feet away Allison could smell the foul air, the sweet stink of rotting meat.

"Treated those boys like they were my own goddamn sons. Showed them every trick of the trade. How to leave an old piece of rug at the head of a canal, warm dark place where snakes will take up residence, come back a week later, lift the rug, there's your snake. Twenty, thirty pieces of rug, on average that gives you fifteen, twenty snakes. Simple things like that, but nothing those two knew when I got a hold of them."

Meriwether gave the glass case a small shake and the beetles swarmed.

"Caught them one day down near Hudson Beach, they were squirting gasoline into rotten trees to flush out rat snakes. Ten bucks apiece. If it wasn't for me telling them that the gas fumes burn up the snakes' lungs and kill 'em within a day or two, they'd've never figured out why the hell all their snakes were croaking on them. Sixteen years old, that's all those assholes were. Orphans, running around in these swamps, totally lost most of the time. I took them in, let them stay around the house any time they had a mind to. Years, that went on. Teaching them what they needed to know to survive out here. Like how all the snake hunters drive the exact same white Ford pickup trucks the sugarcane foremen drive, so they can blend in when they're driving around on Big Sugar's private land, which is prime snake territory in these parts.

"I give them their goddamn college degree in the reptile business. Then one July night, two, three years back, those two shitheads waited till I'd passed out from drinking, comatose on my bed, and they stole every hide, every goddamn skull I had. All my jerky, my smoked mullet. Made off with every damn thing they could carry, down to my granddaddy's old whittling knife.

"Little shits vandalized what they didn't steal. Broke a glass vase of my mama's, a clay pot my granddaddy kept his cigars in. Those measly little fuckfaces. Learned all I had to teach them, then pissed on me like that. Those two would've cut off my pecker if they'd thought there was a market for it."

He set the terrarium back on his workbench, and when he looked at her again, his eyes seemed dimmer, as if his speech had run down his dwindling battery, shaved an hour or two off his life.

"I want you to call them on the phone. Make a proposal. I want to listen in. I want to hear them talk."

Crotch jerked his eyes away from her and winced as if some sharp-fanged creature had just yawned and stretched in his chest. He sucked in a long, whistling breath.

"Well, the problem is," he said, "I'm not rightly sure who I'd prefer to kill. Those fuckfaces, or you."

Allison said, "I'll take you out to the gas station at Monroe Station. You can call from their phone."

Meriwether looked across at Brenda Cougar as he weighed the proposition. Brenda was dicing a bell pepper now, and though she didn't return his look, it was clear she was somehow collaborating with Crotch on this verdict.

Allison's pulse jiggled in her chest, a twinge of pain, as if all her veins had tightened down to pinholes, and an explosive pressure was building within the membranes of her heart. It had been pure folly to come to this place, ask for Meriwether's help. Surely there were a hundred ways to catch these killers that made better sense.

She cast her eyes around the room, and the terrible irony struck her, that she should die in such a place as this. Her enemy's shrine. This foul and airless room, where thousands of animals had been slaughtered or made ready for a lifetime of imprisonment. Surely in her seven years of labor, Allison had not rescued a fraction of the animals that this man had destroyed in any month of his life.

Crotch Meriwether turned around to face her.

"You did a bad thing to me, woman. I turned sick in that prison, and I been getting worse ever since. You did that. Deceived me, shamed me. Broke me in two."

She held his eye, watched a web of veins rise from the yellowed tallow of his forehead. Blue vessels growing into small fingers, clawing upward toward his brain, as though Allison were witnessing the fierce war between Meriwether's heart and mind.

At last the old man closed his eyes, let his head sag. The same submissive posture Brenda Cougar had assumed out in the yard. An Indian gesture perhaps, something he'd learned from her that he must have found frequent use for in his waning days.

He muffled a wet cough with his fist, brought his chin up, fixed his glittering eyes on Allison. Then she watched as they backed down the volume, softened, and she drew a full breath for the first time since she and Thorn had pulled ashore. Feeling this whole moment swinging around, heading off in a hopeful direction.

"We don't need to go to all the trouble," he said. "Hiking way up to Monroe Station."

As Brenda Cougar continued to chop, Crotch shuffled over to his workbench, squatted down, pawed through a cardboard carton underneath it, and came out with two black cellular phones.

"Yes, sir, old Crotch went and joined the twentieth century. Did it at the last possible second too."

Allison shook her head, feeling an urge to go over, kiss the old bastard on his dry, bristly cheek.

"When it starts to ring," he said, "you switch yours on."

Crotch's mouth puckered hard as though he were about to choke on the thick fumes of vengeance.

"Tomorrow night," Allison said. "Have them meet you tomorrow night. You'll lead them to the Shack like you're going to ambush me there, and then we'll capture them, find out what they know."

Crotch squinted at her.

"But the most important thing for now is," she said, "you've got to make one of them say my name."

He didn't ask why, just looked at her, kept staring into her eyes like maybe he was trying to see inside her, catch a last flickering glimpse of her daddy's ghost, Julius Ravenel. One of the rare men Meriwether had once respected.

"I'm sorry, Crotch," she said. "I know it doesn't begin to make up for what I did. But I'm truly sorry for what I did to you. I was full of myself. I thought everything was simple, black-and-white. But I'm seeing a lot more gray wherever I look these days. I hope you can forgive me. It was a shitty thing I did, very shitty. But seven years, that was a long time ago. I'm not that same person anymore."

"No," he said, and looked away at his Indian girl. "I don't reckon none of us are."

Rayon White was on his way out of the office, carrying the ape up to Palm Beach, when the phone rang. He cursed under his breath, debated it for a second, then turned around, unlocked the office door, came back in, shifted the orangutan to one arm, and picked up the phone. Crotch Meriwether calling.

Just like that, "Crotch Meriwether calling." Like it was the very first goddamn time the old man had ever used a phone, he didn't know the proper lingo yet. Then he started right in talking in his jaw-breaking, cornpone accent, asking Ray how the hell he was doing.

Ray broke in, saying, "Whatta you want, you old fool?"

"It's more what you might want, Raimondo. Something I got."

A quick wave of panic passed through him and Ray considered slapping the phone down, but then he could hear from the static that Crotch was at least a hundred miles away, nowhere close enough to actually worry about.

"I think I already took everything I could possibly want from you, Meriwether."

The old man hesitated for a second, then began to laugh, kept at it for a few more seconds. A wheezing whiskey laugh like maybe the bag of worms had forgiven the thievery Orlon and he had perpetrated a few years back, robbing the geezer of every valuable thing he had. Old fellow was probably so senile from all those years of moonshine and fried mullet that he didn't even remember what they'd done to him.

"I'm prepared to provide you with the location," Crotch said, "the exact whereabouts of a certain animal lady."

Ray was quiet.

"You there, Raimondo?"

"What animal lady we talking about here?"

"You know the one, the fucking bitch put me in Raiford. I hear tell she's trying to do the same thing to you boys."

Ray put the orangutan down on the floor.

"Allison?" Ray said softly

"What's that?"

"Allison!" Ray said. "Allison Farleigh."

"Yeah, that's her, that's the one. Allison."

"Why the hell would I care where that slut lives?"

"The way I hear it, you and her are at serious odds over some matter. I thought maybe you'd like to reason with her in private. Use some of your disemboweling skills on her."

"Where the hell did you hear anything about me and Allison, old man?"

"I believe I saw it in a smoke signal blowing across the sky."

Ray listened to the crackle of static for a moment, staring across at the orangutan. The ape had gone into the bathroom and now, all by himself, he'd figured out how to flush the toilet. And he was doing it every few seconds, not even letting the tank reload. The ape was bent over, peering down into the swirling water.

"It so happens I already know where the lady lives," Ray said. "It's not like it's any big secret."

"Not her city place, Raimondo. Her clandestine hideaway out here in the Glades. That's where she spends most of her time."

"Yeah? And what's your angle, old man?"

"Five hundred dollars, that's what it'll cost you to have Crotch Meriwether act as your personal guide, take you directly from your place of business to Allison Farleigh's little bungalow in the woods. Five hundred dollars, not one centavo less."

Ray watched the orangutan step into the toilet, one foot, then the other. Put his hand on the silver lever and give it a flush, squeaking to himself as the water went down.

"I'll think about it," Ray said quietly. "Get back to me later, why don't you, next year or sometime—maybe by then I'll have figured out some fucking use for a guide to that woman's house. Right now, I can't."

"Not just a guide," Meriwether said. "An accomplice too."

"What's that supposed to mean?"

"I'll be there with you, pulling my trigger right alongside you boys."

"Hey, Crotch, if you want to shoot that woman so bad, what's keeping you from doing it your own self? Why you gotta call me up?"

"Sure, sure, I could do it easy enough, but it wouldn't make me five hundred dollars. When I heard you boys were gunning for her, it dawned on me, here's what I've been waiting for, a way I could have my revenge on that woman, plus get some compensation for all them hides and pelts you two fuckfaces ripped off from me a few years back. Two birds with one squeeze of the trigger."

Ray watched as the hair ball flushed the john again, moving his feet up and down in the bowl like he was practicing some kind of toilet ballet.

"You threatening me, old man? Is that what I'm hearing?"

"No," he said. "Strange as it sounds, Rayon, I think we're on the same side of this business."

"Well, I'll think about it," Ray said. "I'll mention it to Orlon, see what he has to say."

"You do that. You just go ahead and do that. But let me tell you, if we catch her out at her house, all isolated like it is, isn't anybody going to hear the shots, the screams, none of it. We could keep that woman alive long as we wanted, wouldn't be nobody to know a thing. We could nail her down to the floor, peel the living skin right off her flesh, do any goddamn thing we wanted. Kill her fast, or take our time."

Ray took a swallow, thinking about it, the image of Allison squirming on the floor, not completely sure if the feeling he was having was desire or revulsion. He swallowed again.

"Tomorrow night is when it's going down," Meriwether said. "You and your brother decide now. I'm an old man, and I'm running out of time pretty goddamn fast. If you can't make it tomorrow night, it isn't going to happen."

"I hear you."

"Good."

"Well, I gotta admit one thing," Ray said. "It's a damn piece of serendipity you should've called at this particular juncture, Meriwether, 'cause it so happens there is one thing you might be able to help me with. A thing more in your neighborhood than mine. Could even make you a little extra cash currency."

"Whatta you lazy thieves need now, an indigo? A gator?"

"Actually, what I'm looking for," Ray said, "is a couple of cats."

"Cats?"

"One male, one female. And I got to have them alive or they aren't any good to me."

"What kind of cats?"

"You know what I'm talking about."

"Panthers? Florida panthers?"

Ray said, "And I don't want any goddamn mountain lion you found in some roadside show. This has gotta be an A-number one genetically correct Florida cat. Gotta stand up to blood tests for authenticity, the whole nine yards. You hear me?"

"I hear you fine."

"I'll go five thousand for the male, six for the female."

The line was empty.

"You still with me, old man?"

"I'll have to see what I can do," he said, sounding shriveled up now, probably a little overwhelmed by that eleven-thousand-dollar offer compared against the measly five hundred he was looking for.

Ray smiled, felt himself getting pumped, showing off for this old bastard, who always came on like he was the world's greatest animal dealer. Meriwether didn't realize Ray and Orlon had moved into the major leagues, playing with the big boys, throwing around much bigger numbers these days.

At the same time Ray was aware, as the bragging words came from him, that he was babbling to this old man. But he couldn't stop himself. Such a golden opportunity to one-up the guy who used to lord it over them, taking all the credit for teaching Ray and Orlon everything they knew about the animal business. Playing like he was their daddy.

"And look here: if you pull this off, Meriwether, maybe we can work out one or two future arrangements.

'Cause, see, I got myself a client these days, this guy's got the biggest goddamn appetite for exotic animals there ever was. Man's prepared to buy just about every goddamn thing on the planet."

# C H A P T E R

# 25

Ray couldn't believe his luck. First Crotch Meriwether calls out of nowhere, offers to solve two of Ray's most pressing problems, Allison Farleigh and Florida panthers. Then Tricia Capoletti, college-trained therapist, agreed to drive along with him up to West Palm Beach to watch Brad Randolph, the famous movie star and breakfast food promoter, get married.

Ray had to pull out all the stops to convince her to go along. First he'd suggested to her that this trip up to West Palm Beach might serve to reveal various important issues about his particular psychological dilemma. Make certain things clear that Ray wasn't able to articulate in her office setting. But on the phone she said she didn't like the idea, didn't consider it professional, going out with him like that. She made a long pause like she was choosing her words to refuse him, but Ray blurted out that the absolute truth was that he was feeling suicidal, wouldn't she consent to spend a couple of extra hours with him, help him through this deep personal cataclysm. And that seemed to turn things around.

Now, an hour later, Tricia Capoletti had, for all intents and purposes, fallen completely and totally in love. In fact, by the time they pulled into Brad Randolph's well-groomed dude ranch west of the turnpike, Ray was fairly sure this smart woman would've been willing to throw away her promising career in counseling, and abandon all her college-educated friends, to run off to a deserted island with that fucking orangutan.

"You absolutely have to sell him?"

"It's done already."

"Has money changed hands?"

"You couldn't afford him anyway," Ray said. "Thing is worth forty-five thousand dollars."

"That much!" she said. "Jeez." Looking out her window for a second or two, then swinging around and coming back with, "Would you consider taking part up front, financing the rest?"

Ray looked over. Tricia smiled like it was a joke, but her voice sounded pretty damn serious. She probably had five or ten socked away, scrimping for a down payment on her first mortgage, and there she was toying with the idea of tossing that all away for the goddamn hair ball. Man, oh, man.

"They grow up," Ray said, driving down the long, narrow road past a half dozen Mercedeses parked on the shoulder, Rolls-Royces, Ferraris, all the other cowpokes getting there early for the shindig. "He's cute now, but in a year or two he'll be so strong, he might just hurl your body right through your own front door for the fun of it."

The ape was sitting on her lap, its head resting against her red cashmere sweater. Soft, soft, soft. Ray looked over as the orangutan shifted, got even more comfortable, nuzzling in between Tricia's nice, medium-large breasts. The little shithead. Ray knew the ape must be aware of what it was up to. Seducing Ray's woman, seducing her right before his eyes. The ape pressing its cheek in there and staring over at Ray with that goddamn look it had, like man, wouldn't you like to be a little hair ball like me, go where I go, have the power over women I have. Sure you would. Sure you would. But you don't, Ray. You gotta just sit there and drive that car. Drive and wish. Drive and fantasize.

"I shot a guy last week," Ray said.

He didn't even need to look over to know Tricia's reaction. He could feel the air in the car get tight.

"I saw this traffic accident happen. Some twerpy kid ran a red light, hit a car, which skidded off and smacked into a woman, an old lady just standing on the sidewalk. Impact sent her flying, and all the kid could do was whine about how bad his truck was bashed up. So I shot him. Yesterday I read where he was released from Jackson Memorial. Legs paralyzed. Bullet hit his spine. Nineteen years old. Ernesto Hervis, he worked in some Kmart in North Miami. A stock boy, I'm guessing."

"Are you serious, Ray?"

There was a black man standing out in the middle of the dirt road wearing blue jeans and a red-checked shirt with a big blue bandanna around his throat like a cravat, a black ten-gallon hat tightened down on his head. He motioned Ray to stop, then started over to his window, probably wanting to check his goddamn Hollywood union card.

"And the weird thing is, I don't even feel all that guilty," Ray said. "The kid was an empty-headed little piece of shit. He didn't have any moral depth. Didn't even realize what he'd done was wrong. People like that, you know, they're barely alive to begin with. A serious thought might go through his head every year or two. I mean, for a kid like that, getting killed is the best thing ever happened to him. Gives him a chance to move up the reincarnation ladder. Maybe next time he'll get a brain."

"Have you been to the police about this, Ray?"

The African cowboy was at the window, Ray looking up at him. Guy in his fifties. Ray believed he recognized him from some movie or another. Played some real badass, a killer, or a bad cop, he wasn't sure. Orlon would know, of course. He'd be able to list all the guy's credits, probably even know which movies he'd auditioned for and didn't get.

Now, there was another thing Ray should file away to ask Tricia about if things got dull again. Why was Orlon so demented about movies? What was the root of that particular neurosis? And how did it connect to his hair plucking and shaving fetish?

"No, I don't consort with cops," Ray said. "Law enforcement officers and I have never enjoyed successful communications."

Ray cranked down the Volvo's window, looked up at the black guy.

"Can I see your invitation, sir?"

"Don't have one," Ray said.

"Then you'll have to turn around right here, and drive on back the way you came."

"I'm supplying the ape."

The cowboy leaned down lower and looked over at the orangutan. The thing was nestled so deep between Tricia's breasts it looked like he might be melting into her.

"Oh," the man said. "You're the entertainment?"

"Yeah, that's right," Ray said. "I'm the organ-grinder. This is my monkey. You want a look in the trunk, see my organ, verify my true identity?"

"Don't, Ray," Tricia said. "Be nice."

Hearing her say that gave Ray a little tickle of pleasure, like she was his wife chastising him, knowing exactly what he was up to, going to push the black guy inside the trunk, slam him in there, let him roast in the Florida sun.

The black Roy Rogers told Ray where to park, back down the line of Ferraris and Mercedeses, where it was a good long walk to the main house. The house itself was showing through a stand of pines and mossy oaks. Pretentious place up on a terrace with eight white columns across the front. *Gone with the Fucking Wind.* Ray could see striped awnings set up out in the grassy front yard, the vodka and liver pâté booths. People milling around, some kind of music coming from over there, a live country band.

He got out and went around and opened Tricia's door.

"The lady that died," Ray said. "The one the kid ran into and sent flying, she looked exactly like my mother. So because of that, I felt it was crucial I do something.

Wasn't any choice for me. A dead-ringer resemblance to my mother."

"Oh," Tricia said.

*Oh,* she said, like that made all the difference in the world. You could murder all you wanted if it was because of mother love. *Oh,* she said. And if Ray wasn't already deep enough in love with Tricia Capoletti, he felt himself sink even farther in. *Oh,* she said. *Oh.*

"Still think I should go to the police?" he said. "Or is this something you and I should work through together? I may be in denial about it or something, I don't know."

"I need to think about this," Tricia said. "This is serious."

"Yeah, I know it is. That's why I wanted to share it with you, somebody I could trust."

"And this is what made you consider suicide?"

"Right," he said. "Exactly."

They walked up the dusty road, Tricia dressed for the air-conditioning in a charcoal blazer over her red cashmere sweater, a black scarf tied at her throat, and a pair of jeans with fancy red stitching. Penny loafers, black socks. Auburn hair appearing redder than usual under the orange November sun.

The orangutan snuggled against her, burying its face in her hair like it might be whispering something into her right ear, telling her secrets. The ape reached out and took hold of a strand of her red hair, almost the same shade as the ape's. He coiled it around his pointing finger, then put that finger in his mouth. Sucked on a strand of the psychotherapist's hair.

Tricia saw what he was doing, then cut her eyes to Ray's.

He smiled at her, at this intimate moment they were sharing, this baby ape that for all the world might be the kind of offspring the two of them would produce. Beautiful red hair, intelligent hungering eyes, like Tricia had. But still an ape, primitive like Ray, a barbarian who never knew which fork went where, which bread plate was his.

Ray and Tricia looked into each other's eyes while the ape peeped between them.

Ray was about to say something to her, find the words that would take them to the next stage of romantic entanglement, when the ape pulled his finger out of his mouth and there, glittering in the sunlight, was a good-size diamond ring. Tricia gasped.

"Jesus Christ. He steal that from you?"

"No," she said. "It's not mine."

The orangutan was pointing his finger at Tricia's nose, the diamond ring on his slimy fingertip.

Ray whispered to Tricia to hold very still, then he edged his hand up, keeping it out of the ape's peripheral vision, closer and closer until he was just inches away. Ray picked his moment, then shot his hand out, grabbed for the ring, but the orangutan was too damn quick. He popped the diamond back in his mouth and gulped it down.

With forty-five thousand dollars in fresh one-hundred-dollar bills arranged neatly in one of Brad Randolph's own personalized cream-colored envelopes, the envelope tucked in his glove compartment, Ray pulled off I-95 at the Sheridan Street exit in Dania so Tricia Capoletti could urinate for the fifth time that afternoon. Though it was possible Ray might've missed one or two back at the wedding.

He located a combination gas station and 7-Eleven in a neighborhood that seemed halfway safe, and pulled into the lot.

"I'll just be a minute."

"No hurry."

He got out with her and followed her into the market. Ray watched her walk back to the bathrooms, suddenly feeling incredibly horny. Watching Tricia closing the bathroom door, he began to picture the rest of it, the woman unzipping her jeans, pulling them down to her knees, sitting, the tinkle of water.

All afternoon he'd been feeling a growing closeness

to her. Getting a vivid glimpse of her biological rhythms, a feel for the cycles of her internal organs. By Ray's standards Tricia had to piss with alarming frequency. Her bladder couldn't be any bigger than a pinto bean.

But still, it didn't bother him. He even found himself liking it. Having to pull over so she could pee, visit new places, and he liked that Tricia wasn't shy about admitting she couldn't hold it, a secret thing like that, moving them into new conversational territory, new stages of intimacy. And most of all he liked the idea of Tricia confessing something to him for a change.

In fact, Ray damn well liked the whole day. Thinking of it as their first date. And a very symbolic one, too, a wedding. Even liking the wedding ceremony, though it was pretty schmaltzy. He liked the way Tricia's eyes got shiny when the orangutan walked away from her and climbed up into Brad Randolph's big ex–football player's arms. Hugging Brad, then hugging his big blond bride, a double for Betty Penski, as far as Ray could tell. Same rubberized body.

The whole time the orangutan was in Brad's arms or his bride's, it was staring back at Tricia with this pitiful look like the ape was headed off to the orphanage instead of a movie star's ranch.

Tricia's eyes watered, but then she caught herself and all at once she set her mouth and turned off the tap, something she must have learned at psychology school. And later during the wedding ceremony, Tricia got a little trickle going from watching the way the ape walked around among the guests while the happy couple was taking their vows, and all those Hollywood types were cooing, smiling, cuddling the thing while the cowboy minister rattled on.

Tricia Capoletti watched the ape, how it climbed into new people's arms and got interested in their hair. And to make it worse, the hair ball kept looking over at her and Ray, giving them one long, sorrowful stare after another like it really wanted to be over with them, but was just being sociable, doing what was expected of it.

Most of all Ray liked the feel of Tricia riding beside him in his old black Volvo, liked the way she'd said, "Could you stop, Ray? I need to use the bathroom." Nothing unusual in the words themselves, but God, it made things seize up inside him. Put a tremble in his hands. Saying it so natural, like the two of them had been married for years.

Ray White stood around in front of the 7-Eleven counter and watched the teenage fat girl ring up gas customers, and guys come in off the street to buy single beers, taking them away in small brown sacks. Ray looked at the magazine rack for a minute, a sports magazine, a soap opera digest. Then he picked up a copy of today's Fort Lauderdale *Sun-Sentinel.*

Read the lead headline: MOTORCYCLE MASSACRE. Then slid his eyes down the page and began reading a different story, something about an airline strike, then in a few seconds he came back to the motorcycle story, eyes running over the words, but none of it really sinking in, 'cause he was thinking of Tricia back in the bathroom. The way she must be looking into the mirror about now, primping, fixing up her makeup, though she didn't wear all that much, at least not compared to the likes of Betty Penski of International House of Pancakes. Ray's eyes slipped down the words, then looked at the photo on the page. A black-and-white picture of a little wooden house with motorcycles out front.

A house Ray recognized. Jesus H. Mother of God.

Then he started to read for real. Taking the words in, digesting them, feeling a flutter begin in his chest, a dizzy spin coming into his head.

Motorcycle massacre. Nine men, three women. Methodically murdered, their mutilated bodies left to decay in their Hialeah clubhouse. Just found late yesterday afternoon, a full twenty-four hours after the slaughter happened. The house in Hialeah, the one where the old woman got killed by the twerpy kid. Neighbors reported seeing a black Corvette parked outside, hearing gunfire, but not reporting it. Wasn't the first time shots were fired in that house. Let them kill each other, one neighbor said.

Ray got to the end of the article just as Tricia walked up. He looked at her blankly, not even recognizing her for a second.

"Ray?"

"You read about this?" He held up the newspaper.

"The motorcycle club?"

"Yeah."

"I saw it on Channel Four this morning. A dozen people shot."

Ray set the paper back in the rack, pushed open the heavy glass door for Tricia. Walked with her over to the car.

"And those poisonous snakes," she said. "Crawling all over the bodies. The victims with their noses cut off. I mean, God Almighty, why would anyone do that, do you think, kill someone, then cut off their nose? I just can't fathom it, can't imagine the landscape of somebody's mind who'd commit an act like that."

"Paper says it wasn't their whole nose," Ray said. "Just the tips."

Tricia studied him as he held the door open for her.

"I guess why he did it," Ray said, "it must've been for revenge. Like maybe what could've happened, a year ago those same motorcycle guys cut his nose, so then he might feel compelled to get them back. A nose for a nose."

She looked at him for a puzzled moment, then her eyes changed and she said his name, a question mark at the end.

"Yeah?"

"Tell me the truth. Did you really shoot that boy?"

He looked at her, the way her head was tilted slightly. He saw a long hair snagged on the front of her cashmere sweater. Maybe one of hers, maybe the hair ball's. Her eyes were waiting for him, wanting to hear the right answer, something big hanging in the balance.

"Did you, Ray? Did you shoot that boy in traffic?"

Ray reached out, pinched hold of that hair on the shoulder of her sweater and drew it off. He cranked open his window and dropped the hair outside, then turned back to look at her again.

"Yes, I did," he said. "I shot him."

She kept on looking at him, things changing in her eyes, her mouth, somewhere he couldn't put his finger on. And he couldn't tell if the change was for the better or the worse.

Then she nodded her head once, twice. Her mouth grim.

"My mother," Ray said, hearing himself speak, but at the same time drifting apart from his body, going off, hovering ten feet up in the air, watching Raimondo White discuss his mother with Tricia Capoletti. "When Mom was dying, one afternoon she made everyone leave her hospital room except for me. She had me get down on my knees, and she held my hand very tight, and she whispered in this croaky voice, telling me she knew she was just on the verge of dying, then asking me to look after Orlon, keep him out of trouble. It was up to me to be her substitute when she was gone. I said I would, sure, what else could I say?

"And ever since she died I've been trying to do it, nudge Orlon in the right direction whenever the chance arose. But now I see the shitty job I've done. Hell, I can't even keep myself out of trouble. And here I got one important job in life, one thing my mother begged me to do above all else, and look how I mangled it up. Look what I did."

"Mangled what up, Ray? I don't follow you."

"Bullying Orlon, making him go in there on his own, into that house. I mean, I might just as well have done that thing myself, butchered all those people. I wound him up so damn tight, set him off in that direction, slicing and shooting."

"What're you saying? What exactly are you telling me?"

Ray started the car, not speaking anything more to

her. Not even looking over to see how she was taking his silence, just wanting to get back home, go up to his room, lock the door, think this through.

"Talk to me, Ray," she said.

But he couldn't. There were some things too awful to confess to anybody, even to your eighty-dollar-an-hour shrink, even to the woman you loved.

Brad Randolph's bride, Windy Li, decided the orangutan should be named Ringo. In a brief and drunken ceremony, she bestowed the name on the orangutan, then immediately turned her attention back to her guests.

Ringo spent his first evening at Brad Randolph's ranch looking out the second-story window. From that perspective, the ape could see into the uppermost branches of the oaks and pines in Brad's front yard. For the last four years the ape had lived almost exclusively in the canopy of the Borneo rain forest, so he was naturally fascinated by the movie star's treetops.

Music played through the early evening, guitars and banjos, drums and fiddles. Lanterns had been hung from limbs around the yard, and dozens of people milled around in their flickering glow. Others hung around the hors d'oeuvres that were set out on the back of a fake chuck wagon. Occasionally Ringo watched the people, but mostly he stared at the tree limbs.

Brad Randolph's assistant had chosen that particular room for Ringo because it contained a single bed but was otherwise empty. With such short notice of the ape's arrival, that room had seemed like the best place to house the new guest. The one room where he could do the least damage.

However, for the last few months the room had belonged to Butch, Brad's five-year-old male rottweiler. Brad owned Butch since his single days, and the dog had once enjoyed the privilege of sleeping alongside Brad in his king-size bed, but since Windy Li arrived he'd been banished to that unfurnished room.

Earlier in the afternoon the dog had retreated to the

room to escape the noise and chaos of the party and had curled up inside the empty closet. When Brad's assistant led the ape into the room and shut the door, he failed to notice that Butch was already there.

The orangutan's arrival woke the dog and Butch lay on his stomach, his chin against his paws, peering out through the half-open closet door. The dog was absolutely still, focused on every move of the orangutan as it paced in front of the second-story window, peering out. The rottweiler's nose was working, his ears pointed up to catch each squeak and peep the red-haired ape made.

As the sun set, Ringo grew weary of the view out the window and walked over to the bed. He tugged on the edge of the flowered bedspread and pulled it loose. He wadded it up and dropped the bedspread onto the floor, then lay down in the small pile and found a comfortable position on his side.

The dog waited a half hour before finally standing up. He came slowly out of the closet. In a crouch he approached Ringo, halting every foot or so, until his snout was just a few inches from the orange ape's feet.

Unlike monkeys, the great apes have no tails. Without a tail for balance, orangutans must rely completely on the strength of their hands and feet to swing through the treetops. Actually the orangutan's feet could more properly be described as third and fourth hands, for they had the same prehensile abilities as the ape's hands and equal strength.

When Butch leaned forward, bringing his nose to within an inch of the strange animal's fragrant soles, the orangutan used its feet in a movement so quick and powerful the dog did not even have time to make a sound.

The orangutan grabbed Butch by the neck, and though Butch outweighed Ringo by forty pounds, the ape held the dog in place as it shifted its grip to the dog's trunk. Then, while grasping the dog with all four hands, Ringo lifted Butch off the ground and held him in the air.

The dog squirmed in the ape's grip but couldn't break free. Lying on his back, Ringo rocked the rottweiler back and forth above him, examining this unusual animal. While domestic dogs were abundant in the villages of Borneo, no wild dogs roamed the jungle. The closest animal to this rottweiler the orangutan might have seen was a common barking deer.

As the ape shifted its grip for a better view of the dog, the rottweiler suddenly twisted its neck, growled, and lurched to the side. It bared its teeth and snapped at the ape's right hand. But the orangutan was too swift. In an effortless motion, he heaved the dog headfirst two yards across the room and Butch crashed through the front window.

Out in the yard, some of the wedding guests screamed.

# CHAPTER

## 26

Brenda Cougar gave Allison two aspirin and made her swallow them down with a jelly glass of Scotch. Then she sat Allison down in a chair and tightened a strip of adhesive tape hard across the bridge of her nose, studiously molding the flesh back into some semblance of its former shape, an operation, it seemed, Brenda Cougar had performed a few times before. Allison's eyes clouded with tears, but she clenched the arms of the chair and was silent throughout the ordeal.

The girl never spoke a word or changed her bland expression. Her dark eyes were empty, but somehow she managed to reveal herself to Allison, let her know without question who ran Mr. Crotch Meriwether's house, and who Allison and her friend were indebted to for walking out of there alive.

When she was done, they went outside and Brenda Cougar lowered a stepladder into the pit, helped to haul Thorn out. She led the two of them to the jon boat and climbed in herself. Brenda poled them all the way back out to the highway, taking a far more direct route than the one Allison had used coming in. She and Allison muscled the boat onto the roof of the Cherokee and strapped it down. As Allison was thanking her, the girl turned away and walked off into the dense woods.

Allison helped Thorn into the Jeep, shut the door,

and he slumped against it. With his eyes closed, he rubbed at his face as if he had walked through a wall of cobwebs.

"So," Thorn said, eyes closed against his pain. "Are they coming for tea?"

"Yes," she said. "Tomorrow night."

"Good," he said. "That'll give me time to grow a new head."

A mile down Tamiami Trail, Thorn was paralyzed by sleep. As Allison watched the black highway unspool beneath them, she was filled with a wild garble of emotions. Dread, sadness, and fury. But through it all a bright, clear voice rang out from the empty sky of her memory. Raimondo White speaking on Crotch's cellular phone. *Allison,* he'd said. *Allison Farleigh.*

Driving through the fading dusk, she compared the lingering echo of those voices in Borneo with this voice, and there was absolutely no mistake. *All-iii-son. Allison.* The same derisive enunciation, turning her name into three syllables, the same shading of the last vowel. The identical hiss at the end, a long, sibilant sneer. *Allie, Allie in come free.*

Yes, it was miles from courtroom proof. Arraignments, grand jury indictments, forget all that. But for Allison it was as definite as fingerprints, as conclusive as a perfect match of the loops and swirls of DNA.

She held the Jeep at the speed limit and kept her eyes on the road, and over and over again she invoked that bullying taunt. *All-iii-son. Come out, come out, wherever you are. All-iii-son!* Winslow lying dead at their feet. Tormenting herself with the image, with the recollection of that haunting voice.

At least now she knew. Not why Winslow had to die, none of the particulars. But she was certain it was them, the two brothers, the White boys. Shabby second-raters. Redneck herpers who until lately had been content with selling fifty-dollar ratsnakes, hundred-dollar kings. Somehow they'd found their way to Borneo, hunting orangutans at forty thousand apiece. Seedy, low-life animal dealers, clearly in the employ of someone a great deal more shrewd. Someone who was buying and selling fantastic numbers of animals. A man like Joshua Bond.

Allison watched a mass of dark clouds pile up in her rearview mirror, the leading edge of another front, driven down the peninsula from the Northwest, a great roiling imbalance in the upper atmosphere as the clean arctic currents clashed with the heavy subtropical air. Wild thunderstorms were on their way, squalls that would shake loose the tons of water that had thickened the air for weeks.

The storm chased them back down Tamiami Trail and caught them as they crossed the Dade County line. The deluge hammered against the Cherokee roof, wipers slapping fast but ineffectual. Headlights on, she drove east into the city through the nerve-racking curtain of rain. It was eight-fifteen by the time they arrived at Baptist Hospital's emergency room, and half past ten when they were released. Ten stitches and a handful of codeine-laced Tylenol for Thorn, another tape job for Allison's nose. And a warning: Go see an ear, nose, throat man first thing tomorrow or you'll snore like a drunken sailor the rest of your life.

She stopped at a Publix, left Thorn sleeping, came out with two bags of groceries. On the ride back neither of them mustered any conversation. It was almost midnight when they reached the Shack again. The rain had died to a drizzle.

Thorn made it twenty yards before he was out of breath, had to drop into one of the front porch rockers. She took the other rocker. For a few moments they sat in silence, Allison staring off toward the east at the faint golden glow of the city. When she spoke again, her voice was parched.

"That's what's wrong."

"What?"

"That," she said, and waved at the shimmer of Miami. "You can almost hear the drone, the hum of voltage. Two million people trapped inside that goddamn grid of freeways, turnpikes, telephone poles, all those wires hooking everything to everything else."

Thorn groaned his agreement, his head propped against a fist.

"Cities are the problem," she said. "That's where it all begins."

"Where what begins?"

"The pet trade," Allison said. "It's cities that make it happen. City people want some reminder, some connection to the world they've lost. And the Joshua Bonds and White brothers are happy to satisfy their cravings. Dismantle the whole goddamn world on their behalf.

"You don't find country people doing it. To them animals are as common as dirt. The idea of keeping a pet, other than a decent hunting dog, going to all the expense to cage some beast, it would never occur to most of them."

Thorn made a noise that he was listening.

Allison went on, feeling the words flood from her. Things she'd never said. No one to say them to.

The way it was going, she told him, if an animal species was to survive it had to become a toy-poodle version of itself. Chimps wearing diapers and sunglasses, doing cartwheels across wall-to-wall carpets, or grinning cheek to cheek with their captors, posing for family Polaroids. Birds that talked, fish that gazed back fondly through their glass cage.

When an animal was impossible to domesticate or was deemed unlovely by current fashion, then watch out —its kind was surely doomed to extinction. These days a species' only hope was to strike some chord with the rulers of the planet. Dewy-eyed, or mesmerizingly dangerous, we spared only what amused us. Only what fit into our busy schedules. Either the damn animal will learn to eat our food, live in our sterile boxes, or to hell with them, let them disappear with the other forty thousand species this year.

Everybody trying to enliven their concrete nightmares, renew their membership in the brotherhood of the wild. Parakeets as bric-a-brac, fish as curios, chimps as cuddly solace for childless couples. Something alive, animated, primitive, a twittering speck of color with its faint drumbeat of jungle blood. Snakes, birds, primates, fish.

And as far as Allison was concerned, zoos were worse than all the hungry consumers together. Zoos wanted only the best. The more exotic the animal, the larger the crowds. If Allison had her way, all zoos would be abolished. Even the best were nothing but camouflaged warehouses, drab and voyeuristic like apartment buildings with one wall torn away.

Oh, some of them tried very hard to pretend they were homey and educational, but in fact they were merely dreary theme parks. With concrete sculptures shaped like trees for the monkeys to swing on, stagnant pools for them to drink, sparsely landscaped viewing stages where they were expected to perform, make the kiddies giggle. Perversions of the natural world where generation after generation of animals would grow obese, listless, dumbfounded, more and more deaf to the powerful messages embedded in their genes. Until they were no longer animals at all, but drowsy zombies. Extinct creatures who were not permitted to die.

And then there were the great white hunters. Those despicable men who slaughtered rhinos, chainsawed loose their horns, left the carcass to rot. All so they might grind that bone into a powder, a dust four times more valuable than cocaine. Murdering the black bear for its gallbladder, the gorilla and tiger for their testicles. Magical potions to the Chinese, the great worshipers of aphrodisiacs. It was as though a plague of impotency had infected a hundred million Oriental men at once, and vast herds of magnificent beasts had to be annihilated to keep their cocks hard.

"Man," Thorn said. "You're angry."

Allison looked away from the glow of Miami, stared at Thorn. His eyes were open now, sitting up straight. Though he seemed to be straining to keep his head balanced on his neck. She could see a small rhythmic wobble.

"I guess I am," she said. "I sound angry, don't I?"

"It happens," said Thorn. "You start off doing something for one reason, it changes into another reason as time goes on. With you it was the orangutans. You loved them, wanted to protect them. Then one day you meet the sons of bitches who exploit the things you love, and you feel an instant hate for them. Who wouldn't? But before you know it, you're making these bad guys your life's work, focused on them, you're seething all the time, running totally on anger. Your love's warped into hate."

Allison shifted in the rocker. Looked over at Thorn, then out at the emptiness. Something was moving out there just beyond the halo of the porch light. A gator, a deer.

"You should go lie down, Thorn. You can have the bed tonight."

"Hey, I'm sorry. I didn't mean to insult you."

She took a moment, then said, "No, you're right. You're absolutely right. I'm going to have to work on that."

He looked over at her, blinked three times, four. Rubbed hard at his eyes.

"I was just getting used to *one* of everything," he said. "And now there's two."

"Two of me?"

"Yeah," he said, reaching out to rest his hand atop hers. "And both of them look pretty good."

She frowned at him.

"God, Thorn, you obviously need some more Tylenol."

She helped him up, unlocked the door, turned on the overhead light, and took a hard breath.

The floor was covered with paper. Hundreds of sheets. She stood and watched as another page unscrolled from her fax machine, angled out of the overflowing chute and fluttered to the floor to join the rest. Then another page began to appear at the opening and in a moment it, too, became airborne and made the short flight to the floor.

\* \* \*

After Ray let Tricia Capoletti off, he drove around aimlessly till after midnight, lost in a stupor of guilt. Trying to figure out what the hell to do. But he came to no conclusion, so finally he just drove home.

He walked in the front door and found Orlon in the living room talking on the phone. Orlon covered the mouthpiece and looked up at Ray and said, "Crotch Meriwether."

Ray took a seat on the couch and listened to Orlon saying, yeah, yeah, yeah. I like it, Crotch, good, yeah. Great. Yeah, Ray just walked in the door. So okay, we can be there by two o'clock—no, you better make it two-thirty. It's a hell of a drive. Yeah, good. Right, right.

After Orlon set the phone down, he came over and sat next to Ray. He was wearing a white terry-cloth robe, and reeked of patchouli massage oil. Orlon smiled and rubbed his hands across his bald head like he was slicking his ducktail back into place.

"Old Crotch Meriwether is giving us Allison on a platter."

"I know, I talked to him this afternoon," Ray said.

"Well, we better get moving. He wants us out there in two hours. Ten miles west of the Shark Valley turnoff. I figure we gotta leave in the next fifteen minutes."

"That's tomorrow night," Ray said. "Friday."

"No, the plan's changed," Orlon said. "Friday night is what Allison thinks. When he was talking to you earlier today, she was there in his cabin, Allison was, standing right beside Crotch while the two of you talked on the phone. She put him up to it, that whole thing about going to her place was a trap. Old Crotch went along, then after she left he sat there and thought it through and decided he'd rather do business with the White brothers than with that bitch."

"A trap? Allison was setting a trap for us?"

"That's right. She must've seen us in Borneo after all. Couldn't get the cops to believe her, so she's taking the law into her own hands."

Ray looked at Orlon, ready to argue, then felt a surge of sadness sweep over him, a dark riptide of melancholy. His brother was a fucking mass murderer. And Ray was a dangerous repeat felon. A couple of life terms at the very least. Caught up in it now, the churn of sad events. You always heard the experts say the best way to keep from drowning in a riptide was just to lay back and ride the current. Fighting was a sure way to tire yourself out and drown. You were supposed to swim along with it, eventually it would slacken, let you go.

Ray rose, went upstairs to change clothes, get ready. Following the experts' advice, going to ride it till it let him go. This dark sadness, this despair that he'd fucked up, let his mother down. Screwed up his own life, and worse than that, he'd let Orlon screw his up too. But for now Ray decided he'd have to ride it, this current of misery and iniquity, just hope it didn't pull him so far out to sea he lost complete sight of land.

# C H A P T E R

# 27

They gathered the pages from the floor, stacked them, went to the couch, Allison reading each one first, passing it to Thorn. Five minutes into it, Thorn looked up, rubbed his eyes, said, "I don't get it."

"I don't either," she said. "Not yet."

Allison went to her desk, found a yellow legal pad, pen, an atlas, came back to the couch, dug into the stack again.

Some of the faxes were newspaper clippings, some were dashed-off notes, a few longer letters. Messages from her membership, the network she'd spent the last seven years developing. On the legal pad she began to make lists, names of animals, locations, people killed. She consulted the atlas, put $X$'s where each event occurred.

Two young mountain gorillas from Rwanda, one male, one female, taken from a nature preserve the month before. An armored vehicle plowed through the front gate of the preserve, two wildlife officers attacked. One died, the other survived to tell the tale. And around the same time, one of her members at his own expense shadowed a crate containing two extremely rare gray-shouldered parakeets, male and female, from Venezuela to Manila, Manila to Hong Kong, where the crate vanished in the back rooms of the customs warehouse. The young man questioned the Hong Kong customs officers to no avail.

That night two men broke into his hotel room while he slept and beat him severely.

Fifteen thousand members. Most were only financial patrons, while a thousand or so were truly active. Of those thousand, it looked like a third had faxed her in the last month. That long since she'd been out here, checked her machine.

Diane Jackson-White in Santa Barbara; Millicent Obergon in Dallas; Harvey Billingsley in Sydney, Australia; Madge Follet in Singapore. Randy Beecher, a banker in Taipei; Vishta Chang, a cardiologist in London; the Donleavys in Missoula, Montana; the Blanchards in Costa Rica; Jonny Izzara from Bali. Nancy and Alex Largo of Cullowee, Georgia. Lieutenant Richard Katz, stationed in Panama. Each with another jigsaw piece.

She was reading a fax from Bettina Marsden, about the recent disappearance of two wild chimps from the island preserve she managed off the coast of Gambia, when Thorn got up, made them a pot of coffee, put the groceries away. She watched him for a moment, moving with woozy deliberation.

Libby Metzler-Davies in Ethiopia; Harrison P. Smithpatrick from Honolulu. Everyone with bits of news, whispers in the wind, pieces of hard evidence. Each caught up in the same agitation.

Thorn eased down on the couch again as she was finishing an article from Singapore's *Straits Times* describing a recent discovery in the rain forest two hundred miles north of the city. The bodies of two Chinese nationals were found lying near a mound of rotting Sumatran rhinos. The men had been shotgunned. Allison added the extremely rare hairy rhinos to her list, marked the location on the atlas and looked up at Thorn.

"This isn't normal, right? All these animals smuggled at once? This much activity?"

She looked to the side, listened for a moment to the night sounds, a distant screech owl, a small plane off to the north.

"No," she said, looking down at her pad. "Not normal. Animals stolen from preserves, from national Parkland, from private collectors, from the wild. So far I've got eleven people killed in the last two months, mostly wildlife agents or park rangers. Murders occurred in six countries, on three continents. No, not normal at all.

"Arabian oryx, black rhinos, Asian small-clawed otters, snow leopards, Indian pythons, Siberian tigers, Andean condors, gaurs, barasinghas, Asiatic wild horses, black-footed ferrets, ruffed lemurs, Humboldt's penguins, lion-tailed macaques. Cheetahs, gorillas, Bali mynahs, white-naped cranes, chacoan peccaries, black howler monkeys, hoolock gibbons.

"Piles of slaughtered animals found in Africa, southeast Asia, Australia, Costa Rica. Rotting carcasses of the rarest and most endangered animals on the planet. Take some, kill some. No, this is obscene. Poaching and butchery on a scale I've never heard of before."

"Has it been in the news?"

"No," she said. "It's too spread out. Too many jurisdictions, too far-flung for anyone to be aware of all of it. Nobody has that kind of global perspective."

"This couldn't be the White brothers, those two doofuses."

"I don't know, Thorn. It may just be some freakish statistical thing. A lot of unrelated incidents that have no common link."

"But you don't really think that."

"No," she said. "I don't."

Sitting beside her on the couch, Thorn studied the atlas she'd marked up. The world spread out on two pages.

"You see this?"

He held the book up. Allison peered at it.

"What?"

"Your marks," Thorn said. "They're all in the tropics. Some subtropics, but mainly tropics. A narrow band."

"That's where the majority of the animals of the world live, and the greatest number of endangered ones."

"But doesn't it seem strange? All this activity, and nothing from the temperate zones?"

"Strange, yes. All of it seems strange."

And an hour later, coming to the end of the stack, Thorn swallowed down another Tylenol with a slug of beer, Allison put aside the pages.

"Well?" He took his seat again on the couch beside her. "What do you think?"

It was after two in the morning. Outside, the Glades was croaking and hooting, the steady whoops of chase and mating, like some great fiesta in the void.

"I don't know," Allison said. "I'm just not sure."

"But you've got a theory. You're seeing something."

She took a moment, staring at the far wall, the old sepia print of Julius Ravenel, his band of hunters. Back when the Everglades was glutted with wildlife, an infinite supply. And the world beyond the Everglades too.

"There are other recurrent patterns," she said.

"What?"

"Always male and female. And the destinations seem to be similar. Despite where the animals were captured, they all seem to be headed toward the Far East. There've been dozens of sightings: Singapore, Djakarta, Taipei, Bangkok. Known animal smugglers sighted with uncustomary frequency in those airports. A surge of activity. Something major is happening in that part of the world."

She was dazed, eyes unfocused. Feeling overtaxed, her circuitry unable to bear the load.

"What is it, Allison? What're you thinking?"

With her fingertips she rubbed hard circles in her temples.

"It looks to me," she said, "like Noah's reappeared."

Thorn put his beer aside.

"He's cramming his ark," Allison said. "Only this time, what he doesn't have room to carry, he's slaughtering."

Ray pulled his black Volvo off the highway behind an authentic Miccosukee tourist trap. Signs out front advertised that old traditional Indian sport of alligator wrestling and genuine honest-to-God Native American snow cones. Ray pulled up alongside what looked like a silver dog-catcher's truck. Crotch Meriwether got out of the truck, came around to Ray's open window. Orlon got out, joined them.

The old man was dressed in dark shirt and pants like some swamp-rat ninja. Frail and yellowed like he was a dozen breaths from the casket.

"Well, she's sure enough at home," Crotch said. Not hello, nice to see you again after all this time, nothing like that. "I hiked back there on foot. She's in the cabin with some guy. Two of them just sitting there reading. Bars on all the windows. I position the truck right, there'll be no way to get out the front door. They're trapped."

"What guy?" Ray said.

"Same one she was with today," Crotch said. "Name of Thorn. But you don't need to worry. I softened him up pretty good with my machete. He shouldn't put up too much of a fight."

"Thorn?" Ray said.

"I told you he wasn't any vet," said Orlon.

"Shit."

Orlon said, "So whatcha bring in the truck, Crotch?"

"Why don't you stick your nose in there, little man, and find out."

Ray got out of the car, followed Orlon over to the truck. On the truck bed there was a big camperlike thing that extended three feet off the end. Rear doors of wire mesh. Orlon edged up to the back door, peered in. Something snorted and banged the cage door, and Orlon jerked away. The truck swayed on its shocks.

"Jesus Christ. What the fuck is that thing?"

"It's two things," Crotch said. "And they don't like each other much. Just some wire mesh separating them. By the time we get down this bumpy road, they're going to like each other even less."

"What the hell are they for?" Ray stepped away from

the truck. "We're just going to keep this simple. Shoot her and leave."

"Ask your brother," said Crotch. "It was his idea."

Ray stepped close to Orlon, got in his face.

"Okay, what's going on? What the hell we need these animals for?"

"For fun," Orlon said. "For the sheer pleasure and dramatic excitement of hearing Allison scream."

"Hey, Orlon, this isn't some fucking movie."

His brother turned from the wire-mesh cage and looked at Ray.

"Sure it is, Ray. Sure it's a movie."

Thorn stripped to his Jockey shorts, lay down on the bed. Allison used the bathroom, stayed in there a long while. He was half asleep, the other half drugged. Not sure if his eyes were still open, not sure if he was dreaming or not when he saw Allison's thin, womanly shape move across the room.

Then a moment later he felt the mattress shift, felt her easing into the double bed beside him, felt the warmth of flesh press close. A polite snuggle, her left arm circling him. He lay still, breathed in her fragrance, a mild sandalwood with a delicate undercurrent of something else. The scent of sunbaked flesh, a warm glow of vanilla.

"Do you mind?" she whispered.

Thorn didn't answer, but relaxed his body, let her fit deeper against his back, both of them adjusting in small nudges and angles till the congruency was perfect. Skin to skin, their bodies becoming a single mass of heat and comfort, a curative blend of flesh.

For Thorn it was as though he were nestling in the protective cradle of Allison's body, a fleshy ark that could carry them safely beyond this difficult world. And he heard in the rhythm of her breath, the deep, soothing rasp of approaching slumber, that she was exactly where he was, the same pulse, the precise other half of his ragged self. Reminding him dimly of that dime-store jewelry heart he'd bought years ago, a bumbling teenager, half a valentine around his neck, its ragged edges matching the other half worn around his first love's neck. Like that, Allison and Thorn, their bodies notch to notch, a mesh that for that moment, in the blackness of the Everglades night, felt more exact, more flawless than any embrace he'd ever known.

It was an hour later, two perhaps. A human noise outside. Thorn lurched awake, sat up, swung his feet over the edge of the bed, set them on the floor. For one flashing moment his head seemed to splinter into two crimson halves along the seams of the machete wound.

Allison came up beside him just as something overturned in the front room. Then an animal snorted and huffed like a lawn mower engine struggling to catch on. A bottle broke, the remains of their wine.

"What is it?" she hissed beside him.

Thorn winced and pushed himself to his feet. Braced himself with a hand against the headboard.

"Were you expecting someone?"

Whatever it was was large, and its odor filled the house like sewer gas, and there was the reek of some other chemical as well, like the sour body odor of a steroid-chewing trucker. The creature was lumbering erratically around the front room, breaking, toppling. For a moment Thorn felt the floor rock, the creak and sway of the walls as if the house were about to capsize in giant swells.

Dizzy, he moved to the bedroom door, which stood a few inches ajar, showing the smallest light coming from the living room, some electric appliance sending out its pale green numbers. Three-twelve in the morning.

He caught the shadowy blur of something low and large trundling beside the couch. And heard the unmistakable snuffle and grunt of a hog.

It was then he saw the bone-white glow of its short tusks as it turned and faced him. After a split second's consideration, the hog squealed once and churned its hooves against the hardwood floor and hurtled toward the bedroom door.

# CHAPTER

## 28

The bedroom door rattled against its hinges and something in the living room crashed, an object as large and ungraceful as a refrigerator. Allison watched the bedroom door shudder as the creature barged against it once more.

The ghost of her dream was lingering. In that dream she'd been at the Shack with her father and his rowdy friends—the first female ever invited along. But for some reason she was banished to the bedroom while just beyond the door the men went wild with bourbon and raucous stories and their muscular rituals, and Allison felt more cheated than ever, taunted by the proximity of all she'd missed, the rambunctious, dangerous world of men, her father and his gang brawling out there, free of civilization, beyond the restraints of mothers and wives and girl children, beyond rules and manners and good taste, doing their lunatic dance around the campfire of masculinity.

As the door jolted again, Allison came up behind Thorn, only barely recognizing him through the last haze of her dream. She touched him on the back and he swung around, bringing a fist with him. But he caught himself in time and the punch fell away.

"Sorry," he said. "Sorry."

Thorn moved past her, went quickly to the single bedroom window, halted, took hold of the bars and rattled them. He turned around, shook his head, a rueful smile.

"There's just that one gun?"

"Yes, just the Remington," she said. "Out there."

"Is it loaded?"

"Yes." She rubbed the vision back into her eyes.

"How many shots?"

"Two."

In the living room a lamp broke. Allison turned and listened. It sounded as if the creature had snagged himself in a knot of electrical cords, and now everywhere he turned he toppled something else. Even in her primitive shack there were a hundred booby traps of modern life, flower vases perched on shelves, walls hung with fragile framed photos, and at ankle level the trip wires of ottomans and coffee tables, with throw rugs lying like patches of slippery ice across the oak floor. Not a place for a frenzied animal to navigate in the dark. A maze of snares, precariously balanced furnishings. A clock, a bell jar, an old transistor radio, plates and glasses, a bowl full of polished stones, her computer, and her fax machine. The animal was reducing them to rubble. Trying to make the room safe for his wildness.

"It's a hog," Thorn said. "Meriwether's hog."

"That bastard. This is his idea of a practical joke."

"I'm afraid it's more than that."

"That bastard."

"I'm going out there," he said.

"Why? We could just stay here, wait it out. It'll leave eventually."

"It isn't leaving. It's trapped in here with us."

Allison felt the shiver rise up her flanks. She walked to the bathroom where she'd dumped her jeans and jersey and she slipped into them. Thorn, still in his Jockey shorts, watched her.

"You can't go out there," she said. "It's too dangerous."

"I don't see there's a choice."

"Okay. All right, then I'll distract it. Throw a pillow or something."

Thorn turned from her and stared at the closed door. The house had become abruptly quiet now. He pressed his ear to the wood, held it there for a long moment, then turned back to her.

"You stay in here. Keep the door shut."

"Screw that, Thorn. I'm not some terrified little girl. This is going to take both of us."

She reached out, put a hand on his ribs, felt the bands of tension across his stomach.

"All right," he said quietly. "But not the goddamn pillow. At least throw something that could do some damage."

Allison drew her hand away, but Thorn caught it and gave her a reassuring squeeze. She squeezed back, and they held hands for a moment before letting go.

"I know just the thing."

Allison went to the small closet beside the bathroom and on a high shelf found the old Kenmore iron.

"That's the ticket," Thorn said. "Okay."

The living room was very still. A breeze filtered through the open window, budged the curtains aside. A gassy draft steeped in sulfur, the rich rotting muck of stranded pools of water. Algae, mildew, mold. A fertile brew, heady as Limburger.

"I go first," Allison said. "Throw the iron, hit the bastard if I can, then I'll duck back in here, hold the door, yell and scream, distract it while you get the Remington."

"But stay clear, be ready to get down," he said. "I may have to fire back in this direction."

"Okay."

"Where's the rest of the ammo stored?"

She smiled.

"What? You don't think you can kill a hog with two shots?"

"Allison," he said. "When we're finished with what's in the living room, we're going to have to deal with what's outside."

* * *

Rayon White was toying with the idea of shooting Crotch Meriwether in the back of the head, then doing the same thing to Orlon. And finish off the evening sucking on the hot barrel himself. A hat trick.

He hated this. Squatting out in the dark fifteen feet from the front porch of the small wood block house, slapping at mosquitoes, waiting for Allison or the guy to come crashing out the front door. It was stupid and sloppy, just the kind of moron stunt Orlon would dream up.

Orlon with the Colt .357, Meriwether with some blunderbuss that looked like he'd stolen it from a Civil War museum, and Ray holding the Glock nine. All of them huddled behind Crotch's truck, waiting for the screams, waiting for somebody or something to try to escape. And without even an idea if the two of them in there were armed. Shit, about the only half-smart thing Orlon had done was to climb up a pine post out in the yard and snip their phone line.

"Nobody's screaming," Ray said. "Or have I missed something?"

"Give 'em time."

"That hog's harder to kill than a mad dog on amphetamines," Crotch said. "Put it in a pen with a pit bull, a gator, and a heavily armed man, I'd bet my last nickel on that hog."

"If you had a last nickel," Orlon said.

"Two of us could go up to the windows," Ray said. "Start firing inside, stir things up. The other one could stay out front, pick them off as they come out."

"What's your hurry, Rayon? Anticipation, man, that's half the fun. Foreplay. Foreplay's where it's at."

"Man, this is completely and totally fucked. I can't believe I'm going along with this. And Crotch, you're as bad as Orlon. I'm out here in the dark with two totally crazy fucking people. We had a simple situation here, a clean kill, and we made it into something that could turn messy in a dozen different ways."

"Yeah," Orlon said. "That's the beauty of it."

"Shut up, you fuckfaces," Crotch said, "before I change my mind and start thinking I should've thrown in with Allison."

"I love it," Orlon said. "I love it. The old man's cracking, Rayon's cracking, that wood cabin is about to explode. Man, I'm about to cream my jeans."

"You wouldn't talk that way in front of Darlene Annette."

Orlon froze. Then very slowly he stood up, raised his pistol, and held it on his brother. He shook his head, mouth twisted.

"Jesus Christ, Ray, you sure know how to ruin a good moment. That's just about the one and only fucking thing in life you're truly good at, spoiling my fun."

Allison stood outside the bedroom door staring into the dark silence. She could see the rolltop desk was overturned, the computer facedown nearby, the couch on its back. There was the shine of broken glass; books and papers everywhere. The same room, but with a completely new terrain.

Thorn slid past her out the door. He followed the east wall, a hand guiding him toward the front door. In the jumble, Allison could see nothing of the hog. There was only the slightest breeze stirring the air, a splinter of moonlight lying across the overturned caneback chairs.

Thorn was three strides from the Remington, going past the east window, when she heard one of the caneback chairs scrape the floor and saw it begin to move along an angle to intercept Thorn.

She took aim, waited till she had a glimpse of pallid flesh, and hurled the iron. The hog squealed and the chair launched into the air. Allison yelled out and stamped her feet, and watched as the moon-pale tusks stopped and turned her way.

By then Thorn had the Remington and was fumbling with its mechanism when she saw a shadow larger than a man suddenly rise up from the floor beside the couch.

"To your right!" she screamed. "Look out!"

And she watched the shadow move, step into the bright spear of moonlight, and saw its shape clarify. A black bear, shorter than Thorn by a foot, but twice as heavy. In the wild they were timid creatures, wary of people. They would run at the slightest human scent. But in such a place as this, trapped with the hog and these two humans, there was no telling what its terror would make it do.

Thorn stepped back from the bear, held the shotgun up, aiming it at the dark shadow. To her right she heard the hard clack of hooves against the wood floor like a card shark riffling the deck.

In the languorous blur of simultaneous events happening impossibly fast, she saw the feral hog trundling toward her ankles, watched the bear take a sluggish swipe with its great paw at the Remington, saw the bright flash of the shotgun, and heard the blast doubled in volume by the small room. Then felt herself fall hard onto her rump in the doorway of the bedroom, and saw the Remington sail through the air, hit the overturned couch and spin away, skid across the floor, saw the black bear lunge at Thorn, watched him duck, all this as the feral hog held still, just a foot from her face, glowering at her with eyes as yellow as rotten corn, its tusks splintered and mangled, and she saw Thorn tossed sideways onto the rolltop desk, heard the air go out of him, and the bear turned and growled and began to lumber toward Allison.

Her body was prickly and numb, muscles useless as if she'd jolted her spine at a crucial juncture. Through a vague fog of rising pain she watched helplessly as the bear waddled toward her, dropping down to all fours.

Hearing its approach, the hog swiveled around to face the dark, foul-smelling beast. Across the room Thorn groaned and began to crawl on his belly toward her. As the thousand needle pricks of a waking limb filled her body, she writhed backward toward the bedroom. But a seam of her jeans snagged on the head of a nail at the doorjamb and caught her there.

The hog lurched forward at the bear, thrashed its

head from side to side, slashing at the animal's forelegs. For a moment Allison thought she could smell the bear's breath, a blast of putrid air. With only a small growl the black bear rose up and swung its paw, then swung the other. Beneath its reach, the hog rushed at the bear's ankles, slammed into it, drove the animal sideways, knocked it off balance into a pile of chairs.

She shot a look at Thorn where he lay a foot from the Remington, one arm outstretched toward the shotgun, gasping like a swimmer washed ashore from a week at sea.

The feral hog charged the fallen bear and the bear flailed at the squat, slippery creature, kicked and sliced its claws as the hog punched its tusks into the bear's thick haunch. Allison sat up against the doorjamb, watching the struggle before her as if from a euphoric mile away.

The feeling was beginning to leak back into her legs and torso. There was a bloody gash on her right ankle and her legs felt swollen twice their size. Thorn had wriggled another foot and his hand was on the shotgun's stock.

"Push it to me, Thorn. Shove it."

With a grunt he jerked his arm straight, slid the Remington a yard across the floor. She reached out for it, lifted it up, fit the weapon to her shoulder. She pressed her back against the wall and watched as the bear swatted the hog with a numbing blow, then gripped it and lifted the writhing creature in its claws.

The bear dropped its shaggy head forward and sunk its teeth into the tight, fat back of the hog's neck. The animal squealed and blood erupted from the bear's mouth. It took another bite and wrenched its head to the side, and the hog went slack.

Allison held her aim, watching the bear stand and drop the lifeless hog to the floor. Watched the black bear waver for a moment, injured, confused, far from any comfort it knew. A thin white strip of bone showed at its ankle, a green-tree fracture with its spray of splintered particles blooming from the bear's damp fur.

The bear stared down at Allison, then shifted its gaze to Thorn. Allison sighted the shotgun on the animal's wide chest, held her aim until the bear shifted its feet and turned its back on her, began a slow, dreary shuffle toward the front window where the moonlight shone the brightest.

There it stopped and took hold of the bars, and held them for a moment as if gathering its strength, then in several awkward heaves it wrenched the entire cage out of its wooden socket, dropped it on the floor, and climbed through the window.

Allison lowered the shotgun, rested her back against the wall. She could hear Thorn wheezing as if he had a punctured lung. She pushed herself to her feet and then she heard the voices outside, men approaching.

Her mind was as flat and bland as it had ever been. No fear, no hope, no anger. She flattened her back against the wall and aimed the shotgun at the door and waited till it was fully open and the silhouette of a man showed clearly there.

And she fired the remaining shot, blew the man's shadow backward out the door. Outside in her yard the men yelled and cursed, and a moment later the roar of an engine sounded nearby, the screech and clashing of gears. And then the long unwinding of the motor's roar.

Allison leaned the Remington against the wall and went to Thorn. He was sitting up, his breath noisy in his throat. She helped him stand, looped his right arm over her shoulder, hauled him to the bed and lay him down.

Between long gulps of air, he told her he was all right. Maybe a broken rib, but nothing worse. She checked him but found no blood. When he was calm, eyes closing, she went out to the living room, picked her way through the debris, and stepped outside into the blanched moonlight.

The man had fallen backward, his legs still on her front steps, but his head and shoulders lay against the sandy ground. At first she couldn't find the wound at all, in the half-dark against his black clothes. But after a moment more she noticed the ragged tear where his right shoulder once had been. A shoulder that had braced the butt of carbines and shotguns and flintlocks and muskets of every kind. A lifetime of bringing down the running deer, of cutting short the lazy flight of birds, of knocking from the trees and tall grasses the game that would fill his stewpot, whose plumage or fur or thick hide he would trade for his livelihood.

Allison stood above the fallen man and watched Meriwether's blood leak into the earth that in his own twisted way he had loved so much.

# CHAPTER

## 29

They buried Crotch Meriwether in an oak hammock a mile west of the Shack. Soft loamy earth, miles of unobstructed view west across the saw grass prairie. They took turns with the shovel, the other holding the Remington, scanning the horizon.

A few minutes past sunrise, when they were done, they stood over the grave, Allison drenched with sweat, Thorn breathing unevenly. After a silent three or four minutes, whatever prayers would be said for Meriwether had been spoken.

Back in the Shack Allison showered, bandaged her ankle, and dressed in fresh wheat-colored jeans, a blue-and-white crew neck shirt. Thorn took his turn in the shower and put on his torn blue work shirt, his khaki shorts. His ribcage was covered with yellowish red bruises, but he said he believed nothing was broken. His breath was coming more freely all the time.

It was nine-thirty when they stopped at a Cuban strip shopping center just inside the Miami city limits. She called Harry at work. His voice was vacant.

"Where were you last two nights?"

"At the Shack."

"Is that how it's going to be now, you're just going to come and go?"

"Look, Harry, I need your help."

"Oh, do you? What is it this time, going after the governor? A senator perhaps?"

She watched Thorn in the front seat of the Cherokee. He was downing another Tylenol with a Budweiser he'd bought in the Cuban market. Breakfast of convalescents.

"Your friend at the State Department," she said. "The redheaded one you used to play golf with. What's his name?"

"Danny Burton," he said warily.

"That's him. I'm sure he could handle this."

"Handle what?"

She said, "I want to know what Americans entered Borneo during October this year. In fact, what I really want is the complete passport and immigration list for the entire month, every nationality. Every port of entry, airports, ships, roads."

"Good Christ!"

"It wouldn't be conclusive," she said. "But I want to see their names. Be absolutely sure they were there. And to see if maybe there's another name I recognize, the one they're working for."

"Whose names are we talking about here?"

"I'll tell you about it later, Harry."

"You're still after Joshua Bond, aren't you? Still obsessed with that man."

"I want to see that list."

"And you think I can do something like that? Snap my fingers, get passport data from a foreign country?"

"Can't you?"

"Why do you have to keep playing cop like this?"

"Will you do it, Harry, or should I call Danny Burton myself?"

"Goddamn it, Allison, immigration records like that, even for a small country like Borneo, you're talking about mountains of paperwork at the very least. Hell, their computers probably can't break out a single month in the first place. I'm sure their data systems are just as backward as everything else in that damn country. And this is not even to mention the fact that the Malaysians would never allow some private citizen to paw through that kind of information."

"I'm sure there're lots of reasons," she said quietly, "why this would be difficult for you to accomplish. Lots of very good reasons you can't help."

He hesitated a moment and when he came back his voice was deeper, more grave.

"You think I can just pick up the phone?" he said. "Call somebody over there, Kuala Lumpur, and they'll drop what they're doing and send me lists of names?"

"Harry, I spent twenty years watching you operate. I know what you can accomplish when you want to. And I know you've got a ton of markers you could call in. So don't pretend with me. If you want to do this, you can find a way."

"All right, all right," he said coldly. "I'll try. But I won't promise anything."

"And Harry," she said. "I won't be home for a few days."

"So what else is new?"

"I'll call you later on, see what you've found out."

"Swell," he said. "I think you know my numbers."

"Thank you, Harry. Thank you for trying."

"Oh, by the way," he said. "Funny you should have called, really."

"What?"

"I just got off the phone with Sean."

"Yes?"

"She's gone. She left."

"Gone?"

The line was silent. Allison watched a construction crew walk past, young men in ponytails and earrings, each of them eyeing her up and down.

"Harry? Where is Sean?"

"I believe it's instructive, Allison, that she called me, not you, at a moment like this. I think that tells us something very important."

"Harry."

He was silent. Traffic sang in her other ear. Cuban Muzak, marimbas and trumpets, a manic beat.

Harry said, "She went back over there. To Borneo. She's with Patrick."

Fifty thousand feet, sixty below zero outside, seven hundred miles an hour, a steady thunder in the Concorde, not too different from riding in an unmuffled, full-race Ferrari, Patrick said. It goes very, very fast, but it's extremely stiff, much bumpier than the slower models, 767's, L-1011's, proving once again that you have to pay in one way or another for every good thing you get.

Only six seats, big leather ones, widely spaced, a creamy color. Then a partition, a sliding door. Behind the door there was a bedroom with soft lighting, smoky gray drapes over the cabin walls cushioning some of the noise. Lights coming from somewhere, Sean wasn't sure.

In the air for hours now, somewhere over the Atlantic, she lay on her back on the bed, a silk sheet covering her. Sean naked, looking up at the vague lights, the shadows, feeling the speed of the airplane, the reckless velocity of the last few days, the sheer wildness of what she'd done, packed one small bag, flown off with this boy from another time, another world, Patrick who lay naked beside her; fifty thousand feet, sixty below zero just beyond those curtains, just beyond the thin aluminum skin of his uncle's Concorde.

Flying against the grain of time, into the rising sun, but with the wind at their backs. Always a trade-off. Lose time, but reap a tailwind. Making love while going against time, losing it one way, gaining it back another. Growing older at seven hundred miles an hour. Later and later and later, every mile they traveled east, every thrust of hip.

Sean was six motel rooms and then some past virginity; two blankets on the beach, and a backseat of an '85 Ford Fairlane, a dorm room, and a beachfront condo. And even from the very first time, with Sammy Parks, parked near the third green of the Gables Country Club, Sean had never once missed her orgasm. She could make it happen quickly, or she could hold it off. Either way, it was predictably intense.

So she'd never understood what the big deal was, how some women could go their whole lives without having one. Like Winslow, who'd had that problem, confiding in Sean that she was in therapy for it, just couldn't let go with a man, repressed, bashful, convinced she was defective, emotionally incomplete.

But not Sean. Ten guys, and even the few who'd been consistently premature, she could come with them all. It was easy for her, like playing a team sport, or slow dancing. Anticipating her partner's move, being there when the ball was passed, harmonizing. Like everything physical Sean had tried, she was good at it almost immediately, got better very quickly, and mastered it within a year or two.

One of them, Tom Lawson, liked to watch porno movies to get in a raunchy mood. Sean had never seen such stuff before and was repelled and fascinated. They'd sit naked on his couch for hours fondling each other, the films running, and Sean watched the California healthies play their Kama Sutra games. But she discovered the films had nothing to teach her. There were no new positions, no anatomical surprises. Somehow in her own instinctive, meandering way she'd already covered the same ground as these fantasy people. A doctorate in sex without any formal training.

But Patrick was different from any man she'd known. Handsome, caring, mysterious, a very light touch. And Sean was beginning to doubt her arrogance. With subtle strokes and nudges, small but crucial shifts in position, he'd been pushing her to places she'd never been. Moving her up a scale of pleasure she had not imagined.

And now, in the shadowy cabin where a vanilla-scented candle fluttered on the bedside table, and Dire Straits seeped quietly from hidden speakers, Patrick sat up, poured two more glasses of cognac, handed one to Sean.

They each took a sip, Sean feeling the golden flush spread through her. After another silent sip or two, Patrick set his glass aside and took hers from her hand, put it on the table. He leaned across her and kissed her shoulder, her throat and breasts as he lowered himself to her again. His body sleek, pale skin as delicate as ash.

With his lips and fingertips he roamed her flesh. She could feel herself begin to lather as she curled to him, moved lower, inhaled the freshly cut hay smell of his cock, so familiar now, taking it in her hands, fondling, and curving down to take it in her mouth. She felt his lips easing down her belly, tongue in her navel, lower through her abundant hair, his lips parting those other lips, tongue dipping into her hungrily as if she were a ripe mango.

For what seemed like the thousandth time in these last few days, one position melted into another, and he was inside her, and they were once again making slow and thorough love. And as he'd been from the first, Patrick was attentive, tender, and exploratory, using a quiet delicacy she'd never felt, as if he were handling an ancient, perilously fragile violin. The background music, the salty taste of him, his deep, slow thrusts flawlessly in time with hers.

As Dire Straits continued to recycle, slowly he drew her off the bed, standing naked at fifty thousand feet, outrunning the speed of sound, a rumble everywhere, clouds exploding around them. He led her to the next contortions, Sean bent over the small couch, then flat on her belly on the gold wall-to-wall rug while Patrick pressed into her from behind, and still later Patrick was atop her again on the bed, supporting himself on straight arms, delicate pushups, only his cock touching her.

And Sean inched to the edge of release again, her cries spiraling upward, calling out as the moment approached. But this time it was different from every time before, a quick jolt that twisted inside her. She stiffened and the back of her head knocked against the headboard. She clenched her eyes, arched back to ease the spasm. Felt something large and feverish moving upward inside her, swelling as it came, a huge warmth spreading through her belly, shuddering into her chest, a ping of lights, swirl of noise.

She made a noise in her throat, gasped, reached up to pull him down against her. It was scary how good they were together, scary to feel this way about anyone, and for all of it to have happened so quickly, as though the other men had only been warm-ups, pale preparations for the real thing. Very scary. Fifty thousand feet, seven hundred miles an hour. Going somewhere far away, getting there very fast.

And those were her final thoughts before it took her. Heavy drugs flooded Sean's bloodstream from glands that had never worked before. Something she hadn't known, hadn't suspected. As if she had never had a true orgasm before, as if before today she'd only been skimming along some shallow pond of feeling.

Allison wanted a few things from the Gables house, clothes, her address book, any new faxes. Thorn said no, it was too dangerous. They'd be watching the house. She wasn't so sure. The way they ran off like that last night. It had to be the White brothers, cowards really. Maybe seeing Meriwether killed like that had scared them off for good.

"Humor me then," said Thorn. "I'll go over there. You stay here."

They were at Snapper Creek Marina in the galley of his thirty-one-foot Chris-Craft berthed on the edge of the shadowy creek. Old Cutler Road ran fifty yards to the east. A hard wind was bending the Australian pines, scudding foam along the fringes of the canal. Another cold front was settling in, the sky gloomy and low, the sun dulled by cheerless layers of clouds the color of oyster shells.

"You need to rest anyway," he said. "Just lie down for a while, take a nap, let me get the stuff, and I'll be back before noon. Then we can take the boat out on the bay, find a cove, anchor up, figure out what to do next."

"Sean flew back to Borneo with Patrick Sagawan."

Thorn opened the small refrigerator beside the breakfast nook. Found a beer, held it up for Allison. She shook her head and he put it back. He looked out at a cabin cruiser headed out of the canal, a man without a care steering from the upper deck, going out on the bay to blow his hair loose, spend a few hundred dollars' worth of gasoline doing it.

"Patrick Sagawan does business with Harry. Some mysterious construction project in Brunei. A very big venture."

"So?"

"Do you know where Brunei is?"

"It sounds far away."

"It's near Djakarta, Singapore, Bangkok, Taipei. Where all those animal smugglers have been congregating lately."

Thorn circled the block twice, saw nothing suspicious, but just to be sure he parked the Cherokee two streets away just off Alhambra, then cut down an alley on foot, jumped over two backyard fences and then was in the Farleighs' backyard.

Frank Sinatra was crooning Christmas carols in the house next door. The smells of roasting turkey, onions and garlic simmering. Only the second week in November and "Silent Night" was filling the neighborhood. As if the cold weather had triggered some automatic response.

It was probably the combination of the Christmas carols, the dreary wind, the raw, sunless day, and all the accumulated wounds and bruises he'd suffered in the last week backing up inside him, all of it with nowhere to go anymore, riding up into his throat, because suddenly Thorn was breathless, and had to sit down on the Farleighs' back steps, his head swirling like a compass needle that's lost its true north.

A few minutes later, when he'd composed himself, he used her key to enter the house. Went upstairs to her bedroom. He selected her wardrobe for the next few days, packed the clothes in a grocery sack. Ms. Allison

Farleigh's personal valet. He took a handful of faxes from
the machine, her toothbrush, deodorant, and filled the
sack to the brim with the assorted tubes and bottles ar-
rayed on the lavatory shelf.

Before he left, he stood in the doorway and took a
long look at her bedroom. Frank Sinatra had moved on to
"The Twelve Days of Christmas," hamming it up on "five
golden rings."

Allison's bedroom reminded him uncomfortably of
his own. A double bed and across from it a desk covered
with the functional paraphernalia of her trade. Muted
beige paint on the walls. No frills, no filigree, no pile of
pillows, no distracting geegaws or romantic watercolors.
All business. A cloister for sleep and toil. The windows
looking out into dull trees.

It was the room of someone who'd lost the knack of
self-indulgence, a person so caught up in the methodical
habits of work, so focused on the minutiae of the problem
at hand that she seemed to have abandoned any last possibility of joy.

Thorn took the sidewalks back to the Cherokee. He
glanced around several times, but saw no one following
him. Only a mail truck making its rounds, one old lady
sweeping her front walk. A yapping dog.

It was eleven-thirty when he got back to the Jeep. He
opened the door, set the grocery bag on the passenger's
seat, and was ducking his head inside when someone
whispered behind him. Pivoting, Thorn saw only a quick
flash. The blur of metal. Though he realized what it was a
half second after the first blow. A rod, tire iron, something
like that. Feeling a second jolt in his gut even before he
registered the first one on his skull. Wondering about that
as he tumbled against the car, how things could get so
scrambled so quickly.

Then another hard shot above his right ear, spinning
him to his right. He snagged his shirt on the Cherokee's
rearview mirror, ripping it, hearing his own grunt as the
scalding zipper opened up the back of his head along the
seam of his machete stitches, a fizzing noise like the spew

from a giant rocket about to lift off. His wound reopening.

Somehow he didn't fall. Somehow Thorn kept his eyes open, the light smudged, growing gray, but his brain still awake. Tottering, he watched the small man, the hairless White brother, peering into his eyes. Through the gray mist, Thorn saw the black crowbar in his left hand. The man was examining Thorn, choosing a spot, as if Thorn were a tree, one good whack away from falling to the forest floor.

Leaning against the door of his car, Thorn let his head loll forward. His eyes slack, but still watching the little guy with the tire iron, and then seeing over his shoulder the next-door neighbor, a white-haired Cuban woman in a yellow apron out on her porch staring in their direction.

Thorn refocused on the small man before him, watched as he drew the iron bar back with both hands, assumed a slugger's stance. The guy was dressed in black T-shirt and jeans. Eyes smiling.

Thorn waited till the bar was coming around, aimed at his head, the little guy going to blast this one over the center field wall, like Mickey, Reggie, Canseco, spray Thorn's teeth across the lawn. The old Cuban lady watched placidly.

At the final possible instant, Thorn jerked out of his slump, dodged the blow, watched the little guy spin halfway around, lose his balance. Thorn stepped in quick, punted him in the butt, kicked a week's shit back up into the little bastard, sent him hurling headfirst across ten feet, into the rough bark of an old oak. Heard the thunk of that hairless skull against the tree.

Thorn met him as he was stumbling to his feet, eyes groggy. Thorn leaned back and cracked him with an overhand right against the bridge of his nose. The guy lurched back, but the tree held him up. Thorn gave him a quick left jab that glanced off his temple, a right uppercut to his solar plexus. Thorn eased off a little, didn't want to kill this guy. Not yet anyway.

Leaning back against the oak, the little man breathed hard, blood leaking from his nose.

"You finished, tough guy?" Orlon White said, his eyes muddy. "You got all that macho bullshit out of your system?"

Thorn stepped in, took a deep grip on the man's shirtfront, straightened him up, fist clenching cloth, his knuckles bumping the underside of the guy's chin. Thorn lifted him a few inches into the air.

"Now you're coming with me. We're going to have a little talk. You, me, and a fence post."

Thorn turned for the Cherokee, swung the guy with him, his toes just brushing the ground. Going to hammer his slick head against the fender till he was unconscious. But he felt the guy wriggle and squirm, then a hard and familiar shape jammed against Thorn's sore ribs.

"I told Ray you were an ape-kisser. I spotted you from the get-go." The small man dug the pistol deeper against Thorn's bruised ribs. Thorn released his grip and the hairless man stepped back.

"So, Senor Muy Macho, where is she? Where's my friend Allison hiding out?"

"Fuck you, Charlie."

"Oh, yeah? Fuck me? Is that your big speech? Your Robert Mitchum tough-guy's comeback? Hey, we're going to have to go somewhere, work on your dialogue, man. You'll never win an Oscar with lines like that."

"Give me a minute," Thorn said. "I'll think of something that'll have you in stitches."

The bald man blinked, then studied Thorn more closely.

"Oh, now, that's better," he said. "You keep working on it, kid, maybe we'll give you a screen test later this evening." He prodded Thorn in the ribs again, pushing him toward a black Corvette parked across the street. "Of course, that all depends," Orlon said, "if later on this evening you're still alive."

# C H A P T E R

# 30

"I've given this a lot of thought," Tricia Capoletti said.

It was Friday afternoon. An hour earlier she'd called Ray at work, and he'd rushed home, changed into better clothes, and gone to her office. "I cleared my calendar, canceled my afternoon appointments. We need to talk, Ray." And bing, he was there, dreading this but at the same time welcoming it. Heart singing. Sloughing off all that shit last night in the Everglades, Meriwether getting shot. The whole mess.

It all felt different now with Tricia, not client and shrink, but Ray and Tricia. She even sat in a different chair, the one behind her desk, and Ray sat in the green one he usually used during their sessions. He wondered if she'd peed before he'd come in. Thinking about yesterday, her bladder, their day together at Brad Randolph's ranch and the 7-Eleven, all of it gave Ray a honey glow in his chest. Things happening between them. Deepening intimacy.

She was in a brown cashmere sweater today. Another blazer, this one hunter green with a bright pin on the lapel, some kind of animal. Beige wool pants, her usual brown loafers. A far cry from Betty Penski and her vinyl miniskirts and red knee-high go-go boots, see-through blouses.

Ray had put on a pair of faded jeans with a hard

crease, a woven leather belt, a blue button-down cham-
bray shirt with the top button undone, red striped tie
worn loose at the throat. A white loose-fitting jacket, new
Adidas tennis shoes. He'd seen some actor dressed like
that in one of the Hollywood magazines Orlon subscribed
to, looking hip but easygoing, arm in arm with his fashion-
model wife. Ray tore out the page and went shopping.
Soft-core preppy, the way Tricia liked, but Ray adding on
a little extra spice—the stripes in the red tie were actually,
if you looked real close, rocket ships.

He was thinking of that, those rocket ships, imagining the moment when he showed them to her, Tricia edging in to see them, her face a few inches from his, Ray
figuring that would be the moment he'd been waiting for,
perfect opportunity to put a hand on her shoulder, draw
her close, kiss her, thinking of the rocket ships, that soft
incredible first kiss, as Tricia said:

"Ray, why did you do this? Why did you shoot that
boy?"

"I told you. 'Cause he hit the woman that looked like
my mom."

"But why did you feel you had to shoot him? Were
you angry?"

"Damn right I was angry. The little shit."

"But that's what I'm for, Ray. When you can't deal
with a situation, when something makes you mad like
that, you come to me, we'll talk it through. You shouldn't
try to settle things with a gun. That's not civilized. It's not
rational, Ray."

Ray sat up straighter. She saw the look on his face
and held up her hand like she was halting traffic.

"Ray, I want you to make reparations for what you
did to that boy."

"Make what?"

"Reparations," she said. "You can't just let this go.
You have to do something, something that costs you in
some major way. Something that's equal to your wrongdo-
ing."

"Reparations."

"That's right."

"What is that actually? I mean, I think I know. It's like an offering at church. Is that what you're saying?"

"Not exactly."

" 'Cause, you know, that really isn't a word in my current usage. I mean, I want to do exactly what you think is the right thing here, but I gotta have a different word from you. Maybe if you just put it another way, a more familiar phrasing, that might be better."

"You're going to have to figure this out yourself, Ray."

"Figure it out myself."

"Yes. Figure out how to make amends, do what you think is appropriate. You'll know when you've accomplished it."

Ray said the word silently to himself. *Reparations.*

"I have to be completely honest with you, Ray. Since you told me what you did, I've given a lot of thought to calling the police, bringing them in on this. Laying it all out in front of them."

"You can do that? I thought it was against some kind of rule in your profession. Unethical."

"After a great deal of thought," she said, "I decided not to proceed in that way. I decided to give you the chance to wrestle with this by yourself. Choose exactly what the appropriate way to redress this crime would be for you. This is not something I think I should solve for you."

Ray stood up, angled over to her desk. Tried to seem at ease, thinking of the Hollywood guy in these same clothes, how comfortable he'd appeared, big tall blond woman on his arm. Tricia looked up at him from a yard away. Ray could smell her perfume, something with a meadowy smell. Sunlight, grass, bees.

He gripped the point of the tie, held it away from his shirt. Looked down at it.

"Rocket ships," Ray said. "That's what these are. From a distance, you know, they look just like ordinary stripes. But if you see it up close . . ."

She squinted at him. A quiver in her chin or eyes, somewhere he couldn't pin down. Hair drawn back today, clamped in a tortoiseshell barrette. Ray preferred it loose, down on her shoulders, a softer look, hair you could spread on a pillow.

"Have I put myself in danger, Ray, saying this to you? Do you see me as a threat now?"

The quiver growing.

"A threat? You? Hey, you gotta be joking."

"I want you to tell me how you feel, Ray. Tell me what's going through your mind right now, okay? Be honest."

He let go of his tie, smoothed it into place against his flat stomach.

"Right now? This exact second?"

She kept squinting at him, the slightest nod.

"A bunch of different things," he said.

"Tell me."

"Are we doing psychology again?"

"I'm asking you not as your counselor, but as a friend. What you're thinking."

"Okay," he said, feeling a sudden creamy warmth flow through him; Tricia, his friend. "I'm thinking, I don't know. I guess I was thinking of going to a bookstore, buy a dictionary. Look up a few words, see exactly what it is you want me to do."

"That's all, Ray?"

"No," he said. "I was thinking about your hair, how the sunlight does different things to the color."

She looked down at her desk, ran her hand over her big green ink blotter in its leather holder.

Ray said, "And one more thing. I guess I was thinking how maybe when this is all over, when I've gotten healthy and normal, maybe the two of us could go out together again. Attend another wedding maybe. Is that something you might be interested in?"

Thousands of lightbulbs. To be exact, fifty-one thousand, four hundred and ninety lightbulbs in that one building. Five hundred and sixty-four chandeliers, some of them as big as compact cars, weighing more than a ton.

Sean was somewhere deep in the interior of the Sultan of Brunei's main palace, Istana Nurul Iman, where according to Patrick roughly two hundred lightbulbs burned out each and every day. Just imagine. Two hundred a day. One servant's full-time job was to unscrew two hundred dead ones, screw in two hundred fresh ones. All day, every day. Week after week after week. One man's lifetime career, to change those bulbs.

Patrick was giving her the tour. The sultan was away in London, visiting one of his hotels, the Dorchester. He wasn't scheduled to return until after the first of the year; both his wives, the queens, traveling, too, and Patrick apparently with the run of the palace. He was dressed in a tight-fitting pale green linen suit, a pleated ecru shirt with a round collar, hair combed straight back. Just before landing they'd showered and changed in the Concorde, been met on the tarmac by a Bentley, and were driven directly to the palace where they were greeted by two of Patrick's uncles, the sultan's brothers, several girl cousins, all of them coolly civil toward Sean. Standing aside as Patrick began to conduct his tour.

From the three outfits Sean had brought along, she'd selected a floral shirtwaist dress with a full, sweeping skirt. Blue background, subdued hibiscus blooms. Half-sleeves, a navy belt. The most conservative thing she'd packed, though even so, Patrick had his doubts. "Don't forget it's changed since you were here last," he said. "The fundamentalists have much more say in things. Everything's more orthodox."

"So what am I supposed to do, wrap myself in a sheet?"

"Sean!"

She told him she was just kidding. Just kidding, really. He studied her suspiciously while Sean tried to rid her face of any trace of irony. Finally Patrick sighed and let his eyes stray away. The moment passed, but it grated on her, lingered. Giving their rapport a chilly undercur-

rent. He was different here in his own land, harder to
reach, preoccupied, more serious. As if perhaps the man
she'd fallen for was a man on holiday, the relaxed version
of Patrick, and now she was seeing the real one.

They walked through the palace, past soldiers with
red sashes, handguns in patent leather holsters, and other
khaki-uniformed guards carrying assault rifles, servants
everywhere, all coming to soft attention as the two of
them approached.

She was deeply exhausted from a string of sleepless
nights, the jarring flight. Rubber-legged, body vibrating,
brain full of nettles. Though she wished only to check into
her room at the Sheraton Utami, lie down and sleep for
days, she followed quietly behind Patrick as he marched
through the palace, sweeping his hands at this or that
amazement. Dutifully she tried to come along on this ride,
share his excited state, but the palace struck her as cold
and bland and at the same time incredibly garish. Like
some sterile concrete parking garage that had been fur-
nished and decorated by drag queens.

According to Patrick, three hundred and fifty million
dollars built it. Oil money, of course, and natural gas. The
Brunei division of Shell Oil working the Seria oil fields
just offshore.

All the money he'd lavished on the palace was little
more than pocket change for the sultan. The man was
worth three times Queen Elizabeth, more than all the
Saudis. By far the richest man in the world. Thirty billion
dollars put safely away, maybe thirty-five by now. Who
could keep track? It grew more mountainous every second. Patrick rattled it off, the numbers, the breezy view of
his uncle. Sean watched him, hearing his voice, a quiet
vibrato of fervor creeping into it.

Though by all accounts, Patrick said, the oil was running out. Within their lifetime the fields would be
pumped dry. The great cash machine forever silenced.

"That's my job," he said. "To help his Majesty diversify. Find other revenue sources for the next century."

The palace was larger than Buckingham Palace or the

Vatican. Two hundred and fifty toilets, eighteen elevators, forty-four staircases. Sewage treatment for 300,000 gallons per day. Enough for a hundred thousand people flushing at once, though on a regular basis the palace housed only two members of the royal family.

"Well, you never know who might drop in," Sean said. Patrick didn't smile.

Sean tagged along. Ooohed the best she could. Nodded as if she were as dazzled by the palace's vital statistics as he was. Perhaps it was her grogginess that was putting the strange shine on the place, a shimmery unreality. But maybe not. Maybe the shimmer was there anyway, and groggy was the best condition for this tour, that or drunk. If she'd been cold alert, surely she would've made cracks she'd regret, shown herself to be an unappreciative snob, too bourgeois to savor the splendor.

Seventeen hundred rooms, over two million square feet of floor space, which worked out to roughly fifty acres. Thirty-eight different types of marble covering fourteen acres of floors. Gold-plated walls. Giant golden domes. Parking for eight hundred. Louis XVI chairs and tables in sleek-windowed, modern rooms. A banquet hall whose ceiling was five stories high, with seating for four thousand. A sports complex that housed a dozen indoor tennis courts, polo practice field, Olympic swimming pools, badminton, squash, handball courts. And this, Patrick said, was only one of several palaces in the royal family.

"Do you have a palace?"

"No," he said, smiling at her. "Not yet." Then, quietly, seriously, "Does it matter?"

They were in the doorway of one of the four kitchens. This one a stainless-steel gymnasium.

"Patrick," she said, taking his hand. "I'd like you even if you were rich."

His smile seemed to weaken around the edges.

"*Like* me? Is that all?"

Sean watched as two servants passed in the corridor, pushing a black handcart with broom handles sticking out. On its side were gold and silver inlays of palm trees and birds in flight. A ten-thousand-dollar janitor's cart.

She said, "You want me to be the first to say it? The magic word?"

Patrick examined the servants walking past.

"No," he said. "Perhaps now is not the best time for declarations of that kind."

He squeezed her hand, then let it go.

Later, when they were finished with the tour, they loafed on the palace's west docks looking out across a mangrove lagoon, a wild stretch of the Brunei River that led into the interior jungles of the country. A half dozen armed guards were spread out on the nearby lawn eyeing the steady stream of outboards ferrying tourists slowly up and down the river so they could snap their photos of the palace.

Just a few miles up that river was Brunei's jungle, lush and abundant, still covering eighty percent of the countryside. With all their oil, the Bruneians had not been forced to strip their land of timber, as the rest of Borneo was doing. Through the luck of the geological draw, a tiny country like Brunei could afford the luxury of rain forest preservation, something her neighbors in the rest of Borneo could not.

Last month, only an hour west of where she stood now, Sean and Winslow and Allison had flown into Kuching, coming in low over the countryside. Sean had seen the wide, depressing vista. Bald hills, thousands and thousands of acres of rough mountain terrain utterly stripped of green. And countless new logging roads were being carved into the few remaining virgin forests.

From above, the rivers were a muddy yellow, clogged with branches and rejected trees, smoke billowing from vast burn sites. Land where some great upheaval was taking place, a war zone. The country was in the midst of swapping its ancient forest for fleeting cash.

"Are you all right, Sean? You're so quiet."

She turned from the river, looked into Patrick's uneasy eyes.

"I was just thinking how strange this all is, being here. The palace."

"Strange? What's so strange?"

"Well, for one thing," she said. "Fifty-one thousand lightbulbs. That's pretty damn strange."

"Yes?" he said. "How?"

"Well, I mean it's amazing," she said. "Someone counted all of them. You knew the exact number."

"So?"

Patrick retreated a half step, regarding her warily. His face was flushed and perspiration stood out on his forehead. It was a hot, clear day, but his sweat seemed to be coming from some sudden inner heat. A flinch in his blue eyes, something close to childish hurt.

"It's nothing," she said. "Nothing, really."

"Go on, make your joke, Sean. That's what you were going to do, wasn't it? Something funny about lightbulbs."

The anger that was roughening his voice had appeared so quickly and unexpectedly that she was momentarily dumbfounded. Two hours ago they'd been making love nine miles up. Now they stood beside a tropical lagoon in the shadow of the world's largest and most expensive palace, the hot, airless breeze more oppressive than a Miami August, and the man she'd fallen in love with, coming with him to the other side of the globe, was now twisting his face into a bitter parody of itself. A sudden stranger. Sean felt it all at once, a pang of fear, the shadowy swirl of sadness and dislocation. Culture shock, lover shock. No longer certain exactly where she'd landed, who exactly she'd landed with.

"What is it you're doing with my father, Patrick? The oil business?"

"Not oil, no. As I said before, diversification. Something for when the oil runs out."

"Diversify to what?"

"Tourism," he said. Rocking his head back and smiling with satisfaction at a patch of sky just above her head.

"Attracting foreigners to Brunei: Europeans, Americans, Asians. People from all over the world."

"What? You're building another Disney World?"

"No," he said. "Something much, much better. Something that no one else has. The only one of its kind in the world."

"But you're not going to tell me."

"Tell you? No," he said. "I'll take you there. Tomorrow we'll fly out to the De Novo site. You can see what your father and I have been up to these last few years. The fruits of our labor."

She was going to ask him more, but Patrick seemed to be elsewhere now, his eyes disengaged, turned inward as if he were savoring some exquisite aroma too private for words.


The movie star himself telephoned Ray White, turned on his considerable charm, but the dealer was unswayed. He was not willing to accept the orangutan back. No refunds. Never. Mr. White listened to the movie star describe a couple of the ape's violent episodes, throwing a favorite dog out an upstairs window, then climbing out the window himself and running amok through the wedding party.

In the middle of the story, and without so much as a good-bye, the animal dealer hung up on the movie star.

Then, after a brief consultation with his tax attorney, who did a half hour's research on his behalf, the movie star determined that it would be in his best interests to make a charitable donation of one orangutan to the primate research facility at his alma mater, a small liberal arts college in central Florida.

The college's research facility was run by a professor whose specialization was behavioral psychology. For ten years the professor had been depending on captive-born monkeys, gibbons, chimps, and crab-eating macaques for his experiments in stress management. Customarily, the monkeys and apes were strapped for twelve to fifteen hours a day into aluminum chairs and were subjected to a variety of noises, lights, movements, and odors. Pulse rates and blood pressure and even cholesterol levels were monitored continually.

In ten years of lab research, the professor had produced forty-three articles on the results of his experiments. They detailed changes of heart function and blood serum as well as a host of other biological changes resulting from the stresses applied.

In all cases, what he found was the same. Stress caused clear and decisive deterioration in general health. While the stages of deterioration varied in individual cases, there was no doubt that when macaques were forced to listen to jet engine noise reproduced at 80 to 100 decibels on a continual basis, their health was negatively affected.

Although some of his colleagues at the college criticized his experiments as facile and predictable, scholarly journals continued to accept his articles, and the professor's career flourished.

Lately, however, he had begun to observe that his laboratory subjects were growing numb to his testing. They showed less and less inclination to react to the loud noises, the bright lights, the foul odors that he discharged into their cages. Their pulse curves had flattened considerably, much smaller swings in their blood pressure. It seemed they were becoming callous and indifferent.

New animals were extremely expensive, and as usual, because of low enrollments, the college was suffering financially. If the college's endowment continued to shrink and the professor's publishing productivity substantially dwindled, there was a very real danger that he might have to begin teaching undergraduate classes again, a fate he had successfully avoided for the last ten years.

So when his dean called him on Friday, November eleventh, to inform him of the movie star's generous gift to the college, the professor was elated. With a new experimental subject, it was possible he could extend his research for years.

Immediately after the dean hung up, the professor

began to consider new stress tests. Air horns, gunfire, ultraviolet sunlamps, the smell of putrefying flesh, sewage. And just as exciting was the prospect that when the orangutan had supplanted his other research animals, the professor might then be free to use the macaques and gibbons in some of the more hazardous experiments in physical stress that he'd hesitated to perform before.

Some years ago, the professor had used grant money to purchase a machine with a compressed-air-driven piston, something like a small jackhammer. It was capable of exerting very precise impact forces up to five thousand pounds. It was his hope to use the apparatus to study impact tolerance. The Chrysler Corporation had awarded him the grant in hopes that the professor could establish the exact breaking point of skull plates, so they could design their newest models without wasting extra steel.

But because the danger of inadvertently killing his experimental subjects had heretofore scared the professor off, the machine sat unused in a corner of his office. Now, with the orangutan's arrival, he believed he would feel comfortable with such a risk.

The professor had long ago sketched out the details of a set of potential experiments. First he would totally immobilize his chimps and macaques in heavy plaster casts, then fix the casts to specially designed steel chairs. Using the jackhammer, he would slam the piston at very precisely controlled impact levels against joints, soft tissues, cranial pressure points. Strike the animals, measure damage, short- and long-term recuperation, measure biological reactions. And of course, try to keep the strikes just below lethal pounds-per-square-inch dosages.

Barring accidents, there was every likelihood that the professor could keep his primates alive for several more years of useful research.

# C H A P T E R

# 31

That Friday afternoon, well into happy hour now, the White brothers' usual quitting time, Ray set the local section of Thursday's *Miami Herald* in front of Orlon and went over to his own desk and sat down. Orlon was dressed in black jeans, a black T-shirt with the sleeves hacked off. Black cowboy boots. Doing his Harley-guy imitation. Ray still in his Beverly Hills cool-guy threads. Rocket ship tie.

Orlon glanced at the newspaper, then looked up at Ray.

"You just reading about this? Man, it happened about six hundred years ago. Lots of water been flushed since then. Lotta shit passed on through the pipes."

Ray fidgeted with the brand-new *Webster's Pocket Dictionary,* fanned the pages, then set the fat book off to the side of his desk. He looked across at Orlon. His brother was going over the article, humming to himself as he read.

Ray looked out at the Mazda place. Watching people arriving to pick up their cars, others dropping theirs off. Ray wondered about Tricia, if this was what she'd had in mind for him, a showdown with Orlon. But then, he thought, no, she'd wanted Ray to figure it out himself. Do it with no help from her. Very mysterious, Tricia telling him he'd know when it was accomplished.

"Tell me why you felt you had to do something like this. Cut their noses, the snakes. Kill all those people. Why, man?"

Orlon looked up.

"Is it my fault?" Ray said. "Did I bully you into this?"

"Bully me?"

"When I said what I did to you about facing your fear."

Orlon grimaced in disdain and shook his head.

"Shit, no, Rayon. The things you say to me, they have absolutely no effect on my behavior whatsoever. Never have."

"Never?"

"You know that movie *Chinatown*? You've seen it, right?"

"We're discussing an important matter here, Orlon. I don't want to talk about goddamn movies, all right?"

"Well, there's that one scene. Roman Polanski directed it. He also acted in it, a little part, some Mafia bad guy. And in this one scene, Roman puts a knife blade into Jack Nicholson's nose, right into his nostril, holds it there for almost a minute. They're having this whole, long conversation with a knife blade in Nicholson's nose the entire time.

"I mean, that in itself is a great moment in filmmaking. First time I saw it, I put my popcorn down, couldn't pick it up for ten minutes. So after Polanski threatens Jack, gives him this long speech, then, like it's just an afterthought or something, very casual, he slices the ever-loving shit out of Nicholson's nostril.

"Now, I been over and over that moment, looking at the video in slow-mo, clicking the frames by one at a time. I scrutinized the hell out of it, but fuck if I can see how they special-effected it. So what I started thinking was, and I'm telling you, Rayon, this is revolutionary in the annals of movie criticism—what I think is, they didn't fake the nose thing.

"What Polanski did was, he cut Jack's nose for real.

And even more wild than that, Jack wasn't in on it. Like maybe they rehearsed the scene with a rubber knife, but then when the cameras were rolling, Polanski put a real blade into Nicholson's nostril just so he could get that incredible look in Jack's face. Jack feels the cold steel in his nose, realizes what Polanski's doing to him, and the fucking fear in his face, man, it's like he's just about to load up his Jockey shorts with yesterday's hot lunch.

"Must've freaked the fuck out of Jack. Polanski flicks the knife, and there's damn blood flying everywhere. Real blood. Jack's genuine, hundred-percent real blood. And imagine what the rest of the cast was thinking, the crew, everybody. They look at this guy, Polanski, their boss, and hey, he just cut the shit out of this famous actor, and now the crew, they see Polanski is as crazy as a tattooed dick. Guy'll do anything for his movie. Any fucking thing he thinks'll make it better."

Ray was staring hard at his brother, shaking his head from side to side in absolute, total disbelief. But Orlon didn't seem to notice. When he'd finished with his movie criticism, he just bowed his head, went back to reading the article again.

"What in fuck's name are you talking about?"

Orlon looked up.

"What? You don't see my point?"

"What fucking point? You got no point."

"I was explaining myself to you, is all." Orlon stood up. "You asked me why I had to kill those motorcycle guys, so that's what I was doing, explaining the psychology of it. I was doing to those people the same thing as Polanski did to Jack. Pushing the envelope. Making the best movie I could."

"Making a movie? What movie?"

"The fucking movie in my head. The one I'm shooting every second of my life. My eyes are the camera. I zoom in, zoom out. I'm the director, writer, producer, best boy, everything. My epic movie. *The Story of Orlon White. Life on the Wild Side.*"

Ray kept shaking his head, and looked back over at

the Mazda place. Kept looking as he tried to sort this out, letting the goose bumps die down. He heard Orlon scoot his chair back, get up, come over. Stand beside him.

"Hell, I thought maybe the Dallas Cowboys cheerleaders were naked out there, the way you were staring."

"I'm looking at the cars, is all. All those Mazdas lined up."

"Place is jumping today, that's for sure."

Ray glanced up at Orlon. His little hairless brother was studying the Mazda repair shop, totally focused on that now. Blipping right from murder to nose cutting, from noses to movies, movies to Mazdas, like everything was equal to everything else.

"You know," said Orlon. "Like I always say, if it's got tits or tires, sooner or later it's going to cost you."

Ray stood up, came around his desk, got face-to-face with Orlon. His brother pinched at a stray hair he'd found on his wrist. Then he brought his wrist up to his mouth and nibbled at the thing, his eyes moving to Ray's eyes as he chewed. Ray could hear his teeth click.

"Listen to you, Orlon," Ray said. "You're acting like this is some kind of goddamn joke. You killed those people. Murdered a dozen American citizens, women included. Do you hear me? This is a Ted Bundy thing. Son of Sam. This is not some fucking movie. It's not something going on in your head. It's out here, out here in the real world where everybody else is."

Orlon squinted up at his brother. Took his wrist out of his mouth.

"Whatta you all worked up over?"

"We got ourselves a problem here, a serious problem."

"What problem? Did I leave a trail of bread crumbs to our door? You see any cops around here?"

"There's other problems besides just the law."

"Yeah? Like name one for me, why don't you?"

"There's scruples. Right and wrong. It's not all just about getting caught or not getting caught."

"Where'd you get a dickhead idea like that?

Scruples? Jesus, you been sneaking off to church or what?"

"Where I got that idea," Ray said, "was from Mom."

Orlon shut up, turned his head away so Ray couldn't see his face, but Ray could picture it, which of Orlon's looks it was. Same expression he got when a woman dumped on him in public. Eyes dull, mouth slack, a bland, snoozy look. Like he didn't give a shit, this didn't hurt, didn't hurt a bit. Go ahead, cut another inch off his cock, see if he flinched.

"We gotta find some way," Ray said, "the both of us, some way we can make up for the evil we've perpetrated. It's what Darlene Annette would've wanted. We've done some disgraceful, evil shit, now we got to find a way to make it right again. Get back to how it was before."

"We do, huh?" Face still turned away, but Ray could tell the expression was still there. Voice dull, a sleepwalking tone. "Make things right 'cause of our dead mom."

"Yeah, that's what we got to do."

"You got some particular idea in mind, or is this just more of Rayon White's hocus-pocus psycho-bullshit. Say it today, forget it tomorrow."

"I'm working on some ideas," Ray said. "Ways to make amends. Reparations."

More cars lining up at the Mazda place. People getting off work, coming directly to the repair shop. Out there talking to each other, waiting to get written up. Comparing depressing stories about what shitty cars they'd bought.

"First off, I want you to go in with me, talk to my shrink."

"Give me a break."

"I'm serious, Orlon. This is important to me."

"Hell," Orlon said. "Before you get it all figured out, how we're going to get all this fucking forgiveness, maybe you should come take a look at something."

"At what?"

"More disgraceful shit you can add to your list."

Orlon headed off into the warehouse without a look at Ray.

Ray closed his eyes, blew out a breath, then followed.

He caught up to Orlon back in the primate room. Orlon stood in front of the empty orangutan cage, only as Ray could see as he got closer, it wasn't empty at all. There was a guy inside it.

The guy from the other night. Kurt Franklin's partner, hunched up, knees up around his throat, arms hugging his ankles. He had blood running down from his hair, little dried trails of it across his forehead. And there were some shit-ugly bruises on his cheeks.

Guy must've weighed near two hundred pounds. Ray would've liked to know how in hell Orlon lifted him up there, three feet off the ground, crammed him inside.

"What the hell!"

"While you were off playing footsie with your brain doctor, I was over at Allison's. Just sitting there, parked, same place as before, when who walks up but this guy. Lying son of a bitch ape-kisser, just like I said. There he is, cahooting with the enemy."

Ray looked in the cage, the guy staring out at him, eyes set on high.

"Why the fuck did you do this, Orlon? Bring him here?"

"So you and me, we could take our own happy time." Orlon poked a finger through the grid of bars, jabbing the guy's knee. "Interrogate the hell out of him, find out where he's secreted Ms. Allison Ballcrusher Farleigh. Then when we're done, we can figure out the exact best method of exterminating the lying ape-kissing son of a bitch."

Friday afternoon, only a few minutes after Brad Randolph's phone call to Hickman College, the orangutan left Brad's compound in West Palm strapped tightly into a child's car seat in the back of a white Cadillac limousine.

By the time the limo was an hour north of Palm Beach, the ape discovered that he could wriggle his finger under a seam in the backseat. Little by little, as the miles went by, he widened the tear and began to explore the batting and springs below.

At five forty-five the chauffeur found his way to the Hickman College psychology lab and parked the car and got out. Watching him come to the rear door, the orangutan scooped up the pile of cotton stuffing, foam, springs, and electrical wiring, and when the chauffeur opened the rear door, the orangutan sat very still until the man ducked his head inside, and the orangutan filled the air with the curious fruits of his afternoon's labor.

It was the eastern diamondback rattlesnake that finally got Thorn's full attention. Orlon held the snake right up against the guy's penis, saying, "So tell us, Thorn. You and Allison are real close, I take it, real bosom buddies. Maybe you're so close, you let the lady handle your pet snake? Something like this."

Orlon rubbed the rattler's head through the guy's pubic hair, jerking it aside when the snake tried to strike.

Ray stood in the doorway of the primate room watching the guy squirm his naked butt on the bare concrete floor. Shorts pulled down to his shins, his hands tied behind his back with a few dozen turns of heavy fishing line. Fingers a dark, oily blue and puffy from how tight Orlon wrapped the line.

The snake hissed, its mouth wide open, hypodermic needle fangs hinged out, its rattles chattering like a field of dried-out milkpods.

"The walls are soundproofed," Orlon told the guy. "So go on, yell the 'Star-Spangled Banner' if you want, scream the pledge of allegiance. Isn't anybody gonna stand up and salute."

Gripping the diamondback by the throat, Orlon bent over the guy again, brought the snake down slowly. The rattler was a six-foot monster, body fully inflated, rough-scaled, big wedge-shaped head, purplish gray body, white X's braiding up and down its length. Large thermal pits between eyes and nose. *Crotalus adamanteus.*

A diamondback that large sold for a hundred and a quarter. Most dangerous snake in North America. Such a mean fucker, brimming over with venom, that even after all these years in the business Ray had never touched one. Always used the loop pole. But Orlon was different. It was a point of honor with him. Point of manhood.

Now Orlon brought the snake lower. Thorn glared at the diamondback like he thought there was chance he could stare that snake down. Orlon moved the rattler close, rubbed its head again through the guy's thick sandy pubic hair, worked it down toward his dick.

"I know Allison's not at home, 'cause I had a nice look through her house just before you got there. So what I need to know now is, where'd you hide the bitch? I got a deal to offer her. A tit-for-tat kind of thing."

Thorn said nothing, staring into Orlon's eyes like he was looking for signs of life. Good luck on that, was all Ray could think. His brother was in the zombie zone. You could set off a stick of dynamite next to him, he wouldn't blink.

Orlon drew the rattler away. Ray watched it all, helpless. A minute ago, quiet as a priest, he had things on the right track, getting it out in the open. Saying *reparation* like he'd used the word all his life. Feeling calm as he explained to Orlon that they'd have to make amends. Now look.

The guy lay on his back still as ice while Orlon slid the snake up and down his thighs. The diamondback squirmed in his hand, extremely pissed. Fucker was hard to hold even on a quiet day. But now it hissed like a pressure cooker, lashing its tail around, Orlon struggling, like trying to one-hand a firehose at full blast.

Orlon bumped the guy's dick with the rattler's nose, yanked it away just as it struck. Thorn's pecker was shriveling, cringing up inside itself, but that was about the only sign the guy was afraid. Orlon kept the snake nosing around, spitting, mouth wide.

"Look, Thorn. We got no case against you. You're a neutral party far as we're concerned. Innocent bystander.

But you got one way and one way only of going on with your productive, healthy American lifestyle. That is, you tell us where the fuck she is. Am I being clear enough with you?"

The guy strained his head up from the floor, licked his lips like he was about to speak. Made a feeble sound and Orlon bent closer. Guy did that again, mumbled something under his breath, and Orlon dropped forward a few more inches.

"Nothing to fear, Thorn, old man. You can talk to us. Nobody ever has to know you told us anything. We cut the fishing line, you walk out that front door. You got my word on it. Just an address, that's all we need. You get to live out your full, rich, allotted time on earth, we go back to making an honest, decent living."

Suddenly Thorn thrust up and butted Orlon in the nose with his forehead, a rugby move. The blood began to pour from both nostrils.

Orlon mashed his eyes closed, shook his head, but nothing more than that. He didn't reach up to massage the pain. He just stood, moved up close to Thorn's head, brought the pointy toe of his black leather boots to his right cheek. Tapped the man's cheekbone lightly like a golfer lining up a drive.

"Don't do it, Orlon. There's no need to fuck with this guy. You do brain damage on him, we'll never find out where she is."

With the blood from his nose streaming down his chin, Orlon glanced once at Ray and sneered, then he looked back at Thorn, lined up his shot, cocked his stubby leg back, and punted the man's head so hard he spun over onto his stomach.

Five minutes later, the guy was conscious again and back in the cage, Orlon washing up in the office. Ray stood in front of the blond guy looking at him through the steel grid.

"Man, you must be fucking crazy," Ray said. "Head-butting him like that, it doesn't improve your position at all."

Thorn glared back at him, right cheek as red and swollen as a tomato left on the vine a month too long. He couldn't lift his head all the way because of the smallness of the cage, thick blond hair pressing into a grid of bars that was also the floor of the cage above him.

The rhesus that came in last week was moving around, exploring its space, and at that moment it had developed an interest in a tuft of blond hair sticking up into its cage. The monkey tugged on the hair, and Thorn smoothed a hand across his head and pulled it from the monkey's hands.

"Listen," Ray said. "I don't know how long we're going to have to keep you locked up in here. So I'm going to leave you a pile of food and water. I'll try to pick up a hamburger later, or something. But for now, this'll have to do."

Ray poured some monkey chow through the cage opening, filled up the plastic dish.

"And I got this for you too. Gets warm in this building sometimes, we're having trouble with the air-conditioning, so you'll probably do some sweating."

Ray opened the cage door quickly and tossed an army canteen inside. Shut the door and padlocked it. New Yale lock, impervious to orangutans or other jailbreakers.

"I got some running around to do," Ray said. "But I'll try to get back over here and check on you from time to time, bring you that Big Mac. Or maybe you'd rather have a Whopper?"

Thorn kept his mouth shut.

"Wendy's?"

The monkey hung from the ceiling of its cage and let go of a stream of bright yellow piss. It missed the newspaper in the corner of his cage and came raining down on Thorn's back.

The guy didn't move, just kept staring at Ray, giving his vicious glands a workout.

"Burger King it is, then. Personally I prefer the fries at McDonald's, but I don't think you can beat that flame-broiled taste."

"It's over, Ray. It's out in the open now." Saying it in a hoarse whisper. "You'd be in a better position trying to make a deal with the police, turn your brother in. Don't let this keep going."

Ray leaned close to the cage door, taking his voice down to a whisper, "That monkey chow, it tastes better than it looks. Nutty flavor."

The rhesus monkey took a good grip on Thorn's hair again, and was now scooting around in circles on its butt while he held to the hair, twisting it into a spike of blond.

# CHAPTER

# 32

As tired as she was, Sean couldn't sleep. Five in the afternoon, Brunei time, while her body was thirteen hours out of synch—four in the morning in Miami, but hell if she could figure out *which* morning. Tomorrow, yesterday?

In bra and panties, she lay on her bedspread and listened to the eerie masculine voice wailing from loudspeakers on the roof of a mosque a block away from the Sheraton. A tenor's mournful chant. He seemed to be lamenting some unbearable loss, but then again, Sean wasn't sure. She knew little about Islam. Maybe the song was about some entirely different kind of suffering. Longing, a passion unfulfilled.

She glanced around the room. From the furnishings, the rug, the bed, the paintings on the wall, she might be anywhere. Idaho, London, Mexico City. Except for the large arrow embedded in the plaster ceiling, pointing the way toward Mecca, and the complimentary *Newsweek* she'd leafed through a few minutes earlier while trying to make herself sleepy. Some government censor with a black Magic Marker had blotted out the breasts of a postage stamp–size photo of the Maja. Much of the accompanying article on sexual harassment was also blacked out, as well as words here and there throughout the magazine.

Though she was fatigued beyond anything she'd

known, her body pulsed with a jittery energy. She twisted and stretched, rearranged the pillow, turned it over to its cooler side. Lay on her left, her back, her stomach, her right, a restless yoga. Stared up at the ceiling and took long breaths, willing her brain to be quiet. But nothing worked. A swarm of furious wasps buzzed in her veins. Something was wrong, something she couldn't name. Blood thronged behind her eyes. A wired, frantic voice seemed to be whispering to her just beyond the borders of her hearing.

At last she could stand it no longer and pushed herself to her feet, went into the marble bathroom, washed her face, brushed her teeth, took her dress from the hanger, put it on, her shoes.

Outside in the warm, musky afternoon, the daylight was dwindling, the western sky filled with a ruddy haze. Without any clear destination, Sean turned left toward the center of town, headed off. In a few seconds she was perspiring heavily.

Beside the sidewalk ran a deep open sewer, blasts of foul air rising from it as she walked. To escape the odor she angled off the walkway, cut across a dusty field toward an open-air market. As she meandered among the food stalls, old women watched her warily from behind their displays of vegetables and fruit. Children played in the dirt at their feet, and groups of young men lounging in the shade eyed Sean, her bare arms, the shape of her exposed calves.

Feet swollen from the long flight, painfully tight in her shoes. Her lower back ached, her calves quivered, on the verge of cramping. The weariness seemed to have seeped into her marrow, taken root, but she marched on, determined to have a glimpse of the Brunei she remembered, even if it meant pushing herself over the edge of exhaustion.

She left the market, went further north, past the concrete landing beside the river where a dozen boys in speedboats hooted at her in English, offering their services for a scenic tour. She circled through the cheerless main shopping district, three- and four-story buildings of prosaic architecture, the shop windows filled with standard foodstuffs and cheap, dreary clothes. She drifted toward Kampong Ayer, the water village where thousands of the city's poor lived in a labyrinth of flimsy stilthouse shacks. It was one of the places she remembered fondly as being extravagantly colorful and exotic. Now she saw what it was, a vast slum at the city's core.

Doggedly she held her course, passed through the water village market, examined the sides of beef hanging in the sun, fish, squid, clams, squeezed through the throng of subdued shoppers bunched around the stark tables. A few yards away the speedboats roared, delivering afternoon shoppers, racing away, the river rocking with their overlapping wakes.

She wandered farther into the village, picking her way along the shaky walkways, boards loose or missing, no handrails, murky water slapping below her at every step, and into the heart of the dense cluster of ramshackle houses built of gray, weathered wood, following the rickety dock past living rooms with doors and windows flung open, exposed bedrooms and kitchens, inhaling the bitter tang of cooking, of sewage, rot, and decay. In the distance she saw the magnificent golden dome of the mosque hovering in the northern sky, and a half mile upstream in the other direction loomed the sultan's palace.

Dismal and discouraged, she retraced her steps through the market, took a narrow bridge back to the city streets, glancing down at the shoreline, which was covered by a rank layer of litter. The plastic containers, Styrofoam, oil cans, and car tires of any garbage dump in any part of the world.

On the way back to the hotel, Sean passed again through the central business district, cheap hotels, pungent restaurants, tiny Chinese-run shops, a museum whose architecture was as flat and spiritless as a hospital. Everywhere the muggy stench of open sewers.

All of it had once seemed so fantastic, so picturesque, had so completely caught the fancy of that fourteen-year-old girl, Sean Marie Farleigh. But now it seemed drab and squalid, a gloomy, oppressive town. The people listless, their conversations muted and tight-lipped. Even the markets were bland. There was no color, no hum, no sense of eagerness in the bargaining. As if the entire country were observing some somber religious observance, or commemorating a grave national disaster. Shoulders stooped, speaking in guarded whispers.

Around her, the streets were packed with new Mercedeses, BMW's, Rolls-Royces, and Jaguars. Even the boys jockeying with their speedboats for taxi fares were well dressed, and on their wrists were gaudy Rolexes and heavy gold bracelets. Their boats and outboard engines were bright and new. And maybe that was it. So much easy money had stunted their spirit. It squared with what her father had frequently said, Sean only half listening as he discoursed on the social history of Brunei.

Over half the population was employed by the government in one of the world's most bloated bureaucracies. They were well-paid civil servants with virtually nothing to do. The rest of the workforce received a minimum wage, which Harry claimed far exceeded the usefulness of their labor. No taxes, free health care, lazy money. No reason to work hard and certainly no reason to revolt. Like Communism with lots of cash.

By the time Sean made it back to the Sheraton she was drunk on gloom. Disgusted with the place, with herself. Beginning to feel that it had been a desperate mistake coming here, still driven by that giddy creation of her fourteen-year-old mind, expecting some romantic, palmy paradise. And what troubled her more was the possibility that her attraction to Patrick, her feelings for him, might be part of the same juvenile fantasy. It wouldn't be the first time that what was merely exotic had been confused for beauty, that lust had been mistaken for love.

She took the elevator to her room, called room service for a gin and tonic. No, make it a double. She was informed stiffly that alcohol was no longer allowed in the country, and in fact had not been permitted for some three or four years now.

She hung up. Lay her head against the throbbing pillow. Closed her eyes and quietly began to weep.

At six o'clock Allison could wait no longer. Thorn's simple task was taking far too long. She got a taxi to the Gables house, asked the driver to wait.

She went inside the house, found no sign of struggle anywhere. Upstairs in her bedroom she saw shampoo and lotion and deodorant were missing. Some clothes. As if perhaps after he'd finished here he'd taken some detour, shopping for himself, clothes, groceries. She was probably worried for nothing. He'd be back at the marina waiting for her, concerned she wasn't there.

Allison was on the front porch locking the door behind her, when she saw it. A small manila envelope balanced on the lip of her mailbox. She drew it out, opened it while she walked toward the waiting taxi.

A dog was howling down the street, as Allison stopped, shuffled hastily through the stack of color photographs. Borneo. Borneo. Coming to the bottom, where she found a dozen enlargements of a single photograph, setting them on top of the stack, angling one of them up to catch the sunlight. And Allison felt the earth lurch beneath her feet.

After a fitful sleep Sean woke, rolled onto her back, and lay staring up into the dark until she was fully awake. She looked over at the red numerals of the digital clock, six-ten in the morning. She struggled for a moment to calculate the true time. Her body's time. But it was hopeless. Her brain wasn't wired for such computations. It was six in the morning in Brunei. That was the only time that mattered.

Reaching over, she switched on the bedside light, and when her eyes had recovered, she picked up the phone and rang the front desk, asked for a taxi to take her to the airport. You're checking out? a woman asked her. I'm checking out, Sean said.

Somewhere as she was drifting away to sleep or waking up, she'd decided what she had to do. She'd leave Brunei this morning. From back in Miami she could sort this out, her confusion, the icy draft blowing across her feelings for Patrick. She would write him a letter, leave it at the desk, call him when she was back home. This had been a mistake. Impetuous, silly. Patrick would be angry, hurt. It would be a difficult phone call. Patrick would say she'd run away from him, and she'd have to admit it was true. She would tell him she needed sufficient distance from him to digest their situation, its seriousness, its future. He would want to join her in Miami, and she'd refuse, at least for now. It would be complicated, messy.

A few minutes later Sean was in the shower when she heard the phone. Pulling the curtain aside, she listened to it ring, seven, eight times before it stopped.

While she was toweling her hair it began to ring again. She walked over, looked down, and picked it up, said hello.

The phone line was silent for a moment. Then echoing down a long, empty corridor from other side of the earth came her mother's voice.

"Sean? Is that you? Sean? Are you okay? Are you safe?"

"I'm looking at it," Allison said. "I swear to you, it's in my hand and I'm looking at it right now. A color photograph of Patrick Sagawan. An orangutan tied to his belt, his rifle aimed up at the trees. Raimondo White, the Miami animal dealer, standing next to him with a rifle too."

Sean said, "I don't believe this."

"There's a date on the photo. Printed in orange down in the right-hand corner, like all of Winslow's snapshots. October 26. The day she was murdered. This is them, Sean. This is a picture of her killers, the last one she took. I heard her camera rewind automatically. These are the men who knew my name."

"Goddamn it, Mother. What the hell are you trying to pull!"

"I'm looking at it, Sean. It's true."

"How can you invent such a thing! Because I ran off, didn't consult with you first? You trying to punish me? Is that what this is?"

"Look," she said. "I'll fax it to the hotel. You find the number for me, then go wait at the fax machine. See for yourself."

"Mother, this is stark-raving insanity. Do you hear me? Can you hear me clearly enough?"

"Find the fax number, Sean. Please, just do it. Go to the office, wait till it comes over. Please, sweetheart. Look at the photo and then call me right back."

"I'm going to hang up now, Mother. Don't try to call me again. I won't be here."

"Wait, there's more."

Allison glanced at the other photos from the envelope. Fanned them out on the coffee table. Her hands quivering so badly, she almost scattered the pile on the floor. The taxi driver was standing in the doorway shaking his head.

"The whole roll is here. All thirty-six. When you and Winslow went off on your own exploring Kuching. Snapshots of the marketplace. A longhouse, bright clothes hanging outside. There's another one of you in the swimming pool at the Holiday Inn, you're making a face at Winslow. Sticking your tongue out. Do you remember that, Sean? Do you remember doing that? It's on the same roll with Patrick and his rifle."

"Mother." Sean's voice had changed, stiff and empty. "Where did you get these?"

"I don't know."

"What do you mean you don't know!"

"I told you, Sean. Someone put them in the mailbox. I was on my way out, and there they were. No stamp, no address."

"In the mailbox. Just sitting there."

"That's right," Allison said. "Just sitting there. Now look, honey, you have to get out of there right now. You can't let Patrick suspect you're aware of any of this. It's serious. Sean, do you hear me? This is very, very serious."

In an empty voice Sean said, "Was there a note? Anything that might suggest who sent them?"

"Just a word," she said. "Someone printed a single word on the envelope."

"What?"

"*Reparation.*"

A white Mercedes taxi was waiting at the front doors of the Sheraton Utama, Sean's bags in its trunk. The hotel's fax machine was streaming out documents from the New York office, weekly communiqués, page after page. One of the desk clerks, a man in his early twenties with Chinese features, stood next to the machine plucking the pages out as they appeared.

"Soon," he said. "Soon be finished. Or perhaps you want to go now, catch plane, I send fax on to you somewhere else."

"I'll wait."

She was in the office behind the registration desk. A dull tingle had replaced her pulse. She looked out at the lobby, every chair filled at this hour of the morning. Businessmen from all over the world, coming here to court the sultan, sell him something, trying to divert some small trickle of the great offshore gushers in their direction. Men of every nationality, most in the same uniform, dark slacks, white shirts, most of them smoking. Businessmen waiting for the sultan to return from his trip, then waiting for an audience with his Majesty. That lobby stank of waiting men. Men with briefcases full of prospectuses, charts and graphs, brochures. Offering the best that money could buy, the crown jewels of the world, the creamiest of the cream.

"It finish," the Chinese clerk said. "Your fax can come now, I think."

Sean moved out of the doorway, came close to the small black box. A moment or two later the phone rang twice and the machine answered. She heard the quiet chatter of electronic connections being made, thousands of silent messages relayed from the other side of the globe, pluses and minuses, positives and negatives. That stream of opposites flooding into the small computer, instantly decoded, and the printer switching on.

She stood beside the machine and watched the first inch of white paper emerge, heard voices behind her. She saw her mother's name printed on the top of the sheet. Allison Farleigh, Wildlife Protection League. And as Sean focused on the paper inching out, she heard behind her a woman politely answering in Malay a man's indignant question. Patrick's voice.

Her eyes fixed on the paper; she felt her knees sag, a blind stab of panic.

"Miss Farleigh," the Chinese clerk said. "There gentleman to see you."

She watched the paper rise from the machine. A smudged copy, but clear enough. Two men surrounded by a dense wood, rifles in their hands, aimed into the trees, a shadowy blur hanging from the belt of one of them. An orangutan.

"Sean," he said from several feet away. "What's going on?"

She heard the machine slice the sheet free and she lifted the single page out of the tray and held it to the light. A tall man held one rifle, and beside him stood a lean young man with wavy black hair. The printer had turned the photo into a murky sketch washed in shadows, but still there was no doubt who the slender man was.

She wadded the paper up, dropped the ball into a half-filled wastebasket. She turned and forced her lips into a smile.

Patrick stood in the doorway, several steps away. In black silk shirt, pale gray slacks, a thin gold bracelet at his wrist.

"What is it, Sean? They called me. They said you were checking out. What's happened? What's wrong?"

She let Patrick lead her out of the hotel office, out into the lobby.

"I made a mistake," she said.

"What mistake? What is it, Sean? You look terrible."

"I *feel* terrible."

A furtive murmur passed through the crowd of businessmen. Idly Sean swept her gaze across the room, watching their flutter of interest in Patrick. If she cried out right now, she wondered if there were any among them who might have the courage to come to her aid. Not likely. Unless perhaps she waved a roll of thousand-dollar bills. Probably not even then, so strong was their focus on Patrick. So great was the wealth he represented, so high in the chain of command.

"I need to go home," she said. "Mother's sick. She needs me."

"She's sick? What's happened?"

"I have to go, Patrick."

He studied her for a moment, eyes becoming shrewd.

"No," he said evenly. "You're not going anywhere."

He turned and spoke in harsh Malay to one of the bellmen. The young man sprinted off toward the cab.

"Now, what is this about, Sean? I leave you alone for a few hours to rest, and you try to run away."

"Mother called. She's in trouble."

"Is she sick? Or is she in trouble, Sean? Which lie is it?"

Stepping across to the elevator, Patrick jabbed the button. The bellman hustled over with Sean's luggage and held the elevator doors aside for her. His hand gripping her arm, Patrick moved Sean inside the elevator.

"May I join you?" Patrick asked. "Upstairs."

She clenched her jaw, stared at him, Patrick's eyes as hard and cold as the grip on her arm.

He spoke again to the bellman holding the elevator doors, then turned away and marched to the front desk. The Chinese clerk nodded solicitously, and held the swinging gate aside. Patrick followed the clerk behind the counter and into the hotel office. He was inside for only a few seconds, then came briskly across the lobby, rubbing his neck as though he had developed a sudden crick.

He stood close beside her in the elevator, his shoulder brushing hers. He stared straight ahead, his face blank, watching the elevator doors shut.

The car began to rise.

"Patrick?"

He slanted his eyes in her direction, and by slow degrees a smile materialized on his lips.

"Yes, my dear?"

"Who are you?"

"You mean you're not sure?"

"No," she said. "I'm not."

"Well, my dear, I suppose we'll have to fix that right away, won't we? I'll have to tell you everything now."

# CHAPTER

## 33

The professor was so excited about the orangutan's arrival, he decided to work late Friday night. But before he could actually begin his stress experiments on the orangutan, he had to chart the ape's baseline physiology. Measurements of limbs, height, weight. Blood tests, pulse readings, body temperature, oral and rectal. Reflexes. Electrocardiograph. Pupil dilation. Ears, teeth, gums, nose, genitals.

At seven-fifteen that evening, when he was finished with the preliminary testing, he put the orangutan back in its cage, and retired to his office to record the results.

The ape's cage was smaller than the one at the animal dealers' warehouse, and much more confined than the movie star's room. The cage was actually closer to the size of the crate in which he'd been stuffed on his airplane ride.

For years animal-rights activists and primatologists had urged the USDA to increase its minimum standards for housing research animals to a square footage of not less than four hundred feet for each primate. While the four-hundred-square-foot figure had not yet been officially accepted, industry standards had improved somewhat in recent years, under pressure from animal-rights groups.

However, colleges such as Hickman regularly received exemptions from even the weak USDA regulations governing cage size. College officials usually pleaded a lack of funds, and claimed that allocating sufficient resources to enlarge their facilities would be impossible and therefore all research would stop and the animals would have to be terminated. Wasn't it more humane to keep the animals alive albeit in confined spaces than to kill them?

The orangutan had only enough space in his cage so he could sit, but could not stand erect. He could turn in a complete circle, but only by tucking his legs tight against his body. He found that he could insert his fingers through the grid of his cage, take a grip, and give it a loud rattle. This was amusing to him. He quickly learned he could produce the loudest noise by shaking the cage's door.

When the ape began to rattle the door, the professor's laboratory assistant, Bernice Shap, a senior psychology major, tried to calm him by cooing and making other baby noises. But it was not her voice that finally soothed the ape. It was her shoulder-length red hair.

The orangutan stuck his fingers through the bars of his cage and reached out to touch the lab assistant's hair. For a while she kept her distance from the ape, following the professor's warnings. The ape peeped at her, made gurgling noises in his throat, rocked his head from side to side, and signed the word *fruit,* until finally the lab assistant, beguiled by the creature, let the ape play with her hands.

After a moment the orangutan reached for a strand of her hair. He stroked it and grew quiet.

With her left hand Bernice reached out to touch the ape's face, but stopped short and gasped. Just a moment before, her hands had been bare, but now on the third finger of her left hand there was a large diamond ring.

Patrick shut the door to her hotel room, walked over to the front window, drew the curtain aside and looked out. Sean settled into the room's one chair, crossing her legs tight. A shiver was growing in her pulse. The room was dark, though neither of them made a move to turn on the light.

"Come here," he said, without turning from the window. "I want to show you something."

Sean drew a breath, came to her feet, crossed the rug to his side. To her right she caught a gleam on the desk, a gold letter opener, a knife with the dullest of blades. Sean turned slightly in its direction, peeked to make sure it was still there, steadied herself with a hand against the wall.

"See out there, just beyond those palms."

Sean felt his hand brush her back, coaxing her closer to him, then his arm snaked around her shoulders, and he drew her to his side.

"That's where your family used to live, that red tiled roof on the hillside. That's where I first saw you. The U.S. consul's compound. You and Winslow, the gorgeous American girls. That is where I first fell in love."

His hand was gripping her left shoulder, arm across her back. She felt him turn his head, but Sean kept her eyes on the view. With his free hand Patrick brushed the hair from her ear, then brought his lips close, murmured the words.

*"I love you."*

Her body was rigid in his embrace. Flesh cold, a queasy coil in her stomach. Her hands were useless, numb. Sweat sprang from her icy flesh. Sean was thinking of the gold letter opener. Thinking of the sweet meat of Patrick's belly. Plunging it there, burying it to the handle.

"I love you," he said again. "I love you, Sean. That's all you need to know about me."

She could see his smile in her peripheral vision as she kept her eyes on the distant hills.

Then he bent close, kissed her ear, touched the tip of his tongue lightly to the rim of it. Turned and with his left hand steered her around to face him. She tried to push away, but he held her around the waist, a mock dance, a waltz of horror.

"You can't know how long I've waited to be next to you like this. It's as though I've been on one of those space flights from one galaxy to the next, the kind you see in movies. My body in suspended animation. I've been moving across empty space, Sean, aging in my crib, all my organs functioning, my vital signs normal, but not truly alive. That's how it has been, making this endless flight to be with you, across vast, cold darkness, all so we could be just as we are at this moment."

His hand combed through her hair, massaged her skull, fingernails lightly scratching the sensitive flesh. She closed her eyes, neck softening, felt the floor giving way.

"No," she said, and pulled back.

"What is it?"

"I feel ill. I'm going to be sick."

She wrestled away from him, her back to the desk.

Patrick smiled, reached out, brushed the hair off her face.

"Do I make you sick, Sean? Does love make you sick?"

He stepped close, brought his hips against hers. She bumped the desk behind her. She pictured the letter opener, its handle toward her. An easy reach.

Patrick embraced her, brought his lips to hers, kissed her hard, and Sean allowed her lips to reshape to his, riding this moment, trying to keep the loathing at bay, not allowing herself to think. She let her mind drift from the mooring of her body. This nameless man kissed her and her lips replied. He kissed the breath from her, began to ease her away from the desk.

Sean stiffened. Dragged her foot on the rug, faking a stumble, a stutter step to the side, broke his embrace, and lurched toward the desk, a hand fumbling toward the golden glint.

But Patrick caught her shoulders, dragged her upright, turned her around.

He was smiling.

"Love has made you awkward as well, Sean."

Gripping her shoulders, he turned her slowly until she was facing the bed. She felt his hands on her back, his fingers beginning to unzip her dress. When the zipper was all the way down, he pulled the dress from her shoulders, let it fall. He unfastened her bra, slid his hands around her and cupped her breasts. A slow twiddle with his fingertips against her nipples, then he tugged the bra off.

When she was naked, he drew her to the bed, pulled the covers aside, lay her down. She swallowed back the acid rising in her throat, watched him undress beside her, watched him move close to her pillow, his penis erect.

Patrick smiled, shifted forward, planted a hand on either side of her head. He swung onto the bed, lowered himself, kissed her lips as he settled between her legs. Balancing on one hand, he guided himself with the other, wedging his cock into the dry space.

"Say it, Sean." His voice hoarse as he began to move his hips. "Say it. You love me, don't you?"

She cringed, closed her eyes, felt the burn of her parched flesh.

"You love me," he said, his voice raspy. Straining above her, grinding in and out, sweat growing on his hairless chest. Breathless and hoarse, he said, "You love me so much, Sean, that one day I know you will forgive me."

He increased his speed, Sean flinching with each stroke.

"Forgive you for what?"

"I think you know," he mumbled.

"Tell me."

"For Winslow. For what I was forced to do."

For a half second Sean tensed. Then she wailed and surged up, tried to buck him off. But Patrick held on, stronger than he'd shown himself to be. She fought him, wrenched from side to side, hammered his shoulders with her fists, grabbed for his hair. He fended off her blows, and the more she writhed and struggled, the more it seemed to rouse him.

Until at last she fell back against the mattress, took hard handfuls of the sheet, clenched her eyes shut, lay as still and cold as a cadaver as he worked above her.

\* \* \*

Seven-thirty, and Harry was in a late conference with the partners. Oh, yes, his smiling secretary assured her, certainly Ms. Farleigh was free to wait for him in his office.

"I need to show him these," Allison said, holding the packet of photographs.

The secretary stared uncertainly at her.

"Of course, Ms. Farleigh. Of course."

Harry's office had a spectacular view of the port of Miami, the cruise ships lined up like a row of great icebergs ready to drift out to sea. His shelves were impeccably neat, his large teak desk with just a single stack of papers lined up at a right angle with the corner of the desk. A minimalist decorating job. Walls pale pink, rug silver-gray. A fishtail fern in one corner, and on the wall across from his desk a painting of the girls at fourteen and fifteen, done the year they'd lived in Brunei. She remembered the painter, a quirky British gentleman. She remembered the five afternoons she'd taken the girls to his house to sit for the portrait. She'd forgotten it existed, and was surprised Harry had hijacked it for his office.

Allison stared at it for a moment, listened to the raucous voices in her chest. A racket of blame, of anger, of grief. She clenched her eyes, held her breath till the throb in her temples subsided and all was silent again.

She set her handbag on the desk, dug through it till she found the scrap of paper where she'd scrawled Sean's number at the Brunei Sheraton. Sitting in Harry's tall black swivel chair, she called the hotel again. Almost nine in the morning there. Two rings, three. Heard the operator's faint and wavering voice. Asked for Sean Farleigh's room.

As the phone rang, Allison pulled apart the neat stack of papers before her. Depositions, titles, abstracts. Architectural drawings, blueprints. And on the bottom was a paper-clipped stack of fax pages.

She pulled them out, riffled through them while she listened to the phone ring in Sean's hotel room in Brunei. She heard the soft chime of a phone beyond Harry's door, the noise muffled by the thick carpeting, and then the hotel operator's voice in her ear, informing her there was no answer in the room. Would she care to leave a message?

But Allison did not answer, her eyes fixed on the list.

"I would be happy to take a message, madam."

Allison set the phone down, picked up the sheaf of papers, held it with both hands to still the shaking. Breath faltering, she stared at the first page, then leafed through the others. Each page with a new heading, a different animal. And below it a thumbnail description.

JAGUAR
Size: Length, 44–73 inches. Tail, 18–30 inches.
Weight: Males, 125–250 lbs. Females, 100–200 lbs.

Distribution: Central and South America as far south as Patagonia; the largest found in Mato Grosso in Brazil.

Habit: Solitary, except in breeding season, when they come together to mate.

Diet: Ground-living mammals, domestic stock, fish, frogs, turtles, and small alligators.

Life span: Up to 22 years.

Related species: Also *P. tigris, P. leo, P. pardus,* and *P. uncia.*

Breeding: Sexual maturity, 3 years
        Mating, nonseasonal in tropics
        Gestation, 93–110 days
        No. of young, 1–4 cubs.

Roam area required: 100 acres. Electric fencing. These cats can swim moats.

And at the bottom of each page there were boxes to fill in.

*Current status (De Novo)*
In captivity: 2
Destroyed: 28
Remaining worldwide population: below five thousand

Allison evened the edges of the papers, placed them back at the bottom of the pile, grabbed her bag and headed for the door. As she was reaching for the knob, the door swung open before her.

"Jesus Christ!" Harry stumbled back. "Scared the holy shit out of me."

She took a breath, tried to speak, but couldn't find the air for words. Allison moved out of his way, watched Harry stroll over to his desk, touch a single finger to the stack of papers, pivot on that finger around the edge of his desk and sit down. He propped his elbows on the desk, clasped his hands in a prayerful pose. He wore a pink shirt, a yellow tie with black polka dots. Burgundy suspenders holding up his gray slacks.

"Well, if you're here about that immigration thing," Harry said. "No luck."

He held her eye for a moment, but a vulture flying past his window pulled his gaze away. He cleared his throat, brought his eyes back to the polished wood. His fingers formed piano chords against the teak. He held them there, an awkward stretch, as he looked up at her again, this time with composure, gotten his story straight, back in command.

"Talked to Danny Burton just before I went out to lunch. He said it was impossible. Immigration information like that, don't ask me why, but countries simply don't share that kind of thing. He said we could try to get a federal subpoena, talk to a judge, try to convince him that the information was necessary to an ongoing murder investigation, maybe he'd issue an order. But still, even then, the Malaysian officials wouldn't be required by international law to obey the subpoena. So it looks like that's a dead end, Allison. Sorry."

She nodded. All she could manage. Standing in the doorway, one hand on the knob. Shifting some of her weight that way.

"You okay? You don't look well. Ankle bothering you? Your nose?"

Allison swallowed, took a long draw of air, glanced out the wide window at one of those twinkling icebergs beginning to inch away from the dock, about to catch the outgoing tide, drift into the Gulf Stream, start its long, slow melting.

"What are you doing?" Allison said. "You and Patrick. What kind of project is it you're working on together?"

"Construction," Harry said, the slightest stiffening in his posture. "Rantel, like always."

"What kind of construction, Harry?" Allison heard her voice leaving her body, a ghostly rattle of sound as if some other person were speaking through her.

"I don't get it," he said. "You never come to my office. Never shown the slightest interest in my work. Disdainful as hell whenever I try to share things with you. Now all of a sudden you've acquired this big fascination. What gives?"

"What kind of project, Harry?" Eyes still on the huge white ship, off on its own now, self-contained, out on the dangerous sea.

"It's a *huge* project," he said. "That's what kind it is. A career maker. The kind of project that when it's finished, a person would never have to pick up his phone, beg his old friends for some paltry favor. It's that kind. The kind that you can retire after. Play golf. Start living your goddamn life for once."

She nodded again.

"Is it so big," she said, "you were willing to sacrifice your own flesh and blood to make it happen?"

"And what the hell is that supposed to mean?"

Allison slid her eyes from the view, regarded her husband. Watched him as he seemed to float inch by inch out of sight. Departing forever from the world she knew.

# C H A P T E R

# 34

Eight-thirty, dark outside. For all the normal, healthy people in the world, dinner was over, the sitcoms starting up. The White brothers, however, were sitting in Tricia Capoletti's office, Orlon saying, "You did *what*?"

"I took Allison those photos, Orlon. Took them over to her house, put them in her mailbox. All of them. Negatives, enlargements, all of them. Now she knows. Now it's over."

"Jesus Christ, man. I don't fucking believe what I'm hearing."

Tricia Capoletti said, "You shouldn't let the anger cloud your thoughts, Orlando. You should tell Ray exactly what's on your mind. Keep it precise. Don't let the anger speak for you."

Orlon stared at Ray, then back at Tricia.

"That what you think, counselor? That your idea of mental health, is it, getting your mind all nice and clear?"

"That's one aspect of it, yes."

Ray loved it. Tricia not taking an ounce of shit from Orlon, just sitting comfortably on the front of her desk, looking straight into Orlon's eyes. She was wearing army-green pants, soft brushed cotton. A light blue shirt, button-down like a man's with a dark blue tie worn loose at her throat. Windsor knot wasn't tied exactly right. Ray, an expert on Windsor knots, half-Windsors, thinking this

was something he might be able to help Tricia with. Get
her knots right.

Orlon made a production of sitting up straighter in
his chair, getting his posture correct for the teacher.
Mocking Tricia, though she didn't seem to notice.

"Okay," he said, looking toward Ray, a couple of
inches away from making eye contact. "Okay, Ray, tell me
something. You gave Allison the photographs, so now
what's supposed to happen?"

"I didn't have a specific outcome in mind. I was just
doing something to make amends. Whichever thing felt
right. And this is what it was: give Allison the photos,
sever our ties with the Brunei guy, both at once. I tried a
couple of other ideas, but they didn't come to anything."

"What else did you try?" Tricia asked him. She
crossed her legs, hands on the edge of her desk, leaning
forward. Ray had never seen her sit on her desk before.
Always behind it. But there she was, sitting there, exposed
to these two guys, madmen a couple of feet away. Tricia
totally collected, serene.

"What I did, I drove over to Hialeah this morning
early, to where the Hervis kid lives. I read they sent him
home from Jackson Memorial. So I went up to the door of
his house, all ready to confess who I was, what I'd done to
their boy. And this guy swung open the door, big man in
underwear, beer gut, rotten complexion.

"I asked him was this the place where Hervis lived,
and right away the guy produces a weapon. Huge black
forty-five, swings it out from behind him, points it at me.
Says for me to get the fuck off his porch.

"But I stood there, asked him again if this was
Hervis's house, the kid who was recently shot in traffic,
partially paralyzed. And the guy cocked that fucking can-
non, aimed it at my face and told me, yeah, this was the
house, he was the father. Father of the paralyzed kid.
What of it?"

Orlon said, "You didn't tell him, did you? You
chicken-shitted out of it. All ready to fess up, but you look
at that gun and you decide different."

"No," Ray said. "I told him the whole damn thing. Start to finish. I told him about you, how you did the motorcycle guys while I was dealing with the Hervis kid. I told him about the yellow parasol, the old woman his kid killed from running the light. How she looked a lot like Mom. I stood there, looking into that gun and told him the naked-balls-to-the-walls truth. Every single little bit I could remember."

"Good for you, Ray." Tricia uncrossed her legs, leaned in his direction, and clenched a fist in victory. "That took a great deal of courage."

"Finish the goddamn story, man. What'd he do?"

"He pulled the trigger," Ray said. "Pulled it three times, then he broke down crying."

"Gun was empty," Orlon said.

Ray nodded.

"Empty gun doesn't fucking count, all that brave bullshit. Doesn't mean a thing."

"Ray didn't know it was empty," Tricia said. "He stood there, faced his crime, confessed his wrongs. Ready to accept responsibility, even death. It took tremendous courage. Tremendous faith."

"Hey, where in the hell you get your psychology degree?" Orlon said. "That's what I want to know."

"Don't," Ray said.

" 'Cause wherever it was, I'm gonna give them a call, let them know the amazing things their goddamn graduates are doing out here, curing criminals of their disease. And shit, the state's attorney might be interested in it too. They could close all the goddamn jails, ship the convicts over here, let pretty little Tricia Italiano cure them all."

"Orlon, you're over the line, man."

Orlon pulled out his pocketknife. Opened it and started digging the point into the wooden arm of the chair. Thing was all nicked and scarred already, Salvation Army stuff, so Ray held his tongue.

Ignoring him, Tricia said, "What did the father do next, Ray? Go on and finish telling your story. Part of the catharsis is to relive this moment, see it in your memory exactly as it happened, reexperience and understand it."

"The father turned around," Ray said, "just went back into his house. I heard him crying. Heard him bawling his brains out in the back of the house. Left the door standing open, anybody could've walked right in, stolen his stuff."

"How did you feel?"

"I felt shitty. I still feel shitty. I went on inside. Walked down this narrow, onion-smelling hallway, looking in rooms till I found where the kid was lying. I pushed open the door, stood there for a minute, and the kid opened his eyes and looked at me. I told him I was sorry."

"Did he respond?"

"He closed his eyes. I believe he thought he was having a bad dream."

"Jesus," Orlon said. "Listen to this bullshit. Listen to you two." Carving in the arm of the chair, Orlon said, "I can't believe it. You took Allison that photograph, didn't even keep one for us. I can't believe you're that dumb, man. That thing was worth money if we'd used it right. A lot of money."

Tricia said, "Something you said a minute ago, Ray. Let's circle back to that for a second. I didn't understand the reference. Something about Orlando doing motorcycle men."

"Whoa, now," Orlon said. "Just wait one fucking second here. If you feel you gotta confess the fucking things you did, Rayon, fine, go ahead, cleanse your immortal soul all you want. But leave me the hell out of it, you hear?"

"Go ahead, Ray. This is bothering you, isn't it, this thing Orlando did?"

"Yeah, it is. It bothers me. I feel responsible, like I did it myself."

"Oh, Jesus." Orlon stood up. Black T-shirt with sweat rings growing in the pits.

"Now look here," Orlon said. He was facing Tricia but talking to Ray. "I came over here tonight 'cause my brother said he wanted me to meet the woman he was going to marry. And I only stayed this long out of respect for Rayon. The man hasn't shown much of an appetite for women over the years, so I thought I should encourage him any way I could. But this is turning out to be a fucking freight train full of dog shit. And I'm not staying around to see it crash."

"Is that right, Ray?"

"What?"

"What your brother just said. Is that what you think I am? The woman you're going to marry."

"Those were his exact words," Orlon said. "Verbatim, ad nauseam."

"I just said that to get him over here. That's all. Make him curious to meet you."

Orlon slid his hand across his smooth head, and said, "Hey, look, I need a quick time-out to pee, okay? Don't say anything good while I'm gone."

He headed for the door, Ray telling him to wait, come back, but Orlon lifted a hand over his shoulder and waved backward at them. Out the door, shut it. Tricia looked down at the rug, shaking her head. Ray just sat there, all the blood drained from his body. Embarrassed, angry. Wanting to run the fuck out of there, strangle Orlon.

Minute later the door to the office opened again and Orlon walked back in, said, "Hi, guys. I'm back," and sat down again.

"So where were we?" Ray said.

"I don't know," Tricia said. "Actually, I think this may be enough for tonight. We've covered some good ground."

Orlon took out his knife again, went back to work on the chair.

"Is that what you want, Tricia?" Ray said. "You want us to leave now?"

Tricia studied him for a long moment, then said, "Do you think facing the boy and his father is enough, Ray?"

"What do you mean?"

"I mean, you've taken care of your personal responsibility, but do you think you have a larger social obligation as well?"

"Oh, man." Orlon rolled his head around, stared up at the ceiling.

"Well, Ray? Do you?"

"She's doing it," Orlon said. "She's doing that exact same thing Mom used to do, thing I hated so much. Asking you questions, but they aren't questions. Backing you into a box."

"What're you saying, Tricia?"

"I'm asking you if you think you're ready now to go to the authorities, talk to them the same way you talked to the boy and his father. Use the same courage."

"See," Orlon said. "See what I'm telling you."

"I don't know," Ray said. "I don't know if I'm ready for that."

"Well, I know," Orlon said. "The answer is no. I'm not ready, and I'm not going to let someone else go and squeal on me either."

Orlon folded up his knife, put it in his pocket. Came back out with his five-shot .25. Black with a small rubber grip. At home he kept it lying beside his keys and sunglasses on the kitchen counter. Whenever he went out, the thing went with him. "Smash, grab, dead on the slab," that's what Orlon liked to say.

Tricia was looking at the pistol. Orlon standing there, pointing the weapon halfway between Tricia and Ray.

"It's okay, Tricia," Ray said. "He gets like this. Don't let him bother you. It's a control thing. When the spotlight moves away from Orlando White, he's got to act like this, pull out a gun, make everybody look at the Big O again. Big Zero is more like it. Big nothing."

Orlon was looking at Ray now. Mouth clamped, eyes flickering.

Ray stood up, reached his hand out.

"Gimme."

"No."

"You're acting that way again, Orlando. You're being a little kid. Just some little kid."

"Look," Orlon said, bringing the pistol up, pointing it directly at Ray's chest. "I already had one mother. Nobody gets to have two. So just shut the fuck up, okay? Let me think what I've got to do."

"Do something, Ray," Tricia said. "Handle this."

"You got a suggestion?"

Looking at Orlon, trying to see into his eyes, see what voltage he was on at the moment. Not much, it looked like. Ray thought of that Jack Nicholson thing, Polanski cutting his nose. How that was Orlon's world view, his way of figuring out how to act, all of it based on some totally fucked-up idea of a movie. Trying to push his own personal movie into new territories.

But then Ray looked at Tricia, saw the way she'd started to shiver as she stared at the gun. Lost all her professional composure; all her psychological training wasn't working for her now.

And where was Ray? Which side of this shit storm was Ray on? Hell if he knew. Maybe it was all just to get laid—his recent adventure into psychology, all that reparation business. Maybe everything he'd been thinking he believed was just because of Tricia's cashmere sweaters. His entire view of life, the reason why he did what he did, based entirely on being a total, complete sucker for cashmere and redheaded women. Not a whole lot different from Orlon believing in *Chinatown* as his sacred gospel.

"So what're you going to do now, Orlon?" Ray said.

"I don't like this," said the therapist. "I don't like what's happening here."

"Mom brought you into her hospital room," Orlon said, eyes bobbing up from wherever they'd been. Looking straight into Ray in a way he almost never did. "There at the end, it was you Mom talked to, not me. I was born two minutes after you, but I'm always the little kid. You're the older, wiser brother. How was that gonna make me feel? You go in there, she talks to you, tells you what to do, the answers, whatever the hell she told you. You come out of that room, it isn't you anymore. It's some other guy.

"I'm standing there, waiting my turn. But I don't *get* a turn. She dies. Whatever it was she said, you aren't talking about it. So there we go, growing up, the two of us, you with the message, me with shit. Nothing. I gotta listen to you 'cause I don't know, maybe this is what she told you. Maybe this is part of the big answer, the thing she was seeing in her fever, because I don't even know where to begin with guessing what she told you."

Tricia slid off the desk. She stepped forward, made the third point on the triangle. She reached her arms out, one toward Ray, one toward Orlon.

"Maybe I can help," she said. "Maybe if you both talked to me, we could work through this."

Orlon looked at her.

"You see what I'm saying to you, Rayon? You see how bad it was to me, not knowing the thing you got told?" Looking at Tricia Capoletti, then back at Ray.

"I've done the best I could," Ray said.

"You should've just told me. You should've said it straight out. Here's what Mom said. She told me this and this and this. But no, you had to hold on to it. It was your secret, the thing that made you the important one. I'm this asshole, this kid, this jerkwipe. I'm never going to grow up. And the reason is—the reason I couldn't grow up even if I wanted to was because I didn't know the thing, the big secret. So I had to make do. I go on making my movie. Never told anybody till I told you the other day. Never let on what I was doing, recording everything, trying to punch up the drama wherever I could. That's what I was doing. That was my secret. That's what I had."

"All she told me, Orlando, was to look after you. Try to keep the family together."

"That's all?" Orlon looked back at Ray. Mouth closed now, gun pointed at Tricia.

"That's every word she said to me."

"Shit, that's not so much."

"No, it isn't. But it's still a hard job."

"You didn't do it very well either, Rayon. You botched it, I'd say. Look at us. The shit we're into."

"Yeah."

"I thought there was more to it. I thought she told you something important."

"I don't think she knew anything important. I think she was just a simple woman. She wanted to travel, but she couldn't afford to. That was her. That was everything I remember about her."

"Why didn't you tell me before now? Why the fuck did you keep it to yourself, Ray? You could've just come out and told me. But no, you had to hold on to it 'cause it gave you the power over me."

"Orlon," he said. "I didn't think you cared. You never asked me."

"Shit," Orlon said. He lowered the pistol. "Shit, shit."

Tricia said, "This is good. We're getting it out now. We're getting to the core."

Orlon looked at her again. He raised his .25.

Saying to Ray, "Mom told you to keep the family together. So is that what you thought you were doing, giving Allison the photographs? Trying to keep us together in jail. Is that what you thought?"

"At that particular moment," Ray said, "I guess I wasn't thinking about Mom, what she said."

"No, you were listening to this one here," Orlon said. "Listening to this shrink, totally disregarding the solemn promise you made."

"I thought it was right at the time."

"But now you see it wasn't."

"Wait a minute," Tricia said. "Your brother is twisting this around, Ray. You had a genuine feeling. You went to that boy's house and you confessed, and what you felt afterward was real."

Ray looked at her. Red hair loose today. That Windsor knot still bothering him, how skinny it was, not a nice triangle like it was supposed to be.

"You're right, Orlon. I should never have dropped

those photos off with Allison. That was dumb. I should've consulted with you at least."

"Bitchcraft," Orlon said. "You were under this woman's spell. That's all it was, bitchcraft."

Orlon shook his head sadly and reached out and pressed the pistol against Tricia's throat.

"Hey!" Ray started for him, but Orlon held up a hand.

"Look at her," Orlon said. "Look at this woman."

Tricia's chin and lips were quivering.

"She's giving out advice, telling you how to run your life, Ray, but what does she know? Book shit. College shit. Has she ever looked into the barrel of a gun? Hell, no. But that guy with the gun in Hialeah, that father out there pointing that forty-five at you, Miss Book Learning here, she thinks she knows exactly what that moment is all about. She tells you, and you fucking listen to her."

Orlon tipped the barrel up, pressing the muzzle into the underside of Tricia's jaw, tilting her face up into the air.

She was trying to speak, trying to say something to Ray, but nothing was working, eyes streaming with tears.

Orlon pulled the trigger, and the hammer clicked on an empty chamber. Tricia tried to pull away, but Orlon kept the barrel hard against her neck and wouldn't let her move.

He pulled the trigger again and again. Empty. Tricia took a long gasp of air, her eyes fluttering shut, and she pitched sideways, hit the edge of her desk, twisted and tumbled onto the rug, faceup, eyes closed. Out, gone.

Orlon bent over her and pressed the gun against her temple and pulled the trigger again and again.

"That's why I went outside," Orlon said. "I took out the bullets."

"You asshole."

"Now she knows about an empty gun. Now what she said is true." Orlon looked at Ray. "Before, she didn't know what the fuck she was talking about, so it was just an accident she happened to speak the truth. But I've furthered her education. Next time it comes up, Miss Tricia can talk about empty guns with some authority."

Ray leaned down and straightened Tricia out, made her more comfortable. She was unconscious. Gone down the long, black slide into slumberland without even a last whoop good-bye.

"Christ," Ray said, and looked up at Orlon. "I love this woman. I do. I love the hell out of her."

"But you see what she was doing, Ray. You see it now, don't you? She was making you betray your solemn oath."

Ray touched her shoulder, her cheek.

"You didn't have to scare her like that."

"She knows things, Ray. You told her intimate family secrets. We couldn't just walk away, her knowing what she does. Not without showing her what the consequences of her actions could be."

Ray touched Tricia's hair, stroked it. More coarse than he'd imagined, crinkly and thick.

"What we got to do now is to start over," Orlon said. "Right from the beginning. Now that I finally know what the hell Mom said, that's what we should do."

"Keep the family together." Ray heard the words come from him, like a dreamer talking. "That's what she told me."

"It's not much," Orlon said. "But it's something."

Ray caressed Tricia's cheek, soft, warm. He guessed now it was over between them. You didn't scare your shrink to death one minute and ask her to marry you the next.

He should've realized a long time ago it would never work with Tricia. It would've been bigamy anyway, 'cause Ray was married already.

Him and Orlon, till death did them part.

# C H A P T E R

# 35

"Allison was just here. She came to my office."

"Harry, you called me on the international phone line at nine in the morning to tell me your wife came to your office?"

"I tried you at home, told your man it was an emergency, he gave me this number. I didn't know what else to do."

"Well, now you found me. Talk."

Patrick straightened the sheets around him, glanced over at Sean. She'd rolled away from him, a tremble in her back. Crying.

Harry's pitiful voice spoke into Patrick's ear.

"She's onto us, Pat. She's figured things out."

"I made arrangements for Allison some time ago. There is nothing to worry about from her. Erase her from your mind."

"What arrangements?"

"Don't worry yourself about it."

"Not those same guys. Those fuckups. Not them."

"Harry, I'm hanging up now."

"This is wrong. This isn't working the way we planned. It's gone way off track."

Patrick was quiet. There was something in Harry's voice he'd glimpsed before. Only then it had been no more than a small vein of weakness, a fissure in the great bedrock of his greed. Nothing to worry about, a trait, in fact, that Patrick could exploit. But now it had grown. A widening crack. His voice almost a screech. Harry's cowardice was souring into full-fledged panic.

"Harry, have a drink. Have several drinks. Relax. Don't worry yourself about this anymore. It will be finished before you know it."

A pause filled with static, then Harry said, "This isn't right. I'm sick of it. I don't want any more killing."

"Neither do I, Harry. I abhor violence. But this is not a conversation for the international phone lines. Do you understand me?"

"Call them off," he said. "I don't want Allison hurt."

Patrick was quiet for a moment, gathering his patience. He fluffed up the pillow, propped it against the headboard, pulled himself up and settled against it. Feeling a twist in his stomach, some knot of feeling. Worry. Worry for having become involved with this family, for staking so much on these people, all of them without backbone. Only Allison was even close to Patrick's equal.

"Harry," he said at last. "I can call them off. But you know what that will mean. If Allison knows what is going on, and if she talks to the right people, it is the end of Rantel, De Novo, your career. My future."

"Goddamn it. Call them off. We'll worry about Rantel later."

"All right, Harry. If that's the way you want it."

"I'm serious. I don't want any more violence."

"If it is important to you, Harry, of course I'll do it."

"Okay. Good."

Harry breathed into the receiver. He was panting. The crackle of cellophane rippling across the line, electronic surf.

Harry said, "We'll find a way to defuse Allison. No one takes her seriously anyway after the Joshua Bond thing. She could talk all she wanted, no one's going to believe her. This isn't the end of De Novo. We can cobble this back together, I know it. I'll take care of Allison.

She'll listen to reason. I can still talk to her, show her how important this is. She's still my wife, for chrissake."

"You know her better than I, Harry."

"Can I trust you, Patrick? You'll rein these people in?"

"Please, Harry. I want what is good for all concerned. As I told you, I abhor what has taken place. I am in total agreement with you that the violence should halt."

"Okay. Look, I'm sorry I bothered you, Patrick. But I feel better. You'll make that call right now. Okay?"

Sean made a move to rise from the bed, but Patrick gripped her wrist, held her down.

"And listen, Patrick," Harry's voice was fraying again. "I know you find Sean attractive. I realize that. But you can't be with her. Sexually, I mean. You can't be with her. Promise me that."

"What are you talking about now, Harry?"

"It's not right," Harry said. "It wouldn't be good."

"I'm hanging up now, Harry. Our conversation is over."

"No, listen. There's something you don't know. When I was over there on my first tour, in Brunei twenty-five years ago, I met a woman. I had a lover there. It was my first posting. I fell in love."

"Touching, Harry. Very touching."

"It was the sultan's sister, Patrick. Your mother. Kalami."

Patrick drew the phone from his ear as if it had stung him. After another moment he brought it back to his ear.

"You're lying, Harry. You're inventing an ugly lie."

"No, it's true, Patrick. It's true, I swear."

"No, Harry. It isn't true. It's a lie. It's a fucking, terrible lie. I never heard you say this."

He put the receiver back.

Sean tried to wrench free, but Patrick held her wrist a moment longer, staring at her. Analyzing her bone structure as if for the first time.

"Let me go, goddamn it."

With a hiss he dropped his hold. Sean rolled over to

face him. Lower jaw jutting out. A vein rising at her temple.

"That was my father."

"Yes."

"Does he know?"

"Know what?"

"That you murdered Winslow."

Patrick sighed.

"I told you, Sean. It was an accident. A ghastly mistake. I never meant for that to happen. None of us did."

"Of course. You meant to kill Allison, but Winslow got in the way. An accident."

"Yes, that's right. I saw her, she saw me. Our eyes met and held for a moment. At that point, I had no choice. I pulled the trigger. It was awful. It was a terrible moment."

"You bastard. You fucking bastard."

"I gave you the absolute truth, Sean, because I want to be perfectly straightforward with you. I could have easily denied the whole affair, pretended innocence, or come up with some other story, an alibi, but I didn't do that. I confided in you because of my love for you. Because of our future together. I don't want our marriage to be founded on lies."

"You're crazy," she said. "You think I'd marry you?"

"You must try to calm yourself, Sean. I realize it is a terrible shock. You are feeling pain now, confusion, anger. Perhaps even fear. But eventually that will all subside, time will wash it away. You'll see things as I see them. And we will be again as we were yesterday."

"Does my father know what you did?"

"Your father," Patrick said, and sniffed at the thought of him. "Your father is a weak man. He has appetites beyond his abilities. He lacks discipline and strength of purpose."

"But does he know?"

With both hands Patrick combed the hair away from his face.

"Sean," he said. "Harry helped plan every facet, every detail. He put me in touch with various men around the world, men I needed for my project. He has been extremely helpful at every stage, from the beginning till today. I could not have accomplished all that I have without his assistance. I am deeply in his debt."

"He okayed the plan to kill Allison? He knew it was you who shot my sister?"

"He knew that a regrettable accident took place in the jungle. That a tragic mishap occurred while reasonable men were engaged in a difficult and crucial enterprise."

Sean turned her face away from him. Stared at the far wall.

"And you actually think I'm going to forgive you for killing Winslow?"

"I don't see what choice you have."

"Forgive you or die. Those are my options."

"All you have to do is continue to feel about me as you did yesterday. Feelings don't simply come to an abrupt halt. We have experienced a setback, a bump in the road of our relationship. We'll recover. Now come here. Make yourself comfortable, lie with me."

She turned back around, glaring at him. Still beautiful, even now, even in her anger, her confusion. Still the staggeringly beautiful teenage girl in the yellow summer dress strolling down the Boulevard Jalang Tasek. Even Harry's awful lie could not taint his vision of her.

"And what if I refuse? What's to keep me from running into the hall, screaming for help?"

Patrick sighed, smoothed the bedspread around him.

He looked off toward the window and said, "If I thought there was no hope, Sean, if I thought you could never forgive me, we could never regain what we had a few short hours ago, if I thought I could not trust you in the presence of others, then I don't know. I don't know what I would do."

"Tell me something, Patrick."

He shrugged away the sad thought he was having, and looked back at her.

"Yes?"

"What's so goddamn important that my sister had to be sacrificed for it? My mother?"

"Tomorrow," Patrick said. "All will be clear."

She turned away from him again, showed him her beautiful bare back. Patrick stroked her shoulders, drew himself up, came close to her and began to massage the tight muscles in her neck and shoulder blades.

"Why don't you just do it," she said. "Put a bullet through my brain and be done with it."

"It's all right, sweetheart. It's all right. You're safe. Don't worry, please. It hurts me to see you this way."

"You fucking bastard."

He let a few seconds pass, then a few more, waiting for her harsh words to break apart, disperse.

"Now rest, sweetheart. I have one phone call to make before I join you. I'll do it in the bathroom so you won't be disturbed."

But before he made his call Patrick took the letter opener from the desk, and searched the room carefully for anything else that might tempt her.

"He phones, we gotta drop everything, clean up after him. Have gun, will travel. The Paladin brothers. Jesus, I'll be glad to be done with all these people."

Orlon was weaving the Vette fast through the traffic on U.S. 1, cutting people off, bouncing from lane to lane, pitching Ray from one side to the other. Nine at night, Friday, most of the traffic was headed out to South Beach, see and be seen. . . .

"And shit," Orlon said, "I don't know why we don't just go to the house, wait there. Less people around."

Ray looked away out the side window, trying not to watch how close Orlon was riding some eighteen-wheeler's bumper.

"He's at the office working late. Nobody's around."

Orlon said, "What's that address again?"

Ray told him for the fifth time. 305 Biscayne. The Columbus Building.

"Hey," Orlon said. "Remember that little office complex, the one used to be around there, near where the Columbus Building is now?"

"No."

"Well, you remember Dr. Krakel?"

"The dentist," Ray said. "The one didn't use novocaine."

"Yeah, guy didn't believe in it. Sat there in his office running fucking Nazi experiments on little kids. See how much pain they could take before they puked or passed out."

"He didn't use novocaine on us," Ray said, "because it was too expensive. Mom couldn't afford it."

"What?"

"Too expensive," Ray said. "Mom told him no. Do it au naturel."

"Is that right? How'd you know that?"

Ray watched as U.S. 1 widened by one lane, turned into I-95, and Orlon gunned the Vette past a dozen cars, touching ninety before he had to brake hard for the exit ramp to downtown.

"I know 'cause I heard Mom arguing with him about it. Trying to get him to throw it in for free. But no, it was ten dollars extra for novocaine. She didn't have the ten bucks, so we didn't get it. No big secret there."

"You telling me all that fucking pain," Orlon said, "a couple dollars more we wouldn't have had to endure it?"

"*Ten* dollars," Ray said. "That was a lot to Mom back then."

Orlon swerved in front of a white Lexus at the light on Flagler, made a quick right with no stop for the red light. Cars honking behind them. Orlon gunned it, jammed Ray's head against the headrest for a hundred yards.

Halfway up the block, letting off the gas, he said, "I bet this guy we're going to see, he always got novocaine when he was a kid. I bet his mom didn't say, no, I can't afford it, go on, torture the shit out of the little tyke."

"On the other hand," Ray said. "This guy had to live with Allison for the past twenty years."

Orlon looked over at him again, an uncertain smile. "What's your point?"

"The universe is fair," Ray said. "You suffer early or you suffer later on. You and me suffered early, and this guy, the one that got novocaine, he got stuck with Allison."

"And now," Orlon said, "he's getting stuck with us."

The ape was strapped into the steel chair, seven monitoring wires attached to him, brain waves, heart rhythm, breath rates, perspiration. Patches of shaggy orange hair had been shaved from his chest and skull so the wires could be implanted, the flesh greased.

The nozzle of the propane torch was attached to one end of an accordion arm that was carefully calibrated to move as close as one inch and as distant as a foot from the orangutan's face. At that moment, the fire burned four and a half inches from the ape's nose, its flame shooting several inches into the air.

The ape had stopped fighting against the straps. He'd even quit watching the fire hiss. He simply sat still as if he were unaware of the danger that hovered so close to his face. He stared straight ahead through the blue flame, making eye contact with the laboratory assistant.

When the professor finished the next notations on his clipboard, he looked up and instructed Bernice to adjust the distance two inches closer. But she didn't move. She was looking into the ape's eyes. The professor cleared his throat and asked the young lady if she heard him. Bernice balked a moment more, then responded that yes, she had heard him.

The orangutan held her eyes as she stepped forward and adjusted the accordion arm, bringing the flame two and a half inches from his nose. A random puff of air might have easily set his facial fur ablaze. The professor studied his assistant for a moment, then shook his head and returned to his gauges, and began to make further notes. There were tears in Bernice's eyes.

The ape closed his eyes and the professor watched

with dismay as the heart monitor showed a sudden steep decline. The orangutan's pulse was quieting. Eyes closed, limbs no longer twitching, hands open and relaxed against the arms of the chair. As though the orangutan were putting himself into some kind of meditational trance.

# CHAPTER

# 36

"Nice view, counselor. Cruise ships, ocean. Everything glittering. Hell, we're up so high you could take a piss, it'd evaporate before it hit the ground."

Harry looked at one brother, then the other. Orlando and Raimondo White.

"Me and Ray, we been meaning to take a cruise. Just never can seem to find the time. Work, work, work."

He stood at Harry's window, pressing his nose against the glass, leaving a two-inch greasy smear. The short one, bald, no eyebrows or lashes, like he'd been dunked in acid. Wearing a black T-shirt stretched tight over his beer gut, black pants, shoes. The other one, Ray, was tall with blond hair swept back, ducktail. Jeans, work shirt, tie, a white sport coat. Dressed like a Sweet Briar professor, but with that hair, that face, he could've been one of those seedy beach boys who put the chaise longues out, and in their spare time picked up elderly women, stole their jewelry.

Harry leaned back in his swivel chair, laced his fingers behind his head, looking over at the blond one.

"Now, how can I help you, gentlemen?"

"Gentlemen?" Orlon smiled, and pulled away from the view. Gave Harry a lunatic grin. "Now, I wouldn't call myself particularly gentle. What about you, Ray? You think of yourself as a *gentle* man?"

Ray was examining the painting of Sean and Winslow at fourteen and fifteen. He didn't turn around, didn't reply.

"Fact is, Harry, my brother here, he's more the gentle type. Ray's what you might call sexually challenged. Inherited a couple of feminine genes, I do believe.

"But me, I'm afflicted with a terminal case of manhood. I gotta go once a month, get dialysis, filter out all the nasty testosterone. Though so far it hasn't done a fucking thing except make me lose my hard-on for a half hour afterward.

"What about you, Harry? Where're you on the manhood scale? Just looking at you I'd have to say you're tipping more toward the ladylike end. You have that fussy-fussy, gotta-get-every-hair-in-place look. But, hey, I guess being married to a ballcrusher like Allison, that's gotta be hard on your virility."

Ray turned back from the painting.

"Just get on with it, Orlon. And let's go."

Harry sat up straight, gripped the arms of his chair. "Did Patrick send you over here?"

"That's right, our mutual associate, the ragin' Asian."

"Wait a minute. I just got off the phone with him an hour ago. What's the matter? What's going on here?"

"Well, counselor, I guess he didn't like what you spoke about, 'cause he called us up on the cell phone, requested we haul our butts over here, put you in immediate early retirement. Maybe help free up some office space around this joint."

*"What?"*

"We're here to kill you, Harry. Set loose your immortal soul."

Harry jerked a hand into the air as if to ward off a blow. Then lowered it heavily to the desk.

"Now, wait just a goddamn minute, you two."

"Sure, whatever you want, counselor. Always got time to shoot the shit before we have to shoot the shit."

Orlon grinned back at Ray, but he wasn't looking.

"Something's gotten screwed up," Harry said. "This is obviously a mistake. A communications mix-up."

"Oh, wow," Orlando said. "Could that be what we have here? A failure to communicate? Classic *Cool Hand Luke* situation?"

"Are you gonna do it, Orlon, or you gonna jerk off all over the man's desk?"

"I'll call Patrick right now, talk to him. Straighten him out."

"I wouldn't recommend that," Orlon said. "I'd probably have to shoot you if you pick up that phone. Then the fun's all over."

Harry set his wrists against the edge of the teak. He was having trouble with his breath. He had a sudden need to piss.

"Yes, sir, after this is over, Ray, and things are calm again," Orlon said, staring out that window again, "you and me, we gotta take a cruise through the islands. Meet some ladies, give them the benefit of our company, have us a shipboard romance. Dance beneath the diamond sky with one hand waving free."

"Now listen to me, you two," said Harry. "Apparently Patrick misunderstood something I said. But I have no intention whatsoever of going to the police. We're all on the same side here. We have the same goals."

"I don't think so, Harry. I mean, nothing personal, but I look around this office, see your taste in things, and I don't see we have a lot in common at all, you and us."

Harry said, "We're business partners, for god's sake. You and your brother, Patrick and me. We have the same interests. Hell, I'm the one who got you involved in the first place. I put you together with Patrick."

"So that was you? Me and Ray wondered who referred us."

"I read about you in my wife's newsletter. You sounded like the men we were looking for."

Ray laughed, shook his head in wonder.

"Now, that's rich. Husband finds jobs for the guys

his wife is trying to lock away. Hey, there's a well-balanced marriage."

Harry's head sagged. He stared down at the grain in the wood. Mind dulling over, going into shock. He'd never really noticed the wood grain before, the swirls where sap had once coursed through the trunk. Drifting away into a thought about wood, trees, the forests of his boyhood in West Virginia, those dense pines behind his house, huge vines strangling them.

When he lifted his eyes, Orlon grinned at him, expectant.

"First thing in the morning," Harry said. "I'll go to my bank, do some rearranging, get you a large sum of money."

"How large?"

Both of them looked into his eyes now.

"I could free up half a million by noon."

"That much?"

Orlon dug into his pocket and produced a small black handgun. Just held it casually down by his leg, gripping it around its girth, not by the handle.

"Seven hundred and fifty thousand," Harry said. "I could go that high."

Orlando let out a wolf whistle.

"You're a prosperous man, Harry Farleigh. You've done all right for yourself. Yeah, sure, we'll be happy to take some cash off your hands, Harry. We can always find a use for American currency."

"Just go on, Orlon, shoot the man, quit fucking around. We're not taking his pathetic money."

"Shoot him, Ray? Just shoot him and walk out? That the way you'd do your movie? A couple of pops through the heart, bang, bang, man slumps over in his chair. Cleaning lady finds him later, swivels his chair around, screams. That the film cliché you got in mind for this fellow?"

Harry pushed himself to his feet. He looked at the door, suddenly picturing himself walking over to it. Take them by surprise—he'd open it, walk out, a dash down the hallway, use his superior knowledge of the office lay-out to lose them.

Orlon was staring again at the window.

"Hey, how high are we, Harry—this office, I forget. Twenty floors?"

"Twenty-six," he said.

Harry looked at the door, his fantasy crystallizing like a dream he was shaping. Sprinting down the hall, gunfire behind him, he ducks through the coffee room, a mad dash down the narrow back hall to the stairwell. Harry the track star, Harry in retreat. Brave Harry. Discretion, the better part of valor. Harry taking the stairs, nimble-legged, going down a floor or two, then hopping on the service elevator, riding to ground level, out through the lobby, breaking through the front door, taking deep gulps of air, fists in the air. Victory cheers.

Orlon picked up a large glass ashtray that lay on the side table next to the client's chair. Shifting his pistol to his left hand, he held the ashtray in his right, took aim. Then the small man rocked back and forth, imitated a pitcher's windup, bringing the ashtray to his chin, pump-ing his leg like Koufax. He hurled it at Harry's window, hit near dead center and the ashtray bounced off, whacked the side of the desk. Not even a crack in the glass.

"What the fuck, Orlon?"

"I suspected that," he said. "Up this high, the way the wind must gust up here. Thing is probably three inches thick."

Harry glanced at the door again. No. If he had any hope at all, he'd have to negotiate his way out of this. Use what skills he had, talk, compromise, finesse. He was a diplomat, after all, a man who had spoken on behalf of his nation, swimming with more dangerous sharks than these. Men with their fingers on powerful buttons. World-end-ing buttons.

"Mr. Farleigh," Ray said. "Before my brother does what we came here to do, the thing that's got to be done, I wish you'd tell me one thing. Something bothering me."

"Look," Harry said. "It doesn't have to happen like this. You don't need to get blood on your hands, put yourself in jeopardy. I can simply disappear. Patrick would have no way of knowing. And anyway, listen, the three of us, we're all Americans. We're not like that man. He's a Muslim, for god's sake. It's like he might as well be from another planet. What he believes, the way he looks at the world, his language, everything. But the three of us, we're Americans, we stick together. We help each other. That's the way it's always been with our people."

"He's good," Orlando said. "The man's got a silver tongue."

Ray's eyes were chilly, squinting at Harry.

"Everybody's tongue turns silver when they face a gun."

"All right, here's what I'll do," Harry said. "I'll walk out the door, no one will ever see me again. Gone, like that. Your job is done, no guilt, no crime, free and clear."

"What I want to know, Harry," the blond one said. "I stand here, I look at the painting on your wall, your pretty daughters. And I'm wondering, just for my own edification, nothing riding on the answer—can you tell me how it could be, a guy shoots your daughter, pretty girl like she was, your own flesh and muscle, shoots her dead, and a month later you're still doing business with the man? How can that be? I want to know this."

Harry leaned forward, thighs against his desk. He tried for a hard look but his face felt rubbery, out of control.

Ray said, "Somebody killed a member of my family, I wouldn't stop till the man was hunted down and dealt with. But you, Harry, you keep on associating economically with this man. This is beyond me. This is truly beyond my psychological scope. I don't believe greed alone can account for it."

Harry opened his lips, closed them again.

"Silver tongue's gone," Orlando said.

Harry closed his eyes, rubbed his forehead, an oily sweat thick as jelly.

"Sure I was upset," he said. "I loved Winslow."

"Upset, Harry? That the strongest phrase you can come up with? 'I was upset.' "

"What do you want me to say?"

Ray said, "I don't mean to psychoanalyze you or anything, but maybe what it is, Harry, maybe you don't have any sympathy for other people's suffering. Could that be, you're just not able to experience anybody else's pain but your own? No compassion? No pity? Got a little faulty wiring in your frontal lobe, maybe.

"I mean, I got my reasons for asking you this. Something similar my own family is working through. So I'd be interested to hear your idea on this."

"Jesus Christ," Orlon said. "You don't ever give up, do you, Ray? Always gotta be tweaking me."

Orlon raised the gun, aimed at the window and fired. A silvery spiderweb erupted around the bullet hole, deep cracks sprouted. Harry felt the blood leave his body.

"Now, that's what I like about a twenty-five," Orlon said. "It's ultraquiet. You squeeze off a few rounds, a room like this, door closed, nice thick carpets, nobody notices. Sounds like somebody's hammering on the wall, maybe hanging a painting. Or they popped a champagne cork, celebrating another big win.

"But then the drawback is, it takes three or four shots sometimes to put a guy away. Or like with that window, something thick like that, one shot won't do it. But then, hey, there's trade-offs, right? Right, Ray? Always trade-offs."

Orlon fired the pistol again and the slug struck a foot from the first one. A single jigsaw piece of glass fell lazily away.

"Go on, Harry, don't mind me. Argue with Ray. Defend yourself. Don't let him bad-mouth you like that. He's always doing that, you know. Does it to me all the fucking time. Mother Teresa White, Saint Ray, Our Lady of the Perfect Life Ray. Go on, Harry, make your case. Stand up to him."

"I don't know what you people want from me."

"Tell him, Harry," Orlon said. "Tell him how it's guys like you and me, mean sons of bitches, us no-pity bastards, when it comes time to shovel the shit, it's gotta be guys like us that do it. We don't even have to pinch our noses.

"Tell him, Harry. Guys like Ray, man, they depend on us. We're the ones pick up their garbage, clean out the monkey cages, shoot the people need to be shot. Maybe we don't make the best party guests, maybe we're a little uncouth around the edges, but hey, we got other virtues."

Orlon fired again, knocked loose a thick platter of glass.

"Shit, without people like us the world wouldn't run at all. Right brain, left brain. Right heart, left heart. Tell him, Harry. It takes the both of us. We can't be like him and he can't be like us. It takes the both of us to make things work. People up here on the twenty-sixth floor, flushing their johns, never thinking of all the work it takes to get their shit where it's gotta go. Never realizing there're guys like us who crawl into the sewer pipes when things stop working right."

Orlon stabbed the pistol toward the window and fired two quick shots. A slab broke free and tumbled away. Wind filled the room, papers blowing from his desk. Lifting his tie.

"Okay, Harry. Time to go," Orlon said.

"What?"

Reloading, Orlon said, "Express elevator is waiting, Harry. You're an attorney, you should be familiar with the laws of gravity."

"Go on, Harry," Ray said quietly. "It'll be all right. Everything'll work out better if you do this yourself."

Harry laughed. He licked his lips, looked at the gash in the glass, felt the cool wind, fresh with a hint of the sea.

"This is a gag, right? To scare me. Okay, okay, you did your job. I'm sufficiently warned."

Ray shook his head sadly, and Orlon fired the pistol once more and knocked loose a sharp incisor of glass. Then he started around the other side of the desk.

Harry edged away from him toward the window.

"Do the right thing, Harry," Ray said. "The honorable thing."

Harry kept backing up, saying, "I don't know what happened out there in the jungle. I mean, I have no way of knowing the truth. All I know is, you two were supposed to kill Allison. Patrick started worrying she'd stumble onto what we were doing right under her nose. But instead of shooting Allison, someone shot my daughter. Sure I was hurt. Sure I was angry. But what could I do? Life has to go on. Business agreements have to be honored. Sometimes things are bigger than a single person."

"That the arrangement, was it?" Ray pulled out the client's chair, sat down, watching Harry. "You saved yourself some alimony, found somebody who'd pull the trigger on her? Patrick's got his reasons for killing her, you got yours, we got ours, everybody's happy. United against Allison Farleigh. That what we walked into here? A domestic war zone?"

Orlon was a yard away, closing in. Harry inched toward the window, eyes on Ray, appealing to him, the one he'd decided was the real boss here, the one with more than a gun. Wind poured into the office. His framed diplomas rocked, the painting of his girls, the papers on his desk swirled onto the rug.

"You can't trust Patrick," Harry said. "He'll use you, then throw you away, just like he's trying to do to me. He'll murder you, and no one will ever find your bodies."

"We know that," Ray said.

Orlon smiled, stepped closer, taking aim with his pistol, sighting on Harry's face.

"If you let me live," Harry said, "I'll make sure Patrick is neutralized. Put away for good. I can expose what he's been doing. The three of us can make a deal with the court, testify against him. We'll walk. I can see to that. I know people."

"Could you get our records expunged, Harry?" Orlon was grinning at him, inching closer. "I always wanted my record expunged. Could you do that? Go all the way back to grade school, clear everything up? Give me good deportment grades. Now, I'd truly like that."

"We don't need your help, Harry," Ray said. "We're going to handle Patrick our own way. We don't need a deal. But thanks for thinking of us."

Orlon beamed at Harry, lost in his ecstasy. Drawing close, a yard between his pistol and Harry's face. Harry could feel the shards of glass beneath his leather soles.

"I could be your attorney. Pro bono, of course. Your own personal legal aid for the rest of your lives."

"We're going straight, Harry. We don't need a lawyer."

"Wow, the man's running low on goodies," Orlon said. "Scraping the fucking bottom of his bribe bag with that one."

Ray, using a dreamy voice, said, "Now why don't you just climb up there, Harry. Into your window. Make it easy on yourself. Just think of your daughter. The dead one. Maybe she's down there in the street, waiting for you. Maybe she'll forgive you for what you let happen to her."

Harry swallowed, took a quick slug of air, all he could manage. Feeling woozy, as if he were dropping already. Dropping through twenty-six stories of air.

Unaccountably thinking again of West Virginia, the woods behind his house. A tree he used to climb for a view of the valley, the spire of the Baptist church, the mines, a handful of dingy houses. Up in the tree, Harry liked to stare out beyond his shabby birthplace, those foggy miles that led to Washington. Harry having fantasies. Tree reverie. Imagining a life beyond the valley, imagining Paris, imagining London and Zurich and Rome. High in the dreamy branches of the tree.

Orlon jammed the pistol against his back. Nudging him to the windowsill. He snapped Harry's suspenders once, twice. The brothers were talking, but Harry heard only a vague buzz. Drawing himself up onto the sill. A strong breeze in his face. Standing before the ragged hole in the glass. Miami spread beneath him, streetlights on.

Buildings lit with colored lights. Biscayne Bay a black emptiness.

Harry stood before the shattered window, high up, like being in that old maple with its easy branches. Much simpler to climb than it appeared at first. Like just about everything had turned out for Harry, easier to master than he'd expected, even the roads leading from his valley. No one was out there blocking his way. Harry had made his escape. Left his town, went swiftly up the ladder. Amazing how easy it was, how effortlessly it all happened. Money, power, luxuries. Amazing how little fun any of it had been.

"You know, Mr. Farleigh," Ray said. "Truth is, sometimes I find myself wishing it was the other way around. It was me that had the cold heart, me instead of Orlon. I gotta say, there's moments I'm jealous of guys like you two. Nothing bothers you. You got no sensitivities.

"I have these thoughts sometimes, lying in bed at night. I think maybe that's where we're all headed, the human race. Like it's actually Orlon who's evolved in the right direction. Guys like him and you, Harry, out on the cutting edge, you've gotten yourselves all ready for the slash-and-burn twenty-first century. No matter how shitty it gets, guys like you will get through somehow."

"Yeah, yeah, there you go," Orlon said. "Same as *Road Warrior*. Me and Mel Gibson, we're the fucking cockroaches, we'll be around no matter what. Bomb goes off, acid rain eats up all the trees, ozone completely evaporates, fucking sun starts scorching everything—shit, we don't care. It'll be Mel and me and the cockroaches slithering around in the rubble. The mean bastards, not the 'Hail Mary, full of grace' assholes like you, Ray. That's good. I like that."

Harry felt the wind on his face, a cool sea breeze, thinking of that tree, that maple. How some days he'd climb up high and jump from the tree just to feel that short, incredible thrill of freedom before the lurch of impact.

Harry Farleigh ducked through the broken pane, out

onto the ledge. He looked at the horizon, that hairline seam that separated heaven from earth. He felt his knees sag. And Harry remembered how it was as a boy, a moment's impulse, a second of bravery was all it took.

Without another thought, Harry Farleigh stumbled forward into the empty air, falling facedown, shirtsleeves rippling hard, gulping gallons of air. His vision blurred, everything below him becoming a watery smudge, so he wasn't absolutely sure, but for an instant it looked to him as though Ray had been right. It seemed that Winslow was indeed waiting for him in the street below.

# C H A P T E R

# 37

It was nine-thirty. The Haitian taximan had made himself a drink, tested all the furniture, chosen the couch. He was stretched out there with the TV zapper, moving through the channels. Allison went upstairs to her room, dialed the long-distance number again. She told the Sheraton operator this was an emergency, just keep ringing till the party in the room picked up. Three, four, five rings.

Allison sat looking at the wall behind her desk, at a framed photo of Broom taken only a few weeks after she'd rescued him from the roadside zoo. Broom, his expression still guarded, sitting in Harry's easy chair, hand on the wood lever, ready to cock it down, recline. A worried look. Waiting for some signal from Allison. Uncertain if he was allowed this pleasure, this strange control over his own existence.

Ten, eleven, twelve.

Someone picked up the phone in Brunei. Allison stiffened, turned her eyes to the desktop.

"Hello?" Sean's voice was strained, groggy.

"Is he there?" Allison said. "Is Patrick with you?"

Faintly, Sean said yes.

"Are you all right?"

"Yes. I'm all right."

"Does he know you know?"

She said *yes* a third time. Voice choked, been crying.

"All right, now listen to me," Allison said. "Listen carefully."

"I hear you."

"You're going to lead Patrick to Broom. Lead him there a step at a time, don't tell him where you're taking him or you might become dispensable. Not the name of the place, nothing about it. Do you hear me?"

"Yes."

"Good," Allison said. "Now let me speak to him."

Allison glanced up at the orangutan again, drew a long, deliberate breath. Hearing the bump of the phone passing, then his voice, coldly cheerful.

"Hello, Allison. How are you? How are things in Miami?"

"Here's what we're going to do, Patrick. Listen to me. I don't care what you and Harry were up to. It doesn't matter to me in the least. Your plan, your project. And I don't even care what your role was in Winslow's death. That's all done. Do you hear me, I don't give a damn about any of that."

"I hear you, Allison. The reception is excellent."

"I have the roll of film Winslow took. Pictures of you and the White brothers shooting your rifles in Borneo. There is an orangutan tied to your belt. Now, this might not prove anything in any court of law. But, Patrick, I am certain the sultan would be deeply shocked to see these pictures, to discover the kind of men you've been consorting with, and what kind of business you've been doing with them."

"Go on." His voice a tight whisper.

"I'll turn the negatives and the prints over to you. I'll put them in your hands only when Sean is safely with me. Sean for the photos. I want her here in Miami on Sunday. That'll give you time to get back here. Sunday at nine P.M."

"You've thought this through," he said.

"Sean for the photos. Sunday at nine. No debate, no negotiating. Sean knows where to meet me. She'll direct you there. If she's not with you, the deal is off, the photographs go to the sultan, to Brunei's religious leadership, to the press, everywhere. Is that clear?"

"Abundantly," he said.

"And if you hire somebody to kill me," Allison said, "the photos are automatically released as well. The animal project you and Harry have been building is finished."

"I see."

"And there's one more thing," she said. "I want Thorn present at the exchange."

"Who the hell is Thorn?"

"I believe your associates, the White brothers, may know where he is. I want him there. Is that understood?"

"And is that all?"

"Let me speak to Sean again," she said. "Then I'm done."

"No," he said.

There was a sharp snap and her head filled suddenly with an unstable electronic buzz as if some frenzied wasp had lost its way in the ticklish inner canals of her ear.

The laboratory assistant was still cleaning the gibbon cages at ten o'clock on Friday evening when the professor left for the weekend. It routinely fell to her to return to the lab on Saturday and Sunday, feed and water the test animals. Giving up her weekends earned her two hours of extra credit.

Tonight after she'd finished her chores, she stayed on in the lab. She sat at the professor's desk, turned the wedding ring around and around on her finger. Nearly a perfect fit.

After a while she got up, went over to the orangutan's cage. The ape was hunkered in a back corner staring at his feet. When she opened the door he did not look up. She tried to tickle some response from him, running her fingers in circles against his smooth soles, but the ape continued to stare listlessly at his toes.

She sighed, then reached inside and clasped the orangutan by the waist and drew him out. He did not resist. Carrying the passive ape in her arms, she paced up and down the aisle between the cages, speaking in low tones, cuddling, cooing, trying to soothe him, revive some of the zest he'd shown when he first arrived.

Nothing seemed to have any effect until by chance she passed close by the storage closet where the calibrated arm was stored. Perhaps the ape could smell the propane, or perhaps he had a sixth sense, the ability to detect trace amounts of danger. However it happened, the ape knew what was behind the closed doors, for he began to chirp loudly and squirmed out of the lab assistant's arms, climbed onto her shoulders and took an awkward grip on her head.

Moving quickly from the closet, Bernice untangled the ape's fingers from her hair, wrestled him safely into her arms again, and once more he fell into a stupor. For ten more minutes she tried to rouse him, but failed.

Bernice took him to the front windows of the lab and let him look at the lights outside. The college gymnasium was across the road, the pool as well. Both were well lit. Groups of students walked by on the road talking loudly. But the orangutan was not engaged by what he saw. He closed his eyes, turned his head from the view, and pressed his face against her chest.

For the last three years Bernice had been an honor student. Only one semester remained until she was to begin graduate work in behavioral psychology at Duke. She was not a rebel, not a malcontent. While she did hold membership in several animal-rights organizations, she was not a letter writer or a political warrior of any kind.

So it made her giddy and somewhat nauseous to carry the orangutan outside the lab with her, lock the door and lug him to her car. It was clearly a mad, self-destructive act to drive with him in the seat beside her, and to park in one of the rarely used parking lots and wait there until she gathered her nerve.

Just after midnight she carried the ape into her dormitory. Once safely in her room, she lay him on her bed and opened her small refrigerator and searched the vegetable bin. She laid out an array of vegetables on her bedspread. Several minutes passed before the ape took any interest in the food. And then only after he'd consumed a bowl of grapes and an entire green pepper, did the animal rouse himself sufficiently to begin to explore her room.

Thorn's fingers were gashed and bleeding badly. He'd pried loose one of the steel bars from its weld and worked it back and forth a few thousand times till it had finally broken free. Then he found the goddamn thing had an edge as sharp as broken glass and before he even felt the slice, blood poured from the fingers on his right hand.

But worse was the fact that all his work served no purpose. He stuck his arm through the opening, wedged it between the bars up to the elbow, but his hand was still several feet from the tools hanging on the opposite walls. A wire clipper, a pair of pliers, hammers and files.

He should have realized from the beginning. It was so goddamn obvious. The cages stood six feet from the opposite wall, laughably far away, but then Thorn wasn't thinking clearly. The blows he had taken had spun his brain around, the rattlesnake torture put a serious dent in his rational process. For the last few hours he'd been so goddamned cramped inside the cage he wasn't getting enough air. Dizzy and sick, bleeding, weak. His head buzzing with a dreamy whirl of voices. Around him the other animals shifted and burrowed, squeaked and rattled, the gibbons hooting their mysterious songs.

He drew his arm back inside the bars, took a couple of breaths, repositioned his butt against the grid of steel. He crammed his torn fingers into the fold of his bent leg, stanched the blood.

He closed his eyes and after a moment or two, willing himself to relax, Thorn felt his breath coming easier. The mist began breaking up, lifting from his mind. Still trapped, still helpless and in danger, but composed now, a growing optimism.

He opened his eyes, peered across from him, took a measuring look to either side, examining the physics of his situation. Just how the hell he'd ever thought that prying a bar loose from the door would help his predicament, he didn't know. The hinges were the only vulnerable spot on the cage. They seemed to be made of thin strips of aluminum fashioned into a nearly closed C. The axle on the door riding in the hollow of the C.

Already the top hinge was slightly bent. The door jiggled loosely as he shook it. Probably twisted out of whack as the White brothers crammed a struggling animal in through the door. Like closing an overstuffed suitcase, softening the hinges in the process.

Thorn tested the aluminum with his thumb. Pried at it. He huffed, his face reddening as the metal gouged his flesh. No good. Keep on trying that and all he'd get was another sliced finger. He drew his hand away, eased back into the fetal ball he'd been assuming.

With a knife, even a coin, Thorn could pry open that hinge in ten, fifteen minutes, be on his way. But in his position, he couldn't even reach a hand to his pocket to see if he had a coin, much less extract it.

Then the answer came to him as answers so often did, not in words, but through his bones and muscles, his body tissues. Shifting his weight inside the cage, feeling the half-inch sway and tip of the unwieldy structure.

Thorn rocked backward, then pitched his weight forward and the stack of cages shuddered and leaned. The monkey above him screamed and began to run in jittery circles around his tight space. Thorn relaxed for a moment more, tried to focus on the gradients and trajectories of his task.

The workbench was six feet in front of him. If he could tip the whole set of cages over, redirect the angle of descent a foot to the right, and if the momentum was sufficient and the angle correct, Thorn's cage door would strike a glancing blow against the corner of the workbench. Whether or not the jolt would be sufficient to wrench the door from its hinges, he couldn't judge. But in any case, it was a hell of a lot better than staying put. Feeling his strength seep away moment by moment.

He took a deep breath, another, then Thorn began to

rock the cages. Heaving forward, drawing back, gradually finding the rhythm and pushing harder on each forward arc. The monkeys in the adjacent cages hooted and wailed, but Thorn kept at it, the cages tottering farther each time, nudging away from the wall, leaning, top-heavy. Thorn kept the tempo going, muscling forward, drawing back as if he were rocking a car out of a muddy trench. The unstable stack of cages lifted up on the fulcrum of its front edge, yawing forward.

Thorn rode the wave one more time, rocked back with all his weight, gathered himself in that half second, and heaved forward, grunting hard as the cages leaned over, tottered at the brink of their balance point, seesawing. He lurched forward, jamming his cheek against the door of the cage, grinding onward, moving every ounce he could into the downward arc.

Lazily the cages fell, and Thorn pitched his weight to the right, pulling the whole structure off center. It crashed against the workbench with such unexpected force he was momentarily paralyzed. For a few seconds the room was utterly quiet, then all around him the monkeys and gibbons broke into an insane, screeching chorus. And the cage itself squeaked and strained as it settled into its new awkward arrangement.

Thorn opened his eyes, saw blood on his hands, on his legs. Touched a finger to his forehead, felt the numb flesh of a new gash. His right shoulder was jammed against the door of the cage, the whole thing hanging a precarious yard off the floor, held in place by the workbench.

It was then he heard two car doors slam out in the parking lot and the voices of the White brothers, their profane banter.

He blinked away the fog, studied the door of his cage. Even though the door had struck a hard blow against the corner of the workbench the goddamn hinges had held. Stronger than they'd seemed. And the padlock was still in place. But on a second look he saw it. What had given way was the solder that held the steel locking hinge to the cages. The padlock dangled uselessly on its broken plate.

Thorn heard the White brothers unlock their front door, come inside the office. The gibbons and monkeys were quieting now. A pant, hoot and an occasional squeal. Thorn jimmied the door open and pried his head out the narrow breach.

He counted to three, then let himself down to the floor, and felt his legs give way under him. He collapsed on the linoleum beneath the half-toppled cages, his legs straight out in front of him.

Furiously rubbing the life back into them, he listened to the White brothers argue, listened to their raucous approach down the hallway. His skin was prickling. Sprawled on the floor, legs dead, Thorn reached a hand up to the workbench, patted around till his fingers bumped a wooden handle. He wormed out from under the cage, sliding along the floor, carrying the ball-peen hammer with him.

There was just time to scoot to the door, force himself into a sitting position. Thorn felt the bile curdling in the back of his throat, the acid rage. Positioning himself beside the closed door, legs still useless. He raised the hammer.

Their voices were a yard from the door, maybe less, when a phone rang in the front office. They halted, the big one ordering the little one to go back, answer it while he checked on the cages himself.

"You can stop bossing me," the little one said. "You got no hold on me anymore, Rayon. From now on, I do what I do, you do what you do. You hear me, man? No more of this mothering bullshit. It's over, man. Fucking over."

Quickly Thorn wiped the slick sweat from his hammer hand, took a fresh grip, raised it again. He could feel the sharp tingle of blood coming back into his legs. He worked his toes, wiggled his feet, bent one leg at the knee.

The big one said something under his breath, so quiet Thorn couldn't make it out. He drew his legs up, pushed himself into a painful squat. He shot a glance down the dark hallway that ran into the reptile room. There was a door back there with a dead bolt, key in the lock. A back door out to the alley, the Dumpster. But there was no way he could make that distance in his condition. No way to outrun those two.

He could hear the big one speaking loud on the phone. Talking to someone a long way off, listening mostly, asking the person to repeat himself. Then a last "Yes, sir. Right away, sir," and he smacked the phone down.

It was the little one who came through the door first. Same black jeans, cowboy boots. Thorn struck him in the right knee. Then the shin. Heard him howl, frozen there in the doorway. Thorn hammered him in the other knee once, twice. Then slammed the toes of his left foot. Struck his foot again and again until the small man crumpled. Thorn raising the ball-peen hammer, taking aim on the man's forehead, a blow between the eyes. The small man writhing on the floor before him, a pistol showing at his belt. And Thorn hesitated a moment, his hammer aloft, poised. Wavered just long enough for the big blond one to get to the door, see what was happening, and wrench the hammer from his hand.

Thorn tried to come to his feet, but his legs gave way beneath him. He made a snatch at the little guy's pistol, but felt the big man's hands on his throat, holding him from above, strangling.

Thorn struggled, but couldn't break free. The small man scooted out of the way, rubbing at his knees, his shin, whimpering.

"Listen to me." The big man rattled Thorn's head, fingers gripping his neck so hard he felt something pop inside his throat. "I want to ask you a fucking question."

"I hear you," Thorn said.

The little one had his pistol out now, and he jammed it into Thorn's ear.

The big one said, "So tell us, Thorn. Who the fuck is Broom?"

# CHAPTER

## 38

Sean Marie Farleigh tightened her seat belt as the helicopter tipped to the side and began a sharp-angled turn, taking aim on a blue-steel mountain range to the east. After leaving the city, they had traveled for half an hour, moving south, roughly following the Brunei River into the Tutong district, the pilot staying low over the jungle treetops.

Patrick was strapped in beside her while the pilot operated the controls from a single front seat. Patrick wore camouflage pants, khaki shirt, brightly shined military boots. Sean was in jeans and a long-sleeved black-and-white checked blouse. The back of her blouse was glued to her seat cushion. Even with the rush of air into the cockpit, sauna sweat poured from her. Not from the jungle humidity or the airless heat alone, but a feverish flush born of the hot brew of hate that was thickening her blood.

In a clumsy lurch, the helicopter canted left, then right, moving swiftly toward a notch in the mountain range. As they passed across the narrow plateau, the pilot swung the chopper hard to the right, then halted its forward motion to hover just beyond the mountains.

The pilot glanced back at Patrick, some signal passing between them, then the ungainly bird tipped forward so that Sean was abruptly presented with an unobstructed panorama. A dramatic trick like flinging aside the curtain. No doubt something the two of them had perfected on previous flights, bringing the sultan or the ministers out here to witness the progress.

At first Sean saw only a vast construction area. A dusty parking lot filled with giant orange earthmovers, dump trucks, rows and rows of pickups and front-end loaders, cranes, scoops, and a vast array of other heavy machines. As if a year's output from the assembly line at a Caterpillar factory had been airlifted to Brunei and set down in neat tiers in the middle of a virgin rain forest.

Patrick spoke a short burst of Malay into his helmet microphone, and the pilot answered him and leveled out the copter, heading south again. A minute or two later he swung them around once more so they could have another clear view, this time of an expansive prairie filled with dozens of concrete buildings, each of them two stories high, and each completely encircled by scaffolding. Snaking between the buildings was a wide, freshly paved road, and alongside the road ran a collection of immense cement columns arranged in an elaborate jumble like the pillars of Stonehenge.

"That will be the monorail." Patrick's voice spoke into her earphones. "The quietest and fastest railway in the world. Moving around the entire two hundred square miles of the preserve in less than an hour. Nothing like it anywhere. The technology is totally new, decades ahead of the Japanese, the French. A great many people will come here simply to marvel at that alone."

Sean was silent, scanning the distance. As far as she could see in every direction there were cranes and earthmovers, long lines of dump trucks, bulldozers, an enormous mobile-home park, the workers' ghetto, dozens of concrete buildings in various stages of completion, lakes, and rolling meadows, a complicated city materializing at the jungle's core. Workers and machines moved at a frenetic pace. The whole scene looked to Sean like those renderings of Egyptian chain gangs hauling inconceivably huge stones up the steep sides of pyramids.

Since Patrick's confession the night before, Sean had been mute with rage, horrified beyond language. But now she struggled to fill her lungs, muster the words. And finally they came, bitter in her mouth.

"What is it?" she said. "What is this goddamn place?"

"It is," he said, smiling to himself as he gazed down at the activity, "the largest, most extraordinary animal preserve the world has ever known."

"A zoo?" Sean said. She turned to face him. "That's why Winslow died? Because you were building a goddamn zoo?"

He stared at her, shook his head sorrowfully.

"Not a zoo," he said. "Far, far more than that."

"What?"

Patrick gave the pilot a short, grumbling order, and the man nodded in reply and brought the helicopter back to horizontal. A moment later he was easing them slowly down onto a football field of asphalt behind several windowless buildings, vast warehouses.

When the engines were shut off, Patrick climbed down, held a hand out for her, but Sean turned her back, used the rope ladder.

He led her across the tarmac into the shade of one of the warehouses, where a guard at the door came to stiff attention. The air outside the building was thick with the musky flavors of a barnyard. And as they passed through the door into the cool twilight of the huge room, the odors ripened drastically. A nearly stifling blend of shit and disinfectant, animal fur and human sweat.

Patrick said, "We are gathering here in this one place, Sean, the most unique collection of animals ever assembled. All of them are on the brink of disappearance. We will perfectly re-create their natural habitats, matching their homeland's flora and fauna precisely."

The room was packed with stalls and cages. Men in gray lab coats and others in jumpsuits of orange and red moved up and down the aisles carrying on their work amid the squalls and barks and hoots and whinnying screeches.

Patrick was smiling broadly.

"This is only one of our twenty-five storage barns. The animals we are amassing will be housed here until their activity areas are completed."

"I don't get it," she said. "What's the big deal?"

"What is the big deal, Sean?" Patrick shook his head and smiled wanly. "Already, only in the last year, we have put together the largest collection of rare creatures ever gathered in one place. This is an historic operation, nothing on this scale has ever been attempted before. Soon we will possess what no one else possesses, what would otherwise be forever lost. By the time the preserve is opened a few years from now, most of the animals before you will be found nowhere else on earth. Except for the ones here in Brunei, they'll be completely extinct."

"You actually think tourists will come to this wretched country to see these animals? Bring their dollars, keep the good times rolling?"

"Wretched, Sean?" He smiled bleakly. "Yes," he said. "I know they will come. Zoos are the most popular tourist destinations in the world, and our preserve, when it is finished, will have no rival. If someone wants to see a manatee, a white-cloud tiger, they will have no choice, they must come here."

Patrick nodded hello to a group of men walking past in white smocks. Clipboards, portable phones, stethoscopes.

He said, "We are saving these creatures, Sean. No one else is even attempting to breed most of these species in captivity. Everyone is so caught up in the politics of the animal-rights groups, international charters and agreements. So frightened of organizations like the one your mother controls. But the attempt to save the world's habitats is failing, and one after another species disappears every few seconds. What we are doing here is a noble service to the world. A bold and gallant effort to change the course of evolutionary history."

"Bullshit," she said. "The only reason you're breeding these things is so you'll have replacements when yours die. That's all. To keep the money flowing."

"Sean, Sean."

"And this is all courtesy of Rantel? My father? Everybody getting rich off this crack-brained scheme."

She waved her hand at the convention hall, the barn, whatever the hell it was.

"Your father was a great help. Yes. Your mother, too, though she doesn't realize it."

"And the sultan? He approves of all this, your methods?"

"Actually, the sultan shows little interest in the particulars of the project, which is probably better for all concerned."

Patrick halted before a tall cage where two white-faced gibbons were housed. One of them was swinging rapidly from one side of the cage to the other, hooting and singing, while the second huddled in a corner, holding a branch with a few parched leaves to its nose as if it were trying to catch a fading trace of its perfume.

Patrick stepped close to her, reached out, swept her hair back, touched a hand to the side of her face. She cringed and twisted away.

"Sean," he said. "I must impress on you how crucial this project is to our country's survival. It will be the cornerstone of our new tourist economy. If De Novo were to fail, the results could be cataclysmic for the region. Believe me, I have consulted with the wisest men of my country and we have all spent a great deal of time considering how best to plan for the next generation of our people, and the generations after that. At present there are a quarter-million citizens in Brunei. When the oil fields are dry, we will have no natural resources to fall back on. We import almost all our commodities.

"Of course, we have investments, a healthy national treasury. But how long could that last, draining away the principal year after year? And we could cut down our forests, yes, despoil our own land for a few years of profit. But that is no long-term answer either. We need De Novo and other things like this. It is critical that we find new ways to capitalize. It is absolutely essential."

"And Allison and Winslow just stumbled into the path of this enormous machine."

Sean was peering out at the cavernous hall, eyes roaming the stalls and cages, catching glimpses of larger animals, tusked creatures, water buffalo, rhinos.

As she gazed out at the animals, she had a quick, herky-jerky image of herself escaping. Sprint down the main aisle, dodge his men, straight-arm them, kick, scratch, throw open cage doors as she went. Leave a wake of raucous cries behind her. Disappear behind the herds and swarms and flocks and tribes of escaping animals. But then what? Where to? Half a world from home.

She shuddered, drew a difficult breath, closed her eyes.

"We should be getting back," Patrick said. "We have another long journey ahead of us. It is finally time that your mother and I resolve our difficulties. If we are to be a family, Sean, you and I, produce a family of our own, it is essential that no impediments to our happiness remain."

Sean felt a catch in her breathing. Her disgust sent a violent flutter through essential valves, a bayonet rammed down the throat.

"I badly want your mother's blessing, Sean," he said, gazing at her with the same naive longing he had had as a boy. An expression that only a few days ago had helped to soften her natural restraint. Part of his charm. But now it seemed to her that all that blind hunger for some girl-child of long ago was no more than the diseased fetish of a stunted boy.

Patrick lay his arm across Sean's shoulders, snugged her near, began to steer her gently toward the bright, open doorway.

"It is my wish," Patrick said, bringing his mouth

close to her ear, "that when Allison stands before her almighty God, she will be comfortable in the knowledge that her daughter has passed into the best possible hands."

# CHAPTER

# 39

As Allison and the taxi driver were leaving the house, the phone rang. A reporter from the *Miami Herald* wanted to know if she had any comment to make.

"Comment about what?"

The reporter cleared her throat and said, "Your husband's apparent suicide."

An hour later the Haitian driver was watching the evening news when the police arrived. Allison brought them into the living room, watched them slosh their styrofoam coffees.

"I know already," she told them. "Jacqueline Bristol called."

They glanced around at the Farleighs' living room, looked curiously at the taxi driver. And one of them asked Allison if her husband had been depressed. Money problems, home life bothering him, anything like that?

"He had plenty to be depressed about," Allison said. "But no, he wasn't. He wasn't capable of it."

The cops slurped coffee, looking at each other through the rising steam. Then one of them stared down at his pad and informed Allison there were signs at the scene that suggested foul play. Did she know anyone who might want to do harm to Harry Farleigh?

*Me,* she wanted to say. *Only if I'd done it, I wouldn't have let him off so easy, such a quick flight, instant carnage.*

Instead she shook her head, and to her great surprise she felt her mouth twist, and she began to weep.

But the crying jag lasted only a minute or two, then she choked it off, looked up at the two suited men, the one uniform. Backhanded her eyes. The lieutenant asked a few more questions, going through the motions. Nothing here. Woman as batty as everyone said. And they left. Three paper cups on the mantelpiece.

She had the taxi driver take her downtown to Harry's building. She saw the yellow tape, the last of the cleanup crew just leaving. In the basement garage she located Harry's Porsche, paid off the taxi man, and took the Porsche west out of the city, heading to the Shack, the one place in the world where she'd known some meager contentment.

Saturday she woke early to the blare of dirt bikes. The Indian boys roared around her house, out into the western fringe of her property. After she straightened the furniture and swept up the broken glass, she sat out on the porch and rocked, watched the clouds form and reform, moving across the Everglades sky. She sat out there most of the day and watched the shadows stretch and pull at the trees and then shrink into nothing. She rocked and held her father's Zippo in her palm, a cool, heavy chunk of him.

That night she slept deeply, dreamless. Woke on Sunday, lay still and listened to the chiding cries of an osprey, coming far inland for a freshwater meal. She rose, found a pair of pinking shears, stood before the bathroom mirror.

She took hold of a strand of her long hair, drew it out from her skull and began to slice the years away. Cut and cut until it was three inches long, a pixie. Using the comb, a smaller pair of scissors, a second mirror, checking her profile, she tried to style it. Not self-mutilation. But feeling a need to simplify. Start over.

She liked what emerged. Trim, honest. Joan of Arc with crow's feet. A little ragged around the ears maybe, a cowlick in back, but still, it highlighted her cheekbones, enlarged her eyes, seemed to brighten them. She felt a vain and foolish spasm in her chest, a flashback of school-girl pride. A new look for a new school year. Maybe this was the year the boys would notice. Maybe now the cloaks would fall away from all the mysteries.

She swept up the bathroom floor, dumped the mound of curls in a grocery sack. Showered again. Doing her makeup, a few final snips to her hair. A fresh bandage for her nose. Dressed in the same jeans, a salmon-colored cotton jersey, moccasins. Feeling younger. Healthy, free.

She ate some cheese and bread, a green apple, drank a club soda. Felt eighteen. As fresh and clear as if she were her own daughter. A feisty calm. Like coming off a three-week binge, hangover finally gone, headache subsided, the world a crystal place. Grateful for every breath, each simple motion a pleasure. Drawing air as if it were pure oxygen.

She sat in the rocker on the front porch all morning, watching the bright spill of daylight ignite the saw grass, the palmettos, the mahogany hammock. Watched a five-foot alligator bask for hours fifty yards east of the porch, a leather log, pebbled, dead. She looked away, then back, and the gator was gone, submerged again in ooze.

A yellow swallowtail twirled past the porch like crepe paper torn loose in the wind, the honks of Canada geese soared overhead. It was morning, it was noon, it was twilight. Her mind transparent. Nothing to rehearse, no speech to prepare, no diagram of action, no plan B. Allison was there, but not there. Like the wind, the gator; like the osprey, the heron, the diamondback. Like the trees and the shadows, the stunning silence. A mirror. Drowsy from the sun, hair-trigger alert.

In the final moments before she drove back into town, she dealt out the stack of Winslow's photos from Borneo, examined each one. Sean's candid looks, pinched smiles, exaggerated pouts as Winslow took yet another snapshot of her little sister. The cheap exoticism of Kuching, food stalls, trash clogging the river, longhouses. And then the jungle shots. Two men aiming their rifles into the trees. Patrick Sagawan and Raimondo White.

She put the prints back in the packet, set it on the porch table. Picked up the Zippo again, opened it, flicked the wheel. She watched the orange flame, a blade of fire wriggling in the easy breeze. She snapped the lighter shut, slid it in her pants pocket. Allison rocked, ran a leisurely hand through her new hair, listened to the nagging cries of a great blue heron. Then the ache of silence filled the distance again. Rich twilight.

She'd been coming to Parrot Jungle for many years. Miami's first tourist attraction had outlived all the rest with its lush landscape, flagstone paths winding through thick stands of bamboo and palm and bushy native dogwoods and mahogany, oaks and ferns, walkways running across coral archways, high bridges.

Even in the total dark Allison knew her way through the maze of walks and pathways. Knew a direct route to the orangutan cages at the westernmost edge of the park. All around her the birds were quiet, mynahs and starlings, parrots and macaws, their cages covered. No breeze, hardly any moon. An occasional passing car out on Red Road left behind the rumble of its exhaust, but that was the only sound. That and the quiet swish of her soft-soled moccasins.

Only a single, distant security light cast its yellow sulfur glow on this part of the grounds. Allison halted behind the stone wall that separated the primate area from the parrots and the cockatoos. In the faint light she saw Sean and Patrick standing arm in arm in front of Broom's cage. The great ape was awake, sitting on top of his broken perch, staring down at these humans who had interrupted his sleep.

When Allison stepped into the patio, Broom coughed and snorted, and with a trumpeting hoot he came swinging down to the floor of his cage.

Patrick was wearing creamy trousers and a white turtleneck, stylish loafers that were a mustard color in the sulfur light. Sean had on blue jeans and a dark crew-neck top, white running shoes. Her short blond hair was rumpled, eyes worn and sleepless, moving like a invalid, each fragile step heroic. She stared at Allison, holding fiercely to her eyes, awaiting some crucial signal.

"Ah, Allison," Patrick said. "How pleasant to see you again."

Allison moved to the edge of the patio. She watched Broom pace the length of his cage, unsettled, making frustrated grumbles. His Allison was standing so close, but she was not approaching, not speaking to him.

"It's just a giant zoo," Sean blurted. "That's what it's all about."

"I know," Allison said.

Sean drew away from Patrick's side, glanced quickly over her shoulder at Broom.

Then in an exhausted voice, Sean said, "He's been collecting animals for the last year, endangered animals. They're building a tourist attraction. A goddamn theme park."

Patrick smiled at Sean. A forbearing look. Let her have her say. The helpless face of love. A bottomless devotion.

He stepped forward, a hand resting on Sean's shoulder, moving her forward with him. Then he turned his gaze to Allison, and she saw the frost glaze his eyes. But still that smile, that vacant smile.

"I wish you could have visited the work site, Allison. I truly wish you could have seen what we're achieving. You would have approved, I'm certain. It's a remarkable project. I've gathered together some of the best animal people in the world. Veterinarians, biologists, primatologists. Someone said the other day that working on this endeavor was like being part of the Manhattan project. I liked that. I like to think we are creating something the world has never seen before."

"Come here, Sean," Allison said. "Come over to me."

"No," Patrick said. "I'm terribly sorry, Allison, but

we can't stay. We just came to retrieve the photographs you mentioned. Then we have to turn around, begin our long journey home. There is still so much to do."

"You get the photographs, I get Sean. That's the arrangement."

Allison held out the packet in her right hand.

"Oh, I'm sure that was your notion of an arrangement, yes. But it was never mine."

Patrick's right hand dipped into his trouser pocket and came out with a small black automatic. One hand on Sean's shoulder, the other pointing the pistol at the ground. Patrick seemed unconscious of its presence in his hand. He would shoot her and fly away unfazed. So powerful was his self-hypnosis, so complete and invincible his detachment.

He said, "You know, Allison, for some time now I've been wanting to give you my sincerest thanks. You don't realize it, but without your help and Harry's, I would never have been able to manage the De Novo endeavor—the zoo, as Sean likes to call it. Truly, it was your newsletters that helped me identify exactly the people I needed to make all this succeed. I wanted you to know that, Allison. Your work has not been in vain. It should give you comfort. The Farleigh family has made a monumental contribution to my country's future."

Broom had picked up two handfuls of straw and was standing at the bars staring out at Allison. Sulking, on the brink of a tantrum.

"Things have been going exceptionally well," Patrick said. He slid his hand all the way across Sean's shoulders, tugged her close. She crossed her arms across her chest as if taken by a sudden chill. "Phase one is almost completed. Except for the unfortunate incident in Borneo, I've managed to collect close to a thousand endangered animals with few significant difficulties."

"Unless you count the fifteen people your men have killed," Allison said. "The hundreds of animals they slaughtered."

He smiled even wider.

"I am very impressed, Allison. You've been busy, haven't you? You have been figuring everything out, just as I suspected you might."

"You told them to kill as many animals as they can to make what you're collecting more precious."

"Yes, yes," he said. "A simple business principle, really. Increase the value of your product by shrinking its general availability. I believe you refer to it as cornering the market."

Sean pulled free of Patrick's grip. She stared down with horror at the pistol in his hand, seeing it for the first time. He glanced curiously at her, blinked, then turned back to Allison.

"It only makes sense," he said. "After all, most of them are professional hunters. A very systematic group, very efficient—very well paid, I might add. By the time De Novo opens, they'll have finished their work, and the species represented in our preserve should be far more precious and rare.

"I know it sounds coldhearted, Allison. But you see, I look at it this way. I'm simply assisting the general trends, speeding up the inevitable. One might even argue that for the last few thousand orangutans or white tigers, it is more merciful to shoot them outright than to leave them in severely reduced habitats. If you think about it logically, cut away all the sentimentalizing malarkey, which is really worse? To have the loggers strip away the orangutans' food sources mile by mile until your precious apes are left to starve, or to end their lives as painlessly as possible?"

Allison watched Broom stalking the perimeter of his cage, his hands still gripping the wads of straw.

"Patrick," she said. "You can annihilate all the animals in the world for all I care, but we had a bargain. And you're going to honor that. That's all that matters to me. Now put your gun away, and let Sean come to me. Take your snapshots and go home. We won't bother you anymore, and you won't bother us."

She held out the packet of photographs, then stepped to her right and pitched them into the orangutan's cage. Broom made a deep grunt.

"It's all there. Negatives, everything."

"What is this!"

"It's very simple," Allison said. "You and I go into the cage together, retrieve the photos. Broom won't hurt you if you're with me. Sean stays outside."

"No," he said. "I can't do that."

"What are you afraid of? If Sean loves you she won't flee. Only if she's your prisoner."

"I'm afraid you must have misunderstood, Allison. Your daughter and I have no intention of separating. Our bond is too strong. Our love."

He turned to her, but Sean's eyes were on Allison.

"You would wake up one day," Allison said. "Maybe not this month, maybe not next month, but someday soon. And you wouldn't recognize the woman lying beside you. Oh, she'd still be my daughter, but you wouldn't know her anymore, because the mirage would have decayed. Not the sweet, unattainable American girl you fell in love with a long time ago. But this other person, a complicated woman. Independent. You'd look at her lying there beside you and you wouldn't know what to do, Patrick. It would terrify you. You wouldn't be prepared for it. This stranger in the bed. This person whose life you've destroyed, who hates you—your captive. All so you could live out some daydream you had as a boy. Some goddamn, twisted hallucination."

"Mother," Sean said. She lifted a hand toward Allison and started forward.

"Don't," he said. "Stay where you are."

Allison took a step forward, stood waiting for Sean.

Patrick raised his pistol, leveled it at a spot a few feet to Allison's left.

"Sean, no," he said. "Stay here, stay with me."

She came forward into Allison's arms, pressed her face into her breast and began to sob.

Patrick marched toward them, stopped a foot behind

Sean, shaking his head in speechless fury. He hesitated a moment more while Sean continued to cry. Then he turned from them and stepped up to the bars and aimed his pistol into Broom's cage.

"You thought you were so smart, Allison. Your little plan to separate Sean from me. But, you see, I don't need you to protect me from some brainless ape."

He fired twice into the cage. The orangutan roared and swung up onto its platform, taking cover behind a railroad tie.

Allison pushed Sean aside, lunged for Patrick and seized his wrist, tried to shake loose the pistol. But Patrick wrenched his hand free, and hooked his arm hard around Allison's head, held her in a grinding headlock. He pinned the side of her face against his ribs, and she felt the cold circle of the barrel jam against her cheek. Behind them Allison could hear Broom raving, a tortured wail as he jumped back to the floor of his cage and stamped back and forth.

"Go back to the front gate, Sean," Patrick said. "Go on. Do it now. Don't disobey me. Wait for me there."

Allison snarled and tried to twist her head free, but Patrick cinched her harder, cut off her air, gouging her cheek with the pistol.

"Let go of her," Sean said. "Let her loose, goddamn you. I'll go with you, I'll go back to Brunei. But I swear to you, Patrick, if you harm my mother, you might as well kill me right now. Because I'll fight you every second for the rest of your life."

In a voice as calm and empty as a sleepwalker's, he said, "I'm going to do this, Sean. Whether you look on or not. It has to happen. It would be better for you, it would be better for both of us if you simply walked back to the front gate now. Wait there for me."

Allison drew the Zippo from her pocket, opened it. She reset her feet, spreading them wide, angling for access.

"Please, Sean," Patrick said.

She felt the pistol cock at her cheek.

Allison flicked the lighter's rough striking wheel, lowered the blaze, and held it steady against the crotch of Patrick's pants.

# CHAPTER

## 40

Patrick Bendari Sagawan screamed and began to fire his pistol wildly. The third of his four shots struck Allison in the thigh. A hard tug, a nasty sting. Slung backward, she crumpled to the flagstone patio.

She drew a painful breath, then forced herself back up to a crouch, gripping the numbed flesh, and watching as Patrick howled and trotted in place, an awkward dance, thrashing with both hands at the faint glow of fire, a low blue halo that wafted from the crotch of his trousers to his belt, then flared again at the midriff of his white turtleneck, moving so erratically he didn't seem to know where to slap next.

In his cage Broom roared and tore at the remnants of his wooden perch, ripping free a four-by-four post and flinging it against the bars.

As Patrick continued to shriek and prance, Sean dashed in close to him, bobbed below his swinging arms, stiff-armed him in the sternum, pushing him aside. She snatched up the fallen pistol, spun away, trotted over to Allison and squatted down beside her. She targeted Patrick, hand quivering.

"Is it bad?" Sean touched a hand to Allison's wounded leg.

Allison sucked in a breath, whistled it out.

"I'm fine," she said, putting an arm around her daughter's shoulders. "Never better."

It was a minute more before Patrick had suffocated all the flames. Sobbing, he stumbled backward, one bare leg exposed, his flesh from thigh to knee was blackened and peeling like the loose, papery bark of a birch. The air reeked of charred meat.

In a whimpering swoon, the young man collapsed against the bars of the cage, began to slide against them down to the ground, but he dropped only a foot before his body halted, then jerked suddenly back to attention. And began slowly to rise, his feet lifting off the ground, going up stiffly.

"No, Broom," Allison shouted. "No!"

She tried to stand, but groaned and sank back.

Broom's giant hand gripped Patrick by the throat, hauling the man upward, his back riding against the rails of the cage. She heard the squeals then, the frantic shrieks of the parrots and mynahs, the screams and croaks and wild machine-gun clicks and chatter of the starlings and lorries and flamingos. A great flutter and thrashing of wings, as Patrick rose higher and higher, moving smoothly as if he were being magically levitated toward the sky.

Allison's leg had stiffened, but she was still lingering in the golden moments of numbness, spared a little longer the pain she knew would soon overpower her. Again she tried to rise, but the leg gave way beneath her.

Sean ducked in close, put an arm around Allison's waist, and hauled her upright. Allison lay her arm across Sean's shoulders, steadied herself against her daughter's sturdy body. It came as a strange surprise feeling the power in Sean's arms and back, the ease with which she lifted Allison upright, maneuvered her to one of the cement benches and settled her there.

No hugs between them for years, hardly a brush of flesh, and now the shock of her daughter's embrace, discovering her substantial firmness, her muscle. This strong woman Sean had turned herself into.

"Jesus, would you look at that. Hoisted on his own petard, or however the fuck it goes."

Orlando White, holding a pistol loosely at his side, gazed up at Patrick dangling in Broom's grip, several feet off the ground. Patrick's back held hard against the bars, his pants still smoldering.

"What the hell is a petard anyway? You know, Allison?"

"It's finished, Orlando. Put the pistol on the ground. It's over."

Sean held the pistol out rigidly, aiming at the small man.

"First of all, my correct name is Orlon. Though on occasion I've been known to answer to Big O. You, Allison, since we're on such close personal terms, you are permitted to call me Big O. But not that other."

"Put the gun down. Put it down now."

Orlon's eyes flicked between Allison and the weapon in Sean's hand.

"What I've found is," Orlon said, angling a step to his right, Sean tracking him with Patrick's pistol. "A lot of people in times of stress, they snatch up a gun, aim it at somebody, they think that person's going to automatically do what they say, shaking and shivering. Oh, Lordy, don't shoot me with your awful scary gun, please, ma'am. That's how people think.

"But the reality is, when it comes the moment to actually squeeze that trigger, make that big old awful explosion and send a wad of hot lead on its way—well now, that's another whole situation entirely.

"I look at the three of you standing there, and I gotta say, you got that L.L. Bean look. You had your weekly manicure, your facial, your fresh-squeezed orange juice every morning, floss and brush, always sleep in clean jammies. That's how you look. Same as your husband, poor Harry. Neat and polished, oiled and vacuumed.

"People like you, you got a natural aversion to making messes. And believe me, young lady, a gun like that one, you hit a human body in the right spot, I guarantee that thing'll make a jumbo mess. Spread bone and blood and gore and shit like you wouldn't believe. 'Cause I've seen it happen. I've been there on site at actual murders. Unlike the two of you."

Out on the edge of her vision Allison saw someone coming down the path. Not letting her eyes move, but seeing the person edge closer.

Orlon had begun to pace in front of them, ten steps one way, ten the other. He was keeping his distance steady, twenty feet, maybe thirty. Allison's pain was seeping into her leg now, the dull ache spiraling up, beginning to cripple her whole body. She could feel her heart struggling to stay with this moment. A serious tremble in her breath.

Orlando halted and faced them. Pistol still hanging at his side.

"It looks to me," he said, "like what we got here is an awfully familiar *High Noon* situation. We have a face-off, we draw. Find out who's quicker, who's the better shot. I mean, I got nothing against the classics, and I guess you could argue what we're doing, we're just acting out some mythical thing, repeating a thousand years of *High Noon*.

"But you know, if it were completely up to me, if I were on my own, Orlon White scripting this from a distance, I'd try to rough up the predictability of it. Throw in some kind of crazy curveball thing. You know, like if in the middle of the standoff, the young lady there, say she pulled her trigger before we'd actually squared up and got ready to draw on each other, and click, click, she found out her handgun wasn't loaded. Now, that would be something a little unique, a little out of left field."

"It's loaded," Sean said. "Trust me."

"Okay, okay. Then fine, let's say it's loaded. If it is, then we definitely need to work out another arrangement here, another variation. See, 'cause I just got a natural aversion to formulas, watching the same old thing coming down the pike again. Not in my movie, man. No, sir, I got higher standards than that. You appreciate what I'm saying, don't you, Allison? I mean, you got some taste and judgment, I believe."

In her peripheral vision Allison could see the man inch closer. Tall, big. Then almost involuntarily she found her eyes straying to the man, seeing who it was.

Orlando caught Allison staring over his shoulder.

"Oh, now, now. How many boring fucking times have we all seen that one? Someone sneaking up on me, I swing around, your little girl shoots. Hey, that's right out of Triteness 101. I mean, Allison, I'm seriously let down with you. I know we can do better than that, you and me. We put our heads together, I'm sure we can improve on that old commonplace."

The man came forward. A grin suddenly twisted Orlon's mouth.

"See, I knew who it was all along. It's just my brother, Allison. My brother Ray."

"Okay, Orlon. Put your weapon down now," Ray White said.

Orlon smiled wider and came around slowly, looking at his brother. Raimondo held the end of a leather leash with a big choke chain at the end. The choker around Thorn's neck. Thorn's hands were lashed behind his back, his face swollen and bloody. In Ray's other hand was a shiny revolver aimed at Orlon.

"Ray, Ray, Ray. What happened, man, you get lost? Hey, you're missing all the fun. We already started without you."

"I'm serious, Orlon. Put your fucking gun down. You and me, we're finished with this shit. We're starting over. This is our chance to break out of this cycle, man."

"Hey, I like the cycle. I'm happy how it's going. You want to turn into a monk, spend the rest of your life in Raiford, shit, help yourself. But I'm not going that way."

"We're not going to hurt these people, Orlon. They haven't done anything. Not even Allison. She's been right all along. A pain in the ass, yeah, but she was doing the right thing—going after our sorry criminal asses. That was right, Orlon. What we been doing is wrong. There's a difference, man. We knew it once, where the exact line was, but then we forgot. We just kept doing the things we were doing so long, we started thinking they were right."

"Listen to you. Man, it just doesn't stop with you, does it? Mother Teresa White. Always got a lecture ready."

Orlon looked up at the stars for a moment, then revolved his head around like he was chasing the flight of an errant bug.

"You remember this place, Ray?"

"What place?"

"Parrot Jungle. Where we are right now."

"I remember it, yeah."

Sean glanced at Allison, frowned a question at her. What the hell should she do? Allison tried to send an answer back with her eyes. Nothing. Do nothing. Just stand there, hold the pistol. Wait. Stay ready.

"This is where Mom used to bring us after the dentist. After the fucking Nazi experiments. Make it up to us, all that pain, letting us walk around here, look at the birds. Tweet, tweet, Ray. Tweet, tweet. Pretend we were off somewhere else, saying the names of places like she was in a swoon. Tahiti, New Zealand, Madagascar. You remember?"

"I remember."

"Funny," Orlon said. "I didn't think of it till now. Standing here, everybody with a gun aimed at everybody —hell, you'd think I'd be concentrating on the difficulties at hand. But no. There's Mom coming into it again. Always old Mom."

At that moment Broom released Patrick and he crashed to the flagstone patio. Rolled two times and came to rest next to a stone bench, faceup. Broom climbed down the bars and waddled to the front corner of his cage and hunched down, staring forlornly at Allison.

Orlon stared at Patrick for a moment, his pistol still hanging at his side.

"I never liked that guy. I'm glad to see him come to a

bad end. I always thought he had shifty eyes and a weak chin."

Still looking down at him, Orlon jerked his pistol up, swung around, crouched, and set his aim on Sean, but before he could fire Sean shot him twice in the belly, and Orlon's body pitched to the left. He rolled onto his face and was still.

With a sob, Sean threw her pistol aside.

"You killed him," Ray said quietly. "You killed my brother. Jesus. There was no need to do that."

"Ray," Thorn said. "Your brother was no good."

"He was my brother. It was my job to look after him."

"He was no good," Thorn said. "The world's better off with him dead. You're better off."

Ray stared at Thorn. Then he broke away, made a half turn, and raised his pistol and aimed it at Sean.

"She didn't even know him. This girl, she just shot my brother without any good reason. She didn't know anything about him. Didn't know what made him do what he did."

Sean froze. Allison pushed herself to her feet, stepped in front of her daughter, into the path of Ray's aim.

Ray cocked the hammer back.

"Orlon was a good man. He just watched too many movies. They confused him. He didn't deserve this."

Thorn dropped his shoulder, lurched to the right, and slammed into Ray White's ribs. He bulled him across the flagstone patio, got him stumbling backward, carrying him all the way to the cage, where Ray slammed his head against the bars. His pistol clattered to the stone walkway.

With Broom roaring behind them, Thorn flopped onto his belly and covered the gun as though it were a live grenade. In a moment, Ray took a long breath, pushed himself to his knees, and crawled across the flagstone patio to where his brother lay.

Ray White squatted beside him, lay his cheek against Orlon's back, and he wept.

# C H A P T E R

# 41

Bernice Shap had never done anything like this before, never in her wildest dreams, but she couldn't help herself, she just couldn't stand to see the young orangutan subjected to torture another minute at Hickman College, so she'd gotten into her car and she'd driven to Miami where she knew there was a woman, Allison Farleigh, who had connections in Borneo or Sumatra, connections that might allow her to send the orangutan back to the jungle over there where it more than likely came from.

Actually, the truth was, she'd known Allison's name for some time because she was a member of Allison's organization, read all her newsletters, never anything more than that, just read them. And no way had she ever done anything like this before, and now what she really needed to know was, was it possible for Allison to keep it a secret exactly where the orangutan came from, how she came by it, because the girl was supposed to start the Duke University graduate program next September, and it would totally wreck her chances for that if it became known what exactly she'd done, not to mention the legal problems, stealing something so valuable from Hickman College, but she couldn't help herself, it wasn't right, the experiments, the way the professor was using this ape, she'd never felt this way before, oh, maybe it bothered her sometimes, but nothing like this, the fire, the tests, the way the orangutan changed so suddenly after arriving.

Allison said yes. She'd take the ape. She thought she might just know where it came from. She'd also try to work out some financial settlement with Hickman for the loss of their ape without revealing to them how the ape was freed.

As the girl was about to leave, Allison noticed the wedding ring on her finger and asked if she could see it. Bernice Shap raised her hand and Allison touched the stone that had once been hers.

"Very pretty," she said. "Who's the lucky fellow?"

"It's over now," Bernice said. Her mouth firm. "I just wear the ring because I like it."

"Well," Allison said, "may it bring you great luck."

The girl thanked her, stroked the orangutan once more, tickled it under its chin, made it smile, then she got in her car and drove away and Allison carried the young orangutan with the silver streak into her house and let it roam.

The sultan was horrified. He'd had absolutely no idea what was going on, the criminal behavior at work behind this important effort. He had bestowed the honor of handling the work of the De Novo project on his sister's son and then left all the details to him.

This was an outrage, horrendous, certainly not at all what the sultan had in mind. Patrick had lied to him, misrepresenting the entire project in the most gross and outrageous ways. As soon as the young man was out of the hospital and free to travel, the sultan would see that justice was served. And of course, as Allison was aware, Islamic justice was far more swift and pitiless than the American version. She could be assured that Patrick would be dealt with in the most severe way.

In fact, Allison was invited to attend the trial. Her presence would be necessary to establish all the facts. And of course, afterward, the sultan would insist on making a substantial contribution to Allison's Wildlife Protection

League, a sum, in fact, that Allison was free to name, if only she would consent to spearhead the effort of returning all the captured animals to their original locations.

Dismantling De Novo would be a time-consuming and difficult undertaking, but the sultan was certain there was no one more qualified, and no one he would trust more to make certain the task was carried out with the professionalism and the good sense that Allison would bring to it. And of course, the sultan assumed that Allison would be extremely diplomatic in accomplishing the task. It was of the highest importance to the entire royal family that the process be carried out as discreetly as possible. Just imagine what the international press might do if they learned of the gross errors of judgment that had taken place, the tragic and unforgivable loss of life. How easy it would be for them to distort the facts and make it appear that Patrick was not the only one culpable. Oh, my.

The sultan and Allison and Sean stood in the buttery light beneath a golden canopy rigged up on the tarmac of Miami International Airport a few feet from his Concorde.

"Ten million dollars," Sean said.

Allison turned and looked at her daughter.

The sultan said, "Ten million dollars?"

Allison smiled, coming back to face his Royal Highness.

"Yes," she said. "We believe that would be the amount necessary to insure the continued viability of the Wildlife Protection League for the next decade or two. We would, of course, give ample credit to you and your countrymen in the newsletter that circulates to our fifteen thousand members."

"You are very kind."

"It would be my pleasure."

"Of course," the sultan said. "Then ten million it is."

Sean said, "Are you sure, Mother? Is ten million enough?"

"It will do," she said. "For a start."

\*   \*   \*

Two weeks later Allison and Sean were met at Miami International Airport by another Concorde. Thorn was there to see them off. They were to fly to Brunei to begin analyzing the scope of the task before them. And on the way there, they would make a brief stop in Kuching to drop the young male orangutan off with Dr. Sidra Tindusiri.

Since the ape was still quite young, its complete rehabilitation was entirely possible. And because Allison and Sean had convinced the sultan to make a further generous donation to Dr. Tindusiri for the purchase of a few thousand acres of virgin rain forest in the regions adjacent to her preserve, the young orangutan now had a reasonable chance of finding a place where he could be alone and live out his life as he was meant to.

As the jet's engines roared a few yards away, Allison and Thorn said their good-byes and she walked across the tarmac to the plane. She was halfway up the stairs when she turned around and came back down and jogged back over to Thorn.

"What did you mean by that?" she said.

"By what?"

"That when we got back you'd take me fishing. Show me your secret spots."

"I didn't mean anything by it."

"Who else have you shown these secret spots?"

"Well, there are a couple," he said, "I've never shown anybody."

"Good," she said, and kissed him briefly. Touched a fingertip to his lips. "We'll start with those."

Special Advance Preview
from the new James W. Hall title

# Buzz Cut

Available July 1996 from Delacorte Press

# C H A P T E R

# 1

In his official Fiesta Cruise Lines shirt, Emilio Sanchez stood before the bathroom mirror squinting at his new tummy bulge. The blue rugby shirt was hugging him tight at the belly, showing off the extra couple of inches of flab.

What it was, was too much cruise line food for the last six months. First time in his life he'd had a chance to eat three meals a day. Here he was, only twenty-four years old, way too young to get a gut. He didn't watch out, soon he'd be looking like all those American passengers. Worse than that, with a big gringo belly he wasn't as likely to score with the ladies.

Emilio was sucking in his stomach, staring at his profile when the door to his cabin opened. Tindu, his Filipino roommate, probably ducking in from the first dinner seating for a quick smoke.

Emilio smoothed his hand over his stomach, flattened it briefly, and decided tomorrow he would begin a diet. Eliminate breakfast. That would be easiest. Eat two meals a day instead of three. Drop ten pounds by the time of the anniversary cruise. No problem. An easy decision. Sex was a hell of a lot more important to Emilio Sanchez than breakfast.

He ran a quick comb through his thick black hair and turned from the mirror, and the first thing he saw was the glitter of the blade. It was not a large knife. He'd seen bigger. Four times in his life he'd faced knives. Taking cuts on both arms and one deep wound to his left shoulder. But in those Juarez street fights he had always possessed his own knife.

The man in his doorway held the knife in a comfortable underhand grip, left hand. Nothing fancy. Clearly familiar with its use.

"The shirt," the man said.

"What?"

The man stepped closer.

"I want that shirt."

"You want my shirt?" Emilio plucked some fabric at his breast. "This shirt?"

"I want it. Give it to me."

He did something with the knife, a little Zorro waggle of his hand. Then he held up his right hand and Emilio blinked. Couldn't believe what he was seeing, here in his own room. A guy with electricity coming out his fingers. Knife in one hand, sparks coming out the fingertips of the other.

"Hey, man, it's okay. You want the shirt, you got the shirt. You can put the goddamn knife away. I give you the shirt, it's yours, man. I never liked the fucking shirt in the first place."

Emilio stepped back, pulled the shirttail out of his pants, crossed his hands over his stomach, ready to drag it off over his head, watching the man.

"You want it, what, like for a souvenir or something?"

"I need the shirt." Saying it very calm. "Like right now."

The man wore a black Fiesta Cruise Lines T-shirt and a pair of new blue jeans. The T-shirt said he'd been a jack-pot winner. The man looked like a movie star, not the super handsome type, but one of those you've seen all your life, in this and in that, the star's brother or best friend. You've seen him a hundred times, but you never know his name. One of those.

Blond hair hanging loose down to his shoulders. A face that looked like the guy might've been playing with his girlfriend's makeup. Lips a little too red, skin a pasty, powdery white. Like you could take a fingernail and scrape some of it off, get down to the real flesh. But still handsome, and despite the knife, still somebody looked like you could reason with.

"I got more shirts, if you want them. In my drawer over there. I got three or four, man. Brand-new practically. You go and take them all. Start your own collection. I don't give a shit. I never liked these fucking shirts."

Still gripping his shirttails, arms crossed, ready to strip off the shirt but trying to talk his way past this, find some way to keep from ducking his head into that blue material, losing sight of the guy in his doorway for even a half second. That knife not moving, just hanging there in front of the guy's belly. The blond man very still, not blinking, nothing.

"Go on, take off the shirt." Voice getting quiet now.

Emilio shifted his feet, brought his right one back a half step, gonna kick the man in the groin if he came forward at all. Punt him up to the promenade deck if he tried anything.

Emilio tugged on the shirt, made a little feint to see if the guy moved. He didn't. So Emilio went ahead, stripped out of it. Losing sight of the guy for a half second was all it was, a half second, couldn't have been any longer than that.

The shirt came over his head and Emilio felt a cold jiggle in his belly, and he heard the noise coming from his throat, and felt himself falling backward against the sink. Seeing the man in his doorway, holding the blue cruise lines shirt in one hand and the bloody knife in the other. No smile on his face, nothing at all. Same look Emilio felt on his own face at that exact moment. Nothing there at all. Never would be again either. Never. Just like the blond guy, a dead face.

Butler Jack strolled through the cruise ship casino listening to the clang of coins, the bells and gongs, the incantations of luck at the crap table, shrieks of joy and groans of defeat.

Butler was tall and rawboned and carried himself fluidly. He wore gray slacks and the blue long-sleeved rugby shirt with a Fiesta Cruise Line insignia above the breast pocket, the uniform for the casino staff. Emilio Sanchez's contribution to the cause. Butler's hair was tucked under a wig. Thick black waves slicked back into a ducktail.

In a corner of the room Butler halted for a moment, leaned against a slot machine, and stared up at the TV mounted overhead. Lovely Lola Sampson in a slinky black dress was standing on the sundeck of the M. S. *Eclipse,* belting out the catchy theme song for Fiesta Cruise Lines, while her husband, Morton, stood below on the promenade deck beaming up at her. The most beautiful sixty-year-old in America. Didn't look a day over forty-five. Body firm, voice lush, face as smooth as a ten-year-old's.

No wonder Morton Sampson snapped her up, made her his wife and a TV star. Two years ago she was an ordinary working woman worrying how she'd survive on her social security. Now look at her, on a first-name basis with America. People in every corner of the televisioned world knew her name. Had her own morning talk show, *Lola Live.* Got buddy-buddy with her new husband's Hollywood friends. Lovely Lola. Singing and dancing, while her low-cut dress displayed her considerable assets. Voice deep and swollen with happiness as she shamelessly pitched her husband's cut-rate Caribbean cruises.

The TV was turned down low, so Lola's song was lost in the hubbub of the casino. But it didn't matter. Ask anyone on the ship to hum the tune, they'd be able to.

Butler watched slender Lola as she swayed and sang, her blond hair swishing. Her new shoulder-length cut. Two years ago, the only singing she'd done was to solo in the church choir. Now look. Like she'd been at this all her life.

When she finished her song, she flashed her best smile at the camera and spoke. Though her words were inaudible, Butler knew her speech by heart. Lola Sampson was inviting one and all to join her and Morton on the twenty-fifth anniversary celebration cruise. A week in the Caribbean, rub shoulders with Lola and Morton and their billionaire pals. A week of *Lola Live* broadcast from on board the *Eclipse*. Only three weeks away, rooms going fast, so make your reservations now.

Oh, yes, Butler Jack had made his already. Wouldn't miss this voyage for the world.

Butler ambled across the smoky room, passing behind a row of blackjack dealers over to the far corner of the casino, where he stood for a moment before the stage where the visiting band was playing their last set of the evening.

Shaggy hair to their shoulders, wearing tight yellow suits with bell-bottom trousers, the four members of the Baby Boomers looked like they'd been beamed down from a sixties hootenanny. Skinny guitars, emaciated bodies. They juked and jived across the stage, trying very hard to make their music fill the big room. But the passengers showed no sign they noticed as they pulled the slot machine levers, slid their stacks of chips across the felt tables, and glanced around with the glazed expressions of men too long on the assembly line.

Butler turned away from the band, and for the second time that evening he visited a blackjack table, this one nearest the cocktail lounge. He waited until the dealer had finished a round and some of the players abandoned their places, then he moved to the dealer's shoulder and the man looked up at him. Butler nodded at his rack of chips.

"Getting a little low?"

The young man stared at Butler.

"Name's Jack." Butler pinched a corner of his counterfeit ID and leaned closer. "I'm subbing for Emilio. His father died and he had to fly off to Pittsburgh for the funeral."

"Too bad," the man said as he opened a new deck of cards.

"You need another rack or not?" Butler asked him.

"Well, since you're here," the dealer said.

He tore a sheet off his pad, signed the chit, handed it to
Butler who turned and worked his way through the hubbub, down several rows of dollar slots, passing the roulette tables, four poker games, and over to the pit boss
station where he filled out his own request form, counter-
signed the dealer's signature, and stapled the two together. Then he headed to the banker's cage.

Butler passed his chits through, waited while the young
black woman with round glasses tore off the receipt and
passed the rack through the window to him. The tray of
chips was sealed tight inside a stiff plastic wrap. Butler
reached for the tray, but this time the young woman held
on to it.

"Wait just a minute," she said. "Do I know you?"

He gave her the Emilio story, dead father, Pittsburgh.
She leaned forward, squinted at his ID.

"Hey, this is my second trip tonight."

"I don't remember seeing you before."

"I'm Jack. You've seen me. From engineering."

"Jack, from engineering?"

"I'm usually covered with grease. That's why you don't
recognize me. They got me filling in tonight."

"Your ID," she said. "It's not right."

"What?"

"I got to call somebody, verify you. Just take a second."

"What's wrong with it?"

Butler unclipped the plastic card and studied it for
flaws.

"They're not issuing those anymore. Five months out of
date. I'm sorry, but we got orders. Some special deal going on."

She had her phone pressed to her ear, tapping numbers.

"I told you," Butler said. "I'm from engineering. I'm
just filling in till Emilio gets back. A last minute thing."

"Just the same, I got to report. Sorry. They're tightening security. Something's been happening, got everybody
spooked."

She gave him an apologetic shrug and he watched her as her face changed, focusing now on the voice in her ear.

Butler glanced around. No one in line behind him, a small crowed gathered around one of the nearby black-jack tables groaning in unison as the last card was flipped.

"Mr. Sugarman?" Annette said.

Butler stared at her. Annette turned her back to him, and cupped a hand around the mouthpiece.

Butler took one more quick look around, then swung back to Annette and snaked his right hand through the bars of her cage and touched the voltage to the nape of her neck. A puff of dark smoke. Her legs sagged, the phone spilled from her hand, and the young woman sunk to the floor.

Carrying his tray, Butler turned away and walked through the crowd. Moving with special care, slow, stroll-ing toward the stage where the Baby Boomers were belt-ing out another sixties favorite. " '. . . two cats in the yard. Life used to be so hard . . .' "

For a moment, as he passed behind their set, he was invisible to the eyes in the sky, the three hundred video cameras that dotted the ceiling of the casino, each one concealed in a small dark globe. Then, directly behind the bass player, shielded from the casino floor, Butler swung open the back of one of their Panasonic speakers he'd customized earlier in the day. He slid the rack inside. One tray crammed in already. Grand total of eighty thousand dollars' worth of chips. Legal tender in any of Morton Sampson's two dozen cruise ship casinos. He drew out the second rack of counterfeit chips and headed back to the blackjack table.

After he'd given the dealer his rack of phonies, Butler glided across the casino, heading casually toward the atrium exit. He was only ten feet from the door when a woman howled from across the room. Annette's replace-ment standing inside the cashier's cage, one hand at her throat.

At the same moment a man about Butler's size, a light-skinned black man, came sprinting down the hall, headed directly toward him. Butler held his ground and the man veered through the doorway and collided headlong with two white-haired ladies, spilling their buckets of quarters. The man stopped short, apologized, helped them scoop up a couple of handfuls of coins. Then Annette's replacement screamed again and the black man apologized once more and hustled off.

Next morning, Sunday, when the M. S. *Eclipse* docked in Key West for a seven-hour shopping tour, Butler was among the first wave of passengers down the gangplank. In gray jeans, long-sleeved blue work shirt, tennis shoes. Black sunglasses. Blond hair pulled back into a ponytail. His hands empty.

Positioned at the bottom of the ramp, the caramel-tinted man was studying the crew and passengers as they disembarked. Beside him was another man in tourist clothes and close-cropped hair. David Cruz, head of security. Butler saw a piece of poster board tacked to the bottom of the railing, the two men consulting it as waves of passengers made their way down the long gangplank.

No doubt a hasty sketch based on Annette's description, a rendering of the man who called himself Jack. Evidently she wasn't up to sitting out in the sun all morning, checking the three thousand faces of crew and passengers. Dizzy and weak, her eyes were probably still blurred. Four hundred thousand volts would do that.

Butler didn't try to strike up a conversation with anyone, didn't try to blend in. Just came striding down the ramp alone, even took off his sunglasses as he approached Mr. Sugarman. The man staring at him, taking a quick look at the sketch, then back at Butler, staring into his eyes. Cruz shifted his position, seemed to pick up his scent. But he kept coming down.

Both men stared at Butler. He was a tall, thin man. Annette probably gave them that much for certain. But the rest of it, his nose, eyes, the shape of his cheekbones, those things were always tricky to describe. Even if she was looking directly at him, trying to put precise words to what she saw, most of it would get lost in translation. The words were the weak point. Most people just didn't have the words.

Butler walked on by. The man called Sugarman giving Butler one last look, then turning his attention back up the ramp. Searching for the next tall thin suspect.

Butler crossed the parking lot, came around the driver's side of his Winnebago, unlocked the door and climbed inside. Four days ago he'd parked it across from Mallory Square in a place where he could easily observe the cruise ship's ramp.

Butler sat back in the driver's seat and settled down, windows open, sunny Key West morning pouring in, the drowsy coconut breeze, that sweet stench of sour milk that always seem to bloom two blocks either side of Duval Street. He watched the shadows straggle along the sidewalk. His mind clear, only a mild ruffle in his pulse.

While he had a minute free, he opened the leather pack on his belt and unplugged the nine-volt batteries. Five of them. Simple store-bought copper tops, impossible to trace.

He tore open the wrappers on five new ones and snapped them into place. He rolled up the right sleeve of his shirt, checked the connections, blew a spray of dust off the voltage amplifier strapped to his wrist. Unbuttoned his shirt, followed the wires where they were taped to his flesh, running to his armpit, down his ribs, out a small incision through the shirt to the battery pack on his belt. He searched meticulously for any nicks in the coating of the two wires, one red, one black. But everything was fine. Everything tight and clean and fully charged. He rebuttoned his shirt, tucked it in, rolled down his sleeve and settled back to wait. Feeling a flood of well-being. A radiance centered in his gut. He was moving down the master list. One through five were finished. The groundwork laid. Ready for number six, the big moment. Halfway there. The slow half done, the arduous half. Years in the making.

It was two hours later when the Baby Boomers finally appeared, towering over the Filipino crew that was spilling out the gangway. The band members rolled their equipment down the ramp. Sugarman and Cruz were there. A little slumped over now. Losing their enthusiasm.

The Boomers loaded the equipment into their Ford van. Butler watched them heave the speakers into the back with the other equipment.

Out Truman Avenue, Butler stayed a car or two behind, fell a little farther back as they headed up U.S. 1. The boys were careful drivers, so it was easy to keep a car or two between them up the narrow stretch of overseas highway through the endless ticky-tack of Big Pine, Cudjoe and Sugarloaf, Layton and Grassy Key, Marathon and Long Key, Matecumbe and Tavernier.

Two hours later, a hundred miles up the road from Key West, at the south end of the nineteen-mile stretch of asphalt that shot straight north through the southern Everglades back to mainland Florida, Butler took a position one car length off the bumper of the van. Bearing down. Saw the driver glance back in the outside mirror. Saw his eyes hold for a second, then let go.

Butler leaned over, snapped opened the glove compartment, and drew out the black plastic transmitter. He thumbed the switch, felt the unit hum in his hand. The sweet fizz of electrons. He raised the unit to the windshield, cocked the aerial toward the white van, leaned to his left, head out the window to check the oncoming lane. He waited till the road was clear for several miles, then drew his head back inside and pushed the red button.

But the van continued to ride smoothly.

Butler rattled the transmitter and pressed the button again. Still nothing. He tamped the plastic case against the dash, then aimed the aerial toward the van once more and mashed the button several times.

And it worked. The circuit breaker he'd duct-taped to the Boomers' steering gear last week was activated by the radio impulse: the circuit switch flipped, released the small bolt holding the idler arm to the relay rod, the bolt fell free onto the highway, skittered away.

A second later the van jerked hard to the right, then swerved left. Sixty miles an hour, a rudderless ship.

The van veered into the oncoming lane, stayed there for a hundred yards, then swung back to the right shoulder. Two more erratic zigzags.

"Shit!" His smile melting away. The thing taking longer than it should have. The van slowing, fifty, forty-five.

Butler leaned to his left, saw in the opposing lane a distant line of traffic caught behind two transfer trucks. Heard the wail of a truck's air horn as once again the van swung across the oncoming lane, bumping along the opposite shoulder.

This time the front wheel slid over the lip of the drainage canal, caught. The van leaned, teetered on two wheels, then went over on its side, skidding along the embankment, hit the water and bounced across the surface like a skipping rock until it came to rest, heavy and dead, settling, the passenger side sinking four feet under water. No doors coming open.

Messier than Butler had pictured, but still workable.

The transfer trucks roared past. Cars screeched and slewed around him as Butler eased the Winnebago off the highway. A hundred yards behind him two cars collided, another plowed into the wreckage, spun twice around and careened into the canal.

Butler got out, jogged across the highway to the Boomers' van. Somebody was there already, a black man in bright pink shorts and an aqua tennis shirt, nice new deck shoes. The man hesitated a moment on the bank of the canal, then lunged forward, splashed up to his chest and went for the driver's door.

Butler waded slowly into the warm water, inched through the thick custard at the bottom. Water rose to his waist, then a few inches higher. He closed in on the van, peered inside the back doors, saw the jumble of equipment and the bodies lying akimbo. No one stirring.

While rubberneckers moved slowly past on the roadway, Butler hauled open the van's rear door. The lead singer's body was draped around the Panasonic speaker, his ear pressed against its cloth mesh as though some echo of music were whispering to him, consoling him in his pain. The man drooled blood, a flap of skin dangled near his chin. Everybody groaning, starting to come alive. Butler shoved the lead singer aside and scraped the speaker back across the floor to the rear doors.

He pried open the backing and took a good breath. The plastic wrap hadn't torn. The chips were still locked neatly in their slots. He drew the two trays out and stacked them, tucked them under his arm.

When he turned, a young man was standing in his way, waist deep in the water. Hawaiian shirt, no tan. Kinky blond hair, Nordic features. A few hours off the plane, taking his Minnesota flesh down to Key West to blister it. Giving Butler a cold glare.

"What the hell you doing, man?"

Butler sloshed forward through the canal, but the man dodged to the right and blocked his way. He reached a hand out as if halting traffic.

"You're staying right there, buddy, till we get this sorted out. You look like a looter to me."

Butler smiled.

*"Loot,"* Butler said. "Good choice."

The young man kept his arm stiff, hand out.

*"Loot*'s from the Hindu *lut,* and the Sanskrit *lotram,* which means 'plunder.' I'm sure you didn't realize it, but it's a very aptly chosen word in this context. An ancient military term. Originally it referred to spoils of war stolen from a captured city. Back in the sweet long ago. It's important to know the words, to know what you are saying."

The young man eyed Butler uneasily but stood his ground.

Butler shifted the trays of chips and lifted his right hand into view. Showed the helpful young man with the pale Yankee flesh the two steel prongs protruding from thick rubber tips on his pointing finger and the middle one. He spread his fingers into a V and Butler Jack made a careful fist to activate the charge.

Between the two prongs a blue spark sputtered.

One of Butler Jack's most useful creations. Parts recycled from three stun guns, the DC thyrister capacitor set at twenty-five pulses a second, the whole thing rewired, voltage doubled. Could put a three-hundred-pound mountain gorilla on its ass for half an hour. Take it anywhere. Zap them and they drop. Sometimes they dropped just looking at him, a hiss of current between his fingers. Like he'd risen from the underworld.

The blond hero stared at the crackling spark and sucked in a breath. As Butler stepped forward, the young man stumbled to his side, went down on one knee. Water to his chin.

Butler released the button, then pressed it again, gunning his engine for effect. One more time showing the good Samaritan the snap and sizzle of voltage writhing between his fingertips.

The man stayed knee-deep in the canal watching Butler as he approached. Butler stretched out his hand, brought the sputtering current to within a foot of the man's face.

"Come on, man." The young man's voice broke into a nervous yodel. "I didn't mean anything. Really. I had it all wrong."

Butler jabbed his fingers against the man's forehead and the current hammered him backward into the dark canal. With his mouth still open, the young man slid below the surface, a few listless bubbles rising from his lips. Eyes wide, their shine dulling quickly.

Butler felt the death. Felt the flutter of it in the air as if a hummingbird had whisked past his face. Standing there above the miracle of death, Butler invoked the image of the girl. The girl in the white dress. Pink and blue embroidery on her lacy collar. The girl in the white dress, on her swing on the wide porch. The angel girl. His uranium, his glowing core. The girl who powered him through all the desperate moments. Butler pictured her and once again she rescued him as she had rescued him for years. Her cool smile, the sprinkle of golden hairs on her arms, the delicate bones in her wrists. Her perfect blue eyes. Urging him forward. Urging him away from the dead canal water, back to the Winnebago. Back to his seat behind the wheel. The girl he would see soon. Number six on the list. When everything was in place. Almost there. His angel. His glowing core.

An hour later Butler Jack exited the Palmetto Expressway onto the Tamiami Trail, drove a few blocks east and stopped at a Cuban market. Butler went inside, walked straight back to the storage room. There he traded the two trays of casino chips to a smartly dressed young woman for fifty-one thousand dollars in used twenties.

Loaves and fishes. Water to wine.

# CHAPTER

# 2

"Cruise ships?"

"Yeah, you know, those big white things, like *Love Boat*. Gopher and the gang."

"Gopher?" Thorn said.

"*Love Boat*. It was a TV show. People always falling in love on this big white cruise ship." Sugarman looked out at the glassy flats. Cast his lure thirty feet out, the six-pound line melting against the still water with barely a trace. "Jeez, never mind. I forgot for a second who I was with. Only guy in America never heard of *Love Boat*. Mr. Pop Culture himself."

"Hey, I try to keep up. But it's hard."

"Yeah, without a TV, a radio, newspapers, I expect it is."

"I read books," Thorn said.

"Like I said, totally out of it."

Thorn picked up his paddle, realigned the canoe so they were facing away from the early afternoon sun.

For most of August and September, Thorn had puttered in his downstairs workshop, trying to construct the canoe without benefit of blueprint or model. Just a vague image in his mind. The canoe had emerged after a month of trial and error. Bending the water-soaked slats of birch until they bowed. Stretching the canvas across the birch. Twice he'd misaligned the keel, cut the canvas short, snapped innumerable ribs. But finally it came together, everything flush, riveted tight, ready for its shakedown cruise.

Neither he nor Sugarman had fished from a canoe before, but they were getting the hang of it. No leaks. Well-balanced. Of course, later on this afternoon would be the real test, returning to the docks at Flamingo. Five miles of open water.

Thorn's back muscles were burning already, a blister had broken open on his right thumb from the trip out. Sugar soaked through his khaki shirt in the first ten minutes as they'd paddled through the cool dawn.

But they didn't complain. It was worth the effort to fish those southern Everglades flats, a place no powerboat could reach, not even the shallowest draft skiff poling with its engine tilted up. On those secluded shoals there were large areas with barely enough water at high tide to dampen the sand, closer to a beach than a bay. But some of the finger channels that webbed the sand were choked with fish. Grouper and trout, redfish and snapper. Even a few tarpon were laid up back there.

"How the hell you get hooked up with a cruise ship company?"

"Out of the blue," Sugar said as he drew in line. "Last month the head of security for Fiesta Cruises called up, wanted to know if I'd hire on for a month or two, work undercover. I asked him how he picked me, he wouldn't say. Just that my name wound up on his desk."

"You got a mysterious benefactor."

"Appears that way."

Thorn watched his Lab puppy sleeping under the center seat of the canoe. Leaning forward, Thorn waved away a mosquito that had settled on the dog's nose. Add that to the list of good reasons for having a dog around—mosquitoes preferred their blood to human.

"Fiesta Cruise Lines," Thorn said. "That's Morton Sampson's company."

Sugarman swung his head around, peered at Thorn. "Jesus! How the hell—"

"Hey, I know a few things. He's famous. Morton Sampson, the guy with the missing daughter. Monica."

"You never heard of Gopher, *Love Boat*, but you know Morton Sampson."

"Handbills," Thorn said. "You remember. Someone dumped a stack of them in the ditch out by the highway. Back when they were looking for the girl, couple, three years ago. I used those posters to light the evening cook fire for about six months. Pretty girl. They ever find her?"

"No. Her old man must've spent a million dollars on posters, private eyes, TV ads."

"Damn good-looking young lady. It bothered me to light her up every night. But I couldn't just throw those things away."

Thorn watched a hawk strafe the mangroves to their east, warding off some interloper.

"This new job," Sugarman said, "I get all the free cruises I want. Except it's wasted on me. I never had any aspirations to cruise. Big ship like that, it's like some skyscraper's fallen into the bay and floated off. And man, the ships smell like damn Greyhound buses. Too many people been there, the upholstery, the rooms, everything reeks of body odor. Smell you can't get out. Every week the boat docks, passengers get off, cleaning crew comes aboard, dusts and waxes the floors, an hour later more passengers are lined up to get on. Thing never has a chance to air out."

"That what they hired you for? A body odor detective. Catch who's stinking up the place."

Sugarman looked up at the empty sky.

"I'm after a thief," he said.

Rover woke and began to whimper. Thorn reached over, lifted him up, and suspended him over the side of the canoe, and a moment or two later the dog let go a stream of pee. Damn good boat dog. When he was done, Thorn set him back on his pillow.

"This guy, he's been hitting this one ship for around fifty thousand dollars every month for the last seven months. The M. S. *Eclipse*. Uses a different approach every time. They think it's somebody in the crew, so they brought me in. Want to keep it all hush-hush. Bad for business otherwise."

"High adventure on the high seas."

"High seas is right," Sugar said. "Couple of weeks ago I'm prowling the casino all night. Boat's tossing and pitching in that tropical storm Edgar. Twelve foot swells. But does that stop the goddamn gamblers? No, nuh-uh. Room is full. They're pulling the slot machine arms like one set of robots making love to another set. They can barely stand up, but they're keeping at it. Place is smoky as hell. That's the worst part. Gamblers gotta have their cigarettes."

Thorn leaned forward and scratched Rover's ears. The puppy groaned with pleasure.

"Middle of that tropical storm, I notice this guy. I don't know why. He's dressed like everybody else, with his plastic cup full of coins, same as all the rest. But there's something about him. Way he moved, I don't know."

"Furtive gestures," Thorn said.

"Yeah, something like that. Guy had sneaky eyes. He wasn't looking around, glancing over his shoulder or anything. In fact, maybe that's what caught my attention. Just kept his eyes down. Dark glasses, baseball cap. He'd work one machine for a long time, a half hour or so, he'd move on to the next one. Going like that all night, one machine to the next."

"Yeah?"

"It was an accident I caught on. He left a quarter in the payout tray. I picked it up, and bingo-bongo, I know he was pulling something."

"He was using slugs."

"No," Sugarman said. "Much better."

"I'm supposed to guess?"

"You'd never get it. Even after I had the thing in my nd, it was a few more days before I figured out how he orking the scam. By then the cruise was over, the disembarked, long gone."

Thorn picked up his paddle, sculled them away from the small island they were drifting toward.

"Don't you want to know what it was? The scam."

"I'm all atwitter."

Sugarman said, "He milled the edges off the quarters."

Thorn looked over at him.

"The rough, serrated edges, you know. Smoothed them off."

"And what the hell would that accomplish?"

"Exactly," Sugar said. "What difference does it make, grinding the edges off the quarters? The casino people had no idea, so they fly in one of their hotshot engineers, he meets us in Nassau, one of the stops. This kid, he looks like a movie usher, long greasy hair, some loser you'd find hanging around a video game room, but no, he's their resident electronic genius. Smug little bastard.

"So anyway, we sat around, dropping that quarter into machines. It registered like any other quarter. No difference. Bing, bing, pull the arm, you get two cherries and an apple. Nothing. Open up the machine, take it out, try it again on another machine. Same thing."

Thorn watched the puppy sleep. His paws jerked as he chased a rabbit through the tall grass of his dream.

"The video kid, he gets out his laptop computer, starts banging away, doing computations, analyzing the specs. The cruise people are yammering among themselves. So I get up, walk around looking at the slots. I've been mulling this thing over for days, coming up with nothing, but then out of nowhere it hits me. I don't know diddly about the mechanics, except the little I just overheard as these guys were talking. But what I do know is the win rate is four percent on slots, but on that particular cruise the win rate went up to seven percent. Either a lot of people got real lucky, or somebody was rigging things.

"So without completely understanding it, I go back over and announce that I know how the guy pulled it off. They all look up. And I hear myself—I'm off to the races but hell if I know how I know any of this.

"I say, look, what if the milled quarter goes in, registers

like the real quarter. But its weight is just different enough from a real quarter that maybe, for some reason, it doesn't register when it comes out."

"I'm not following this."

"See, the machines are set to pick up slugs or foreign coins. They have a very precise measuring scale for entering coins. So a scam artist couldn't adjust the coins too much, or the machine won't take them. But just milling the edges off, apparently that isn't enough to trigger the alarm."

"I guess I'm just dense," Thorn said.

"Okay, the crook comes in with a bucket of milled quarters. He goes up to a machine, starts playing. Puts them in, loses, loses, loses. His milled quarters are in the machine now, circulating among the real ones. Then he wins a small jackpot, four or five real quarters. He keeps on playing, feeding the machine the milled quarters, and he loses, loses, loses. Then finally when he hits another winner, this time in addition to the eight or ten real quarters he's supposed to win, one of his milled quarters is in line next to them and it slips out too. Only it doesn't register going out. Its smooth edges allow it to slip past the exit counter. The exit counter isn't so precise. If you catch the slugs going in, there's no need for the exit to be finely tuned.

"So what happens, instead of winning eight quarters he wins nine. Eight of theirs, one of his. Keeps feeding the milled quarters, and whenever he wins, his special quarters don't stick. So he keeps playing one machine long enough, he's got all his milled quarters back and he's milked most of the real quarters out of the machine too.

"Then he moves on to the next one and does the same thing. Careful to keep his customized quarters separate from the real ones. Very patient. Very low tech. No big jackpot or anything. But little by little over the course of an evening, he can walk out of there with a sizable take. Do seven thousand a day for a whole week of the cruise, he's got his fifty."

"Fifty thousand. It's this guy's magic number?"

"That's been his take. Poker or slots or roulette. Then last week he got away with eighty thousand bucks' worth of chips. He sells them somewhere, makes sixty, seventy percent of the face value. So there it is again, hitting around the same figure. Fifty thousand. That was the trip one of the casino workers was killed, slashed open. His shirt was stolen."

"That's connected?"

"The bad guy used the shirt to impersonate a casino worker."

"Killed a guy for his shirt."

"Yeah, it looks that way."

Thorn stared out at the still water for a while.

"How'd you figure it out? The milled quarter thing."

"That's what they wanted to know. All of them looking at me suspiciously, you know, like maybe I was in on it. But I couldn't tell them. I heard it come out of my mouth, babbling away like some part of my brain figured it out, while the rest of my brain didn't understand it. A gift from the gods."

Thorn nodded. He knew a little about those.

"Anyway, we tested it out. Went into the ship's machine shop, filed off the edges on fifty quarters, played them, and sure thing, they didn't stick in the machine. If they were in the chute next to a payout, they came out too. You keep playing long enough with money that slips out on its own, you could skim every quarter out of that whole casino."

"Impressive," Thorn said.

"It would have been," Sugarman said. "Except the guy got away. His face didn't come out on the video cameras. We checked and the guy kept his head down, very aware of being watched. Had on that baseball cap, big dark glasses. He was tall, that's all we could tell.

"The cruise ship people, they were happy I'd figured out the quarter thing, sure, but it didn't get them any closer to the guy. Then a week later he stabs this guy to death. So now it's serious. Not just money anymore."

Sugarman ran his finger through the water, seemed to be writing a word there.

"I had no idea how much money flows through those ships, the casinos. Hell, every Saturday those ships leave port with two and a half million in the casino bank. A week later they come back with close to three mil. All you need, the average passenger loses fifty dollars a day for a week, there's your half million. So somebody steals fifty thou, it's chicken feed really, compared to what's actually on the stagecoach."

"Chicken feed? Hell, I'm in the wrong business."

"You're not in any business, Thorn."

Thorn smiled.

"Yeah, well, thank God for that."

Thorn watched a small hammerhead sliding along the bottom.

They broke for lunch. Drank a couple of icy Foster's and swallowed down the peanut butter and jelly sandwiches Sugarman's wife had packed. Big gooey things that leaked around the edges.

Afterward, Thorn leaned back against the canvas seat in a half-doze, listening to a distant osprey's shrill lament, his rod at his feet. He heard Sugarman casting, felt the gentle wobble of the canoe as he worked his line.

Thorn drifted down into the dusky light of a snooze. Picturing Rochelle's face. Her striking face behind the pages of a book. Turning pages. Reading in the bed beside her. Smelling her cinnamon scent. Hearing Rochelle breathe. The dream shifting suddenly to a conversation. Dreaming soundless words. A stream of them coming from Rochelle's mouth, one of her theories. She had dozens of them. A theory about dreams. Why we dream. Why we remember some, don't others. Something to do with physics. Thorn following her words, her idea, then things becoming more and more intricate until he was lost and found himself watching her lips shape the words, not hearing her theory anymore, just watching the stream of beautiful words coming from her intriguing mouth. Exotic words, wide exotic mouth. Rochelle.

Sugarman let out a whoop that jerked Thorn upright.

Sugar's reel was revving, and twenty yards to the east the silver water humped and surged and a monster snook flopped hard on its side, shook his head savagely against the six-pound line.

Sugarman rose to get leverage on the fish, but the canoe wobble precariously and he squatted back down. For the next ten minutes Thorn watched him fight that same impulse, until the snook made a sudden reel-melting run and Sugarman came to his feet again, hauled back on the rod, and tipped the canoe.

Everything went overboard. Their gear, the remains of their lunch. The puppy splashed around, then started swimming in delirious circles licking at the water as he went. Up to his knees in muck and soft sand, Thorn laughed and cursed, and after a moment's bewilderment, Sugarman joined in. The two of them wallowed about until they got the canoe righted, the provisions and the puppy back inside, Sugarman one-handing his rod the whole time, keeping the line taut on his fish. Thorn steadied the canoe while Sugar climbed back inside, then Thorn slid over the side and settled into his seat again.

Finally Sugar hauled the fish to the boat. While Thorn held the tippet high, they examined the brute. Close to forty pounds. On Sugar's light line, the snook might even be a world record if they wanted to take it back, weigh it on official scales.

"Gonna keep it?"

Sugarman gave Thorn a quiet look, and pried the barbless hook from the fish's jaw, eased him back into the water, moved him gently back and forth till the fish recovered and glided away into the labyrinth of tidal channels.

As they were drying out in the sun, Sugarman lifted his hand and gestured at the deep-water cove twenty feet away. A pod of dolphins had rolled into the inlet. Thorn counted half a dozen dolphins circling the cove.

A moment later the water boiled with bait fish. For several minutes the dolphins worked together, herding what must have been a very large school of mullet tighter and tighter until they had them clustered in a thick mass. Then the dolphins moved in, the water churning briefly. Lunch.

"Damn mullet never had a chance."

"Makes you glad dolphins are on our side," Sugar said.

Thorn stared at the last flutters of water.

"Only reason they're on our side is 'cause they don't know us that well."

They watched the dolphins move away, an undulating line.

"We ought to get out here more often," Thorn said, leaning back, stretching out his arms. "Blow out the arteries."

"Some of us got jobs, man."

"Go on," Thorn said. "Give me some more shit."

"Naw, it's too easy."

"Well, anyway, that explains where the hell you been these last few weeks. I was beginning to worry about you, man."

"It's good to be missed."

"Actually what it is, I'm running a little low on hair."

Sugarman scowled.

For the last few months Sugar had been grabbing handfuls of hair out of the trash can behind the Hairport Beauty Salon next to his office. Dropping the hair off at Thorn's so he could experiment with it in his bonefish flies. Thorn had discovered that pinches of frosted hair worked the best. The frosted stuff stood up to saltwater almost as well as boar bristle.

"You been kind of engrossed lately," Sugar said. "I didn't think you'd notice I wasn't around."

"You mean Rochelle. Engrossed with Rochelle."

Sugarman shrugged.

"Yeah," Thorn said, smiling. "I guess you could call it that. Engrossed."

"Tell me something, Thorn. Why the hell'd you name that dog Rover? All the names you could've picked, you couldn't do any better than that?"

"It was Rochelle's idea. It's ironic."

"Ironic?"

"Well, actually she's got another name for it. Postmodern. It's a postmodern thing. Like an intellectual joke."

" 'Ironic' I've heard of."

"That year of Harvard," Thorn said, "it gave her a peculiar sense of humor. Some of the books she reads, I can't pronounce their titles."

"Well, making your dog the butt of a joke, I don't know about that. Seems like bad karma."

"He doesn't mind. 'Rover' seems to suit him fine."

Rover was curled in a ball in the shade of the middle seat.

Out in the center of the cove, a single dolphin rolled. Lingering behind to clean up the scraps. Thorn watched it surface and dive, surface again, its sleek gray hide blending perfectly with the water. It made one more round of the cove, then headed toward the bay to catch up with its buddies.